TH

B
O
SECRETS

Tom Harper was born in Germany and studied medieval history at Oxford university. He has written eight novels, including *Knights of the Cross* and *Lost Temple*. He lives in York with his wife and son.

Also available by Tom Harper

The Mosaic of Shadows
Knights of the Cross
Siege of Heaven
Lost Temple

THE
Book
OF
SECRETS

TOM HARPER

arrow books

Published in the United Kingdom by Arrow Books in 2009

3 5 7 9 10 8 6 4

First published in the United Kingdom in 2009 by Arrow

Arrow Books
The Random House Group Limited
20 Vauxhall Bridge Road, London, SW1V 2SA

Addresses for companies within The Random House Group Limited can be found
at: www.randomhouse.co.uk/offices.htm

The Random House Group Limited Reg. No. 954009

www.rbooks.co.uk

A CIP catalogue record for this book
is available from the British Library

ISBN 9780099545576

The Random House Group Limited supports The Forest Stewardship
Council (FSC), the leading international forest certification organisation.
All our titles that are printed on Greenpeace-approved FSC-certified paper
carry the FSC logo. Our paper procurement policy can be found at
www.rbooks.co.uk/environment

Typeset by SX Composing DTP, Rayleigh, Essex
Printed and bound in Great Britain by
CPI Cox & Wyman, Reading, RG1 8EX

for Owen

Art and Adventure

I

Oberwinter, Germany

Thick snow covered the village that morning. A cold silence gripped the streets. The cars parked opposite the hotel were shrouded with frost – except one, where a gloved hand had scraped a rough circle clear on the driver's window. Behind the black glass, the red eye of a cigarette blinked and glowed.

A young woman came round the corner and hurried up the hotel steps. She was dressed as if for a run: a hooded sweatshirt and jogging trousers, running shoes, a woollen hat and a small rucksack on her back. But it was not a morning for running, and no footprints had left the hotel since the overnight snow. She let herself in the front door and disappeared. The cigarette in the car glowed faster, then went out.

Gillian reached the top of the hotel stairs, tiptoed across the landing and slipped into her room. A dirty half-light seeped through the curtains, making the shabby room look even shabbier. It stank of nicotine: in the thin mattress and untouched sheets, the heavily varnished furniture, the

1

threadbare rugs slung over the floorboards. The black laptop on the dresser was the only sign of change in the last thirty years.

Gillian pulled off the hat and shook out her raven-black hair. She glimpsed herself in the mirror and felt a faint pang of surprise: the new hair colour still didn't feel right. If she couldn't recognise herself, perhaps others wouldn't either. She unzipped her top and stripped it off. Mud streaked her pale arms; her fingers were cracked and bloody from climbing in the dark, but she hardly noticed. She'd found what she'd gone for. She crossed to the computer, flipped up the lid and turned it on. Down on the street, a car door slammed.

As the machine clicked into life, something gave inside Gillian. The adrenalin drained away. She was exhausted – and shivering with cold. Too tired to wait for the computer, she went to the bathroom and undressed, peeling the damp fabric away from her skin. She left the clothes in a heap on the floor and stepped into the shower. The old hotel might lack some comforts, but at least the plumbing worked. The hot water blasted her face, slicking her hair flat against her scalp. The sharp droplets pricked warmth back into her skin; her muscles began to relax. She closed her eyes. In the dark space that opened, she saw the castle on the cliff; the icy rock face and the tiny crevice; the terror in her throat as she pushed against the ancient door . . .

Her eyes snapped open. Over the white noise of steam and water, she'd heard a sound from the bedroom. It might have been nothing – the hotel had its share of creaks and bumps – but the last three weeks had taught Gillian new fears. She left the water running and stepped out of the shower, wrapping herself in a skimpy hotel towel. Wet footprints pooled on the floorboards as she tiptoed through to the bedroom.

There was no one there. The laptop sat on the dresser between the two windows, chattering away to itself.

The sound came again – a knock at the door. She didn't move.

'Fräulein – *telefon*.'

It was a man's voice, not the hotel owner's. Gillian looked at the door. *She'd forgotten to attach the safety chain.* Did she dare slip it on now, or would that only alert him to her presence? She grabbed the hooded top from the bed and zipped it over her breasts, then pulled on a pair of pyjama bottoms from under the pillow. That made her feel less vulnerable.

'Fräulein?' The voice was harsh, impatient – or was that just her imagination? No. In horror, she saw the door handle start to turn.

'I'm here,' she called, trying not to sound frightened. 'Who is it?'

'*Telefon*. Is important for you, Fräulein.' But it didn't sound important – it sounded false, a rehearsed lie at the wrong moment, dialogue out of sync with the film. The handle was still down, the tongue of the lock bumping the frame as the man pushed against it.

'I can't take it right now,' said Gillian. She snatched the laptop from the dresser and stuffed it into the rucksack. 'I'll be down in five minutes.'

'Is important.' An ill-fitting key scrabbled in the lock. *It was opening.* She flew across the room and slammed the safety chain home. She grabbed the handle and tried to hold it, but the grip on the other side was remorseless. Her fingers went white; her wrist was twisted back.

With a pop, the lock gave. The door sprang open, flinging Gillian backwards onto the floor. The chain snapped taut, bit – and held. The door shuddered to a standstill. Gillian heard a muffled curse. An unseen hand pulled it back a fraction and thrust it forward again. Again the chain held.

Dazed and desperate, Gillian pushed herself up. Blood ran down her cheek where the door had grazed it but she didn't notice. She knew what she had to do. She slung the rucksack over one shoulder, pulled open the window and climbed out onto the tiny balcony. A rusting ladder, the fire escape, ran down the side of the building. She'd insisted on a room next to it, though she hadn't expected to need it. She'd thought she'd lost them after Mainz. She pulled her sleeves down over her hands and reached for the nearest rung.

A second before she touched it, the whole ladder shivered. The snow on the rungs shook loose. With her arm still outstretched, she looked down.

The icy air seemed to freeze in her lungs. Through the swirling mist and snow, she saw a dark figure climbing towards her. From inside the room she heard another crash: the impact must have almost torn the chain from its housing. Perhaps someone had heard the noise, but she doubted it. She hadn't seen another guest since she checked in.

She was trapped. Only one thing mattered now. She ducked back through the window, ran to the bathroom and locked the door. It wouldn't hold two minutes, but perhaps that would be enough. Trembling, she perched on the edge of the bathtub and opened the laptop. In the bedroom, she heard a splitting crack as the chain finally gave. Footsteps ran in, paused, then headed for the window. That would buy her a few more seconds.

But not enough time to write – to explain. She reached behind the machine and turned on the webcam built into the lid. The light on the data card blinked as it established a connection; on screen, a new window opened with a list of names. She cursed. All of them were greyed out, dead to the online world. Probably still fast asleep.

Out in the bedroom, voices conferred for a moment, then approached the bathroom. A heavy boot slammed against the door, so hard she thought they'd kick it off its hinges. But the door held. She scrolled frantically through the names. Someone must be up. The light on the data card blinked orange and her heart almost stopped, but a second later the connection re-established itself and the light turned green. Another kick; this time the door buckled.

There. At the very bottom of the list, she found what she was looking for: a single name rendered in firm bold letters. *Nick* – of course he'd be up. A flash of misgiving shot through her, but more pounding on the door drove it out instantly. He'd have to do. She clicked the button next to his name to open a connection. Without waiting to see if he answered, she found the file and clicked SEND. The light on the data card flashed a furious pulse as it started streaming the information out of the computer.

Come on, she mouthed. She waited for Nick's face to appear on screen so she could warn him, tell him what to do with it – but the box where he should have been stayed black, blank. *Answer, godamit.*

'About 1 minute remaining,' the status bar said. But she didn't have that long. There was a small window behind the bath: she reached up and jammed the laptop into the opening. Her fingers scrabbled on the keyboard as she typed two brief lines of text, praying that the message would find someone. Another kick. She pulled the shower curtain across the bath to hide the computer.

The door smashed open. A man in a long black coat and black gloves stepped through the splintered frame and advanced towards her, the cigarette glowing like a needle in his mouth. Unthinkingly, Gillian tugged up the zip of her top.

Outside, a faint scream drifted down the street until the cold mist smothered it. Loose snow filled the footsteps outside the front door. The car drove away, the chains on its tyres clanking like a ghost. And on the other side of the world, a handful of pixels flashed up on a screen to announce that a message had arrived.

II

The Confession of Johann Gensfleisch

> The Lord came down to see the city, and the tower which mortals had built. And the Lord said, 'Look, they are one people and they all have one language; and this is only the beginning of what they will do; from now, nothing that they propose to achieve will be impossible for them . . .'

God have mercy for I have sinned. Like the men of Babel I built a tower to approach the heavens, and now I am cast down. Not by a jealous god, but by my own blind pride. I should have destroyed the cursed object, cast it in the river, or burned it in a fire until the gold leaf melted off the pages, the ink boiled away and the paper charred to ash. But – beguiled by its beauty and its creator – I could not do it. I have buried it in stone; I will write my confession, a single copy only, and they will lie together in eternity. And God will judge me.

It begins – I began – in Mainz, a town of wharves and spires on the banks of the river Rhine. A man may bear many names in his life: at this time, mine was Henchen Gensfleisch. Henchen was a childish form of Johann; Gensfleisch was my father's name. It means goose meat, and it suited him well. Our family's fortunes had grown fat and he had grown with them, until his belly sagged below his belt and his cheeks drooped around his chins. Like a goose, he had a sharp bite.

It was only natural that my father's financial interests led him eventually to the source. He became a companion of the mint, a sinecure which catered perfectly to his vanities. It gave him a pension and the right to march in pride of place on the St Martin's Day procession, and demanded little in return except the occasional inspection of the mint's workings. One day, when I was ten or eleven years old, he took me with him.

It was a black November day. Cloud had settled on the pinnacles of the cathedral, and rain pelted us as we scurried across the square. There was no market that day; the rain seemed to have washed every living thing from the streets. But inside the mint all was warmth and life. The master met us himself; he gave us hot apple wine, which burned my throat but made me glow inside. He deferred constantly to my father, and this also made me happy and proud (later I realised he ran the mint under contract, and hoped it would be renewed). I stood close beside my father, clutching the damp hem of his robe as we followed the master into the workshops.

It was like stepping into a romance, a sorcerer's laboratory or the caverns of the dwarves. The smells alone intoxicated me utterly: salt and sulphur, charcoal, sweat and scorched air. In one room, smiths poured out crucibles of smoking gold onto guttered tables; through a door, a long gallery rang with pealing hammers as men on benches pounded the sheets flat. Further along, a man with a pair of giant shears cut the metal as easily as a bolt of cloth, snipping it into fragments no bigger than a man's thumb. Women worked them against wheels until the corners and edges were ground into discs.

I was entranced. I had never imagined such harmony, such unity of purpose, could exist outside the heavens. Without thinking, I reached for one of the gold pieces, but my father's heavy palm swatted me away.

'Don't touch,' he warned.

A small boy, younger than me, collected the pieces in a wooden bowl and brought them to a clerk at the head of the room who tested each one on a small pair of scales.

'Each must be exactly the same as the others,' said the master, 'or everything we do would be worthless. The coinage only works if all its pieces are identical.'

The clerk swept a pile of the golden discs off his table into a felt bag. He weighed the bag and made a note in the ledger beside him. Then he passed the bag to his apprentice, who carried it solemnly through a door in the back wall. We followed.

I could tell at once that this room was different. Iron grilles covered the windows; heavy locks gripped the doors. The moneyers, four huge men with bare arms and leather aprons, stood at a workbench striking iron dies like miniature anvils. The apprentice brought the bag to one of them. The moneyer tipped it out on the bench beside him, slipped a disc into the jaws of his mould, then raised his hammer and struck. A single blow, an eruption of sparks, then the die was popped open and the newly minted coin added to a fresh pile.

I stared. In the heavy lamplight, the coins gleamed and winked back perfection. My father and the master had their backs to me, examining one of the moulds through a lens. At the bench, the moneyer concentrated on aligning the gold blank in the die.

9

I knew it was wrong – but how could it be theft to take something that would instantly be replaced a hundredfold? It was like scooping a handful of water from the river to drink, or plucking a wild berry from a bramble. I reached out my hand. The coin was still warm from the impress of the die. For an instant, I saw St John's embossed face in a reproachful gaze. Then he vanished in my clenched fist. I felt no guilt.

It was not greed – not for gold. It was a longing such as my child's mind had never known, a lust for something perfect. I understood – dimly – that these coins would enter the world and be changed and changed again – into property, power, war and salvation – and all this would happen because each was a perfect duplicate, triplicate, replicate of all the others, members of a system that was unbreakable as water.

They were done. My father shook the master's hand and offered some approving words; the master smiled hungrily and proposed schnapps in his lodgings. While he turned to say a few words to the moneyers, I tugged my father's sleeve and pointed to the door, squeezing my legs together to imitate discomfort. He looked surprised to be reminded I was there. He tousled my hair, as close to affection as he ever managed.

I knew I had been caught the moment we stepped through the door. The clerk was standing behind the desk, the apprentice opposite, both staring at the balance in incomprehension. One pan lifted the velvet bag high in the air; the other sat immovable on the table, pinned down by a copper weight. I felt the lightness like a hole in my stomach – though even then, I marvelled at a system so precisely tempered that it could detect the absence of a single coin.

The master ran to the table. Angry words followed; the clerk lifted off the weight and replaced it, the scales swung, but the judgement remained the same. The moneyer was summoned and furiously protested his innocence. The clerk tipped open the bag and counted out the coins one by one, assigning each a square on his chequered cloth. I counted with him silently, almost believing that the missing coin might miraculously reappear. One row of ten crept across the table, a second followed, then a third and the beginnings of a fourth.

'Thirty-seven. Thirty-eight. Thirty-nine.' The clerk reached inside the bag and pulled it inside out. 'Nothing.' He consulted the ledger. 'There were forty before.'

The clerk glared at the moneyer. The moneyer stared at the master, who glanced anxiously at my father. Nobody thought to look at me – but that made no difference. I knew that the all-seeing eye of God was upon me, could feel His angry gaze. Sweat trickled down into my palm. The gulden became lead in my hand, bearing down the full weight of my guilt.

My hand opened. Perhaps it slipped, perhaps I wanted to let it go. The gulden spilled out, dropped at my foot and rolled away. Five heads craned to follow it across the stone floor, then slowly turned back to me. One was faster than the others. A stinging blow hit the back of my head and knocked me to the ground. Through my tears, I saw the clerk bend down to pick up the errant coin, dust it off and place it lovingly in the final square of its row. The last thing I remember before my father dragged me away was seeing him lick his pen to record the outcome in the vast ledger at his side.

My father beat me again that evening, thrashing me with his studded belt while he damned my sins to everlasting hell. I cried readily – stoicism only made him angrier. But as I bent over the chair and stared into the hearth, all I saw was an endless cascade of gold gulden, each one a bright fragment of perfection.

III

People used to have circles of friends, Nick thought: now they had lists. Thumbnail photographs tallied on a web page like a fighter pilot's kills, or ladders of contacts displayed in real-time league tables of how recently you'd been in touch. Never mind how you felt: if you didn't keep talking, your friends fell ruthlessly into social purgatory. Part of Nick found it unsettling, but he still used the programs. He was looking at one of those lists on the monitor in front of him now, at a green button flashing next to a highlighted name. The name had been anchored to the bottom of his list for months, down among the former colleagues, old classmates and vague friends-of-friends. But that didn't begin to tell the story.

Gillian. Nick leaned back in his chair. His apartment was dark: the only light was the purple glow of the monitors on his desk, and at the opposite end of the room, an answering beacon where the unwatched television played a late-night movie. He'd longed for this moment for months: checked his cellphone, his voicemail, his instant messages and his different

12

email accounts, even got his hopes up when the mailman came each day – a dozen ways to be ignored. And now here she was.

The cursor hovered over the green button, still flashing. Nick's heart had kicked into overdrive. He took a deep breath to steady himself, tugged on the neck of his sweater to straighten it. He should have shaved. He clicked.

The scream ripped through him like a knife. His first thought was it must have come from the TV, but that was on mute. He waited a second for it to come again. Nothing. Had he imagined it? On screen, a grainy image had appeared in the window. It looked like wallpaper: a grey-white wall with small green Christmas trees stencilled on it. Or perhaps a curtain – the trees seemed to ripple and sway in front of the camera. The picture was so jerky it was hard to tell.

'Gillian?' he said to the microphone above his computer. 'Are you there?' He squinted into the camera. 'Is this some kind of joke?' A sourness began to spread inside him. He should've known it would be a disappointment.

But someone must be there. He heard voices – men's voices – and some sort of commotion. Suddenly, the Christmas trees shot back. A man's face appeared – dark Mediterranean features squashed like a potato where the camera lens distorted it, a glowing cigarette jammed between his lips. There seemed to be splash of blood on his cheek – perhaps he'd cut himself shaving. Nick could see brown tiles and a small bathroom mirror over his shoulder.

The man shouted something furious that Nick couldn't understand, then reached forward as if to drag Nick through the window. The hand filled the screen, blurry and pixellated but so vivid that Nick pushed back from the desk in panic. Then the image went black.

Nick looked at the screen, dazed. The video was blank, but

13

the message panel was still open. For the first time, he noticed the two lines of text that had come through underneath.

use this. bear is the key
help me theyre coming

Beside it, a flashing icon showed that a file had been downloaded.

Naples, Italy
The black Mercedes prowled through the cobbled streets. The morning half-light made the world a grim place: men and women in sober coats and suits scurried to work under the clouds, sometimes glimpsing their reflections in oily puddles. Cesare Gemato watched them from the back seat of the car, through tinted windows that made the world almost black. He liked this time of day, this season. He'd lived all his life in the shadows.

A sudden squawk of opera broke the silence in the limousine – a tinny Pavarotti singing Puccini through a mobile-phone speaker. Gemato's grandson had changed the ringtone when his back was turned; for all his undoubted power, Gemato hadn't yet found a way to undo it.

The young man sitting beside him fished a phone out of the calfskin briefcase on his knee, spoke a few words, then passed it to Gemato.

'Ugo,' he said.

'*Si*.' Gemato listened. 'Good. You found anything with her? The book?'

He frowned.

'Is it possible he saw you on this machine?' Through the window, he noticed a young woman in a white raincoat pedalling hard on a bicycle. Black hair tumbled down her back; the wind blew her coat taut against her body.

'Send it to our friends in Tallinn. Find out who, where, what this man knows.'

He ended the call and passed the phone back to his assistant. That was the problem with doing favours, he thought, even for someone he owed as much as his patron. There was always one more thing to take care of.

'Get me Nevado.'

New York City

Nick sat on the bench in the diner. His laptop lay open on the table, next to a sheet of paper and a vanilla milkshake in a stainless-steel shaker. At four in the morning the place was almost empty, but he liked coming here when he couldn't sleep, liked the neon and chrome, the leatherette and Formica and the dollar-fifty bottomless cup of coffee. It felt authentic – though he knew he only thought that because a hundred Hollywood movies had perfected the fiction. Gillian had pointed that out to him.

Gillian.

He stared at the laptop. The Greeks who ran the diner weren't so old-fashioned that they hadn't installed wireless Internet when they noticed their customers drifting to the coffee shop down the street. Nick had been logged on for an hour, watching the screen with tired eyes to see if Gillian reappeared. Her name had leaped to the top of the list, but the icon beside it stayed grey, lifeless.

Last seen: 06 January 07:48:26

He sipped his shake. 7:48, that put her six hours ahead of

15

him. Where was that – somewhere in Europe? What had she been doing there?

Help me theyre coming.

It had to be a joke. With Gillian, anything was possible. But if anything was possible . . .

Why would she go all the way to Europe to play a prank? He replayed the video in his head: the scream, the snarling face filling the screen, the hand reaching out to the camera. It hadn't looked like a joke.

With Gillian, anything was possible.

And then there was the file she'd sent. He slid the printout across the table and studied it. He'd expected it to be the answer, some sort of punchline that would explain the whole charade. Instead, it only added confusion. There was no writing, just a black-and-white picture showing eight hand-drawn lions and bears in various poses: stalking, crouching, sleeping, roaring, digging, climbing. One of the lions sat up on its haunches and licked its jaws; it stared out of the page at Nick, holding his gaze, daring him to come closer.

Closer to what?

It must be something she'd been working on. But why send it to him? Was it valuable? *Bear is the key.* He'd tried clicking on the bears in the picture, but nothing happened.

He tried another tack. He opened the web browser and pulled up sites he knew she'd frequented, a sad lover drifting around his old flame's former haunts. Blogs she'd posted on, forums she might contribute to. There wasn't much. A review of a book he'd seen her reading not long before she left him; something about goldsmithing on a discussion board for medievalists. He tried to read it, but the words blurred in his brain. There was almost nothing since July, the last time he'd seen her. Was that a coincidence? Maybe it had affected her worse than she'd let on. The thought was strangely comforting.

Almost as an afterthought, he tried a social networking site he knew she'd used. Like a lot of people, she'd signed up, spent two weeks constantly updating her profile and cajoling her friends to join, then decided she had better things to do with her life. Nick had never known her spend any time on it since. But she must have come back to it quite recently. At the top of the page, in the space where users could upload pithy one-line commentaries on what they were doing, he read,

Gillian Lockhart
is in mortal peril ☺
(last updated 02 January 11:54:56)

Was that another joke? It was the sort of melodramatic overstatement she specialised in. But she also loved the slipperiness of irony, things that were simultaneously true and not true. She teased you with possibilities but never gave answers.

Nick sucked the last drops of his milkshake out of the cup. The air frothed and popped in the empty straw.

IV

In my youth I saw two men burned alive. It was in Frankfurt, a day's journey from Mainz. My father had some business there at the Wetterau fair and brought me with him, three months after the incident at the mint. He was in a merry mood, laughing with his companions at the hucksters and cripples who thronged the road. I laughed too, though I did not understand the jokes.

The crowd thickened as we reached the town square, but my father used his bulk and his staff to push through to the front so I would have an unbroken view. My eyes were wide with excitement, wondering what entertainment could draw such an audience. I hoped it would be a dancing bear.

The gallows stood in the middle of the square like the frame of an invisible door. Even at that age, I knew where it led. Bales of straw were piled underneath it. I wanted to cry but knew my father would not allow it.

Two sergeants led the prisoners out of the crowd. One wore a long black gown and a white mitre on which was painted a

18

string of devils holding a banner that proclaimed 'Heresiarch', the Archbishop of Heretics. The other man was bareheaded, his skull shaved, his wrists and ankles chained together.

'What has he done?' I asked.

'This man was a mint master,' my father explained. 'He debased his coins, like a wicked brewer watering down his beer.' He squatted down beside me and pulled out a gulden. He turned it in his fingers so that the gold faces winked at me. 'Who do you see?'

'St John.'

'And on the other side?'

'The arms of the prince.'

My father smiled his approval. My heart glowed. 'The saint and the prince. The power of God and the power of man. The two pillars of our world.'

He gestured to the mint master. The sergeants had manacled his hands to an iron hook in the crossbar, and were now trying to attach his chained legs to a second hook at the far end. One of the sergeants stood with the condemned man's legs straddling his shoulders, while the other crouched and heaved from underneath. The crowd whistled and shouted lewd encouragements.

'Against whom was his sin, Henchen?'

'Against the prince, Father.'

'And?'

'God.'

He licked his fat lips and nodded. 'If the coinage is not kept perfect – if even one grain of gold is missing – no man will credit it and God's order will collapse. Even one grain,' he repeated.

Up on the gallows, the two sergeants had finally managed to sling the mint master between the hooks, a carcass suspended from a spit. This would make him burn for longer before he died. The heretic was more fortunate: he was bound upright to a post, where the flames would quickly consume him. From this I judged that his crime was the lesser.

Bailiffs brought wood and tinder from the corners of the square and piled them over the straw. The sergeants sprinkled them with oil from a flask, making sure that some splashed over the prisoners. The magistrate stood on a box and read the charges from a great sealed scroll. I could not hear what he said, though my father took great pleasure repeating it to me. That the heretic had denied that Christ was the son of God and the Church was the path of salvation. That he had called for the Church to surrender its property. That he had summoned Lucifer himself in a black rite at midnight; mingled the communion wine with the ashes of stillborn children; fornicated on the altar and committed incest with his sister. It was hard to believe, looking at that mild-faced man with his pronounced Adam's apple; but, as my father said, the devil delights in disguise. Perhaps I should have listened more carefully.

Clouds gathered; the wind rose. The torch in the sergeant's hand grew brighter as the day darkened. The condemned men whimpered frantic prayers. The magistrate's face went purple as he bellowed to be heard above the noise of beasts, bells and onlookers. The moment he had finished, he jumped off his box and signalled the sergeant to set the fire.

It took in seconds, racing over the piled wood and licking at the wretches above. The heretic died instantly, or perhaps fainted; the forger lasted longer. I saw flames tear open his shift where spots of oil had soaked in, almost as if the fire were consuming him from the inside out. Screams and the crackle of wood mingled with the shouts of the crowd.

I felt something strike my back and looked up. It was my father. His bandy legs were splayed apart, his eyes turned to heaven, his face burning with righteous glee as his staff rained down blows over my shoulders, beating the memory into me.

Later in my life I watched other men burn for their unnatural sins. And each time, a small part of my soul withered in sympathy.

V

New York City

Even in New York the weather could get to you. Nick was woken by rain, ice-hard needles lancing against his window. He rolled over, clinging to the comfort of the last shreds of sleep for a few seconds longer. Until he remembered.

His eyes snapped open. The watch on his bedside table said ten to eleven, though the sky outside was so dark it could have been any time. No wonder he'd overslept. He swung himself out of bed and crossed to the open laptop on the shelf by the window. He'd left it running all night, the volume turned up in case she called again. There was nothing. He scanned the emails that had come in, not even bothering to delete the junk. Nothing there either. A dull pain began to throb behind his temples. He needed coffee.

He knew he was up too late the moment he saw Bret. His room-mate was sprawled in front of his computer in an easy chair, tapping a keyboard with one hand while the other dangled a limp slice of last night's pizza.

'What're you up to?'

'Captchas.' Bret spoke through a mouthful of pepperoni. 'This site gives you free porn for every hundred.'

When machines took over the planet, Nick thought, Bret would be their fifth column. He was a bottom feeder, a parasite nibbling at the Internet's underbelly. Harvesting email addresses for spammers, bidding up prices in online auctions, advertising the benefits of dubious medications or, now, deciphering the distorted letters that websites used to block automated registrations: there was nothing Bret wouldn't do for a few cents. If there was such a thing as an anti-Internet pressure group – Nick supposed they existed somewhere – Bret would be their Exhibit A. Nick still wasn't exactly sure how they'd ended up sharing the apartment.

'You went out late,' said Bret. 'Your pimp call?'

Nick went to the kitchen counter and flipped on the kettle. 'I had a message from Gillian.'

'Mmmm.' Bret licked grease off his fingers and reached for the mouse. 'Is she back in town?'

'I think she's in Europe.'

'One hundred.' Bret clicked. The letters disappeared, replaced on screen by a grappling pair of naked women. Their mouths hung open in frozen masks of delight. 'She is nice.'

Nick splashed hot water over the coffee grounds, then decided he couldn't face the wait. He'd get one at the store on the corner.

'I'm going out.'

Bret waved. The pizza flapped in his hand like dead skin. 'I'll be here.'

Nick rode the A train to 190th Street and walked up Fort Washington Avenue. The rain had softened into a fine freezing mist that seeped down his collar into his bones. The last time

23

he'd come here it had been midsummer, leafy trees shading the street and kids chasing each other with water pistols. He'd bought Gillian an ice cream from the Good Humor van. Now the trees were bare, the street empty. On the grey hill in front of him the stone tower of a medieval monastery poked above the forest, a fragment of a foreign place and time resurrected on the tip of Manhattan. The Cloisters museum. Beyond it, the slope fell away to the Hudson, the bluffs on the far shore little more than shadows in the mist. The bass roar of traffic crossing the George Washington Bridge lingered in the air like distant thunder.

The museum was all but deserted. Nick paid his admission and wandered across to a guide, a white-haired lady poised like a hawk to pounce on visitors. The brooch on her lapel tagged her like an exhibit: 'PAM'. Manhattan, mid-20th century, possible Jewish origin. Her eyes gleamed as Nick approached.

He pulled out the picture Gillian had sent.

'Do you recognise this?'

The docent's gaze flicked over the page. Four lions and four bears stared back at her.

'I don't know.' Nick could see her disappointment. 'Maybe you should try Dr Sutherland.'

'Where can I find him?'

'*Her*. She's probably in the Unicorn room.' She pointed to the cloister through the open door. 'Down to the end.'

The Cloisters was a strange place. A chimera, Gillian had called it: a museum stitched together from the dismembered pieces of other buildings brought over from the Old World. A Romanesque corridor leading to a Gothic hall, a Spanish chapel next to a French chapter house. Nick walked down the empty arcade, ducked through a twelfth-century doorway and entered a long, dimly lit room. Its walls were almost invisible behind the seven vast tapestries that covered them. A young woman knelt in front of one, examining the threads with what looked like a small torch. Above her, a horde of dogs and men with spears surrounded a unicorn, who had impaled one of the dogs on its horn. Its sad eyes brimmed with desperation.

Nick's shoes squeaked on the polished floor and the woman started.

'Dr Sutherland?' She looked as though she'd stepped out of a black-and-white photograph: black hair tied back with a black ribbon, smooth ivory skin, a neat black skirt-suit with a white blouse buttoned close to the neck. The only colour came from her shoes, glossy red patent leather.

'My name's Nick Ash. I'm sorry to bother you . . .' He hesitated. 'I'm a friend of Gillian Lockhart.' A blank. 'She used to work here.'

'Oh.' An apologetic smile. 'I've only been here since October. I don't know . . .'

She sounded British. 'Perhaps you can help me anyway.' Nick unfolded the printout and passed it to her. He saw something flicker in her dark eyes. 'I got sent this yesterday, sort of, um, mysteriously. I was hoping someone here could tell me what it is.'

She studied it for a moment, her lips mouthing silently. 'It's fifteenth century. Copper engraving by a German artist, probably of upper Rhenish origin. Datable to around 1430.' She saw confusion on Nick's face and laughed, embarrassed at herself. 'It's a playing card.'

'Shouldn't there be hearts or clubs or something?'

'The lions and bears are the suit.' She tugged a stray lock of hair back behind her ear. 'Actually, I think it's wild beasts. The number of the card is shown by the number of animals on it.'

'You obviously know a lot about it.'

She shrugged, embarrassed again. 'Not really. Art History 101 stuff. My research is more to do with animal symbolism. But these cards are famous. They're just about the earliest examples of printing from copper engraving we have.'

'Who made them?'

'That we don't know. Most medieval artworks aren't signed, and there are no records for where these came from. Art historians call him the Master of the Playing Cards. There are some other engravings that we attribute to him on stylistic grounds, but the playing cards are the main thing that's survived.'

'Are there others?'

'There are a few dozen that have survived in Europe. Mostly in Paris, I think. The deck's very unusual: it has five suits, instead of the usual four. Deer, birds, flowers, men . . .' She tapped the printout lightly. 'And wild beasts.'

An awkward pause hung between them. In looking at the printout he'd crowded her, pushing her back so that she now stood in the pool of light cast by a stained-glass window high in the wall. The glass splayed a mess of colours across her chest like a wound. In his mind's eye Nick saw the snarling face lunging towards the camera. He shivered.

'Can I keep this?' She held up the paper, watching him curiously. He hesitated.

'Sure.'

'I'll see if I can find out anything more when I finish work.' She nodded to the tapestry. 'I should really . . .'

'Right.'

Nick fumbled in his wallet and pulled out a card. Her fingers brushed his as she took it – slender and white, the nails daubed scarlet. She read it.

26

'*Digital Forensic Reconstruction*?'

'I piece things together.'

It was an old line, something to use when he wanted to seem interesting. Now it just sounded hollow.

On his way out he saw the guide again. Still without any visitors to enlighten, she was standing in the cloister, watching the rain trickle off the fluted roof-tiles into the garden. A stone saint on a pedestal watched over her shoulder.

'Did you find Dr Sutherland?'

'She was very helpful.' He wasn't sure if that was true. 'But I wanted to ask you something. Have you been here long?'

She drew herself up a little straighter.

'Seventeen years.'

'Did you know Gillian Lockhart? She used to work here.'

Behind the glasses, her heavily shadowed eyes narrowed. She pretended to examine the sculpted saint behind him. 'Is she a friend of yours?'

'She was. I – I lost touch with her. I just wondered if you knew where she went after here?'

The guide swung back towards Nick, looking him firmly in the eye. Seventeen stern years of educating ignorance and dispelling error was channelled into her fearsome stare. 'We lost touch with her too. I don't want to be telling tales out of school, but in my opinion that was a darn good thing. Pardon my French.'

Nick tried to hold her gaze and found he couldn't. Before he could think what to say, the trill of his cellphone gatecrashed the rain-pattered still of the cloister. The guide's look could have turned him to stone. Blushing furiously, staring at the floor, he pulled it out of his coat pocket and flipped it open. He barely caught a glimpse of the incoming number flashing on the screen before he jammed it off. The phone went dead.

'This is a *museum*.' Her voice was possibly louder than the phone had been.

'I'm just going,' Nick promised. 'But if you could tell me anything at all about where Gillian might have gone . . . Anything you know.'

The prospect of seeing him off was obviously too much to resist. 'I heard she applied for a job with Stevens Mathison.' She looked to see if it meant anything to Nick. 'The auction house. They have a showroom down on Fifteenth and Tenth. I'm sure Ms Lockhart was just what they needed.'

Nick wondered what she meant, but didn't dare ask.

VI

Mainz, 1420

'When Sarah saw her son Isaac playing with Ishmael, she said to Abraham: "Cast out this woman with her son; for the son of this slave shall not inherit along with my son Isaac."'

The lector's voice drifted out of the refectory. Through the arched door, I saw him reading from an enormous Bible spread out on a lectern, while rows of monks sat on benches and ate up their lesson in silence. I could only hear him intermittently, for out in the cloister the judge was giving his summary.

'The fundamental question in the case before this court, the division of the inheritance of Friedrich Gensfleisch, is the question of *precedence.*'

Weak April sunshine made pale shadows on the cloister. In the dim arcades, the business of the monastery went on as usual around us. Lay brothers hurried about their chores. Down a passage, I could hear the rumble of a barrel being rolled to the buttery. But in the middle of the courtyard, all attention was on the judge. He sat facing us behind a table stacked with books which he never consulted. One hand rested in his lap and played with a rosary; the other stroked the fur of his robe as if it were still alive.

'On the one hand we have the claims of the deceased's children by his wife Elsa.' He gestured to the bench where I sat with my brother Friedrich, my sister and her husband Claus. 'Nobody would doubt that the deceased loved his wife, the shopkeeper's daughter. Nor does anyone dispute that in willing his considerable estate to these three children, he was following the dictates of his heart.'

My father had died in November, his death sudden but not especially tragic. He had lived out his three score years and ten, vigorous to the last. So vigorous, in fact, that he thought nothing of getting out his leather strap to punish the chambermaid who had left tarnish on the silver. Rumour had it she was so fearful she waited a full ten minutes after my father collapsed before turning around to see why he had paused the beating. I had been away, but those who were there said they had never seen such a look of peace as they found on his face.

'But the head must rule the heart, as the husband rules the wife and as Christ rules the Church.' The judge rolled his gaze across to the other bench, where my half-sister Patze sat with her uncle and her cousin. 'And that is why we must also consider the claims of the other party in this case, the deceased's daughter by his first wife.'

My brother shot Patze a murderous look. She bowed her head as if in prayer.

'Nobody disputes that Friedrich's widow Elsa is a virtuous woman who grieves her husband deeply. But a shop built of stone is still a shop.'

This was a laboured play on my mother's maiden name, which translated as 'from the stone-built shop'.

'Whereas it would be remiss of this court to ignore the character of his first wife. Can anyone forget that she was the daughter of a magistrate and the niece of a chancellor? Truly an *ancient* family. And this court has learned that in the spirit of service and obedience that characterises that family, her daughter Patze now intends to take holy orders and join herself to Christ in the Convent of the Blessed Virgin Mary.'

In a strange way, it reminded me of the way I felt when I learned my father died. An exhalation, a sense of something that I had never quite possessed being taken away from me. My brother was faster to react: he balled his fists so hard his nails almost drew blood.

'In recent times much has been spoken of a changing order in Mainz. That the ancient families who have always administered this city's liberties should share their burden with new men, craftsmen and shopkeepers.' His face hardened in contempt. 'In this city, we have always recognised and supported God's order. But equally, we protect the humble and the lowly, as was ordained by Christ. For this reason, the court awards the house Zum Gutenberg, its furnishings and as much as may be necessary for a comfortable life, to the widow Elsa for the rest of her days. To Friedrich's three children by her, out of respect for his affection for them, we award the sum of twenty gulden apiece. The rest of the inheritance we award, according to the laws of precedence, to his first-born, best-loved and most virtuous daughter Patze.'

He tapped his staff on the table, hammering the nail of his verdict.

I did not feel angry – not yet. I was twenty years old, and my future had been taken away from me. I had a lifetime to let my resentment bloom.

My brother Friele, thirteen years older and his future already more than half spent, felt it more urgently.

'Bastard thieves. Whore-mongering, gold-grasping boy-fucking Jews.'

In an alcove in the cloister, a brightly painted St Martin leaned off his wooden horse to offer a beggar his cloak. I said nothing. Friele had moved out of the house a year after I was born. In our case, the bond of brotherhood was a bar that fixed us at a set distance, no closer.

'They've waited thirty years to get their revenge on Father for marrying a shopkeeper's daughter. Now they have it.'

Since I had been old enough to understand why my mother spent so many days in the house, why our neighbours found other errands to run whenever she encountered them in the street, I had wondered why my father married her. In a lifetime calculated for his own profit, it was the one act that brought him no gain.

Friele's face burned with baffled fury. I thought he might pull St Martin off his horse and smash him to pieces on the cloister floor.

'Mother will live comfortably enough, and Elsa's husband will look after her. I at least have made a small name for myself in commercial circles, where a man's ability is valued more than his inheritance. But you.' He looked at me with half-sincere concern, seeing, I suppose, a proxy for the war he was waging in his mind. 'You have no wealth, no craft and no standing. What will you do?'

I was my father's son – one thing at least I had inherited from him. I knew what I loved best.

'I will become a goldsmith.'

VII

New York City
The A train rattled through the tunnel somewhere under Harlem. Electricity flashed off the walls, tossing up images of dusty cables and rusting pipes. Nick tipped his head back against the scratched glass and closed his eyes.

Gillian was the only person he'd ever met on a train – probably the only person he could have. Mid-afternoon on the Metro-North coming back from New Haven, no one around except a few private-school kids and a family heading into the city for the theatre. She'd got on at Greenwich, and with a whole empty carriage to choose from had parked herself in the seat opposite him. He'd avoided her eye, a true New Yorker, concentrating extra hard on the laptop balanced on his knees. But Gillian didn't let you escape that easily.

'Did you know that "commute" comes from the Latin word commutare? *It means "to change completely"?'*

Straight in. Nick shook his head and stared at the screen.

'Kind of ironic, don't you think?'

Nick gave a non-committal grunt. It didn't deter her.

'Nothing ever changes if you're a commuter. You take the same train at the same time, sit opposite the same people going to the same job. Then you come home to the same house, same wife and kids, same mortgage and retirement plan.' She looked out the window, at the strip-suburbs sliding by. 'I mean these places – Rye, New Rochelle, Harrison – do they even exist? Did you ever meet one person who's been there?'

Nick vaguely remembered he'd been to an amusement park in Rye when he was a kid. 'Not that they admitted.'

She bounced on her seat like a toddler. 'You know what else you commute?'

'A death sentence?'

She beamed. 'Exactly. I'm Gillian, by the way.' She stuck out a hand with exaggerated formality. Everything with Gillian was overdone, he found out later, a casual way of telegraphing her ironic detachment. Later still he realised it was a way of protecting herself. 'You must be . . .?'

'Nick.' He reached awkwardly around the laptop lid and shook her hand. She wasn't beautiful in a Maybelline kind of way: her chin was too dimpled, her arms too long, her auburn hair unglossy. She looked like the sort of person who scorned make-up. But there was something in her that defied you to look away – an energy or an aura, a sense of possiblities.

'I'm not a commuter,' he added. Feeling the need to justify himself.

She pivoted around and slid onto the seat next to him. 'What are you working on?'

Nick slammed the laptop shut, then laughed awkwardly. Casting around, not knowing where to look, his eyes met hers. Green and brimming with mischief, staring into him without apology.

'Would you believe me if I told you it was classified?'

She rolled her eyes, a give-me-a-break look that dissolved into a squeal of delight as she saw he was serious. 'No way. Are you a spy?'

'Not really.' He cleared his throat. 'Actually, I, um, piece things together . . .'

The subway's wheels screamed as it braked into Fourteenth Street station.

Nick followed the crush of commuters up to the street. The rain had started again, streaming down the steps so that he felt like a salmon battling up a leap. By the time he reached the auction showroom, two blocks away, he was drenched. At least he'd worn his good coat. Nobody else in the building seemed touched by the rain. All he saw were crisp shirts and sharply pressed pleats, as if these people inhabited a world where it was always seventy degrees and the sun always shone. A polished world of glass and steel and marble, if the lobby was anything to go by. A hard world. It seemed so unlike Gillian.

'Can I help you, sir?' The receptionist was a young man with floppy hair and rimless glasses, a trace of a European accent behind his English. His smile seemed to say that he was taking pains to put Nick at ease.

'I'm trying to track down a friend of mine – Gillian Lockhart. I was told she might be working here?'

'Let me just check for you.'

He tapped at the computer terminal on his desk. 'Miss Gillian Lockhart. In our Late Medieval Manuscripts and Printed Materials department.' Another tap. 'She works out of our Paris branch.'

'Does she have a phone number there?'

'I can give you the showroom number.' He took a fountain pen and printed a number across the back of a card. His cufflinks clacked on the desk as he wrote. 'Of course you know you need to dial 011 for international calls.'

Nick glanced at the row of clocks mounted like trophies on the wall behind the receptionist. Four p.m. in New York, ten in Paris. 'I guess they'll be shut now.'

Another tap at the computer. 'You might be in luck. They have an evening sale tonight. A manuscript of the Duc de Berry – it will be very popular. I would think Miss Lockhart should certainly be there.'

Nick went to a coffee shop across the street. His cellphone was switched off – had been since the museum. He turned it on and dialled the number on the card.

'Stevens Mathison, *bonsoir*.' A woman – not Gillian.

'*Bonjour*.' That was wrong. 'Um, is Gillian Lockhart there, please?'

'*Moment, s'il vous plaît*.'

A Vivaldi concerto took her place. Nick tried not to think how much each note was costing him. What would he say to Gillian? Where to begin?

A beep from his phone alerted him to an incoming call. He pulled it away from his ear and looked at the screen. He recognised the flashing number, though it took him a second to realise why. It was his apartment. Bret?

The Vivaldi cut out; he diverted the other call to voicemail and whipped the phone back to his ear, just in time to catch a man's voice asking, 'Who is this?'

He tried to keep his disappointment in check. 'My name's Nick Ash. I'm trying to reach Gillian Lockhart. Your New York office said she might be working there tonight.'

'Have you heard from her?' The accent was British, refined. In the background Nick could hear the murmur of conversation and clinking glasses.

'An email. She didn't say where she was.' He paused. 'I'm actually a bit worried about her.'

'So are we. We haven't seen Gillian for almost a month.'

'Do you mean she's quit?'

'I mean she's disappeared.'

Again Nick saw the face lunging for the camera. *Help me theyre coming.* But that was only yesterday. 'You said she's been gone a month?'

For a moment all he heard was hiss, Atlantic waves echoing through the cable.

'I'm sorry – who did you say you were?'

'Nick Ash. I'm a friend of Gillian's. From New York.'

'You said you had an email from her yesterday?'

'Uh huh.'

'Well at least she's alive.' The British accent made it impossible to tell if he meant it as a joke. 'Did she say where she is?'

Nick wondered how much to say. 'It was very short. She sounded like she may be in trouble.'

'Oh God.' Again, the accent bleached all depth from the words. It could have been profound distress or simply boredom. 'Have you called the police?'

'I don't really have anything to tell them.'

'Well I did. Utterly useless. They told me young women wander off all the time. Said it was probably an affair of the heart – particularly when I showed them the photograph. You know how the French can be. Though speaking of our Gallic friends, the Duc de Berry is about to go under the hammer and I'm afraid I ought to be—'

'Just one more thing.' Nick rushed the words out. 'Have you heard of the Master of the Playing Cards?'

The man sounded surprised. 'Of course. Fifteenth-century German engraver. Those curious cards.'

'Gillian mentioned him in her message.'

'Did she?'

Nick hung on, waiting for another question. None came.

'Was she working on anything to do with the playing cards?' he prompted. 'Anything for sale or auction?'

'I'm not aware of any new works by the *Meister der Spielkarten* to have appeared in the last hundred years. They certainly haven't come through our door.'

Another pause. The waves crashed and rolled down the line.

'I really must go and look after our customers. But thank you very much for your call. Do get in touch if you find out anything else. We're all very worried for Gillian.'

It was only when he hung up that Nick realised he hadn't got the man's name. He swore and thought about calling back, but he had a feeling he wouldn't get an answer. Outside, darkness had already brought a premature end to the short January day. He'd finish his coffee and go home.

Lying on the table, his cellphone suddenly glowed blue and let off a series of outraged beeps. 'Seven missed calls, one new voicemail,' the screen announced. He checked the numbers. All the calls had come from his apartment.

He ignored the voicemail and rang Bret. He picked up on the first ring.

'Nick? Is that you?' He sounded breathless, close to tears. 'You need to get back here. It's Gillian.'

Nick forced himself to be calm. 'Did she call? Is she OK?'

'Um, Gillian called, yeah. Listen, you need to get back here pronto.'

'Did you speak to her? What did she say? Is she in trouble?'

'Trouble? Yeah I'd say she's in fucking trouble. It's – listen, you can't even—' He broke off with what sounded like a sob.

38

A second later: 'Sorry. Just get back here now OK? And buzz me when you arrive.'

It took Nick twenty-five minutes. On a wet Friday night in the city there wasn't a cab to be found: he ran almost the whole way. By the time he arrived outside the apartment building his wool coat was soaked through. He bounded up the stairs into the lobby, past the steel mailboxes and dimly lit buzzers.

Buzz me when you arrive.

But why buzz when he had his keys?

Nothing made sense, hadn't since Gillian's message arrived. Maybe if he stopped to think about it . . . But he couldn't stop, didn't *want* to think about it. He wanted answers. Everything else could wait. He punched the elevator button, then decided the stairs would be faster. He took them two at a time, past the startled faces of familiar, anonymous neighbours. He reached the third floor and pushed through the fire door.

The corridor was dark. He punched the switch on the wall. The low-energy bulb jumped into life with a buzz.

Buzz me when you arrive.

Why did Bret sound so panicked? What had Gillian said to him? What would he care? So far as Nick could tell, Gillian had never been any more to Bret than a redhead with nice tits.

Help me theyre coming.

And in the twenty-first century there was more than one way to buzz someone.

Afterwards, he couldn't say why he did it – only that his world had gotten so strange that even the weirdest things seemed normal. Nick pulled the laptop out of his bag and flipped it open on the floor. This close to the apartment, it had no trouble connecting to his wireless router. He clicked an icon on the taskbar. A new program filled the screen.

His contacts were listed underneath, Gillian still perched at the top.

Last seen: 06 January 07:48:26

No change. Nick scrolled down until he found Bret.

Last seen: Online Now

Feeling ridiculous kneeling on the linoleum floor almost outside his own front door, Nick clicked the VIDEO button.

A hazy image of his apartment appeared on screen. Bret's face filled the foreground, slumped back in his chair. His eyes were open as if he was trying to scream, though no sound came through the duct tape plastered over his mouth. Blood dribbled from a gash in his temple. Over his shoulder, in the middle of the room, Nick could see a man in a leather jacket and black balaclava waiting opposite the door. He swung his arms, shifting his weight impatiently. A long-barrelled pistol flashed in his hand.

Help me theyre coming.

Whoever they were, they'd come.

VIII

Cologne, 1420

'Is everything satisfactory?'

I sat at the workbench and tried to concentrate on the sheet of paper laid in front of me. I wanted to impress my new master with my diligence, but everywhere my surroundings seduced my attention away. It was as though all the dreams of my imagination had exploded into this one room. Tools beyond number hung from nails on the walls: burins and polishers, scrapers and chisels, and many whose names I did not know but would learn. One whole beam was given over to a set of hammers, ranging in size from a sturdy mallet to a gem hammer so small it could have beaten angel hair. A rack on the opposite wall held more treasures: glass and silver beads dangling on long strings, fragments of crystal and lead, vials of antimony and quicksilver for alloying the gold, pink coral that forked like antlers, long iron fingers loaded with rings. In a lattice-fronted cabinet by the window, gold cups and plates awaited their owners. Even the scorch marks on the table by my elbow seemed to speak of wonders. Outside the shopfront, across the square, buttresses and scaffolding rose around the unfinished cathedral.

Konrad Schmidt, master goldsmith and now also my master, sighed to draw my attention back.

'For seven years I undertake to school you in the ways, crafts and mysteries of the goldsmith's guild. You will live under my roof, eat with my family, and do all the work I command you in accordance with the laws of the guild. I will not demand anything below your dignity as an apprentice. You will draw water for quenching iron but not for drinking; you will fetch wood for the forge but not for my wife's oven. In return, you will pay me ten gulden now, and another gulden each three months for your food and lodgings. You will conduct yourself as befits a member of this noble guild. You will not divulge the secrets of our craft to any man. You will not steal from my shop or my family. You will moderate your appetites and bring no shame on my household. You will not commit any immoral or heinous act under my roof, nor insult my family. Is this satisfactory?'

I snatched the reed pen from the inkpot and scrawled my name large across the bottom of the page. Flush with the desire to impress my new master with my learning, I signed in Latin. *Johannes de Maguntia* – Johann of Mainz. Henchen Gensfleisch, the boy I had been, was gone, abandoned on the wharf at Mainz six days earlier.

Konrad Schmidt was not a man susceptible to enthusiasm. He took the paper, sanded the wet ink and left it to dry.

I took a moment to examine the man who now owned my future. He was about fifty, his eyes dark and deep, his cheeks hollowed out by age. He wore a high-necked wine-coloured gown with a fur-trimmed jerkin over it, and a fat ring on his left hand which was rich but not gaudy. Grey curls poked out from under the velvet cap he wore; sobriety seemed written on every line of his face. When he smiled, which was rarely, it only made him seem sad.

And what did he have in return? I saw myself over his shoulder in a silver mirror on the wall. Surely I was the model of a young apprentice. I wore the fresh white shirt I had bought in Mainz and kept wrapped for a week while the barge brought me downriver. My hair was brushed and trimmed under my cloth cap, my skin scrubbed in the bathhouse, my cheeks freshly shaved. All my belongings were gathered in a sack by my feet. From the moment I had set foot on the dock at Cologne and seen the cathedral on its hill like a blade of glass, I had felt free, beyond my father's reach at last and released from the suffocation of my family. This, I knew, was where I would make my mark.

Schmidt saw me staring but did not comment. 'I will show you the rest of the house.'

I picked up my sack and followed. A door at the back led into a small yard which contained a privy, a storeroom, a woodshed and a large furnace set against the back wall. A man in a leather apron worked a pair of wheezing bellows by the furnace. He turned as he heard us approach.

'This is Gerhard,' said Schmidt. 'He finished his apprenticeship this past summer. Now he works here as a journeyman.'

I disliked him at once. His big hands looked far too clumsy to have created any of the delicate pieces in the shop. His face was fat and red, sweaty from the forge, with puffy skin around his narrow eyes. He reminded me of my father, though he could not have been more than five years my senior. He nodded at me and grunted, then turned back to his task.

'Gerhard will supervise you while I tend the shop.'

43

My shining mood dimmed. Konrad Schmidt was everything I had expected from my master: solemn, authoritative, easy to obey. Gerhard, I knew instantly, was an oaf who would teach me nothing. It was with a sullen face that I followed Schmidt up the wooden staircase on the outside of the house to the next storey.

'This is where my wife and I live.'

This level was divided into two rooms, a hall and a bedchamber. Green hangings covered the stone walls, and three dark chests lined the edges of the room. Sitting on one of them, next to a cradle, a fair-haired woman in an unlaced dress suckled an infant.

'My wife,' said Schmidt gruffly. Just before he pulled me back to the staircase I saw her shoot me a welcoming smile. She must have been closer in age to me than to her husband, and time had been kind to her figure. I understood now why Schmidt had put such emphasis on my moral obligations.

'Do you have other children?' I asked as we climbed to the attic chamber. We were high up now: rooftops, chimneys and spires stretched away all around us. Down in the courtyard, even Gerhard looked small.

'A daughter, apprenticed to a weaver, and a son. You will meet him soon enough. The guild has just approved his enrolment as my apprentice. You will share the room.'

We reached the platform at the top of the stairs and ducked into the attic. A window in the gable admitted a cool autumn light. Otherwise the room was bare save for a lamp, a chest and a single bed.

'This is where you and Pieter sleep.'

I crossed to the window and looked out. Directly opposite rose the half-built cathedral – the needle-thin chapel the only part rising to its full height. The city stretched away from it in a broad crescent, mirroring the bend in the river which ribboned away to the south, back to Mainz. The view reassured me. Perhaps Gerhard's tutelage would not be such an ordeal.

The door banged open and I turned, thinking the wind had blown it in. A youth, not much more than a boy, stood on the stair outside and peered in curiously. He had soft white skin, unmarked by any line or flaw, and a cap of golden curls. For a moment I thought he must be an angel. Then I saw the resemblance with Konrad. They were as alike as two clay vessels moulded by the same potter's hand, one fired and cracked, the other moist and smooth, untouched by the kiln. He smiled at me.

Schmidt made a gesture between us. 'This is my son, Pieter.'

That moment, I felt the demon enter my soul.

IX

Bret's eyes opened wider – at least he was alive. He stared out of the laptop window and jerked his head back over his shoulder. The gunman's gaze was fixed on the door; he hadn't noticed Nick's face on Bret's screen.

Nick's mind spun; he wanted to vomit. *What was this?*

A door banged open behind him.

'Nick? What are you doing?'

Nick turned. It was Max, his neighbour from across the hall, an eight-year-old latchkey kid whose mother worked all hours at some big legal firm. Nick had helped him with his home-work a couple of times. He was peering out his apartment door, sucking on a soda and looking down curiously at Nick. 'Did Bret lock you out again?'

'I—'

Nick heard the gunshots through the wall. A split second later the noise repeated through the speakers, a digital echo almost louder than the original. By then, Bret was dead. His body convulsed under the impact of the bullets, jerky and unnatural, as if the enormity was too much for the camera's connection. The man in the room was staring at the monitor, watching Nick on screen. For a moment their eyes met, artificially opposed in virtual space. Then the gunman moved for the door.

Max screamed and slammed his door shut. Nick picked up the laptop and ran. Sick with shock and adrenalin, he burst into the stairwell. Up or down? Downstairs was the street, people, safety – would the gunman expect that? Was there someone else waiting for him there? If he went up, would he be trapped?

The door to his apartment opened and he decided. Down. Slipping and sliding, hanging on to the rail for dear life as he corkscrewed around. He passed the door to the second-floor corridor and kicked it open, hoping to confuse his pursuer. But he was the only person on the stairs: his footsteps must have clattered all the way up to the roof. There was no way the gunman could mistake it.

Nick skidded to a stop at the bottom of the stairs. The lobby was empty, but through the glass doors that led onto the street he saw movement. A man was loitering outside, keeping just out of range of the light over the door. He had a black coat draped over his right arm, covering the hand and whatever it held.

It could have been anyone: someone waiting for his date, a smoker getting a fix, a driver making a pickup. Nick didn't want to find out. An animal instinct seemed to have taken over. Everything else – the horror, the confusion, the terror – had been locked down. Footsteps were pounding down the stairs.

Nick threw himself into the waiting elevator. His thumb hammered on the button; the footsteps were almost on top of him.

The doors slid together with a grumble. In the narrowing crack, Nick saw the gunman race into the lobby. He'd pulled off his balaclava, revealing a closely shaved head and a row of gold studs gleaming from one ear. His head turned; their eyes met. Then the doors shut and the elevator began to rise.

He was heading for the top floor. Instinct had made the decision again, the basic desire to go as far as possible from danger. But how far was that? All the corridors were dead ends. There was a door onto the roof – he'd taken Gillian up there in the summer to stargaze, though all they'd seen was the navigation lights of planes dipping into La Guardia. But where then?

The elevator stopped. From below, Nick could hear footsteps clattering up the stairwell once more. He turned down a short corridor that ended in a door with a green FIRE EXIT sign nailed to it. Nick slammed straight into the metal bar and barged it open. He stumbled out onto the roof.

An angry, high-pitched whine erupted behind him, the building itself protesting against his trespass. *The fire alarm.* When he'd come up with Gillian, they'd used a credit card and a roll of tape to disarm it. Now it was in full roar, filling the cold night with its siren. *Good.* Help would come, the fire brigade or the police.

But until then . . .

Raindrops spat against his face. A shiver of despair knifed through his body. He had come out onto a small square of Astroturf that some optimist had once laid to impersonate a lawn. All around him were the water tanks, heating vents and satellite dishes that crusted the roof. Plenty of cover – but nowhere to hide for long.

The fire alarm hammered against his ears. He couldn't even hear if the killer was coming up the stairs. He stood there on the soggy fake grass, stiff with indecision. All his life had been based on reason: methodical, boring, safe. Now he had nothing. No framework. No time to think. Whatever instinct had driven him up there was spent. He had nowhere to go.

Strangely, in that moment of emptiness he didn't think of Gillian, or his parents, or his sister. He thought of Bret, lying dead in an easy chair four floors below him. Bret who had told thousands of men how to go all night without ever, to Nick's knowledge, bringing a girl back to the apartment. Bret who had bid for countless auction items he had no intention of buying. Bret who had sat with a gun held to his head and still managed to warn Nick. *Buzz me.*

Nick ran across the wet roof and threw himself down behind an air-conditioning unit. Puddled water soaked into his shirt. At least his coat was black. He peered around the corner, between the struts supporting a water tank.

For a moment he thought his pursuer might have given up. In the pink half-light that passed for night he saw the stairwell door swaying loose in the wind. The fire alarm wailed. The damp shirt pressed against his chest like a heart attack.

Then Nick saw him, crouched in the doorway as he scanned the cluttered rooftop. The pistol swept over Nick's hiding place and carried on around. He was a short, heavyset man and looked out of breath. It was the first time Nick had supposed he might be anything less than superhuman.

Almost because he knew it was expected of him, Nick felt a powerful, suicidal need to run. He fought it back. They couldn't stay like this for ever. Even in New York someone must have heard the shots, called the police.

The gunman knew it too. He edged away from the door, tracking the pistol in sharp sweeps across the rooftop, silent under the shriek of the alarm.

Then, as suddenly as it had started, the alarm cut out. A desolate silence filled Nick's ears. Even the gunman was caught off guard. He paused, glancing around uncertainly.

Nick reached inside his coat pocket and felt his keys, cold and wet. He balled them in his fist and pulled them out. The background roar of the city at night was beginning to filter back over the ringing in his ears, but he didn't dare risk being heard. Across the rooftop, the gunman was still edging closer.

Nick reached out. His arm was frozen and weighted down by the sodden coat. He had it to do it. Throw the keys, distract the killer, tackle him and get the gun out of his hand. If he just came one step closer . . .

Nick was trembling. He'd never done anything like this in his life.

The gunman took a half-step nearer and turned. Nick tensed his arm for the throw – but now the killer was looking straight at him. If Nick moved he'd be dead before the keys left his hand. Even if he didn't move . . . He held his breath, feeling the pressure build in his lungs, pushing against his chest and throat. All he wanted to do was scream.

And then the gunman turned away and walked back to the door. Nick waited, still not daring to breathe. He squeezed the keys in his fingers and closed his eyes. Was now the moment? He'd never thought he could be so terrified.

He opened his eyes again. The gunman was kneeling beside an air-conditioning unit, glancing over his shoulder. He had his back to Nick – if ever there was a time to take him, it was now, Nick told himself.

He drew a deep breath and tensed himself to spring. His muscles felt locked stiff with cold. What if he was too slow? What if the man heard him coming across the fake grass?

The killer stood up. He took one last look at the rooftop,

straight over Nick's head again, then stepped inside the door-way and vanished. Nick heard him jogging down the stairs.

Nick waited until he was sure the man was gone, then picked himself up. The moment he was on his feet his whole body shuddered uncontrollably. He could hardly stand – thank God he hadn't tried anything dumb with the gunman. He peeled off his coat and staggered across the wet grass to the door, keeping a nervous eye on the stairs in case the man came back. He almost collapsed on his knees next to the air conditioner as he tried to see what the gunman had been doing.

A dark crack showed where the maintenance flap hadn't been shut properly. Nick pulled it open. Inside, a black pistol nestled among the dials and tubes.

Nick reached in and picked it up. It was heavier than he'd expected; his stiff fingers almost dropped it. Was there a safety catch? He hadn't touched a gun since Scout camp, and this was very different from shooting .22 rifles at paper targets. Even holding the pistol in his hand he felt frightened by its power. This was the gun that had killed Bret.

He laid it down on the artificial grass and moved away. Blue and red lights flashed off the canyon walls of the apartment blocks, reflected ten-to-a-floor in the stacked black windows. Only then did he hear the sirens.

X

Cologne, 1420–1

Through the autumn of that year, I made a number of discoveries about Konrad Schmidt.

He was a fair master, but a hard man to impress. I was a more than able apprentice. When he taught us the device for drawing out gold to make wire, my first length came through supple and straight. Pieter spent an afternoon – and a considerable quantity of his father's gold – producing length after length that stretched and bunched and snapped like wet dough. When we hammered gold between parchment sheets to make leaf, mine emerged airy and gossamer thin; Pieter's was lumpy as porridge. When Konrad showed us how to fire silver sulphide onto an engraving to make the lines leap out, mine were sharp as glass. Pieter's looked as if he had left it standing in the grate too long.

Yet Konrad Schmidt resisted my precocity. Whenever I showed him a piece of work, he merely grunted and gave me another task before going back to the laborious task of correcting his son. When I suggested – after many hours' observation – a way to improve the gold wire puller, he heard me in silence and then dismissed me with a shake of his head. At first I ascribed it to a father's love for his son – but the more I watched them together, the less plausible that seemed. Konrad rarely criticised Pieter's work, but beat him for the most minor lapses: leaving a bucket of milk in the sun, forgetting to doff his cap to a customer, putting a hammer in the wrong place in the rack. Eventually I decided that the one was a substitute for the other – that Konrad found so many other faults because he could not admit to himself that his son would not succeed him in his trade. That, I supposed, was why he had had to on take his own son as an apprentice, a practice frowned upon by the guild. And, perhaps, why he resented my skill.

Gerhard resented me too, though that I put down to obvious rivalry. His fat hands were surprisingly fine at working metal – far more than I had credited – but he did not have my instinct for gold. At first he tried to hold me back by giving me lesser tasks, flattering Pieter with responsibility, but this quickly rebounded on him when he had to take responsibility for Pieter's mistakes. Thereafter he decided it was better to take credit for my work than blame for Pieter's, and satisfied himself with thrashing me whenever I gifted him an excuse.

There were other things I learned about Konrad Schmidt and his household that year.

I learned that his wife was the third Frau Schmidt. She praised me often and extravagantly – my diligence, my honesty, my artful skill – and I was flattered, until I realised she did it only to humiliate Pieter, who was not her son.

I learned that Gerhard could not afford the gold he needed to produce his master-piece, and therefore could not gain full membership as a master of the guild. Rather than save, he spent what he had drinking out his frustrations in the river-front taverns.

I learned that Konrad kept the key to his cabinet on a string around his neck and never removed it, except once a month when he visited the bathhouse. When I knew that, I followed him there, and while he bathed took an impression of the key between two wax blocks softened in the steamy air. That evening I cast my own copy in the forge, and after that would creep down at night when Pieter was asleep to fondle and caress the pieces inside.

It was not a happy household, but nor had been my home in Mainz, so I did not mind. I was happy in my work. Once I learned that my skill only fuelled envy and resentment I kept it to myself as much as possible, and took my delights in solitude.

The only person who admired my ability was poor, artless Pieter. Four years younger, he venerated me with the unthinking awe of a brother. It was a new feeling for me, always last and youngest growing up. Though it was sometimes a burden, more often it made me glow with possessive pride. I took to protecting Pieter, slipping him pieces of my work to pass off as his own, neglecting my own tasks to show him again and again how to perform some simple piece of skill. Though it sometimes earned me a beating, I did not care. Each time his knee brushed mine at the workbench, each time I cupped my hand over his to guide his graving tool, the demon inside me thrilled with delight. Of course I suffered agonies and shame – but they were vivid agonies, the sweetest shame, raging like fire in my body. On Sundays in the cathedral I stared up at the cross of Our Saviour and begged for release, but I knew in my heart I did not mean it. At night we lay in our shared bed and I dug my nails into my palms until they bled like Christ's to resist the

54

wild temptations that assailed me. Some nights, especially in winter, Pieter would burrow against me for warmth, half asleep, and I would have to roll away before my risen lust betrayed itself. Eventually, I reasoned, the demon would see that he could not overcome me and would depart my body for a weaker vessel. Until then I basked in the heat of my lust and the glory of my suffering, quivering in sublime stasis.

In spring, a year after the verdict in Mainz, I made another discovery. It was a warm day in April and there was little work to do, so Konrad decided to teach us a lesson. While Gerhard kept the counter and watched for customers, Konrad brought me and Pieter to the workbench and laid out a bottle, a small piece of paper, a saucer and a spindle of signet rings.

'All our skill and artifice – where does it come from?' he asked.

'From God, Father,' said Pieter.

At the front of the shop I saw Gerhard smirking. Perhaps he thought – as I did – that God's glory was hard to discern in Pieter's craftsmanship.

'All art comes from God and we learn it as best we may.' A grimace at Pieter. 'The greatest tribute we can pay perfection is to perfectly imitate it.'

He took a ring off the spindle and slipped it onto his forefinger, just above the knuckle. Then he did something I had not seen before: he took the bottle, poured a little pool of ink into a dish and touched it with the ring. It came away black and sticky. He wiped a finger across its face, then pushed it hard with his fist into a scrap of paper on the table. When he lifted his hand, the wet image of a running stag was pressed perfectly into the paper. Another touch, another wipe, another impression and a second, identical stag appeared beside the first. Konrad tore the paper in two and handed Pieter and me half each, together with blank rings from the spindle.

'There is your design. A penny to whoever produces the more perfect copy.'

The penny did not interest me: I knew I would win it. Something about what Konrad did had chimed false, though I did not know what it was. I pondered it while I worked on the ring. First, I took a flimsy piece of parchment that had been soaked to become translucent and traced the image on the paper with a leaded stylus. I washed a thin layer of wax over the face of the ring, and rubbed the back of my parchment with the lead. Then I put the ring in a vice, overlaid the parchment and retraced the image, bearing down hard with the stylus. When I took the parchment away, a light grey stag had appeared on the wax-coated ring.

I reached for the original ring and held up the two to compare. I saw what was wrong at once.

'Herr Schmidt,' I called. 'Which image did you mean us to copy?'

He turned away from his conversation with Gerhard and scowled at me like an idiot. 'The image on the ring.'

'It was just that . . .' I faltered under his gaze, but gathered strength to carry on. 'The deer on your ring is facing right, but the deer on the paper is facing left. A truly perfect copy . . .' I trailed off.

'The image on the ring,' he repeated, and turned away.

Now my mind was hungry with the challenge. I scraped the wax off the ring, erasing the wrong-headed deer, and started again. I took another, bigger ball of wax and worked it on the tabletop until it was flat and smooth. Pieter watched wide-eyed but said nothing; his own effort looked more like a lame dog than a stag.

I retraced the image onto the wax plaque. I carved it out with a burin, then I dipped the wax in the bowl of ink and pressed it out on the paper, as Konrad had done with the ring. When I pulled it away, I had a second copy of the stag, who now stood back to back with the first, facing left. Hot with success, I traced the new image and then transferred it back onto the ring with the stylus.

But the more I examined it, the more dissatisfied I became. The stag was facing the right direction now, but in every other respect he was inferior. His antlers were a muddied tangle. One leg was spindly and another like a ham, while his tail looked like a protrusion of his rump. His nose had completely disappeared.

I studied his lineage, strewn across the table on paper, parchment, wax and gold. The changes were apparent across every generation. With every copy the stag moved further from the perfection I sought, until it became the unrecognisable monstrosity I had on the ring, fit only for the pages of a bestiary.

Across the square the cathedral bell tolled the hour. Customers were beginning to gather at the counter; I knew that soon Konrad would call us away to some other task. There was no time to try again. I carved out the animal as he was, mending his deformities as best I could with the graver. It made him a little more like a deer, but further still from Konrad's prototype.

When I was finished, I took the ring to my master. He examined it briefly, grunted, and threw a penny to Pieter. Pieter's face glowed with rare success; my own was red with shame. I struggled to fight back tears. Konrad must have seen it for he told me, gently, 'True perfection exists only in God.'

But I knew I could do more.

XI

Bret had never been so popular as he was in death. Nick stood in the corridor, a blanket around his shoulders, and watched an army of police officers and technicians go in and out of the apartment like ants picking over Bret's carcass. How could it take so many people to figure it out when he'd seen Bret die himself? They wouldn't even let him in, but kept him in the corridor with only a cup of coffee and the blanket. A token strip of black and yellow tape barred the door.

He was exhausted – he just wanted to collapse. He'd already told his story twice to two different officers. They hadn't looked as sympathetic as he'd expected. They'd told him a detective would want to talk to him soon – but that had been half an hour ago.

Two men appeared in the doorway, one in uniform, the other in a grey suit that looked more expensive than anything Nick owned. The uniform pointed at him and muttered something that Nick couldn't hear. The suit nodded, ducked under the tape and walked over.

'Mr Ash? I'm Detective Royce.'

Detective Royce was lean and far too tanned for January; he looked like he ran marathons. He had close-cropped hair that was probably going grey, and pointed sideburns that crossed his cheeks like spurs.

'I hear you've got quite a story to tell.'

Nick leaned back against the wall and pulled the blanket closer around him. He felt faint.

'Is there any way of getting another cup of coffee?'

'It won't take long at this stage. If you could just tell me in your own words . . .'

Who else's words would they be? 'Bret—'

'You mean the deceased? Mr Deangelo?'

'He rang me on my cellphone.'

'Approximately what time was that?'

'About five, I guess. I can check my phone.'

'We'll check out the phone company records anyhow. You weren't in the apartment at this time?'

Was Royce even listening? 'I told you, he rang me on my cellphone. I was out.'

'Do you remember where you were?'

Nick thought back a couple of hours. It seemed forever ago. 'A coffee shop by Fifteen and Tenth. I had my phone switched off. When I—'

He stopped. Royce had turned to look down the corridor, where a man in a white boiler suit, white hood and facemask was walking towards him. He looked as if he'd just walked out of a nuclear reactor. In his gloved hand he carried the killer's pistol wrapped in a clear plastic bag.

'We found this on the roof. We'll get it checked for prints and ballistics.'

Nick started. 'Wait a minute. It'll have my fingerprints on it.'

Royce looked at him with more interest.

'I picked it up where it was hidden, behind the air conditioner. I told you.'

The technician jerked his head at the detective. 'Put it in the statement.'

He wandered off into Nick's apartment. Royce turned back to him with an out-of-my-hands grimace.

'I'm sorry. I know you think this probably isn't the best time for all this. Believe me, it never is. You've heard the line that ninety per cent of murders are solved in twenty-four hours or never?'

Nick nodded wearily. 'I guess.'

'It's bullshit. But the more we get now, the quicker we can make it later.' There was a high-caffeine energy about Royce, restless and impatient. 'I'll get the rest of your story tomorrow at the precinct. For now, I just need to know: to your knowledge, was Mr Deangelo involved in anything of an illegitimate or criminal nature?'

Nick hesitated. What could he say about Bret that wouldn't condemn him? Sleazy, disreputable, maybe even offensive – but not criminal.

Royce saw his uncertainty and drew his own conclusions. 'We need to know, Nick.' He was standing too close, staring down at Nick, his voice too loud for the cramped corridor. 'This wasn't an angry girlfriend or some crackhead thief who screwed up. The guy who did this had a motive. Was Bret into drugs?'

Nick squirmed, but at the rate they were dismantling the apartment they'd find out soon enough. 'He smoked some pot. A lot of people do.' He meant it to sound casual, no big deal, but it came out defensive.

'Do you?'

'No.' Nick pulled the blanket tighter across his shoulders. 'Not really.' How convincing did that sound? 'I don't think this was about Bret. I think it was me they wanted.'

'*They?*' Royce pulled out a slim notebook and flipped through it. 'The sergeant said you told him there was only one perpetrator in the room.'

'There was.' Nick felt overwhelmed with tiredness. His head ached and his eyes felt vacant. 'I meant *they* . . .' He flapped his hands vaguely. 'You know . . . Whoever.'

'Right.'

'Listen.' Nick grabbed Royce's sleeve. The blanket slid off his shoulder and fell to the floor in a heap. 'Last night I had a message – online – from my ex-girlfriend. She sounded desperate, like someone was after her. When I turned on the webcam all I heard was a scream and then a guy shut it off.' He saw Royce's look and realised how crazy he sounded.

Royce pulled his arm away and smoothed out the crease Nick had made. 'We'll look into it. Does she have a name, your girlfriend?'

'Ex. Gillian Lockhart. She works in Paris now for Stevens Mathison. The auction house.'

Royce put his notebook away without writing anything. 'We'll get a full statement from you tomorrow. Right now, I think you should get some rest.'

Nick stepped back as two more men in boiler suits came out of his apartment carrying a large silver box wrapped in plastic sheeting. It took him a second to realise what was inside.

'That's my computer.'

'Evidence,' said one of the technicians. The facemask deadened his voice. He thrust a clipboard into Nick's hands. 'Sign here.'

'Bret never touched that machine.' *I'd have killed him if he did*, Nick almost added – but didn't. 'He was using his own computer when he . . . when it happened.'

'We've got that too,' said Royce. 'But if the killer was after you – like you said – then maybe it's got something to do with something. And it was in the same room as Bret when he died. If the camera was turned on or something . . .' Out of the corner of his eye, he saw one of the other officers beckoning him from inside the apartment. 'We'll see what we find.'

He nodded to the man by the door, then turned back to Nick and fixed him with a pitiless stare.

'We're going to get the guy who did it. I promise you that.'

Nick had never realised how much bureaucracy attended the taking of human life. It was midnight before they let him go. He spoke to a police artist, who took a description of the gunman. He saw the lab technician, who brushed his hands for gunpowder residue and stuck a cotton swab in his mouth to get a DNA sample. 'Just so we don't waste our time,' he reassured Nick. He got signed off by an earnest woman from Victim Support who gave him her card and told him to call any time. By the time it was over he was beyond exhaustion. It was all he could do to drag himself the few blocks to find a bed. There were friends he might have stayed with, but even the thought of the explanations he'd need to give made him feel ill. He checked into a hotel by Washington Square and collapsed into bed.

The moment his head touched the pillow the tears started flowing.

XII

Cologne, 1421–2

Konrad Schmidt was a generous teacher, but there was one aspect of his trade he never spoke of. He never told me how much profit he made. I never asked; I did not have to. My father's wealth had always been vague – dispersed in warehouses and barges the length of the Rhine – but the goldsmith's was tangible, displayed for all to see in the iron-bound cabinet in the shop window. Month by month, my midnight expeditions turned up fewer and fewer treasures. Pieces disappeared and were not replaced; those that remained were pushed to the front so that customers would not notice the empty shelves behind. One day, I caught Konrad on his hands and knees in front of the melting hearth, his arms black with soot as he sifted through the cold ashes. When he noticed me, I was shocked by the wild look in his eyes.

'The gold that overflows the mould when we make castings – what happens to it?' he demanded. 'There ought to be a treasure trove down here but I cannot find one grain. Do you know anything about this, Johann?'

I kept silent. Sweeping out the grate was Pieter's task, but I did it in his place. I told him it was so he would have more time to finish his work in the shop, that if his father found out he would only assign him some other chore. I picked up the crumbs of spilled gold, and kept them in a bag under a floorboard in the attic – not a treasure trove, but enough that when the time came to make my master-piece I would not want for material.

Konrad's mood matched the decline in his fortunes. He beat me and Pieter for trivial offences, and abused Gerhard viciously for imagined shortcomings. Gerhard took out his frustration by beating me and Pieter even more. We did not sit down much that winter. At night, we would lie naked on the bed and compare our bruises while I tried to hide my longing.

Strange things started to happen in the house. New vials and jars appeared on the shelves in the workshop, daubed with cryptic symbols that meant nothing to me. Konrad forbade us even to open them. Once a month, often around the time of the full moon, he would send us to bed early while sounds of earnest conversation drifted up from the workshop late into the night. We never saw who visited. One night, when I went out on the stairs to relieve myself, I looked down and saw the forge glowing hot in the yard. Konrad crouched in front of it, bare-chested. He seemed to be holding a large, egg-shaped crucible in his tongs which he thrust into the fire, muttering words I could not make out. He did not see me watching.

One night in May I discovered Konrad's secret. He had gone to meet a friend at a tavern. I waited until I heard Pieter's familiar little snores on the pillow next to me, then crept out of the room and down the outside stairs to the workshop. I took my purse, and also my key. Konrad now insisted on watching while Pieter cleaned out the melting hearth, but he had to wait until morning for the embers to cool. I had discovered that if I went down in the night, I could pick out the biggest nuggets of gold for myself and still leave enough to convince Konrad he was not being cheated. Sometimes it singed my hands, especially if we had been casting late in the afternoon, but the blisters and calluses were a price I happily paid.

I lay on my belly in front of the hearth, holding my hand over the ashes to let it warm to the heat. I was just steeling myself to delve in when suddenly I heard sounds at the front of the shop. Footsteps, several pairs approaching our door, and a dry cough I had heard a hundred times in the workshop.

I leaped to my feet, scalding the back of my hand on the grate, and ran to the back door which I had left open. But curiosity stayed me. Two water barrels stood in the corner of the room: I dived behind them, just as the front door swung open.

Someone lit a lamp. The cheap oil spluttered and fizzed, casting a diabolical glow around the shop that thankfully did not penetrate my corner. I peered through a crack between the barrels.

Four men stood around the table. My master, with his back to me; a hook-nosed man I recognised as an apothecary from the neighbouring street; a deacon from the cathedral whose name I did not know; and a fourth I had never seen before. He was a dwarf, or short enough for one, with a bristling black beard and a slanted cap. As I watched, he dragged a stool across from the hearth and jumped up on it so that he could look the others in the eye. He unhooked a small bag from his belt and laid it on the table.

'The apothecary told me you have suffered many setbacks. Perhaps I can supply what you lack.'

His voice was harsh and screeching, like an owl. He pulled back the cloth. His hands blocked my view, but between his fingers I made out the shape of a small box.

'I bought this in Paris, in the shadow of the Church of the Innocents.' A nasty chuckle. 'The man who sold it to me did not know what it was worth. But I do – and you will, if you can persuade me to part with it.'

'Can we see?' The deacon reached across the table. As his hand passed the lamp it cast a monstrous shadow over the far wall, trembling in a way I did not think was caused by the light.

'Any man can look,' said the dwarf dismissively. He handed the box to the deacon. Only when the cleric opened it did I see it was not a box but a book. Bronze straps across the cover gleamed in the lamplight.

The deacon turned a few pages and passed it wordlessly to the apothecary, who examined it more closely.

'This was all Flamel used?' he asked cryptically.

'All his secrets from the *Book of Abraham*,' was the dwarf's equally mysterious answer.

The apothecary gave the book to Schmidt. 'What do you think?'

Konrad waited a long time. I could not see his face, but I saw the way he hunched over the book, the knots in his hands as he gripped the table. My knees ached; my thigh began to spasm from my awkward posture.

At last Konrad spoke. 'If everything you say is true, why are you offering the book to us?'

The dwarf laughed – a harsh, braying noise. 'Why do men sell you raw gold when they could sell you a goblet for a higher price? Because I do not have the craft or the ingenuity, nor the tools nor indeed the materials. All I have is this book. And that is all you need to perfect your art.'

He fixed Konrad with a wicked smile and reached across the table to slide the book away. Konrad slapped his hand down heavily to stop him.

'We will take it.'

He pulled the key from around his neck and unlocked the cabinet. The dwarf hopped off his stool and followed, staring up at the chalices, cups, plates and bowls displayed on its shelves. He licked his lips. He pulled one piece down and examined it, then another. Sometimes he had to point to something on the upper shelves for Konrad to reach. There was something in the way he touched the precious objects that I recognised: a jealousy, a kindred spirit.

'This one. This one for the book.'

He held up a richly enamelled chalice. The base was embossed with scenes from the life of St John, the cup supported by arms of intricately braided wire. An abbot had commissioned it and then died; his successor, a more ascetic monk, had refused to honour the contract. Konrad had been furious, but I think a part of him was relieved to keep hold of it, for it was a rare piece of work. The one I would have chosen.

Konrad swallowed, then nodded. The lamp flame flickered, darting around the bowl like a serpent's tongue. The dwarf stuffed the cup into a sack.

'You have made a fine bargain.'

The others did not linger long after he had gone. The deacon and the apothecary excused themselves; Konrad sat at the table for some minutes staring at the book, then reluctantly closed it and locked it in the cabinet. I waited. When he left, I listened to the sound of his footsteps mounting the outside stairs and crossing the ceiling, the squeaky board at the threshold to the bedroom, the creak as the bed took his weight. I counted to one hundred. Then I crept out from behind the barrels, lit the lamp and opened the cabinet.

The book was small and worn, the edges of the binding frayed and the pages shrivelled. A brass clasp kept it shut, but otherwise there was nothing to suggest why Konrad should have paid so much for it. I unhooked the clasp.

It was written in Latin in a small, hurried hand, with many corrections and notes in brown ink in the margins. Seven of the pages were given over to drawings: a snake curled around a cross, a garden sprouting a forked tree, a king with a giant sword watching his soldiers dismember children into buckets. I shuddered and wondered what story they could possibly tell.

As I turned the pages, phrases leaped out at me from the text. *'I have opened the Books of the Philosophers, and in them learned their hidden secrets.'* Then: *'The first time that I made projection was upon Mercury, whereof I turned half-a-pound, or thereabouts, into pure Silver, better than if it had come straight from the Mine.'* And eventually: *'In the year of the restoring of mankind 1382, on the five and twentieth day of April, in the presence of my wife, I made projection of the Red Stone upon the like quantity of Mercury, which I transmuted truly into almost half a pound of wondrous, soft, perfect Gold.'*

I spent the next day in a dream, my head dizzy with possibilities. I was a virgin with a new lover: I could not wait for night to come again. Gerhard thrashed me for spilling too much gold when I poured it out of the crucible, and thrashed me again when a careless slip of my burin left an ugly scar on a brooch I had been engraving. Konrad was little better. His face had aged ten years overnight; he wandered around his shop like a ghost, fingering the key around his neck and checking the cabinet three times an hour.

Konrad went to bed late that night. The cathedral bell sounded out the hours, and I counted every one. At last I heard the creak of the stairs, the muffled squeak of the bedroom floor and a sleepy murmur from his wife. Still I waited, until the loudest sound in the house was Pieter's soft breathing beside me.

At last I crept downstairs. By then, I knew every inch of the way in darkness. The fifth and eighth stairs which creaked too loudly, the way to lift the bolt so it did not rasp, the precise amount of pressure to use on the lock of the cabinet to prevent it making a noise when it opened. I felt inside. My fingers brushed across the shelf, tracing familiar contours of plate, until they felt the leather binding.

There was a sound behind me and I froze. I listened to the night, unconsoled by silence. It was probably just coals settling in the grate, or Konrad turning over in his bed – but I needed to concentrate. I also needed light, and I did not want a zealous watchman peering through the windows that night.

I climbed back to my attic. It was only when I reached the top of the stairs that I realised I had left the cabinet open. I cursed, but it did not matter. I would have to replace the book before morning anyway. I lit the lamp by my bedside and trimmed the wick low. Pieter turned and murmured something in his sleep; he thrust out an arm as if falling. It settled on my thigh and I did not remove it. It only added to the perfection of the moment.

I do not know how long I lay there, puzzling over that mysterious book. It made no sense to me. It told the miraculous story of how the author, a Frenchman, had toiled for decades to unlock the secret of the Stone, which seemed to

69

be not a rock but an element by which quicksilver was turned to silver and gold. But how he had done it, despite the dwarf's assurances, was a mystery. He spoke of snakes and herbs; the moon and sun and Mercury; red and white powders and even the blood of infants. But what he meant by it all I could not fathom.

'*The Jew who painted the book figured it with very great cunning and workmanship: for although it was well and intelligibly painted, yet no man could ever have been able to understand it without being well skilled in their Cabala.*' I stared at the pictures until my eyes ached, but I knew nothing of the Jewish Cabala. The secrets buried in plain sight remained hidden.

At some point, I must have fallen asleep. All my dreams were golden. I stood on a mountain bathed in hot sunlight that turned the grass, the rocks, the hills and valleys gold. A golden cross stood behind me. Then I looked down and saw two snakes slithering through the grass towards me. I cried out – but instead of attacking me the snakes turned on each other. One devoured the other, then chased himself, slithering in a circle until he blurred into a haze. He fastened his jaws around his tail and began swallowing himself whole.

I looked again and saw that the snake had become a golden ring. I picked it up; I put it on my head as a crown, and the moment I did so I felt a shaft of golden light well through me like a fountain, connecting the mountain at my feet with the heavens in perfect oneness. An angel with a trumpet appeared in the likeness of my father. He touched my forehead, and the seal of the prophets was set on my brow in gold. I fell to my knees and embraced the golden earth, which was soft and warm and infinitely forgiving.

I woke from my dream. To my horror and delight, I found

that Pieter's outstretched arm had drifted across my waist, his hand cupped between my legs. I had been rubbing myself against him in my sleep. A golden pleasure suffused my body.

Alas, the demons who possess us know our weaknesses and bide their time. My dreams had intoxicated me: I knew I should stop but could not. Whether the same demon had possessed Pieter, or whether he was too sleepfast to recognise what he did, he responded willingly, even eagerly. I kissed him all over his body; I ran my fingers through his golden hair and pressed his face against my chest; I kneaded his soft skin until he gasped. He rolled me onto my side and pressed himself against me, kissing the nape of my neck. We fitted together like two spoons in a drawer. My whole body shuddered with desire and my blood flowed hot like molten gold.

With a crash of thunder, the attic door flew open. The gold in my veins turned to lead. Konrad Schmidt stood on the stair outside, a lantern in his hand and his face slack with bewilderment. I do not know what he expected to find, but surely not his naked son tangled with his apprentice in the most wanton abomination imaginable.

Confusion turned to fury. He stepped into the room, touching the place on his waist where his knife should have been. The attic was narrow and confined; there was no way past him to the door.

I took a final, longing look at Pieter, cowering naked on the bed and screaming it was not his fault. Then I leaped out of the window.

XIII

New York City

For five or ten seconds Nick didn't remember. He lay between the stiff hotel sheets feeling warm and dislocated, drifting between worlds. The rain had gone; sunlight shone through the white curtains.

Then it came back to him, and he knew the world would never be the same. He rolled over and buried his head in the pillow, as if he could smother the thoughts that overwhelmed him. He sobbed; he tossed and thrashed under the sheets like a drowning man. Images repeated themselves in his mind: Gillian, Bret, the killer chasing him up an endless flight of stairs. He felt broken.

The ring of his cellphone cut through his grief. He groaned and ignored it, wishing it away. It persisted.

He reached out and scrabbled on the bedside table.

'Nick?'

A woman's voice. British. Did he recognise it?

'It's Emily Sutherland.' She waited. 'From the Cloisters?'

'Right, yes.' There was some part of Nick that could still

72

function. 'Listen, it's not really—'

'I did some research on that card you brought me. It's . . . intriguing.'

'OK.'

'Can I meet you to talk about it?'

'Can you tell me now?'

She hesitated. 'I – It would be easier in person. It raises some interesting questions. I need to be at the Metropolitan Museum this afternoon. Can you meet me on the roof terrace there?'

'Sure.' Anything to get her off the phone.

'I'll be there at four.'

He mumbled a goodbye and hung up. He still had the phone in his hand when it rang again. He dragged it back to his ear. 'Yes?'

'How you doing this morning?' It was Royce, a voice from his nightmares. He carried on without waiting for an answer, 'We need you to come down to the precinct to give us a statement about last night?'

Another wave of tiredness hit Nick. 'What time is it now?'

'Twenty after nine. Come as soon as you can.'

The police station on Tenth Street was a squat block that must have been modern once, flanked by two grey towers. Nick was expected. A uniformed officer led him from the lobby through a beige labyrinth of corridors to a small room somewhere deep in the building. There were no windows, only a wide linoleum-framed mirror across one wall. Nick glimpsed his reflection in it and winced. He was still wearing his clothes from yesterday. Something he'd lain in on the rooftop had left an oily smear all across the front of his shirt. A thin itch of stubble dishevelled his cheeks. His eyes were baggy, his hair limp despite the best

73

efforts of the hotel shampoo. His heart sank when he saw a video camera poised on its tripod to record him.

Royce kept him waiting for a quarter of an hour. The moment he entered the room Nick felt himself wilt. Royce was a vampire, feeding off other people's energy. He flopped into the chair across the table from Nick and leaned forward on sharp elbows.

'Thanks for coming in. I know it's a tough time for you.' He pushed his chair away and leaned back, crossing his legs. He drummed his fingers on the side of his shoe while the technician fiddled with the camera.

'OK.' Underneath the lens, a dark red light blinked at Nick. 'Let's go. Could you state your name and occupation for the record.'

'Nick Ash. I work in digital forensic reconstruction.'

Like most people, Royce looked blank. 'What's that?'

'It's trying to piece together documents that have been torn or shredded beyond recognition. I work on systems that scan the pieces and then digitally reconstruct them using algorithms. The idea is they might be used as evidence.'

'Do you do that for us?'

'For the federal government – the FBI, other agencies.' Again, it sounded good when he wanted to impress someone. For Royce, it was just another opening.

'Do you have access to classified documents?'

Nick shook his head. 'It's still a research programme. The technology's unproven.'

Royce lost interest. 'Let's get to last night. First of all, please describe your relationship with the deceased.'

Nick told them everything he could, starting from when they'd moved in to the apartment. The message from Gillian, the panicked call from Bret, his decision to check on the webcam and what he'd seen. His pulse rose as he described the chase up the stairs, the panicked moments on the rooftop when he thought he'd die.

Royce listened to it all folded up on his chair like a bat. Unlike the night before, there were no interruptions. If anything, Nick found the silence more unsettling. No noise penetrated the room; all he could hear was his own voice and the whine of the video camera.

He finished and looked up. Royce seemed to be examining some blemish on the corner of the table.

'That's quite a story.'

What did that mean?

'Would you say you were close to your room-mate?'

'We're – we were – very different people. We got on OK.'

'The lab had a look at the PC we recovered from your apartment. Couldn't find much because apparently half your hard drive's encrypted.'

'I told you; I work under contract to the FBI.'

'While your friend's machine,' Royce continued, 'that really opened our eyes. Would it surprise you to hear he had a significant number of indecent images – really, a lot – stored on his computer?'

Nick was too tired to pretend. 'Bret liked looking at porn. He's not the first guy to do that and it's not against the law.'

'Did he ever share his stash with you?'

It was so hard to get a handle on Royce. One minute he was aloof, a prick with a badge – the next he was trying to be your big brother.

'I had a girlfriend.'

Royce looked unimpressed. 'Did you see what he was looking at?'

'Tried not to.'

Royce leaned closer. 'Why? Was it really bad?'

'No. Just . . .'

'Did Bret ever talk about it?'

He never shut up. 'Sometimes, I guess.'

'Did you ever hear him mention underage girls?'

That took Nick by surprise. He did his best to let his shock show while his mind raced. There were no black-and-white answers where Bret was concerned, only sludgy shades of grey. But even he had limits.

'Bret would never have done anything illegal.'

'You admitted yourself he was a drug abuser. If he was still alive we could have gotten him for possession with intent, with all the pot we found in your apartment.'

'What are you—'

Royce pushed back his chair, almost knocking over the video camera. He spread his arms and leaned over the table. The flaps of his suit jacket stretched behind him like wings. 'Bret's death wasn't an accident. Someone tied him to that chair and killed him because they wanted him dead. At this stage in our investigation we don't need to look too fucking far to find a motive.'

Nick said nothing. Royce was trying to pen him in, confirm his prejudices.

'I don't think you're right,' he said at last. 'I told you what happened. The killer must have broken into the apartment and tied Bret up. Then they got him to call me to get me home. He only killed Bret when he realised I'd seen him on the webcam.'

'Did you do that often? Spy on Bret?'

It was like talking to a ten-year-old. They heard what you said but took a completely different meaning.

'I never spied on Bret. He told me to *Buzz* him.'

'Excuse me?' Royce sounded perplexed, though his

76

expression said he knew exactly what Nick was going to say.

'Buzz is a communications interface – software. It's sort of instant messaging, Internet video and voice calling all in the same package.'

'Sounds great.' Royce switched again. 'We'd like you to unencrypt the contents of your computer.'

'I can't do that. My contract with the FBI—'

'Forget it. We can get a warrant, but it'll look better if you cooperate.'

Nick stared at him. 'Look better to who? I came down here to answer your questions. Am I under arrest?'

'No.' Royce pulled back. 'You're just giving us a statement. Everything's cool.' He glanced at the video camera. Had he slipped up? Nick began to wish he'd brought a lawyer with him.

'Look at it from my point of view,' Royce said, more reasonable now. 'We've got the gun that killed Bret and it's got your fingerprints all over it. We're still waiting on the samples from your hands for gunpowder traces.'

Gunpowder traces? Did they think he'd fired the gun? Could it have got on his hands when he picked it up?

'We've got witnesses who place you at the scene of the crime—'

'Of course I was at the scene of the crime.' Nick was almost shouting. 'It's where I fucking live.'

'And you're giving me this – frankly – incredible story about some masked guy who chased you onto the roof with a gun, then changed his mind and vanished into the night. Leaving the gun behind for you.' Royce rested his hands on the back of the chair and leaned forward. 'I want to believe you, Nick. Really, I do. But you're not making it easy for me.'

Nick's mind raced, trying to think of something that would exonerate him.

'Max.'

'What?'

'Max. The kid across the hall. He was talking to me when Bret got shot. He'll tell you I had nothing to do with it.'

For the first time that morning, Royce looked uncertain. He excused himself and left the room. When he came back, he slumped into the chair.

'We haven't interviewed the kid yet. His mom says he's in shock, won't let us near him.'

That sounded right. Max's mother was a force-five hurricane of a woman who made up for never seeing her son by being ferociously protective of him. If he tripped on his shoelaces she'd probably have sued the sneaker manufacturer.

'Did the kid see the gunman?'

'I don't know. It all happened so fast.' Nick cleared his throat. His mouth was dry as bone. 'I'd like to go now. Can I do that?'

XIV

Upper Rhine, 1432

The traveller walked his horse to the bluff and looked out over the valley. What did he see? The river below him, of course, quickening as it squeezed around the promontory, then easing out again into a smooth ribbon between the wooded hills. Fish basked in the shallows near the bank, flitting among the weeds that writhed like smoke in the water. Dragonflies hummed over the surface, and golden sunlight warmed the sandy bottom.

Just behind the promontory, the river lapped into a shallow bay where a tributary joined it, young and lithe in comparison to the stately Rhine. Looking down, the traveller would have seen a clearing near where the lesser river flowed out, and – if the sun was not in his eyes – a crude hut made of branches and mud. In front of it, where the shore sloped down, a table with two of its legs sawn off tilted steeply towards the water. Planks had been nailed across it in a series of ridges, like steps. The whole structure glistened with wet mud. Beside it, a hollowed-out tree trunk formed a crude trough.

The traveller twitched the bridle and guided his mount back into the trees. The path was steep, but not treacherous. Dappled sunlight brushed the forest floor; the woods hummed with the buzz of bees and insects, gradually giving way to the rush of flowing water. Soon enough, he arrived at the bank of the tributary river. It looked deeper than he had thought. He slid down from the saddle, looped the bridle around a branch and strode out into the water a few paces to check the ford.

The strong current tugged at his legs as he tried to balance on the slippery stones underfoot. Downstream, a forlorn pile of boulders marked the remains of an attempt to make a breakwater. The river had broken through, and the stones meant to stem the flow now urged it on, drawing it through the gap. Still, the traveller thought, his horse should manage it.

As he turned to go back, a beam of sunlight flashed through the trees and struck his eyes. He threw up a hand to block it, but that unbalanced him; he lunged to keep his footing, but the rock that held his weight betrayed him and toppled over. With a splash, he pitched headlong into the river.

The current seized him immediately, propelling him forward towards the channel in the broken dam. He lashed out, but the river was too strong. It spun him around like a twig. He felt himself sucked under, swallowed a mouthful of water and rose gasping to the surface. Then his head dashed against a boulder and the world went dark.

Out in the bay where the two rivers joined, a dark speck broke the silver sheen on the water. An observer from the bluffs above would have taken it for nothing, a ripple or perhaps the shadow of a hovering hawk. Closer to, however, the shadow resolved itself into something like a man. He was a wild sight. His hair reached down to his shoulders, his beard almost to his chest: both were matted with so much grime you could hardly tell the colour. He stood waist deep in the water, swaying easily in the current, his feet planted in the ooze where eels and weeds twined themselves around his legs. He scooped mud from the riverbed into a cracked wooden bucket. When the bucket was mostly full, he half-carried, half-floated it back to the shore and clambered out.

He was naked. Mud caked his chest, his arms and his face like a potter's effigy, cracked in the sun; below the waist his skin was washed clean and white by the river. He hauled the bucket up to the slanting table and tipped it out. Mud slithered down the ladder, slopping over the rungs and leaving a residue of white clay clinging to the boards. The man scooped it off and deposited it in the trough, which he then filled with water from his bucket and stirred with his hand. White clouds billowed and swirled in the water, but where sunlight touched the bottom, through the whorls and eddies, he caught the unmistakable sparkle of gold.

Something at the mouth of the river caught his eye. At first he thought it was a log, then perhaps a dead fox, or even a sheep swept down from a distant pasture. Only when it was almost past him did he recognise it for what it was.

He hesitated a moment, but only because he was not used to urgency. Then he ran into the bay, kicked off from the bottom and dived forward. He was a strong swimmer: a dozen strokes took him to the body. He grabbed a fistful of the man's sodden shirt and pulled him back. The current was stronger here, hurrying him towards the open river; he let his legs sink but could not touch the bottom. The drowning man jerked under his touch, flailing and choking. He might have killed them both in his frenzy to live. Kicking furiously to stay afloat, the mudlark wrestled him down. He hooked one arm over his

81

shoulder, another around his waist, and hauled them both back to the shore. When he had dragged his prize up onto the bank he pulled him into a sitting position, took his hands and bent him double, pumping the water out of him like a bladder.

The man-who-had-not-drowned spat, groaned, retched, then rolled over and lay heaving on the leafy ground. The mudlark left him to dry in the sun. He brought bread and honey and left them a little distance from his guest. He blew life into the fire that smouldered by his hut and warmed some milk in a bowl. By the time he returned to his guest, the food was gone and the man was sitting propped against a log. He squinted up at his saviour.

'Thank you.' He made an appreciative gesture with his hands. 'If not for you . . .' He trailed off.

'What is your name?' said the mudlark. He spoke slowly, unused to speech, his tongue searching his mouth for the sounds.

The guest smiled. 'Aeneas.'

The name was like a stick poked into the past. Memories bubbled up through the mud: sunlight pouring through a schoolroom window, a monk in a grey cowl, an ancient book of stories.

'*Multum ille et terris iactatus et alto.*' *A man tossed about on land and sea.*

Aeneas sat up in surprise. He studied the mudlark, then laughed curiously. 'What a strange fellow you are. You haunt the woods like a faun or a wild man; you swim like a mermaid and rescue travellers from their doom; and then you quote Virgil at me. Tell me, what is your name?'

The mudlark looked confused – frightened, almost. There had been so many names over the years: names called in anger, in derision, in ignorance and fear. Names given, never owned. But before them all there was:

'Johann,' I said.

Aeneas stayed that night in my hut. He was remarkably cheerful for a man who had almost died. By mid-afternoon he was able to stand with the aid of a staff I cut him from a willow. By dusk he had accompanied me back to the path to fetch his horse, and when night fell he built up the fire and shared the bottle of wine he had in his saddlebag. He also gave me a mirror, a silvered piece of glass set in a cast-iron frame.

'It came from Aachen,' he told me. 'It has absorbed the holy radiance of the relics in the cathedral there. Take it. Perhaps some day it will bring you a blessing, as you have saved me.'

Aeneas loved to talk and delighted in company. Words poured out of him like a spring, overflowing with energy. He was particularly curious about me, though I avoided his questions. When he asked where I came from I simply pointed down the river; when he tried to discover how I had ended up dredging my miserable living from the Rhine mud, I threw another log on the fire and said nothing. Much had happened in the last ten years, but only in the way that a man falling down a well may strike the walls many times. Though each blow agonises at the time, all he remembers afterwards is hitting the bottom.

So Aeneas told me about himself. He was five years younger than me, though any observer would have looked at my face and guessed twenty. He had been born in Italy in a village near Siena; his father was a farmer of little standing, and Aeneas had rejected the fields in favour of the university.

He leaned forward so that his face shone in the firelight. 'Did you ever feel that God made you for a purpose? I did. I knew I was destined for higher things than my father's pastures. I studied everything I could. When the plague drove the scholars out of Siena, they could not carry all their books. I bought them for a pittance, taught myself everything they had to teach, then sold them back for five times what I had paid when the plague was over. Truly, there is nothing so profitable as knowledge.' He chuckled at his own joke, then thought for a second. 'Or perhaps, "Nothing profits a man like learning"? Which way sounds better?'

I shrugged. I could not help but wince at the comparison: the patrician's heir rooting in the riverbed like a pig, and the farmer's boy who had made more of himself. But he had not reached that part of the story.

'At first I meant to become a doctor, or perhaps a lawyer. I have always been good with words.' He was utterly immodest, but so sincere it did not seem boastful. 'I tried many things – none seemed right. Then, a year ago, a man passed through our village. A cardinal, on his way to Basle.'

He squinted at me, clearly expecting some reaction or recognition.

'You are aware there is currently a great council being held in Basle to address the wrongs of the Church?'

If I had ever known it, I had forgotten.

'I took service with the cardinal and accompanied him.'

'But you are not a priest?' I asked. He did not seem like one. The first thing he had done after rescuing his horse was delve into the saddlebag for a clean shirt and hose. Even drowning in the river he had somehow managed to keep on his soft leather boots, their tops fashionably turned over to show off both their green silk lining and his calves.

He laughed. 'Whatever God intends for me, I do not think it is holy orders. I am too much in love with the world. No – I interrupted myself. I joined this cardinal as a secretary, and he brought me to Basle. I soon found out that his riches were stored up in heaven – he did not have the money to pay me. I left his service, but I found another.' He winked at me. 'It was not hard. There is so much work to be done in the council that any man who can write his name is guaranteed employment.'

He rested his hand on his chin and stared into the fire, a caricature of thought.

'You should come with me.'

Of course I resisted. But Aeneas had been right – he was clever with words. He argued with me through the night, until the fire burned low and the birds sang. He would not be refused.

The next morning, I left my hut behind and set out for Basle.

XV

New York City

A stiff wind hit Nick's face as he walked out of the elevator onto the roof terrace. A memory of the night before seized his mind: water tanks and fake grass and the terror he would die. This was very different: bone-white paving slabs and a glass-boxed café, now shuttered for the winter; a huge spider sculpted from twisted iron, taller than he was. Beyond the box-hedge balustrade stretched the lifeless trees of Central Park, a dead forest. He could just see the reservoir through the branches. It reminded him of a poem from school:

> The sedge has wither'd from the lake,
> And no birds sing.

He found Emily Sutherland sitting on a steel bench, waiting for him. There was something anachronistic about her – not like the medieval studies majors he'd known at college, with their pre-Raphaelite curls and flowery dresses, but the formal elegance of the mid-twentieth century. She wore a fitted black skirt that ended just above her knee with a high-collared red coat. Her glossy black hair was tied back with a red ribbon, her hands folded demurely in her lap. She looked lost.

He sat down beside her. The cold steel bench pressed against the back of his thighs. 'Sorry I'm late.'

'I wasn't sure if you were coming.'

I almost didn't. After Royce let him go, he'd wandered aimlessly for almost two hours. The thought of having to speak to anyone made him ill. What could you say when your whole world had been torn apart? The people he passed on the streets – the hot-dog sellers and traffic cops and tourists pouring out of Macy's – they had nothing in common with him. He was a ghost among them. But eventually the shock and self-pity had worn itself out. If he retreated into his shell he'd go mad: he needed to act, to *do*. So he had come.

'You said you'd found something?'

Emily pulled a book out of her purse and laid it open on her knee. Nick's printout was folded flat inside it. The book seemed to be in German.

'*The Oldest Surviving German Playing Cards.*' Nick read the title at the top of the page. Emily glanced at him, surprised.

'You speak German?'

'I worked in Berlin for a couple of years.'

'Then you should have a look at this book. It catalogues all the surviving works attributed to the Master of the Playing Cards.'

'And?'

'Your card isn't in it.' She slid a fingernail between the pages and turned towards the back. A menagerie of finely engraved lions and bears stared up at him, two cards pictured side by side. The animals were shown in various poses.

'These are the two surviving copies of the eight of beasts.

One in Dresden, one at the Bibliothèque Nationale in Paris. Do you notice anything?'

Nick studied them for a moment. 'They're different.' He pointed to the top-right corners. Where the Dresden card showed a standing lion with its head tipped back in a defiant roar, the Paris lion sat on its haunches, staring imperiously off the page.

He reached across and pulled out the printout. The layout was the same – four bears and four lions in three rows – but this time the top-right animal was a bear scratching itself.

'You said the cards were printed. If they all came from the same plate, shouldn't they look the same?'

'At some point in their history, the original plates were cut up. You can actually see it sometimes on the cards.' She traced a fingernail around one of the lions on the Paris card.

Nick leaned over. He could see a faint, irregular outline around the animal, almost as if it had been cut out of a magazine with scissors and pasted on the page.

'Why would anyone do that?'

'The best theory is that the original cards were so successful he wanted to make more. Copper plates wear out pretty quickly if you take too many prints from them. Maybe the engraver cut up the ones that were still usable so he could mix and match to make a new deck.' She laid the palm of her hand flat across the page so that it hid the two lions in the centre. 'Take them away and your eight becomes a six. Add another and it's the nine – which is true, incidentally.' She turned to the next plate in the book, the nine of the suit. Here the animals were in three rows of three, with an extra bear added.

'In a way, it prefigures the use of printing text from movable type,' Emily added. 'Breaking the page elements down into smaller units to give you more flexibility.'

Nick peered closer. 'There aren't any of those outlines from the cut-outs on this card.'

'No,' Emily agreed. 'Though it's a printout of a digital image of . . . who knows what. Faint lines could easily be lost. Where did you say you found this?'

Nick looked around the roof terrace. The sky had clouded over again; most of the other visitors had gone back inside. A couple of students were examining a piece of sculpture and trying to sound knowledgeable, while an Orthodox Jew in a black suit and a Homburg was doing a crossword by the railing. A janitor brushed some dead leaves off the paving stones. Otherwise, there was no one.

And no birds sing.

He realised Emily was watching him, waiting. Her pale cheeks had flushed rose pink in the cold air. What could he tell her that didn't sound crazy?

'Gillian Lockhart – my, ah, friend – sent me the file two nights ago.'

'Can't you just ask her where she got it from?'

Nick ignored the question. 'Do you think she discovered one of these original cards? One that nobody knew about?'

'It's a possibility. Or it could be a fake. Either a physical forgery that she's found or a digital fake that she's created as some sort of joke.' As if she could read his face, Emily added, 'I asked around the museum about Gillian Lockhart when you said you knew her. Apparently she had quite a reputation for being unpredictable.'

A gust of wind whipped the words away. Nick felt a chill shiver down his back. A joke? It had seemed the only explanation when the card arrived. Part of him still insisted it must be. But seeing Bret die; cowering on a rooftop while a man with a gun hunted him; sitting in a police station being interrogated: those were real enough. And they had all started with the card.

'If the card *is* real, how much would it be worth?'

Emily frowned. 'I really don't know. I don't work in acquisitions. I don't think any of the cards have changed hands in decades, so there's nothing even to compare it to.'

'Ballpark. Are we talking millions of dollars?' He could see the question offended her. He felt embarrassed, as if he'd offered money to sleep with her.

'I've seen Dürer engravings offered privately for under ten thousand dollars. He's later, but better known. For the Master of the Playing Cards . . .' She thought for a moment. 'You'd be talking tens of thousands. Maybe a hundred thousand at the most.'

'Worth killing for?'

'I'm sorry?'

Nick took a deep breath. Part of him was desperate to say it, to give voice to the thoughts that obsessed him. Every second he didn't say it made him feel a fraud. Part of him was terrified she'd think he was nuts.

'Gillian sounded like she was in some kind of trouble when she sent me the card. I haven't heard from her since. Then last night my room-mate was murdered.'

She gasped. 'I'm so sorry. How – terrible.' She stared at the book in her lap, her arms pressed tightly against her side.

'I think they – whoever did it – were after me.'

It sounded ridiculous – and presumptuous, appropriating Bret's tragedy for himself. He glanced at Emily. She didn't look at him.

'Have you been to the police?'

'Of course. They think it's crazy.' *They think I did it.*

'It's not crazy.' The words were quiet but clear. 'I don't

know what happened to Gillian Lockhart, but . . . You can see it when you mention her name in the museum. People react, like you've opened a room you're not supposed to go in. They don't say much, but . . .'

A flock of birds rose squawking from the trees by the reservoir. They wheeled against the towers on the far side of the park. Emily tugged on the collar of her coat.

'Then there are the cards. They're so strange. None of the animals look happy. As for the people . . .' She turned to another plate in the book. Five miniature people danced and strutted across the page, though the closer Nick looked the less human they seemed. Some were as hairy as animals; on others, the skin seemed to hang off them like leaves. They blew horns, aimed arrows, swung cudgels. One strummed a lute, a fool oblivious to the mayhem around him.

'This is the fifth suit, wild men. There's something so unsettling about them.' She gave a sad laugh. 'Now you probably think I'm crazy.'

'No.' Nick touched her arm to reassure her and immediately wished he hadn't. She shied away like a frightened bird, hugging her arms across her chest.

'Sorry.' He wished he hadn't said that either. It made him sound guilty.

She got to her feet, smoothing her skirt behind her. Her face was almost lost behind her high collar. 'I should go.'

Nick stood, keeping an awkward distance. 'Be careful. I'm really grateful for your advice, but I might not be the guy you want to help right now.'

XVI

Basle, 1432–3

My father once said there is no change a man cannot get used to given a fortnight. Not in his soul, perhaps, but in his actions and routines, his choices and expectations. The first night of my journey with Aeneas, I slept on the floor of the inn and ate only bread. Midway through the second night, I crawled into the common bed and wrapped myself in a corner of a blanket. On the third night, I ate as much as any other man in the tavern, drank my fill and thought nothing of sleeping on straw rather than earth. Aeneas paid a barber to cut my hair and my beard, and that alone shaved ten years from my face. An hour's scrubbing in a bathhouse removed another five.

'Although,' Aeneas told me, 'you should certainly seek out the Holy Baths in Basle. They think nothing there of men and women bathing together quite promiscuously. The sights you see . . .' He made an obscene gesture with his hand; I tried not to shudder. Some memories take more than a fortnight to heal.

*

By the time we reached Basle I was a new man. I had a new pair of boots, a new hat and a tunic that Aeneas had bought for three pennies from a French merchant. Even so, the city terrified me. It reminded me of Mainz: a rich town by the Rhine, a city of tall houses and high towers whose weather-cocks and crosses sparkled like dew in the dawn sun. A ring of stout walls circled it, beyond which its tributary villages stretched almost unbroken in every direction.

The city was crammed to its rooftops with men there for the council, but Aeneas' silver tongue soon found me lodgings in a monastery. He took me there, then excused himself – having been away for two months, he had much to learn and report to his masters. I lay on my pallet shivering, feeling abandoned in that strange city; I thought I must run down to the river and leap on the first barge that would carry me back to my hut in the forest. But the terror passed, I slept, and the next morning Aeneas bounded in, beaming with excitement.

'A splendid opportunity,' he enthused. 'A countryman of yours, a most remarkable man. His secretary has just eloped with a girl from the bathhouse.' He winked. 'I told you they were promiscuous. But he is a prolific thinker: if he does not find a scribe to tap his words soon they will flood his mind until it bursts. I saw him this morning – no sooner had I mentioned your name than he told me to fetch you without a moment's delay.'

One of Aeneas' most appealing traits, then, was his utter lack of inhibition. He had as fine an instinct for politics as any man I ever knew, but he could praise others with unthinking generosity. I had no doubt that in his description I had become the greatest scribe since St Paul. I only feared that I could not possibly satisfy my prospective employer if he believed even half of what Aeneas said.

The man in question inhabited a small room on the upper level of a whitewashed courtyard at the house of the Augustinians. Aeneas did not wait for an answer to his knock, but pushed straight through. I followed more tentatively.

There was little in the room except a bed and a desk. The desk was the larger. Two candlesticks gave it the appearance of a sacred altar. Sheaves of paper covered every inch of its surface, weighted down with anything that came to hand: a penknife, a candle end, a Bible, even a brown apple core. There were three inkpots for red, black and blue ink, a selection of reed and goose-quill pens, a bull's-eye glass for magnification and a half-drunk cup of wine with a dead fly in it. Stacks of books surrounded the desk like ramparts – more than I had ever seen in one room. And behind it, the lord of this paper kingdom, the man we had come to see.

He barely seemed to notice us, but stared at an icon of Christ that hung on a nail on the wall. His eyes were pale blue and pure as water. There was something ageless about him, though in the course of my employment I learned he was actually a few months younger than me. His head was shaved bare, revealing an angular skull whose bones seemed to press out against the skin. I remembered Aeneas' joke about his mind bursting with words, and wondered if it might be true. Ink stained the white sleeves of his cassock, though his hands were surprisingly clean.

Aeneas did not wait. 'This is Johann who I told you about. Johann, it is my honour to introduce Nicholas Cusanus.'

I gave a small bow and steeled myself for the inevitable questions about my past.

'Can you write?'

'He knows Latin better than Cicero,' Aeneas insisted. 'Do

you know the first thing he said to me after he fished me out of the river? He said—'

'Take a pen and write what I dictate.' Nicholas pushed back his chair and stood. Barely looking, he picked up the cup and sipped it. I did not see whether he drank the fly. I took his chair, sharpened one of the pens with the knife and then made a clean cut in the point. My hands were shaking so much I almost sliced it in half.

Nicholas walked around the desk and stood with his back to me, still contemplating the icon.

'Because God is perfect form, in which all differences are united and all contradictions are reconciled, it is impossible for a diversity of forms to exist in him.'

He waited while I wrote. There was something profound in his silence which hushed even Aeneas. The only sound in the room was the scratch of my pen. My cheeks pricked with sweat as I tried to remember how to form the words. I had barely picked up a pen in ten years. As for remembering what he had actually said, I felt as if I was stumbling blind. *Absolute.* The words hemmed me in like a fog.

The instant I put down my pen Nicholas spun around and picked up the paper.

'Because God is perfectly form in which all differences are different and all contradictions united, it is impossible for him to exist.' He threw the paper aside. 'Do you know what my words mean?'

I shook my head. I felt hot: all I wanted was to be back in the river, feeling the cold current close over me.

'It means that God is the unity of all things. Therefore there can be no diversity in God – and certainly no diversity when we *write* about God. Diversity leads to error, and error to sin.' He turned to Aeneas. 'I need a man who can record my words as if my tongue itself was writing on the page.'

Aeneas looked crestfallen. But he was not a man to abandon his enthusiasm so easily. 'There are saints in heaven who would struggle to grasp your words. Johann is out of practice and overawed by your intellect. Let him try again.'

Nicholas turned back to face the icon. Without even waiting to see if I was ready, he began:

Lord, to see you is to love; and as your gaze watches over me from a great distance and never deviates, so does your love. And because your love is always with me – you whose love is nothing other than yourself, who loves me – thus you are always with me. You do not desert me, Lord, but guard me at every turn with the most tender care.

He might have continued, but my pen had stopped moving. It rested forgotten above a half-completed sentence while tears streamed down my face. I felt like a fool – worse than a fool – but I could not help myself. Nicholas's words were like a hammer, shattering the walls I had built around my soul with a single blow. The echoes reverberated through me, shaking loose the foundation stones of my being. I felt naked before God.

In the corner of the room, Aeneas looked surprised but not angry. Nicholas was harder to read. Though he could be passionate in his faith, he struggled with emotions on the lowly human scale. I saw the shock in his eyes, his struggle to find an appropriate response. In the end he took refuge in procedure. He slid the piece of paper off the table and read it quickly. There was not much to look at. I waited for him to discard it again, and me with it.

He frowned. 'This is better. Not perfect – you misspelled *amandus* on the third line – but definitely improved. Perhaps even promising.'

I looked up at him. Hope shone in my tear-rimmed eyes.

'I will retain you for one week. If your work satisfies me, then I will keep you on for as long as the council sits.'

Aeneas clapped his hands. 'I told you he would not disappoint you.'

And that was how I – a thief, a liar and a debaucher – came to work for one of the holiest men that ever lived.

For the churchmen at the council, I suppose it was not a happy time. They did not lack ambition – many of them, including Aeneas, wanted nothing less than the complete subordination of the papacy to the decisions of the council. But that goal remained elusive. They met in committees and debated resolutions; they passed those to the general congregation to be ratified, and they in turn sent them to the Pope. The number of couriers crossing back and forth that autumn must have worn a new pass in the Alps. But I never saw anything to change the impression of my first day in Basle: that there were too many beggars and not enough rich men to make it matter.

I did not care. Nicholas had offered me work while the council sat, and I would have been happy for them to deliberate until Judgement Day. I was satisfied with my lot, simple though it was. Every day I went to Nicholas's study and dutifully recorded whatever he dictated; every evening I returned to my room and read, or prayed. Occasionally I met Aeneas in a tavern, but not often. He was a busy man, constantly on some errand in the service of his ambition. I enjoyed hearing his stories, and did not begrudge him his progress. I felt a serenity, a feeling that the great tides that tossed me in the world had ebbed.

The council ground on through the winter. Blocks of ice

appeared in the river, hard as stone: one cold morning I saw a lump strike a coal barge and smash it in two. In Nicholas's study, I wrapped rags around my hands so that my fingers could grip the pen. My master never seemed to notice the cold. Day after day he stood staring at his icon, his only concession to the season a fur stole over his cassock.

'In the beginning was the Word, and the Word was with God and the Word was God. Do you know where it went wrong, Johann?'

As he got used to me, his lectures became more conversational, using me as an anvil for hammering out his ideas. Like the anvil, I could not understand the intricacy of the work being made on my back – but I served my purpose.

'The Fall? The serpent in Eden?'

'For mankind, undoubtedly. But Adam's sin was disobedience, not ignorance.' He moved across to the window, silhouetted against its harsh cold light. 'The greatest blow the Word suffered, when the world was young, was the disaster at Babel. When men could no longer understand each other, how could they understand the Word?'

'I thought the tower of Babel was an affront to God.'

'It brought its builders closer to God. The sin He punished was not ambition but overambition. And now look how the legacy spreads. What is the first fruit of the heresy that the Hussites and Wycliffites preach?'

I kept silent. That too was part of my job.

'They preach that the Bible itself should be split apart – rendered in English or Czech or German or whichever language they prefer it. Imagine the errors, the bitter confusion and the arguments that would follow.' He glanced out of the window, towards the spire of the cathedral where the general congregation of the council met. 'God knows we find enough to quarrel over already.'

He looked back to the icon. 'God is perfection. As I told you once before, there can be no diversity in him. So why do we tolerate diversity in the Church? We cannot even agree on a liturgy. Every diocese has its own devotions and ceremonies, and strives to make its own rite more splendid than its neighbour's. They think thereby they will obtain greater favour with God – when in fact all they do is fissure his Church.'

My pen still hovered over the desk, dripping drops of ink on the page. 'Shall I write that?'

He sighed. 'No. Write: "We must make allowances for the weaknesses of men, unless it works contrary to eternal salvation."'

He dismissed me at noon for my dinner. I had arranged to meet Aeneas that day – we had not spoken in a fortnight – and hurried through the streets to the tavern at the sign of the dancing bear. It was a busy, cheerful place, buried in the cellars beneath a cloth warehouse near the river. Laughter and songs echoed off its vaulted ceiling; in the hearth, a pig turned on a spit. Fat dripped into the fire and flared into smoke.

I searched through the various rooms for Aeneas but did not find him. He was often delayed, though no one ever bore it against him. I bought a mug of beer and perched on the end of a bench. A group of merchants from Strassburg occupied most of the table: they greeted me briefly, then ignored me. A single glance at my dress told them I had nothing profitable to sell.

I watched the crowd while I waited. There were a few men I recognised – a priest from Lyons, two Italian brothers who sold the paper that my master used so freely – but none I wanted to speak to. The cellar was warm, the beer mixed with herbs and honey.

And then I saw him. He was sitting on a bench two tables away, on the fringes of a conversation with a group of goldsmiths. One hand clutched a mug of beer; with the other, he fed himself bites of an enormous pork chop. The fat smeared around his lips glistened in the candlelight; his puffy eyes scanned the room with a suspicious resentment that a decade had not dimmed since he beat me in Konrad Schmidt's workshop. Gerhard.

I should have dropped my gaze at once and hoped he would not notice, but shock had me in its grip. All I could do was stare, like a rabbit in a trap. The lank hair had receded, leaving a patch of red skin like a blister on the top of his head; his back had developed a stoop, perhaps from too many years bending in front of a furnace. But it was certainly him. And if I could recognise him, he could surely do the same to me.

Our eyes met. I cursed myself for shaving my beard, which might have been enough of a disguise; I touched the pilgrim mirror that I kept in my purse and prayed that a decade of suffering might have aged my face to the point where he did not remember it. But Aeneas had restored my life too well. Stupefied, I watched surprise give way to disbelief, then harden into certainty. And triumph.

He pushed back the bench and rose. I looked at the hearth, at the spitted pig twisting in the flames and the fat oozing out of its body. I knew what would happen to me if Gerhard reported my crime.

A maid with a tray of mugs crossed in front of Gerhard, blocking his path. He stumbled back a step and in that moment I made my decision. I jumped up from my seat and ran to the stairs, careless of the attention I drew. Hot fat spat onto my hand as I passed the fire and I flinched – but my greater fear was meeting Aeneas. I could not bear for him to learn what sort of man he had helped.

I reached the street and ran up a narrow alley towards the cathedral. When I reached the market in the square, I ducked behind a tanner's stall and doubled back on myself, down a narrow row of shops towards the river. It was almost deserted. If Gerhard had followed me, he would certainly have no difficulty seeing me now.

I came out on a wharf just below the bridge. Few boats dared risk the river that early in the season but, to my shining relief, there was one at the foot of the steps, a small barge whose captain was just casting off the ropes. I skidded to a halt at the edge of the wharf.

'Where are you going?' I shouted down.

'To Aachen, and then to Paris.'

It was not the captain who answered but one of the passengers. He wore a short travelling cloak and a hood, and carried a long walking staff – though if the barge was taking him all the way to Aachen, he would not have to walk a step for weeks. A small knot of men and women stood around him on the bow, all dressed for a pilgrimage.

I glanced nervously over my shoulder. Was Gerhard even now summoning the guard, telling them what manner of criminal they harboured in their city?

'Can I join you?'

The pilgrim consulted with his companions a moment, then looked at the captain, who shrugged.

'If you have two silver pennies to contribute to the costs of the journey.'

I scampered down the steps and leaped aboard. I rummaged

in my purse and found the two coins – most of what it held. I did not even have a hat with me.

The bargeman gave me a curious look but said nothing. He cast off the ropes and poled the vessel away from the landing, until the current picked it up and began to drive it forward. I sat on the bow with my back to the city and did not look back.

XVII

Kingdom of Iskiard

The inn stood on a wind-blown hill above the great river, tall and crooked like the blasted trees that surrounded it. The sign that hung from its gable swung like a noose in the breeze. In the far distance, the four Castles of the Guardians stood silhouetted against the setting sun, watching over the realm as darkness descended. The lone Wanderer hurried his pace, tapping his staff on the road. He did not want to be abroad after nightfall, when the wargs hunted.

He climbed the stairs and entered the inn, surveying it from the deep shadows of his cloak. The candles had burned low, and the fire in the hearth was no match for the surrounding gloom. Three swordsmen, still in their armour, sat drinking horns of mead and boasting of their deeds. In a corner, two merchants – one a dwarf – muttered and counted coins. Otherwise the hall was empty, apart from from a wench in a low-cut blouse behind the bar. She edged her way to serve him.

'Prithee, what is thy desire, stranger?'

'I seek Urthred the Necromancer.'

Her face didn't move, but the tone of her voice spoke of awe. 'Urthred keeps to his chamber upstairs. Be warned, stranger: he is fearsomely guarded.'

The Wanderer nodded. He made his way to the twisting stair at the back of the room and climbed: past narrow, barred windows laced with cobwebs, through a wizened door into a dark corridor. Shafts of moonlight tiled the floor through the windows; at the far end, a blue skein blazed and crackled in front of another door.

The Wanderer took a step towards it, then halted. Had he heard something?

'*Ni-yargh!*' A figure came charging out of the shadows. The Wanderer just had time to glimpse a hooked nose and savage fangs, the gleam of a sword in the moonlight. But the Wanderer was the hero of a thousand battles in this land. He stepped to one side and tilted his staff like a lance, straight into his assailant's body. The goblin flailed back, off balance; the Wanderer stepped forward, swung the staff around and with two swift blows dispatched him.

'Who trespasses in the Necromancer's abode?' The voice came out of nowhere, echoing in his ears. The threads of light at the end of the passage pulsed like the strings of a harp.

'Nicholas the Wanderer.' He pulled back the sleeve of his cloak to show the mark of the Brethren seared onto his wrist. 'In the name of Farang, let me pass.'

The glowing tendrils pulled away. The door swung in noiselessly. The Wanderer stepped through.

The room beyond was a dim stone chamber, lit only by moonlight and a pair of naphtha torches bracketed to the wall. The ceiling above was so high that the rafters, where bats roosted, were almost invisible. Magickal and alchemickal apparatus filled the corners of the room – siphons, flasks, jars of dragons' bane and unicorns' mane. And behind a stone table, staring at his uninvited guest, an old man with piercing eyes and a straggly grey cloak, a silver circlet enclosing his long white hair. Urthred the Necromancer.

'Nicholas the Wanderer. Many moons has it been ere you crossed the threshold of these lands.'

'Sorry,' said Nick. 'I've been kind of busy.'

Urthred's face stayed expressionless, but Nick knew he didn't like the irreverence.

'Listen, I'm sorry I don't have time for the formalities. I need to talk to you.'

'Then why didn't you pick up the phone? This isn't a chat room.'

'I didn't want to be traceable.'

Urthred sighed. 'Job making you paranoid again?'

'My room-mate was murdered last night.'

It was unnerving to say it to the avatar, to look for shock or sympathy in the digitally drawn face and see nothing. Its blank eyes just stared at him.

'Shit, man, I'm sorry.' Urthred's portentously Anglicised voice was gone, replaced by the Midwestern twang that, somewhere in Chicago, belonged to a geek named Randall. 'How did it happen?'

Nick told him, starting with Gillian's message. He added in what he'd learned about the card. 'If it's real, it's worth something. But it could just be a fake.'

'Want me to take a look at it?'

'Please.'

In the Necromancer's chamber, the Wanderer reached inside his cloak and pulled out what looked like a giant marble, a glass globe filled with swirling coloured mists. He handed it to Urthred, who placed it in a rack on the wall with other, similar spheres. Somewhere on a server farm in Oregon or China, a file copied itself from Nick's account to Randall's.

'I'll just run it through.'

Randall's avatar went still as he dropped offline. After a few seconds, the Necromancer began to shuffle on the spot and swing his arms, a sort of human screensaver. It was odd, Nick thought, how although nothing had changed on screen, the mere knowledge that Randall wasn't looking out of that rendered face made him feel alone in the imaginary room. Even odder, he supposed, since he'd never seen Randall in the flesh.

They'd met at an online conference a couple of years back, both participants in a Web symposium. Randall had just made a name for himself by convincing a judge that a tabloid photo of a supermodel entering rehab was actually a fake. The supermodel had received an undisclosed sum from the newspapers; Randall had earned a reputation as one of the smartest researchers in the field. Informed rumour had it he'd also taken a juicy cut of the damages. Scurrilous rumour added he'd enjoyed a more personal thank-you from his grateful client.

'The reliability of digital evidence is one of the biggest challenges for law enforcement in the twenty-first century,' he'd told the conference. 'With a fifty-dollar camera and a PC, there's almost nothing that can't be faked. But there is hope. The moment you change a digital image, you leave fingerprints on it. It's almost impossible to combine two pictures realistically without rotating or resizing something. Those are mathematical manipulations, and they make marks in the data like ripples when you toss a rock in a pond. If you could measure all the ripples, their height and wavelength and velocity, you could work backwards to figure out where the rock went in and how big it was. This is the same idea.'

It was an idea that required some chunky mathematics – maths that turned out to be as useful for piecing together real documents as detecting fakes. Nick had emailed him afterwards to compare notes, and from there they'd become occasional collaborators. Randall had also brought him into Gothic Lair. For several months they'd roamed across the online fantasy kingdom almost every night: killing dragons, saving princesses and storming castles filled with unimaginable treasures. Before Nick swapped the company of the princesses for Gillian.

A nimbus of white light flared around Urthred the Necromancer as he came alive again.

'Any joy?'

'All I got was garbage.'

Nick had spent enough frustrated hours waiting for a computer to deliver its verdict to know not to expect much. But this wasn't just another exercise. He squeezed the mouse in frustration, accidentally sending the Wanderer scuttling across to the far corner of Urthred's chamber.

'It's not the algorithm. The picture's completely screwed up.'

'What do you mean?' Nick guided the Wanderer back to the centre of the room. 'Is the file corrupted?'

'It's not the file.'

Belatedly, Nick realised Randall was trying to tell him something.

'You know my analogy about the ripples in the pond? Well, imagine you pull up a sample and it turns out the pond's not even water. That's what I'm talking about.'

'I don't—'

'Someone's done something to this file. The picture's still there, obviously – I can see it fine. But something's going on under the surface that's completely changed the file coding.'

Nick finally got it. 'Encryption.'

'Exactly. Someone's buried something inside this file that doesn't show up when you look at the picture. There are over five million individual pixels in that image, each one stored as a string of six characters. All you have to do is change a handful of them so that those numbers and letters spell out a message, and you can hide a whole string of text without anyone knowing. Invisible to the naked eye.'

Nick knew how it worked – he'd come across it before. *Why didn't I think of that?*

'Would Gillian have known how to do that?'

'Sure. There are a bunch of programs you can get to do it for you. Figure out which one she used, run the file through and it'll just pull the data back out. It's probably password-protected though.'

Bear is the key. 'I'll get right on to it.' For the first time since Gillian's name had lit up on the screen, Nick felt hopeful again.

'You could try to her IP address as well,' Randall suggested. 'See where she got to?'

'She Buzzed me. Peer to peer. I thought that was impossible to trace.'

'Someone must have managed it.' Urthred turned and looked at him. 'Otherwise how did they find you?'

On screen, Nicholas the Wanderer leaned on his staff and stared across the moonlit chamber at the Necromancer. In a busy Internet café on lower Broadway, Nick leaned back on the stainless-steel barstool. The place was full: no dwarves or magicians, but just about everyone else. Filipinos and Indians checking in with their families back home; European backpacker-types bragging to their blogs; some Mexican kids playing Counterstrike. A tiny, infinitesimal fraction of the chatter shooting around the world over wires and airwaves. Yet through all that hubbub, someone had traced a message from a frightened girl in Europe to an apartment in New York. Nick glanced over his shoulder. A Korean man with pimpled cheeks and a buzz cut seemed to be waiting for a free machine. Was he familiar? Had he seen him before?

'Are you at home now?' Randall asked through the earphones.

Nick shook his head, then remembered Randall couldn't see. 'Home's a crime scene. I'm not allowed back there.'

'That's probably a good thing.' Urthred came around the table to stand right in front of the Wanderer. 'You've got to be careful. You and I, what we do, we're so used to seeing this illegal shit as paper, pictures, numbers we hack up. But this is real. Real people, real bullets. Don't fuck around.'

'I'll be careful.'

Nick hit ESCAPE and dropped out of Gothic Lair. Into a world where there were more than monsters to fear.

XVIII

Paris, 1433

Aeneas once said that a man's life is a blank page on which God writes what He will. But paper must be formed before it can take the ink. I considered this while I waited in the paper maker's workshop. The whole room stank of damp and rot, like an apple store at the end of winter. A woman sat at a table with a knife and a pile of sodden rags, cutting them into tiny scraps. These went into a wooden vat, where two apprentices with long paddles beat them into a porridge. When this was ready it would be pushed to the side of the room to fester for a week, then beaten again and again until the original rags were utterly obliterated. Only then would the master paper maker scoop out the paste in a wire form, squeeze it dry in his press, harden it with glue and rub it with pumice to make it smooth beneath the pen. So must a man's life be dissolved and remade before one drop of God's purpose can be written on it.

The paper maker brought me a bale of paper bound with string. Behind him, one of the apprentices turned the screw on the press. There was a slurping sound as water oozed out of the

110

wet paper into the interleaved layers of felt. In a moment of whimsy I imagined the water as ink, as if words themselves could be squeezed out of the paper, destiny unwritten.

'Your master must keep you busy.' The paper maker took the coins I gave him.

I shrugged. 'We sell salvation to sinners and knowledge to the ignorant. We never want for customers.'

I carried the paper back to our workshop, across the bridge so thick with houses you never saw the river. The only sign of water was the grumble of the milling wheels in the arches below. I passed under the watchful gazes of the twenty-four kings of Israel carved into the face of Notre-Dame cathedral, and crossed the invisible river again into the warren of streets around the church of St Severin, in the shadow of the university. This was my home. Goose down and parchment shavings drifted in the air like snow; even to breathe was to take in great lungfuls of them. Copyists sat by open doors and windows with books propped open on stands beside them; illuminators called new and fabulous beasts into being in the capitals and margins of their manuscripts, and students in threadbare finery haggled with the stationers, trying to save their coins for the whores across the rue St Jacques.

The shop was about halfway down a lane, with a cloth awning and a few battered books laid out on a table in front. A large poster nailed next to the door advertised the stationer's many hands: heavy blackletter with ornate initials; fine cursives whose stems twined like a tangled garden; thickset minuscules that only a glass could read. On the corner of the house, the figure of Minerva sat atop a pile of books and peered down at the street.

'There you are.'

111

Olivier de Narbonne – stationer, bookbinder, my employer – looked up from the Bible he had been poring over with a customer. I was about to sidle upstairs to begin work on a piece I had promised him that day, but he beckoned me over, steering his customer so that he could introduce us.

'A countryman of yours. Allow me to present Johann Fust. From Mainz.'

I knew where he came from. I knew where he had lived, where he had attended church and where he had gone to school. I knew he was two years older than me, though with grey already flecking his dark hair it looked more. I had fled the length of Christendom to escape my past, each calamity toppling into the next like dominoes. Yet here in Paris a face from my childhood stood in my shop, smiling curiously.

And he knew me.

'Henchen Gensfleisch.' He crossed the room and embraced me awkwardly. I held back, searching his face for any sign of what he knew, trying to hide my panic from Olivier, who was beaming with surprise. After I fled Cologne I never knew what was said about me, how widely my crime was reported. Perhaps Konrad had kept it secret to protect his son. Certainly there was no hint in Fust's face that he had heard of it – only honest shock at finding an old acquaintance so far from home.

I returned his embrace. 'It is good to see you.'

We had never been friends. Fust, ambitious and clear-sighted, attached himself to boys of untainted patrician stock, boys who were not descended from shopkeepers on their mother's side. He must have prospered: his blue coat was of a rich cloth, trimmed with bear fur and golden thread. It was not the fashion of the day, but the sort of coat an older man might wear, the dress of a man impatient with his contemporaries.

'Why are you in Paris?' I asked.

He lifted up the little Bible. 'Buying books to take back to Mainz.'

'I did not expect to see you as a bookseller.'

He gave a tight-lipped smile. 'I earn a living here and there. I have several ventures. But what about you? The last I heard you had gone to Cologne to learn goldsmithing.'

'The wrong craft for me.' I smiled blankly. 'I came to Paris to work as a copyist.'

'There is nowhere better.' Fust seemed genuinely enthusiastic. 'So many books, and such quality. I buy everything I can.' He pointed at the dog cart outside. 'I will fill that by tonight, and soon come back for more.'

'And you must take that Bible,' broke in Olivier. 'To anyone else I would demand seven gold écus, but as it was copied by your friend I offer it to you for four *sous* less.'

'As it was written by my friend I will pay you the seven écus – if the balance goes to the scribe.'

'Of course. Indeed, he has copied many other works for me. Perhaps I could show you—'

'Not today.' Fust closed the book. 'I must go. I have other appointments before dusk, and tomorrow I set out for Mainz.' He turned to me. 'I will be back in the spring.'

'Perhaps I will see you then.'

'I hope so. It is always good to see a familiar face.' He started for the door then paused, remembering something. 'Forgive me for being slow – I should have said at once. I was so sorry to hear about your mother.'

I was so eager for him to go that I heard the words without the meaning. 'My mother?'

'She was a good and Christian woman. There were many mourners at her funeral. God speed her to Heaven.'

*

113

I sat at my desk and willed the tears to come. My soul ached, but my body was too numb to answer. I had not seen my mother since the day I went to Cologne, a stiff figure in a grey cloak on the riverbank. I had thought of her in the intervening decade, but not often. If I had not met Fust, I could have lived for years happily believing she was alive. I did not even know if it was her I mourned, or the reminder of a life I had lost long ago. I felt a great well drain inside me.

Too many thoughts crowded my head. I looked back down at the desk, at the parchment, ink and book waiting for me. Work would not heal me, but it would bring the comfort of distraction. I rubbed the parchment with chalk to make it white, then ruled it, scoring heavy lines with my lead to show it had been done with care. I blocked out a box for the first initial and left two lines for the rubric.

I positioned the book on the reading stand. It was a slim volume: it would not take me long. I sharpened my pen, turned to the first page and received my third great shock of the day, another fragment of a long-lost life: a belligerent dwarf and the book of marvels he had sold Konrad Schmidt.

I have opened the Books of the Philosophers, and in them learned their hidden secrets.

XIX

New York City

Download complete

Nick glanced at the screen as he swirled the last piece of waffle around his plate, soaking up as much syrup as he could. He was back in the diner's neon cocoon, eating his first proper meal of the day just as night fell. He'd taken a corner booth near the back, keeping a wary eye on the customers coming and going. It was the usual after-work crowd: finance types in suits, secretaries, a few students. Nobody stayed long. By the counter, the Charlie Daniels Band played 'The Devil Went Down To Georgia' out of the jukebox.

He licked the syrup off his fingers and pressed a button on the laptop.

Are you sure you want to install Cryptych?

Yes

It was the third program he'd tried, another free one. He chewed the end of his straw while the progress bar inched across the screen.

What could have driven Gillian to do something like this? When he'd known her she'd been . . . not a Luddite, but someone who pulled a face whenever the conversation got too technical, who wanted computers to work without wanting to know how. Now she'd found ways to encrypt data that even Nick was barely aware of.

Would you like to launch Cryptych now?

Yes. A new window opened on screen, a simple interface of three white boxes in a row. Nick clicked in the middle.

Please select a file to DeCrypt

Another couple of clicks brought up the card, eight animals penned in the centre box. That was the easy part.

With a deep breath, Nick clicked once more. The screen blinked.

Enter Password:

It worked. Nick punched the table in his elation. The empty plate rattled on the Formica. At the next table, a little girl looked up in surprise before going back to her ice cream. Nick tried to fight back the hope that raced through him.

Bear is the key.

Here goes nothing, he thought. He pushed the plate aside, pulling the computer in front of him so that there was no danger of misspelling. B E A R.

Password incorrect
Enter Password:

He tried again, lower case this time. His anxious fingers scrabbled on the keys; he had to repeat it three times before he could be sure he'd got it right. Each time, the same rejection.

The hope was unbearable. The password prompt sat there, an empty space, a keyhole waiting for the right key. If he could only unlock it . . . He tried again and again, changing capitals, adding numbers – Gillian's birthday, even (though he felt pathetic) their anniversary. He wanted to punch a hole in the screen, to reach through the pixel wall and snatch the secrets within. Find reasons for all the questions that had turned his life inside out in the last thirty-six hours.

He plugged in his headset and logged back in to Gothic Lair. Randall must have been looking out for Nick. He appeared out of nowhere in a cloud of sparks a second after Nick arrived.

'It's Cryptych,' Nick said at once. 'The program,' he clarified, in case Randall had misunderstood.

'I know. I took a look.'

'Is there any way to crack it?'

A pause. 'That program's pretty solid. You won't get it out of there in a hurry without the password. Didn't Gillian send you anything to unlock it?'

'She said, "bear is the key".' Nick typed it out. In the moonlit chamber, the Wanderer took a sheet of parchment from inside his cloak and handed it to the Necromancer.

'There's four bears in the picture. Maybe that's what the clue's about?'

Nick swapped programs. Four bears cavorted with the lions

in their digital box. One seemed to be digging an invisible hole. He clicked, and received the dreaded password prompt.

He typed: f o u r

Password incorrect
Enter Password:

'How about . . .' Randall thought for a moment. 'You said these cards were from the Middle Ages, right? Didn't they speak Latin back then?'

'What's the Latin for "bear"?'

Urthred walked to a dusty shelf and opened up a large, iron-bound book resting on a lectern. He studied it. On Randall's machine, Nick knew, the action would have opened up a window on the Web.

'*Ursus.*' Randall spelled it out. 'Any good?'

Nick tried it: capitalised, lower case. 'Nope.'

'How about—'

The muffled bleep of Nick's cellphone penetrated through the headphones. 'Hang on.' He unhooked the headset and picked up the phone. 'Yes?'

'Nick, buddy.' Royce, as ebulliently unpleasant as ever. 'We got a few more questions for you. You want to come back in?'

Nick looked at his watch. Almost as if he could see him, Royce added, 'Not now. I'm heading out. Tomorrow morning. Bring a friend.'

When Nick went back into the game, Urthred was gone and the Wanderer held a new parchment scroll.

Had to go. Good luck hunting bears.

Nick didn't smile. He ordered another soda and reopened

118

Cryptych. He tried every variant of 'bears' and numbers he could think of, every combination of dates. In the corner of the screen time moved on, the seconds tapped out by the click of keys. He wondered if 'bear' was a mistake Gillian had mistyped in her panic. Beat? Neat? Near?

'Nowhere near.' Nick slammed the lid of the computer and waved to the waitress for the bill. He tossed his credit card onto the plate and stared into neon-lit space while she ran it through the machine. The password prompt had branded itself onto his brain: he knew when he went to bed he would see it in his sleep, dancing in front of his eyes.

'Sir? Excuse me, sir?'

The waitress had come back with his credit card. He reached for the pen to sign, but there was no slip.

'I'm sorry, sir. Your card was declined.' Her tone was so bored she could have been listing the specials. Nick was bewildered.

'Can you try it again?'

'Three times already. You should call your bank. You got something else?'

'How much do I owe?'

'Twenty-seven seventy-five.'

He peered inside his wallet. A twenty and a ten. He pulled them both out and laid them on the table. The waitress saw the tip and popped her gum in contempt.

'Have a nice day.'

The moment he was back in his hotel room he rang the phone number on the back of his credit card. He punched in the card number when the computer asked for it, then settled back on his bed for the long, on-hold purgatory. To his surprise, an operator picked up almost straight away.

'How may I help you today, Mr Ash?' she asked, after the usual security checks.

'I just tried to pay for a meal with my card and the waitress said it was declined.'

'That card's been cancelled, sir.'

'Cancelled?'

'It was reported stolen three hours ago.'

'Stolen?' Nick's mind spun. 'Who told you that?'

A hollow clacking of keys on the other end of the phone. 'You did, sir.'

Nick lay flat on the bed. He felt weak, a shadow snatching at things he couldn't grasp. 'I, uh, the card wasn't in my wallet so I assumed it must have been stolen. I guess I panicked.' How guilty did he sound? 'But I found it again now. Can I get it reactivated?'

'I'm sorry, it's not possible to reactivate a cancelled card. You should receive a replacement within seven to ten working days.'

Nick ended the call. He was shaking. How could they do that – whoever *they* were – just phone up and cancel a part of his life?

Maybe it wasn't anyone. Credit card companies make mistakes, the wrong cards get cancelled . . .

What about the hotel? They'd swiped his card when he checked in. Would that show up on his statement? If it did, they'd know where he was. And his cellphone. Was that safe? There were so many base stations in New York City they'd get a fix on him in an instant, if they had that kind of access.

They.

He jumped off the bed. He had to get out of there. There was nothing to pack except his laptop and the previous day's clothes still balled-up damp in a corner. He stuffed them into

120

a laundry bag he found in the closet and turned out the light, then turned it back on again in case anyone was watching.

He let himself out into the corridor. At the far end, by the elevator, a bellboy with a room-service trolley was waiting outside another room. He heard Nick and glanced up, watching him for a second longer than was necessary.

Is he one of them? Did he recognise me? With a spurt of embarrassment, Nick realised what he must look like: unshaven, unkempt, with a laptop slung over one shoulder and a laundry bag in the other. No wonder the guy looked suspicious.

An invisible guest opened his door. The bellboy pushed the trolley into the room, shooting Nick another doubtful glance. The moment he was out of sight, Nick ducked back into his room. He leaned against the wall, shivering as sweat beaded on his forehead.

He couldn't check out of the hotel without paying. Then Royce really would lock him up. But he couldn't pay without the card – and if *they* were monitoring it, they'd know at once he was on the move. Where would he go? He had friends, but each time he thought of them he imagined them like Bret, slumped dead in a chair. He couldn't do that to them.

He double-locked the door, shot the chain and put a chair under the handle. He checked the windows didn't open. Then he stripped off and crawled into bed.

It was a long time before sleep came, and when it did it brought no rest. He dreamed he was running through a forest, thick and tangled like something from Gothic Lair, chasing a creature that crashed unseen through the undergrowth ahead. However fast he ran he never seemed to get closer. The forest was filled with noise, other hunters chasing the same animal – or were they after him? He knew Royce was among them. He

121

ran faster, tripping on rocks and tearing his face on branches.

He came out into a clearing, a long meadow that ended at the foot of a sheer cliff. Now he could see his prey, a black-backed bear breasting through the high grass in long, sinuous bounds.

'Shoot him,' said Gillian, next to him. He hadn't seen her come. 'Bear is the key.'

He looked down and saw a gun in his hand. It was surprisingly heavy. He had the terrible feeling he was doing something wrong, but he didn't know what it could be. He lifted the gun and aimed it at the bear, who had rolled into a ball and seemed to be tickling itself, oblivious to the danger.

'Poor bear,' said Emily, who had appeared out of nowhere. But it was too late: Nick had already pulled the trigger. Except that the bear wasn't a bear any more – it was Bret. It slumped against the cliff, drowning in blood.

When daylight finally dawned outside he'd already been awake for hours. And he still had no idea what the password might be.

XX

Paris, 1433

The cloaked man stood in the churchyard, glancing between the arch above him and the book in his hand. To anyone watching – anyone but me – it must have seemed some sort of piety, the book perhaps a Bible or a book of hours. I knew better.

I had spent half the night copying the book by candlelight, thrilling to the phrases that flowed through my pen. I should have abandoned it to another scribe – told Olivier I did not have time and forfeited the fee. But I could not. The words crept into me, seizing me the same way they had that night in Cologne. I had found out the customer's name from Olivier: Tristan d'Amboise. When he came to collect his manuscript I lingered on the stairs at the back of the shop, and the moment he left I followed, all the way to the churchyard.

I stood behind a gravestone and watched. The sun setting behind the spire of St Innocent's flung a long shadow across his shoulders. Above him, seven painted panels adorned the great arch over the churchyard gate, set there by Nicholas Flamel, the magician who crossed Mercury with the Red Stone and produced half a pound of pure gold. The pictures returned to me like a long-forgotten dream: the king with the sword, the cross and the serpent, a lonely flower on the high mountain guarded by griffins. Flanking the arch, painted on the walls, two lines of women in coloured dresses processed solemnly towards the gate.

I looked back down. Tristan d'Amboise had gone. Before I could blink, a rough hand reached around my shoulders and pinned my arms; a knife pressed against my neck. Stubble scraped my cheek as he put his mouth to my ear. 'Who are you? What are you doing?'

'Pr . . . praying,' I whispered, terrified that if I so much as swallowed he would slit my throat.

'You followed me all the way from the bookseller's shop. *Why?*'

'The book,' I gasped. My eyes swivelled in their sockets, desperate for some sexton or curate to rescue me. The churchyard was empty.

'What about the book?'

'I know what you seek. I – I want to help.'

He pulled the knife away and spun me around, holding me at arm's length. The knife lingered between us.

'How?'

It was the first time I had seen much more than his back. He was beautiful, with a head of dark curls and creamy skin that flushed easily. His eyes burned with the fire of youth. Despite the situation, I felt the long-dormant demon stir in my loins.

'I trained as a goldsmith. I know how to alloy metals and how to purify them with quicksilver. I can fire them with powders, hammer them thin as air or carve them with mystic symbols. And I know the ways of gold.'

The knife wavered. He hushed his voice, though there was no one to hear us but the dead.

'Do you know the secret of the Stone?'

'No,' I admitted. I fixed my gaze on his and stepped towards him, daring him to either drop the knife or impale me. He lowered the blade. 'Let me help you.'

'After long errors of three years or thereabouts – during which time I did nothing but study and labour – finally I found that which I desired.'

So wrote Flamel in his book. I did not persevere for three years, but after six months all I had discovered were his errors. The further I delved into the secrets of the Art the further I seemed from it. Yet I could not abandon the quest. At first I assisted Tristan one or two evenings in the week, but in those early, heady days our progress seemed rapid, success imminent. Evenings gave way to long nights spent sweating over the forge, both stripped to the waist, until dawn came and I slunk back to Olivier's house. With so little sleep my eyes became unreliable. My scripts grew ragged and irregular, feeble imitations of the proud specimens by the door. Olivier, proofreading, spilled so much red ink on my manuscripts it became an embarrassment.

Inevitably, he soon realised how little I went to my bed. The first time he caught me trying to creep in just after sunrise he warned me not to repeat it; the second time he threatened to expel me from his house; the third he pleaded with me not to ruin my livelihood. I resented his kindness even more than his anger. Deep in my soul I knew he spoke the truth.

I left the next day. Tristan gave me a room in his house, and

125

there I devoted my every hour to breaking Flamel's secret. I slept only when exhaustion compelled me, ate little and left the house so rarely his neighbours must have taken me for a ghost. After six weeks I realised I was, to all effects, a prisoner.

XXI

New York City

They were back in the same room, with its police-issue plastic table and folding metal chairs. This time the door was open, offering a view into the busy corridor beyond. Perhaps that was what made the room feel safer. Perhaps it was because he'd brought Seth Goldberg. He'd been an idiot for ever coming here without a lawyer. But then, he hadn't thought he had anything to hide.

Seth sat at the table and flipped through some papers in his briefcase. Nick had always assumed defence lawyers were magicians – wise, grey-bearded, irascibly benevolent – but Seth was only in his mid-thirties, young enough to have been at college at the same time as Nick. The difference might as well have been a decade. Where Nick felt like a perpetual kid trying to get served in a bar, Seth moved with a bow wave of authority that seemed to impress itself on everyone he met. They'd known each other at NYU, connected in a loose sort of way by overlapping acquaintances and softball. Nick had never imagined they'd end up in a police station together as client and attorney.

Nick glanced out of the door and felt the fresh scar on his chin. The first thing Seth had done that morning was buy Nick breakfast. The second thing he'd done was send him to the drugstore across the road for a razor and some shaving gel, which he'd then insisted Nick use in the coffee shop's cramped bathroom.

'Rule number one: you're only as innocent as you look. If they play the tape of this interview back in court and twelve jurors see you looking like the Unabomber, they're not even going to care what you say.'

'What happened to not judging a book by its cover?'

'Did you ever buy a book with a shitty cover?'

The door banged against the wall as Royce blew in. Today's suit was grey again, but sliced with white pinstripes that made him look like a stockbroker.

'Thanks for coming back. We won't take too much of your time.'

Royce sat and waited while the technician adjusted the camera.

'We've spoken to your neighbour's kid. He confirmed that he saw you in the corridor at approximately the time the shot was fired.'

'*When* the shot was fired,' Nick corrected him.

'He wasn't able to confirm the presence of the masked gunman you described, because he ran inside his apartment as soon as he heard the shot. But he heard footsteps.'

For the first time since Bret had called, Nick felt the knots inside him begin to unwind. He sat back, so relieved he barely heard what Royce was saying about other lines of enquiry, potential connections, different angles. Only when he heard a name –

'Could you please describe your relationship with Miss Gillian Lockhart.'

Nick blinked with surprise. Gillian's name still produced a physical reaction, even now. A part of him was always ready to talk about her, desperate even, a sad drunk at a bar. Seth shot Nick a look that said, *Be careful.*

'I met Gillian about a year ago, on a train. We got talking. I gave her my number, we kept in touch, eventually we started . . .'

Started what? Nick had dated girls where he'd have known the exact word, each phase of the relationship analysed and classified in earnest conversations. *Dating. Going steady. Boyfriend and girlfriend. Married. Divorced.* A complete taxonomy. With Gillian, things just sort of happened.

'We got together.'

That wasn't good enough for Royce. 'Was it a sexual relationship?'

Nick blushed. It was like being back in the cabin at summer camp, adolescents in the dark desperately bragging about who'd *done* who. He glanced at Seth, who simply shrugged.

'Yes.'

'Were you living together?'

'Gillian kept her own place. Somewhere on the East Side. She had a room-mate from hell – we never went there.'

That was another wound. He'd always been emotionally a step ahead of her, always ready to commit. But she'd been adamant. 'I need my space, Nick. I've opened myself up before. I need to take it slowly.' And he'd sworn to himself that he'd prove he was different, that she could trust him.

'And what was her occupation at this time?'

'She worked as a conservator at the Cloisters museum.' He would have bet money Royce had never been there. 'Up in Fort

Washington Park. It's where the Metropolitan Museum keeps its medieval collection.'

'Was Ms Lockhart acquainted with your room-mate, Bret Deangelo?'

Nick checked with Seth, who nodded and made a note on a yellow legal pad.

'Sure. Bret and I were in the apartment together while I was going out with Gillian.'

'Did they get along?'

'I guess.' Though it was a small apartment and Bret didn't often leave, Nick couldn't remember more than a couple of times when the three of them had been together. He remembered how awkward it had been: Bret trying not to be caught looking at Gillian's breasts, Gillian sitting stiff on the couch, and Nick bustling about trying to break the ice with inanities. Otherwise, Bret had somehow contrived to make himself invisible whenever Gillian was around. The best part of six months. It occurred to Nick that Bret had been doing him a favour.

'When was the last time you saw Ms Lockhart?'

'Some time last July.' *July 23, around half past ten.*

'Did she dump you?' Again, the sudden lurch into high-school crudeness. Nick flinched, but Seth was quick off the mark.

'Would you like to rephrase that question, Detective?'

Royce adjusted his tie. 'Did your relationship end acrimoniously.'

'No.'

There had been a lot of fights with Gillian. Sometimes he thought she provoked them deliberately, because she couldn't resist the drama. She'd threaten to leave him, and he'd be up until four in the morning begging her to reconsider. Other times it just seemed to be the inevitable eruption of two tectonic plates colliding or moving apart – those were the ones that could last days. It kept him on a knife-edge.

But there'd been no fight the night she left him. She'd cooked him dinner, teased him about his new haircut and gone to bed with him. She'd been subdued all evening, which was unusual but not unheard of. The next morning he woke alone to find a note on the pillow.

It's over. x G

No apologies, no explanation, no tears, no way back. A one-night stand that lasted six months.

'Did you try to contact her again?' Royce asked.

Nick shifted uncomfortably in his seat. 'A few times.'

Those were memories he didn't want to relive: dark days of phones that rang and were never answered; emails written, re-drafted and abandoned; meals forgotten; work ignored so long that even Bret started to worry.

'So – just so we can be clear – when exactly was the last time you communicated with Ms Lockhart?'

'Last July. Then nothing until I got the video call from her three days ago.'

'So you weren't aware that she had moved to Paris and got a job with an auctioneers?'

'I learned that after I got the message.'

'Even though you'd shown no interest in finding it out for the previous six months?'

'I was worried. I told you what I saw on the computer.'

Royce leaned closer. 'And did you then call Ms Lockhart

131

from your cellphone about an hour before Bret Deangelo was murdered?'

The room seemed closer, the lights too bright. 'I got the number of her office in Paris and called it.'

'Paris is six hours ahead of East Coast time. Did you really expect she'd be there?'

'The auction house told me there was a late-night sale going on. I thought it'd be worth a try. You can check that with Stevens Mathison, if you like,' he added. Too defensively, judging by the look Seth gave him.

Royce powered on. 'Was it?'

'What?'

'Worth a try.'

'She wasn't there, if that's what you mean.'

'But you spoke to someone? Someone who'll confirm your story.'

'I don't remember his name. I – I don't think he gave it. He sounded English.'

'We'll look into it.' Royce dismissed it and moved on. 'Now, when Ms Lockhart contacted you via email—'

'It was Buzz,' Nick interrupted.

'Right. The same thing you used for snooping on your room-mate.'

Seth raised his pen, a silent objection.

'OK, she Buzzed you – have I got that right?'

Nick nodded.

'Did she send anything with her message?'

He was trying to be casual, but Royce couldn't really manage low key. *He knows*, Nick thought. *Did I tell him?* He didn't think so. They must have looked on the computer they'd taken.

There was no point stalling. 'She sent me a file – a picture of

132

a medieval playing card.' He saw the next question coming and cut it off. 'I have absolutely no idea why. I wish I knew.'

Something in the hopelessness of his voice seemed to check Royce's momentum. Seth took advantage.

'My client's been very cooperative in answering all your questions. Would you mind informing him why you're so interested in his former partner?'

Royce stood. 'I think, Mr Goldberg, you and I should have a moment alone.' He held the door open and gestured Nick to go out. 'We'll just be a minute.'

In fact they were ten. Nick watched them through the window in the door, the wires of the safety glass like prison bars. He could see both men standing, facing each other across the table and arguing intently. When they were finished, it wasn't Seth who came out but Royce.

'Your lawyer wants you.' He smirked. 'I'll be by the coffee machine.'

Nick went back in the room. The video camera had been turned off. Seth gave a weary sigh.

'They want you to surrender your passport. They think you might be a flight risk. They seem really hung up about this call you made to Paris just before Bret was killed.'

'Do they think I hired some French guy to kill him?'

'Keep your voice down.' Seth glanced at the windows. 'Rule number one: never use sarcasm to the police. Same goes for irony. That stuff is filet mignon to prosecutors – they slice it up, serve it to the jury any which way. This whole thing is a mess. You should've talked to me before you told them anything, especially that story about the assassin on the roof. Did you expect them to believe that?'

'It's the truth,' Nick protested.

'That's not what I said. Royce is convinced you're either

half-crazy or guilty as hell. The only thing keeping you out of jail is the testimony of an eight-year-old kid. Bret's not an easy case for the defence. And they've got something on Gillian too.'

'What?' Nick felt dizzy. Had the police cracked the picture? What else did they have?

'I've done the best I can for you,' Seth was saying. 'Royce was ready to arrest you right there. I convinced him to go easy for the moment. This passport thing's his compromise.'

'It's at the apartment. Will they let me in there?'

'I'll come with you.'

XXII

Paris, 1433

Tristan's house was an enormous *hôtel*: a square stone-built mansion near the church of St Germain. It could have been anywhere. The moment you passed its gate the city was relegated to a distant smudge of smoke and spires behind the wall. Tristan's father had a role at the court of King Charles, from where he had been dispatched on some diplomatic errand to Constantinople. He had been gone some months and would be away for many more. He had taken his wife, his two daughters and most of his household, leaving Tristan with an almost-empty house and stern instructions to behave himself.

If Tristan's father feared that his son might consort with prostitutes, idlers and gamblers then he had every reason to worry. If the secret of the Stone could have been discovered through fornication, or won at cards, Tristan would have had it within a month. But the whores and drinking and gambling were merely diversions from his true aim. With three older brothers and two sisters who would soon need dowries, he knew his days of living in the grand house – all he had ever known – were drawing to their end. The knowledge seemed to tear him apart, pitting the two halves of his soul in war against each other. He squandered his inheritance ever more savagely in couplings and wagers whose only pleasure was defiance, but he also pursued the Art with the obsessive conviction that it would free him from his father's legacy.

Tristan had made his laboratory in a tower that had been added to the east wing some years earlier. The first time he brought me there it took my breath away. With the sort of architectural absent-mindedness that only the nobility can afford, the inside of the tower had never been finished: you could stand on the ground and stare all the way up to the coned roof, so high it seemed to funnel into eternity. Broad windows for chambers that were never built pierced the stone walls above, while at our level the whole surround was painted with perfect copies of Flamel's panels in St Innocent's. Only a brick furnace set into the far wall, and the door opposite, broke its sweep.

Tristan pointed up into the giddy darkness. 'Truly a place to dream of grasping the secrets of heaven.'

I thought of Nicholas and the tower of Babel. *The sin God punished was not ambition but overambition.*

Tristan was a humourless and petulant collaborator, neither master nor friend. I did not care. I was back in my element. All I thought of was unravelling Flamel's riddles. The fever I had felt in Cologne was returning – and with it came other feelings, harder to resist. I disliked Tristan; sometimes I hated him. But on sweaty nights when we worked the furnace half-naked together, or when his hand brushed mine as I held the pestle for him to grind our powders, the worm inside me thrilled with perverse lust. The tower became my prison, then my world. Flamel's paintings were my horizons, the dark roof my heaven, the bats and swallows who nested in the rafters its angels.

One day, very excited, Tristan brought a stooped old man back to our workshop. He had white hair down to his shoulders and a white beard that touched his chest; he hobbled on a stick, poling himself like a barge. Blindness clouded his eyes, yet still there was something vigorous and watchful in his bearing.

Tristan sat him on a bench amid our apparatus and fetched him wine.

'This is Master Anselme,' he said. 'How old are you?'

'Seventy-eight.' His voice was thin, but he smiled when he spoke.

'Tell my friend what you told me in the churchyard at St Innocent's.'

'Many years ago – before my father died, God rest his soul – when I was young and eager, I delved into the secrets of the Art. As you yourselves do. And so it pleased God that I met the greatest adept of this age – of any age – a man who blazed over the rest of us as the sun vanquishes the moon. Nicholas Flamel.'

I sat bolt upright. Even the figures in the paintings seemed to straighten. 'You knew Flamel?'

'I sat in his workshop as I sit with you now.'

'For how long?'

'Many years. He died, God rest him, fifteen winters ago.'

'And were you there when he produced the gold?'

The old man shook his head. Wine stained the hairs around his mouth like a gash. 'Perenella, his beloved wife. She was the only one.'

'But afterwards,' Tristan prompted him, 'he told you his secret?'

Master Anselme held out his glass for more wine. Tristan waited.

'The Art is not magic. Do you know what the Stone really is? It is medicine, a tonic for all the diseased matter of this world.'

He lifted his left arm, which I saw was stunted and withered, quite useless. 'This limb is still a part of me, however frail it becomes. The soul that unites my being runs through it as much as anywhere else. So with metal. What you call lead or tin are no different from gold and silver, except in the degree of their perfection.

'There is one perfect substance in this universe – ether, quintessence, first matter, call it what you like. In its truest state it is without form. Only when it allies with the material of this world does it take shape. It is a principle, an *idea* that animates. It runs purest in the noble metals, and weakest in the base. You do not transmute lead into gold like a street magician changing an egg into a kitten. You purify it. You alloy it with the Stone, so that the seeds imprisoned in the metal blossom, until in the unity of perfection it can take any shape you command. Not for wealth or riches, but to perfect the universe.'

Tristan, whose interest could blaze and cool like air over coals, looked suspiciously at Anselme's limp arm. 'I heard that the Stone could also cure men. If you knew Flamel so well, why did you not heal yourself?'

The old man coughed. 'I am a feeble vessel. The Stone is valuable beyond measure. I would not waste it on such humble flesh. Flamel himself believed that – used correctly – the Stone might work on our human forms so profoundly as to render us immortal. But he never discovered that art.'

'Obviously,' said Tristan.

'But how did he find the Stone?' I rubbed the blisters on my hands where I had been too eager to pick up vessels fresh from the fire. 'I have read that it can be extracted from gold.'

'Yes. Yes, precisely.' Spittle flew from his mouth. He regathered some of it by licking his lips prodigiously. His tongue was truly enormous. 'Gold is where it is most abundant. But even gold is filthy as mud when set against the Stone. It must be purified in the three furnaces. You must extract the seeds of sulphur and mercury, then combine them in the Hermetic Stream. That is what Flamel did.'

'But how—'

'You must watch the colour. In the fire it will change seven times, until in the moment of perfection it casts a light like a rainbow. That is the sign.'

Tristan leaped to his feet. Master Anselme glanced around fearfully.

'You are a *liar*. Get out.' Tristan kicked the table; the jars, bottles and flasks arrayed on it shivered and chattered. 'Did you think you could come here and recite half-remembered lies you picked up from Flamel's gutter – if you ever knew him? Get *out* of my house.'

He grabbed the old man by his shoulder and flung him halfway to the door. If I had not been standing there to catch him he might have broken his neck.

The incident with Master Anselme put Tristan in a strange mood for the next fortnight. Once when I came back into the tower I found him standing over shards of a broken bottle. Blood was beading around his wrist, and when I tried to bind it he shook me off angrily. His nights with the whores became more frequent. Sometimes he invited me to join them – at first half-heartedly, when he thought I might accept, then with malicious pleasure when he realised I would not. He called me 'monk' when he was kind or 'eunuch' when he was not, though he never guessed the real reason for my abstinence.

Perhaps Master Anselme was a fraud, haunting St Innocent's churchyard and preying on the dreams of those who came to study Flamel's figures. But something in his babble had struck home, a thread through the labyrinth. I followed it day after day, sometimes stretching it almost to breaking, sometimes tangling my mind in knots. And I began to understand.

All my life I had been captivated by gold. In the depths of my fall I had scrabbled to claw a few precious grains out of the river mud; even in Basle I had defined myself by the renunciation of my obsession. Yet now I saw it was not its glitter that bewitched me, as it did other men. Even in my ignorance I had seen through its surface, had sensed something of the divine universal housed within. I had felt it in the perfection of the gulden, in the gold leaf we hammered out in Konrad Schmidt's workshop and in the wisdom of Nicholas Cusanus.

I knew why these things had obsessed me. It was because I could imagine perfection, as real as a dream, and the world would not be whole until I had grasped it.

I redoubled my efforts. While Tristan gave himself over to his dubious pleasures, I took Flamel's book back to St Innocent's. *'In the churchyard in which I put these Hieroglyphical Figures,'* wrote Flamel, *'I have also set on the wall a Procession, in which are represented by order all the colours of the Stone as they come and go.'* The wall paintings in Tristan's tower showed the seven panels from the arch, the same seven pictures as were drawn in the book. But there were others he had not bothered to have copied, the women on either side of the arch processing towards the centre.

I studied them in the light of what Master Anselme had said. 'You must extract the seeds of sulphur and mercury.' By then I knew that sulphur and mercury were not the substances commonly called such, but wise names for mystic elements, the two opposing principles of heat and cold.

'You must watch the colour. In the fire it will change seven times.' I counted the women in the processions: seven on each side. As I looked at them, I began to realise they were all the same. Artfully painted so that no two *seemed* exactly alike – some turned to face the churchyard, others looking away or staring straight ahead, smiling, frowning, laughing, desolate – but all incarnations of the same woman, differing only in the colour and length of their hair. Sometimes it was white as the moon, sometimes black as night; brown, bronze, amber, honey-yellow or steel-grey. And at the front of each procession, where two identical women with knowing smiles faced each other across the open arch, red like cedar bark. The colour of the Stone.

And so I scoured the apothecaries' shops and tapped their lore. I sought learned men and wise women. I pored over Flamel's book until I could recite it word perfect and draw the figures in my sleep. I teased meanings from his riddles, mined the pictures until I struck new seams of understanding. I melted, alloyed, quenched and boiled. I learned more of the ways of metals than I would have in seven years in Konrad Schmidt's shop. With many errors and missteps, I followed Flamel's progress.

Along the way I made some curious discoveries. I burned copper oxide, reduced it with litharge and produced a liquid that was black as sin, yet dry to the touch in a very short time. Another time I alloyed lead, antimony and tin to create a wondrous new metal that melted easily over a flame, yet hardened like steel as soon as it cooled. When I showed it to Tristan he only grunted and asked if it brought us closer to the Stone.

It was not a happy time. When fatigue or Tristan's petty cruelties drove me close to tears, I cursed my fate and despaired. What evil drove me on? I had spent ten years curing myself of my immoderate desires, years of agonies and mortification that drove me at last to the river ooze. In Basle I had been happy with a cell and a pen, a faithful servant to the ambitions of worthier men. A chance encounter and a single sentence in a book had undone it all. I felt as if I was stumbling through a dark tunnel, with an enormous burden crushing my back and chains dragging around my ankles.

But I was making progress. Gold turned black, then bronze, then a cloudy grey, then wine-red as I found ways to tinge it according to Flamel's scheme. Silver resisted me longer, but after weeks of frustration it too yielded. At last, one night deep in November, I lifted my grinding mortar and, trembling, beheld a reddish powder the colour of cedar bark.

I dabbed a few grains on my fingertip and held them up to the lamp. It was very fine, like dust, sweet-smelling but dry as salt to the touch. There was terrifyingly little. All my weeks of labour had reduced to not much more than a thimbleful of the stuff.

I covered the bowl with an upturned jar, took the lamp and went to fetch Tristan. The house was dark, its filth disguised. As the costs of our experiments mounted, Tristan had dismissed the servants one by one until we were alone in our squalor. It made the cavernous house even more frightening.

Rats played among the cobwebs just beyond the reach of my lamp; terrible creatures stalked me from the tapestries hanging on the walls. Once I knocked over a wooden stool and almost died of terror. My whole body was sunk in grim exhaustion, yet at the same time I thrilled to the wonder of the moment.

I found Tristan in his bed. A scrawny prostitute lay sprawled over him. Both were naked and half-asleep; I could see the scabs of flea bites down the backs of her legs, and something moving in her hair that looked like lice. Evidently the servants were not the only economy Tristan had made.

He propped himself up on his elbow. The prostitute rolled off him, revealing a meagre pair of breasts and a great deal of hair.

'Have you come to join us after all?' leered Tristan.

'I have it.'

He pushed the whore aside and leaped out of bed, kicking over a glass of wine on the floor. He grabbed his father's sword, which rested on a shelf in its scabbard. 'Are you sure?'

'There is one way to prove it.'

We returned to the tower, under the gaze of Flamel's inscrutable figures. Black infinity yawned above us. Working in silence, I heaped up the powder on a fold of paper. I had wanted to hold some back in case the first projection did not work, but there was so little I did not dare spare a grain. I twisted it shut and sealed it with wax. A silver mirror lay on the bench from when I had tried to trap the sun's rays: I glimpsed my reflection in it and trembled. My skin was grey, my hair thin and my eyes sunk beyond sight. The skin on my hands was pink and shiny, smooth as a baby's from all the burns I had suffered in my haste. A splash of vitriol had seared a crescent scar into my cheek.

Tristan brought out an egg-shaped vase made of blown glass. He filled it with powdered lead which he measured in a balance, then sprinkled it with a few drops of quicksilver. Then he fitted a crystal plug to its end and burned the edges with a taper. While he did that, I shovelled coals into the furnace and worked the bellows. I watched the colours of the fire change, from red to orange to a brilliant white too painful to behold. When I saw that, I knew we were ready.

I grasped the glass egg with a pair of iron tongs and thrust it into the centre of the fire. Tristan rested his arm on my shoulder and leaned forward to look. Though the night was cold, we were both soaked in sweat.

'How long will it take?'

'We will know when the moment comes,' I told him.

We stood there and watched, our bodies pressed together so close our sweat mingled into one. I hardly noticed. Steam began to curl out of the metal in the vase. The lead softened, melted and bubbled, drinking up the quicksilver.

I pulled away from Tristan and squeezed the bellows, building up the fire to new fury. The heat seared my face; smoke billowed into the tower. Tristan stumbled away with his hands over his eyes, but I stayed rooted in front of the furnace.

Something flashed in the glass and I knew the time had come. I reached in and knocked out the crystal plug with a poker, then lifted the paper twist in the tongs and flung it in. It dropped through the opening, fell onto the boiling metal in the base and burst into flame. It was the purest, whitest flame I ever saw, like sunlight on snow. And as it burned I saw an aura, an iridescent halo that filled the vase with colours. The rainbow.

I cried out to Tristan. He must have seen it too for he ran to my side. Together, we dragged the vase out of the fire and stood it upright on the floor. Tristan drew his sword, raised it and struck. The glass egg cracked in two and fell apart. Through the smoke and sweat that stung our eyes, we stared down at what we had created.

XXIII

New York City

Going back to the apartment was worse than he'd expected. A uniformed officer gave them plastic gloves and elasticated bags like shower caps to wear over their shoes, then lifted the tape that barricaded the door. Nick and Seth ducked under it into the living room.

The last time he'd seen it, Nick realised, had been on Buzz. He looked at Bret's desk, then back where the video camera had pointed, trying to figure out where the killer had stood. Bret's computer was gone, as was the chair he'd been tied to. So, thankfully, was the body, though there were stains on the carpet that might have been Bret, once. How long did you have to preserve the evidence at a crime scene?

He went into his own bedroom. The police must have been in here, too: it was tidy enough but disarranged, a product jammed back in its packaging. He made to sit on the bed and thought better of it. His whole body crawled with the fear that he would contaminate anything he touched. He crouched in front of the bedside table and pulled out the drawer. A leather travel wallet, a graduation present from his parents, lay buried at the back under the usual debris of aftershaves, paperbacks and condoms. He took the passport out, then slipped the wallet into his jacket pocket. You never knew what might prove useful. A gold eagle with a sheaf of arrows in its claws glared at him from the passport cover.

'Nick?'

He pushed the drawer shut and turned around, trying not to look guilty. Seth was standing in the door, the policeman beyond watching over his shoulder. Had they seen him? Did the wallet make a bulge?

'Got it.' His voice sounded lifeless in the still apartment. He tossed the passport to Seth. 'Let's go.'

He took a last look around the room. A balled-up sock sat on the floor where he'd left it three nights ago. A magazine lay open to the article he'd been reading over dinner that night. Two creased shirts he'd meant to iron hung on the closet door. His former life. He remembered an article he'd seen once in *National Geographic* about a caveman found frozen in the Alps. He'd been perfectly preserved, even down to the bowl of berries still clutched in his hands. The scientists thought he must have fallen asleep next to the glacier, swallowed by the advancing ice. Nick had always wondered about him. Did he realise what was happening? Was there a moment when he woke up, too cold, and found himself trapped? Was the ice clear enough for him to see the sunlit world outside? Did he scream, or had the ice frozen his lungs?

He glanced at the alarm clock by the bed to get his bearings, but even that had fallen victim to the spell in the room. 00:00. 00:00. 00:00. The blue numbers flashed their non-time at him. The police must have unplugged it when they searched the room.

'C'mon.' Seth was waiting.

Nick walked slowly to the door, trying to cram in as many memories as he could. That was when he saw the picture of Gillian. She sat on his dresser, watching from behind the bottles and aerosols. Somehow he'd never got round to putting it away. He reached to get a closer look.

'Don't,' said Seth. He waved the passport. 'You've given the police enough help.'

Nick hadn't used his passport since he came back from Berlin eighteen months ago. He wasn't even sure if it was still valid. But now that he'd given it away he felt trapped without it, as if he'd handed his jailers the key to his cell. Locked out of his home, locked into the city. Almost.

With nowhere to go, he wandered the streets. The temperature had dropped overnight; the radio was forecasting snow. Gusts of steam billowed out of the manhole covers; Haitian street vendors tried to sell him ice scrapers and black leather gloves. The buildings reflected the concrete sky.

He knew he needed to go to the bank but kept putting it off: he dreaded the thought of another rebuff, more suspicion. He invented other things to do, department-store windows to stare at or bookstores where he could flip through the magazine racks. One had a coffee shop; he searched his bag and dug out enough change for an espresso.

The coffee shop was hot and crowded. Nick couldn't get a table of his own, but had to share with a young woman who was working her way through a three-inch stack of fashion magazines. She gave him a discouraging scowl when he sat down, and afterwards ignored him completely.

He perched the laptop on the edge of the table and booted it up. He had vague thoughts of doing some work, but most of it was held on the servers at the FBI, and the rest was in the police station on Tenth Street. Inevitably, he went back to the card, scratching a scab he'd already dug raw. *Bear is the key.* Except it wasn't. Nor was grizzly, panda, koala, polar, Kodiak, Yogi, brown . . .

Nick killed the program. His head was beginning to ache. He searched his bag and found a nickel but no painkillers. There were some back in the apartment, but he doubted Royce would let him back to the crime scene for that. He could almost script the conversation. '*Do you have a painkiller addiction? Did you supply drugs to Ms Lockhart? Why did you keep a photograph of her on your desk when – by your own admission – you broke up six months ago?*'

The photograph. He opened a new folder on the screen. In the real world it would have been covered in dust and yellowing at the edges, perhaps blotted with a few dried tears. In the digital realm it was just one among a dozen identical icons, as fresh and sterile as the day he'd created it. Inside were a couple of dozen photographs, perfectly aligned like pinned butterflies, all he had of Gillian. For a woman who could make a date with a stranger on an empty train, she'd been surprisingly self-conscious when it came to cameras. He hit the SLIDESHOW button and let the images segue across the screen. Six months of his life played out in less than a minute.

The photograph from his room came near the end. He remembered exactly when he'd taken it. He'd gone out to lock up and come back into the bedroom to find Gillian curled up on the bed wearing nothing except the old college T-shirt she used as pyjamas. It wasn't exactly an unusual sight, but something about that moment had captivated him: the low light from the bedside lamp and the shadow between her thighs where the T-shirt rode up, the swell of her breasts under the torn V-neck, the auburn hair tangled around her throat. It caught her perfectly: beautiful, irresistible and his. He'd seen the camera on the bookshelf, grabbed it and squeezed off the photo before she could object. Later, he'd had it printed and framed. Gillian had complained, of course, but he didn't care. It was the first time he'd felt confident enough to display a trophy of their relationship, and he felt the pride of ownership.

It hadn't lasted long after that.

But for the first time in months, he didn't care; he stared at the picture and barely noticed Gillian. He magnified the picture, zooming in on the T-shirt. A dark blue shield filled the screen, the single word BROWN blazoned on it across Gillian's chest. Behind, wrapping his vast forearms around the shield, loomed an enormous brown bear.

The bookshop had an Internet connection but it was down. Nick ran to the stairwell and checked the store directory. EDUCATION AND CAREERS: BASEMENT. He took the elevator. There was hardly anyone down there: people coming back from Christmas vacation hadn't yet had time to remember how much they hated their jobs.

He found what he was looking for in a dead-end aisle near the back of the store: *Inside the Ivy League* by J. B. Morford. He flipped through the photographs of gothic cloisters and blonde girls with too-perfect teeth clutching copies of Shakespeare. He didn't have to go far.

Brown University
Student Body: 7,740 (approx.)
Mascot: Bruno the Bear

He squatted down on a rubberised grey stool and balanced

the laptop on his knee, checking there was no one to see him. The Cryptych program opened at once. Nick clicked on the picture.

Enter Password:

b r u n o

Password incorrect

Enter Password:

B r u n o

Password accepted

XXIV

Paris, 1433

I woke on bare stone. My skin was clammy and cold, my bones stiff as iron. I was naked except for a short cloth around my waist. My head ached, and when I opened my eyes the harsh winter light made me wince.

I heaved myself up. I could not find my clothes, so I pulled a hanging off the wall and wrapped it around my shoulders. It trailed behind me, dragging a broad road in the dust as I walked barefoot through the empty house. When I came to the tower door I paused. The ache in my head pounded to a new intensity. I knew what I would find.

I had not realised how bad the tower had become in those last frenzied weeks. Everything was filthy. Black residues crystallised in jars that I had not washed out; the ghosts of failed experiments congealed where I had abandoned them. Several parts of the table were crusted with bird droppings. On the floor in front of the cold furnace lay our broken egg. Shards of glass glinted like a shattered crown, the fallen sword beside it.

I heard a sound at the door and turned. Tristan stood there wearing a brown cloak, a fresh cup of wine in his hand. Heavy circles rimmed his eyes. Half of me expected him to pick up the sword and slice off my head, like Herod in the painting. Half of me would have welcomed it.

He looked at the slug of cooled metal among the broken glass. It was dull and grey, little different from the lead we had filled it with. Of the powder which I had laboured so long to produce, there was no trace.

We had failed.

I spent the day picking through the detritus of the laboratory. I swept the grate. I filled a barrel with water and scrubbed out every cup and vessel I had touched. The chill of the water made the ache in my head worse, but I forced myself to continue until everything was clean. Then I went outside and tipped a bucket over my head to clean myself. I arranged the tools in racks and put the remains of my materials in boxes and jars. There was nothing else I could do. The day was a void, an empty space between the ill-fitting fragments of my life. I could not stay there. But I did not know where to go.

That evening, three of Tristan's friends came to play cards. He lit a fire in the hall and fetched a barrel of wine. Normally I would have avoided them and locked myself in the tower, but I could not go there that night. Nor did I want to retreat to another corner of the house. Now that I was alive to my surroundings again, they terrified me.

I had nothing to say to Tristan's friends. I gathered they were all younger sons of more or less noble families, idle youths with no purpose but to spin out their fortunes until their brothers inherited. I said nothing and concentrated on my cards. Not on the game – I gambled as little as I could, though more than I had, and endured the hilarious cries of 'Alms, alms' every time I reached out my hand. But the cards themselves entranced me. They were beautiful: a wild menagerie of birds, beasts, flowers and men that flitted in and out of my hands with the firelight. In the ashes of my soul I felt a small ember begin to glow again. Twice I lost games I might have won by holding on to cards just because I wanted to examine them more closely. The creatures were drawn with rare skill, delicate lines so sharp they almost seemed to be carved into the paper. They reminded me of the figures I had incised in gold at Konrad Schmidt's workshop.

That thought stirred a memory, though not one I could quite grasp. I worried at it while I lost the next two hands, then decided to concentrate on the game.

It was not complicated. The goal was to husband your cards until you held either five consecutive numbers from the same suit or four identical numbers across the five different suits. On each turn a player discarded one card in his hand and took another, either the one the previous player had discarded (which he could see) or one from the deck (which he could not). When he had taken the card he could raise his bet, and if he did the next player had either to match it or to forfeit the round.

All night I had been playing in the most perfunctory way, offering tiny bets on my own account and then surrendering at the first challenge. The others had quickly noticed, and made a separate game of offering derisory bids, clapping and cheering me to match them and then abusing me when I refused. And yet now, as I looked at my cards, I saw that fate had dealt me a tantalising hand. Three eights – beasts, birds and stags – and the ten and Jack of stags.

I bet my usual pittance and watched the other players, wondering if I should pursue the set of eights or the sequence of stags. Tristan took the two of birds and discarded the five of stags – a good sign. His friend drew a card from the deck I could not see, made a sour face and discarded the nine of stags.

'No bet.'

I tried to be calm. I pretended to study my hand, to hover between the deck and the discard pile. I took the nine. Now I had the eight-nine-ten-Jack of stags, but also the three eights. The thought that one more card could win it was like liquor in my blood: not for the money, but for the joy of beating Tristan and his friends. Just once would be enough.

But I could not pursue one path without sacrificing the other. The cards were hard to read: I counted and recounted the images to be sure I had the right numbers. Somewhere around the table were two eights, either one of which would complete my set. Equally, the seven or the queen would complete my run of stags. The decision paralysed me.

'How long does he need to decide to give up?' asked the player to my left. His name was Jacques; the deck was his. I longed to find out more about it, but could not bring myself to ask him.

I looked at my hand again and noticed that one poked slightly above the others. The eight of birds. I pulled it out and threw it down on the table, followed by a quarter penny. On such fine quantities do the balances of our lives tip.

The other players reacted with predictable hilarity to my bet. They made great sport of rummaging in their purses, scratching their heads and crossing themselves in mock distress. All except Jacques beside me, who had stiffened the moment I played my card. I would not have noticed if I had not been so alive to the possibility of winning myself. While the others were still distracted he smoothly palmed the eight of birds and raised my bet to a penny.

155

The game went round the circle. On my next turn I drew blind from the deck, praying for the seven or the queen. I cupped the card in my hand and tilted it up to the firelight.

Eight wild men leaped out at me, brandishing cudgels, exposing themselves, making cruel mockery of my hopes. If I had not given away the eight of birds on my previous turn I would have won.

I threw the card back on the table, not even pretending to consider it. Despair took hold of me: out of pure devilment, I tossed another penny into the betting pot. It prompted an unguarded glance from Jacques as he swept up the card. Now he had two eights thanks to my mistakes, plus whatever he had originally been dealt.

I sat and watched the other players, wondering if they held the cards I needed. Two of Tristan's friends clearly had nothing, and soon threw in their hands. Those were shuffled and returned to the deck. With Tristan I could not find the pattern in the cards he chose to take or leave; he never raised the bet, but met every increase with a cool stare. As for me, I drew blind every time and prayed. All I got were a succession of birds and flowers. My only consolation was that Jacques seemed to do the same. He never took the card he could see, but tried his luck like me in the deck. And I knew that so long as I held my two remaining eights, he could not get the four he needed.

My small pile of coins shrank to nothing and still I did not have the card I wanted. I drew another and threw it back almost without looking. Jacques drew from the deck, made a pretence of shuffling it into the cards he held, then threw it back. A piece of silver followed it onto the table.

'Anyone to raise?'

Tristan swore and put down his cards. I looked at mine – a

run of four stags, including the eight, and the eight of beasts. I had no doubt Jacques meant to raise me out of the game. It was as close as I had come to winning all night. And I had no more money.

'Here.'

A second silver coin landed on the table, rolled across the varnished wood and fell onto the pile. I looked at Tristan.

'That is for you. Now no more bets. Play to see who wins.'

I loved him more that moment than ever before – though afterwards I thought he did it to annoy his friend. They were a pack of wild dogs who would tear into each other at the least sign of weakness.

But for now it was just the two of us. Jacques moved to the other side of the hearth so that he sat facing me. Half his face glowed in the firelight; the other half was lost in shadow. The others sat on the sidelines and made bets among themselves – what suit the next card would be, how many turns it would take to win, whether the card I threw down would be higher or lower than Jacques'. With no gambling of our own to do we played quickly. Our hands darted over the table like flies on meat, peeling off the cards and getting rid of them almost in one movement.

Jacques picked up the five of stags and discarded it. For a moment I wondered if I should take it and hope for the six – but then I would have to surrender one of my eights to him. I peeled another card from the deck, tipped it up, and was halfway to discarding it when I registered what it was.

The eight of flowers. I felt a pain in my stomach; somewhere in heaven, God was surely laughing at me. For the third time that evening I held three eights – and I could not do anything with them. I threw the card back onto the table.

Jacques picked it up, as I knew he would. He tucked it into

157

his hand and plucked out another with a flourish. I watched it go down on the table. A queen sat in a meadow admiring her reflection in a mirror, while a dwarfish stag grazed on the hem of her outspread skirts. The queen of stags.

My hand shot out to take it – but was held in mid-air. Jacques grasped it, squeezing until my knuckles cracked. He held it while he laid out his other cards with his free hand. Four eights. Flowers, wild men, birds – and beasts.

Tristan kicked the table leg in anger. His two friends whooped and crowed. Still holding my fist, Jacques swept the pile of money towards him.

'Wait.'

My hand was in agony, but I barely noticed the pain. I clenched my teeth and put my cards face up on the table. Four stags and the eight of beasts. *Another* eight of beasts.

I shook off Jacques' grip and slid the two cards together. They were the same. Not similar or alike – identical. Perfect copies, two coins struck from the same die.

Tristan realised first. The other two were slower, but quicker to react once they understood they'd been cheated. They flew at Jacques and knocked him off his stool; they tried to pin him down but he was stronger. He sent one reeling back with a kick to the groin, clubbed the other with a fire iron and sprinted for the door. Tristan sprang after him, the others limping behind as best they could.

I picked up the card and followed. I found Jacques in the muddy yard in front of the house, held down by his friends as with cries of 'Cheat' and 'Jew' they kicked, punched, beat and bit him. Tristan, in particular, was possessed by a relentless frenzy that I feared would kill Jacques.

I could not let that happen. I ran to the writhing mass of bodies and forced my way through, ducking the indiscriminate blows. The others thought I wanted to join in the attack, and that this would be hilarious – they pulled Tristan away, shouting that the servant should have his revenge. One of them sat on Jacques' legs, though there was no need for it. His shirt was soaked in blood; his lip was split, and one eye could hardly open. The fingers on his left hand had been crushed under a boot.

I knelt astride Jacques' chest and held up the card. My breath steamed in the cold moonlight.

'Where did you get this?'

Jacques twisted his head and spat a gob of blood onto the ground. A tooth rattled on the stones.

'A man in Strassburg.'

'What was his name?'

He shook his head.

'How did he do it?'

Jacques misunderstood my question. 'He sold them to me.'

The others were getting bored. 'Kill him,' one shouted.

I ignored them. 'Where can I find this man?'

'At the sign of the bear.'

He coughed out a spray of blood. Several droplets landed on the card and I pulled it away hurriedly. I pushed myself up and walked away, trying not to listen to the gleeful screams behind me. I felt dizzy with blood and wine. I stared at the card in my hand – all that mattered in that vast cursed house.

How many others existed in the world? And how had their creator made them so perfect?

XXV

New York City

The card divided, dealing itself out into the left and right panes of the window. One showed a copy of the card indistinguishable from the encoded picture in the centre. In the other panel, three lines of text appeared.

```
177 rue de Rivoli
Boite 628
300-481
```

'Excuse me?'

Nick looked up so fast he almost knocked the laptop onto the floor. A sales assistant was looking down at him with a pile of revision guides stacked in her arms. He leaned over the laptop screen to shield it.

'Can I help you find something?'

Nick snapped the laptop shut. 'I'm fine.'

'There's an Internet connection in the café,' the girl said helpfully.

'Thanks.'

He walked slowly back up the stairs to ground level, hugging the laptop to his chest. Already, the elation of breaking the password had been overtaken by confusion. When the phone in his pocket vibrated against his hip, he almost didn't notice it.

The screen announced two missed calls, both in the last ten minutes. There must have been no signal in the basement. He checked the numbers. One was Seth, the other a local number he didn't recognise. He rang Seth.

'Nick?' He answered almost at once. 'Thank God.'

'What is it?' Seth must be in a car. Nick had to shout to make himself heard over the rumble of traffic in the background.

'Bad news. The kid's changed his story.'

Something that sounded like a rocket roared past Seth's phone.

'Now he's saying he maybe didn't see you in the hallway when the gun went off. Maybe it was just before, or just after.'

'What do you mean? It was the gunshot that made him run for cover. He— Hello?'

A blare of silence cut him short. When Seth came back, his voice was disjointed, almost unintelligible.

'You need – Royce – Gillian – arrest you –'

'I can't hear you,' Nick shouted.

'I'm just heading into the Holland Tunnel. Traffic's pretty bad. I'll call—'

The signal died in a flat drone. Nick stared at the handset. Feeling numb, he hit REDIAL, just in case. Seth's voicemail answered at once.

His head was beginning to ache again; his whole body shivered with fatigue. Why would Max change his story? Was it his mother trying to protect him? Getting revenge for all the nights she'd complained of Bret's pot smoke creeping out from under their door. It was so unfair he wanted to hit something.

The phone rang again. Shoppers browsing the tables of discount paperbacks shot him disapproving glances. He looked at the number displayed on the phone – a local number. What if it was Royce?

The ring forced him into a decision. He answered.

'Nick? It's Emily.'

'How are you?' The words were reflexive, an unthinking verbal handshake. It was only as he said it that he realised something seemed wrong.

'I'm terrified.' She sounded it. 'Nick, someone's following me.'

Her voice was barely louder than a whisper, the words tumbling over themselves in her anxiety. He thought he could hear a hiss like running water in the background.

'Where are you now?'

'The ladies' room at the public library.'

'Is that the one with the lions outside?'

'Yes. Fifth Avenue and Forty-Second Street. '

'OK.' Nick's mind raced. 'The man who's following you, what did he look like?'

'I didn't see his face. He had his hood up. He—' A small gasp. 'Someone's here. I—'

He heard the bang of a door, then a rushing clatter that ended in silence.

'I'm coming,' said Nick. But he was speaking to an empty phone.

New York is an unforgiving city if you don't have money. Nick didn't have enough for a cab: he ran to the subway on Washington Square Park and dropped his last token in the slot. Would it have been faster to walk? He stood on the platform and stared into the tunnel, willing the train to come. The seconds ratcheted round on the grimy station clock.

There'd been no more calls on his phone when he came up at Forty-Second Street. He sprinted the block from the station to the library, pushing against the wind and the cramp in his side. Two stone lions, Patience and Fortitude, watched him race up the steps. He found an information desk on the first floor.

'Where are the restrooms?'

He choked the words out through gasping breaths. The woman behind the desk must have thought he was deranged, a drug addict maybe. She glanced over his shoulder at the security guard, then raised her eyes to the ceiling.

'Third floor.'

He took the steps as fast as he dared, trying not to attract attention while he scanned the faces he passed. *He had his hood up.* But it was a cold day, and half the people on the stairs wore hooded coats. Up ahead, he saw a man in a white shirt and jeans coming round the second-floor landing; his mind flashed back to the rooftop and the gun. He almost slipped on the stairs. But the man was a Nordic type, blond and fair, not the man from the roof.

He reached the third floor. Through a wood-panelled rotunda that he barely noticed, down a sparkling white corridor signposted for the restroom. He stopped outside the door.

What now? He couldn't just burst in to the ladies'. *Royce would love that.*

The door swung in. The blast of a hand dryer intruded on the quiet of the library. He tensed, but it was only a pair of college-age girls.

'Excuse me.'

They slowed but didn't stop.

'I wonder if you could help me. I lost my girlfriend – can't find her anywhere. Do you think one of you could check . . .?'

'Sure.'

One of the girls gave him a brisk, happy-to-help smile and poked her head back inside the door. 'There's nobody in there,' she announced.

His heart sank. 'Thanks anyway.'

The moment they were out of sight he slipped inside the restroom. It was empty. No trace of Emily, just white tiles, white handbasins, white lights reflected in stark white floors.

One of the cubicle doors hung shut, not locked. Still gripped by a sense of unholy trespass, he nudged it in. The stall was empty, but in the toilet bowl something gleamed. He peered in. Just where the bowl funnelled away into darkness, he could see a corner of a silver cellphone poking out of the waste pipe like sunken treasure. Was it Emily's?

An electric trill broke the silence. He stared at the sparkling phone in the water for a second, stupefied, before he realised it was coming from his own pocket.

'Hello?'

'Nick?'

His whole body seemed to unclench as he heard Emily's voice. Weak with relief, he sank against the stall partition. 'Where are you?'

'The payphone in the stairwell.' An embarrassed pause. 'I dropped my cellphone in the toilet.'

'I just found it. Are you OK?'

'I think so. I think the man lost me. Where are you?'

'Heading over to you now. Stay on the line.' He shouldered through the door, glad to be back on legitimate ground. A well-dressed woman walking up the corridor shot him a nasty look: he grinned and tapped the cellphone against his head like an idiot.

'Wait a minute.' Panic rose in Emily's voice. 'I think he's coming back. I'll meet you in the Salomon room on the third floor.'

Nick started running. As he came around the corner he saw a flash of red disappearing into the gallery off the main rotunda. Was that her? He slowed his pace for a second, watching. Five Japanese tourists followed her in. An elderly couple came out. A short, well-built man in a black parka hurried past them, almost tripping on the old man's stick. His hood was down, revealing a shaved head with a row of gold glinting from his left ear. A face Nick had seen before.

He ran.

The Salomon Gallery was a dim room lined with book-shelves and display cabinets. A single glass case stood in the centre of the room like an altar or a tabernacle; inside, reverential lights played over an enormous spreadeagled book. The creamy pages shone back off the glass case, while the black print created holes in the reflection allowing a mosaic view beyond. A small figure in red shimmered in and out of sight behind. Nick wondered if she could see the man in the parka striding through the shadows towards her.

A guard sat in the corner keeping a lazy eye on the visitors. Nick crossed to him.

'Excuse me, but that man over there, I think I saw him carrying a gun.'

The panic in his voice gave truth to the lie. The guard hauled himself out of the chair, unclipped the flap of his holster and advanced across the room, murmuring something into his radio mic. Nick followed, splitting off around the display case.

There was Emily, pretending to peer at the open book while darting nervous glances around the room. She was so frightened she didn't see him until he was almost on top of her.

'Nick!' She flew across to him and wrapped her arms around him. Her thin arms gripped him surprisingly tight. 'I was terrified.'

'You're not safe yet.'

Nick put his hand on her shoulder and steered her to the exit, skirting the edge of the room. In the centre, a second guard had arrived, both deep in conversation with the man in the parka. Nick gestured towards them.

'Was that him?'

Emily nodded.

They slipped out of the door and hurried to the elevator. None of the men in the room seemed to notice them go, and Nick didn't look back. Only when they were out on the front steps in the stiff wind coming down Forty-Second Street, did he dare relax.

'I'll take you home.'

They caught a cab. Nick let Emily pay. Home for her turned out to be a tidy street in Midtown, whose closely planted trees and plain facades didn't quite disguise the quiet wealth behind the windows. Emily saw Nick taking it in.

'The museum owns it.' An apologetic smile. 'Just an apartment. I get it for six months, then I have to move into the real world. My time's almost up.'

He scanned the street for danger while Emily fumbled with the front door. It led into a gloomy hallway, full of stairs and doors. He followed her up to the second floor. He wasn't sure if he was invited, but she didn't object. Their footsteps padded on the carpeted stairs; the whole house seemed to be asleep.

166

A cry from Emily broke the silence. Two steps behind her, Nick looked up. She was standing in front of the door to what must be her apartment, staring at something. She stood aside so he could see.

The door was open. Only fractionally, but wider than any door should ever be left open in New York city. A nest of splinters around the lock showed where it had been forced.

For a long moment they both stood there, frozen like dust in a beam of light. Then they turned and ran. Down the stairs, out the door, along the street past the long row of grey trees. It was only when they reached the intersection that they paused and looked back. The street was empty.

'Call the police.' Nick leaned forward, resting his hands on his thighs. 'Don't go inside until they arrive. Does anyone else live there?'

Emily shook her head. She looked close to tears.

'One more thing. Please don't tell the cops I was here. They already think I'm guilty as hell.'

Emily was horrified. 'Aren't you going to wait with me?'

'It won't do you any good if they find me here.'

'Please.' Emily half-stretched out an arm, like a bird with a broken wing. 'I won't tell them you were with me.'

Nick glanced across the street. From halfway down the block, the aroma of grilling hamburgers wafted out of a Burger King.

'Let's go somewhere warmer.'

Emily perched on the edge of the plastic seat among the screaming kids on their way home from school and sipped a bottle of water. She didn't take her coat off. Nick played with an empty paper cup left on the table.

'Do you know who it was in the library?' she asked.

'No.'

'The last time I saw you, you warned me you weren't the sort of person I should be helping.'

'Not *shouldn't* help. *Wanted* to.'

'I wondered what you meant by that.'

Nick thought for a moment. 'The card's like a virus. Everyone it touches . . . First Gillian, then Bret. Now you.'

'And you?'

She turned the question round with a flick of her head. Her eyes were as dark as a summer storm.

'My apartment's been broken into; I was almost killed and my friend was shot dead. Someone's managed to cancel my credit card. The police have confiscated my passport, my computer, and they're probably about to arrest me for murder. And robbery, if they find out I was here.'

He'd started to rush his words, spilling out the grievances and injustices that were swilling around inside him. He felt energised, purged. 'All because of that card.'

'Because of the card,' Emily repeated. She looked shocked by his outburst – but less than he'd expected. 'I looked at it some more last night. Of the eight animals on it, three don't appear on any of the other cards.'

'It could still be a forgery.'

'Or else Gillian Lockhart made one of the most valuable finds in the field in the last twenty years.' She spoke solemnly, no trace of exaggeration.

'I thought you said it would only be worth ten thousand dollars.'

Emily's look made Nick cringe. 'That card would be one of the first ever printings from copper engraving. It's also an impressive work of art in its own right. The money you'd pay for it doesn't begin to describe what it's worth.'

'Worth someone killing for?'

Emily retreated a little. 'Maybe it's not the card. Maybe that's only part of something else.' She tipped her head to one side and examined him as she might a medieval tapestry. 'There's something else, isn't there?'

Nick had always been a hopeless liar. 'I can't tell you that.'

'Can't – or don't want to?'

'Believe me, you don't want to know.'

She leaned forward over the table. 'I do.' Again her naked stare. 'What else did you find?'

Nick swallowed. The laminated sides of his paper cup were as wizened as tree bark from being mangled in his hands. He looked out of the window, listening for the squawk of sirens.

'Gillian sent me another message. The same time as the card, but I only just got it.' He didn't elaborate how. 'It gives an address.'

'You think Gillian might be there. Or have left something there?' Emily's face was alight with excitement, painfully vulnerable. 'You're going to find it.'

Nick didn't deny it. 'Please don't tell the police. Not until tomorrow, at least.'

'I won't.' Emily spun the water bottle on the table. She had a habit of tucking her arms in close to her sides when she was thinking, Nick had noticed. When she looked up, her gaze was clear and strong.

'I'll come with you.'

It would be a lie to say he hadn't thought of it. Part of him desperately wanted her with him – a companion, a confidante, a friend he barely knew. But it was madness.

'No.' He tried to sound definite.

Emily just stared at him, manipulating the silence.

'It would be too dangerous. For both of us. We don't know each other. For all you know I'm a thief and a murderer.'

A flicker of Emily's eyes dismissed the idea.

'And it's not like we're just hopping over to New Jersey. It's . . . a long trip.'

'It's in Paris, isn't it?' Emily bit her lip. 'I thought you said the police confiscated your passport.'

Nick marvelled at how someone so delicate could be so relentless. 'I'm not interested in the card. I just want to find Gillian.'

'Of course. I want to help you.'

'Why?'

'Because I don't want to stay in New York, coming home every evening and wondering if that's the night they'll come back for me. Because I want to find out if that card really exists. And because I think you'll need all the help you can get.'

She put the bottle down. It rang hollow on the plastic table. 'How do we get there?'

'There's a Continental flight departing JFK for Brussels Zaventem at six thirty tonight.' The agent tapped on his computer. 'That has availability.'

Nick couldn't remember the last time he'd been in a travel ʾency – probably not since college, when the Internet got invented. He'd forgotten how slow it could be. He tried not to peer over his shoulder too often at the traffic crawling down Forty-Second Street.

'I just need to see your passports.'

Emily snapped open her purse and slid her passport across the desk. Nick reached inside his coat for the travel wallet, feeling the stiff lump of the booklet inside. He fished it out and laid it on top of Emily's, slightly fanned out like cards, waiting for the dealer's verdict.

The travel agent flipped through it and checked the photograph. 'You're British?' he asked Nick.

'On my mother's side.' He'd applied for the passport when he'd gone to Germany, to save the hassle of getting a work permit. He'd never imagined he'd use it to sneak out of his home country. He still wasn't sure if it would work.

It seemed to satisfy the agent, at least. He handed them back. 'Enjoy your flight.'

XXVI

Strassburg, 1434

Strassburg – the city of roads. Roads from the north, from the rich cloth markets of Bruges, and London beyond; roads south from Milan, Pisa and across the Mediterranean to the dark coast of Africa; roads which came from the west, from Paris and Champagne, and continued east into the heartlands of empires: Vienna, Constantinople, Damascus and the spiced cities of the East. And a few miles distant the great flowing road of the Rhine, the warp of my life.

The roads were the arteries of Christendom; Strassburg was its heart. It stood on an island in the river Ill, a tributary to the Rhine, which necessity and human ingenuity had channelled into a many-stranded necklace of canals ringing the city with water and stone. Merely entering the city was a bewildering journey across bridges and moats, through gates, towers and narrow alleys that seemed to lead nowhere but another bridge, until at last you turned a corner and came out in a great square. There, where all roads met, stood the cathedral of Notre-Dame. There I found what I sought.

I arrived on the road from the west. It was a perfect spring morning: a gentle sun in a smalt blue sky, following rain the night before that had washed the streets clean. A dewy freshness lingered in the air and brought colour to my cheeks. I was unrecognisable from the wretch who had prostrated himself before Tristan's furnace. The scalds and blisters on my hands had healed, with only a telltale gap in my beard where the vitriol had burned my cheek. I had a new coat of sober blue cloth and a new pair of boots I had bought in Troges with money I had earned copying indulgences over Christmas. I felt a new man. Strangers no longer recoiled or crossed the road when I stopped to ask them my way. And so I found my path to the house at the sign of the bear.

I would have found it anyway. It stood opposite the cathedral, across the square, which had become a field of stones for the building of the new tower on the cathedral's west front. I weaved my way between the vast blocks. On the far side, a gilded bear climbed an iron vine hanging over the door of a goldsmith's shop.

I took the card from the bag that hung around my neck and held it up. I hardly needed to look. After four months every image was stamped on my being, as perfect a copy as the card itself. The bear in the top-left corner was the same, though on the card the vine was invisible.

I approached the shop nervously. It was too familiar: the rings on their spindles, the boxes of beads and corals, the gold plates and cups gleaming from the shadows behind the cabinet bars. Even the man at the counter reminded me of Konrad Schmidt, paternal in a way my own father never was. He offered me a wary welcome as I approached.

I held up the card and saw at once that he recognised it.

'Did you make this?'

Paris

A fine mist hung in the Gare du Nord at eight o'clock that morning, as if steam was still settling from a hundred years ago. A policeman loitered by the café at the end of the platform and watched the passengers just arrived off the early train from Brussels. There weren't many on a Saturday morning: clubbers not yet sober and football fans not yet drunk; a few solitary businessmen; gaggles of backpackers wearing shorts and sandals in their perpetual adolescent summer.

Last off the train came a curious couple – a man of about thirty in jeans and a long black coat, and a young woman in a high-necked red coat and bright red shoes. The policeman watched them. They were clearly travelling together, but there was an awkwardness between them that suggested unfamiliarity. They spoke without looking at each other; when the man had to squeeze past a pillar and brushed the woman's arm, both apologised. A one-night stand, the policeman decided – two colleagues who had got drunk on business, too young to have made a habit of it yet. The man probably counted himself the luckier of the two. The girl was beautiful, in a prim sort of way. The policeman undressed her with his eyes, following the curve of her slim legs to the hem of her coat, then to the small, tightly belted waist and the full breasts above, to the dark eyes, disarranged hair and provocatively scarlet lips. The man just looked scruffy and dazed. Perhaps he had a wife to face.

Nick's stomach tightened as he caught the policeman watching them. Had he been recognised? Was he on some sort of watch list? Had the NYPD circulated his photograph to Interpol? His movements felt more and more unnatural as he walked towards the policeman, his body seizing up under the pressure. He half-turned towards Emily and muttered something irrelevant; she nodded and looked uncomfortable.

174

At least the jet lag helped: it was hard to look too tense when you were still half asleep. Nick had spent the short night cramped upright on the plane while Emily dozed under a blanket next to him. Fear kept him awake right across the Atlantic: fear of what he had left behind, fear of what he would find waiting for him. Just as he'd begun to nod off, the cabin crew had turned on the lights to begin their descent into Brussels. Then it had been a rush through the airport, a taxi into the city and the first train to Paris. That had been Emily's idea. From Brussels they could travel anywhere in Europe without having to show their passports again. Though there were other ways to be discovered.

Nick looked around and realised they were past the policeman. He was too tired to be relieved. At the back of the station they queued ten minutes for a taxi.

'*Cent soixante dix-sept rue de Rivoli*,' Emily told the driver. Nick looked at her in bleary-eyed surprise.

'I spent six months here for my doctorate,' she explained. 'It's hard to do much original research if you can't speak the language.'

It reminded them both how little they knew each other. Emily clutched her bag on her lap and leaned against the door; Nick looked out the car window.

Number 177 rue de Rivoli was an anonymous building, a bank sandwiched between an American chain store and a shoe shop. A guard was just rolling back the iron security gate when they arrived. They got a coffee and a croissant in a café across the road and waited for other customers to arrive. Lost in their weary thoughts, they barely spoke to each other. Nick felt as if he was limping over the finish line of a long nightmarish race. All he wanted to do was give up and sleep.

175

At half past nine they walked into the bank. A receptionist behind a grey desk greeted them, and listened patiently while Emily explained that she had a valuable necklace her grandmother had given her and needed somewhere safe to store it while she pursued her studies in Paris for six months.

The receptionist nodded. They had deposit boxes available for just such a purpose.

'Are they secure?'

The receptionist gave the sort of shrug they surely taught in all French schools. '*Oui, je pense.*' She saw Nick looking blank and switched seamlessly to English. 'You have a card which opens the door to the safe room, and a pin number to open your box.'

'*Et ça coûte combien?*' Emily persisted in French.

'Now you pay five hundred euros, and then each month one hundred euros.'

Emily affected indecision. 'Is it possible to see the safe room?'

The receptionist pointed to a glass-panelled door in the back wall. '*C'est là.*'

They walked over and peered through. Behind the door was a small carpeted room with rows of anonymous steel cabinets running from wall to wall. Red numbers glowed from digital readouts on their faces. Nick tried to find box 628 but couldn't make out the numbers through the thick, bulletproof glass. Though the door looked like wood it was cold to the touch – three-inch steel.

'I guess we're not breaking in there,' he muttered.

They went back to the receptionist. Emily reached in her purse and pulled out five hundred-euro notes and her passport.

The receptionist gave an apologetic smile. 'You have to pay in advance six months. Another six hundred euros.'

Nick winced. Emily handed over the money and waited while the receptionist tapped the details into her computer. A machine under the desk spat out a plastic card, which she handed to Emily with her passport and a sheet of paper.

'That is your PIN number. You have box 717. *Merci beaucoup*.'

Emily swiped her card. The steel door opened with a hiss of air, then closed with a heavy click the moment they'd stepped through. They walked silently across the carpeted floor. The red numbers on a thousand doors blinked from the sidelines, every one slightly out of sync with the others. Together with the harsh fluorescents above, Nick felt as if he'd stepped into a migraine.

Emily stopped in front of one of the deposit boxes. 'This is 628.'

Nick angled himself so that he stood between Emily and the door, fighting back the urge to check if anyone was watching. Emily pulled on a pair of black leather gloves. With sharp, birdlike movements, she pecked out the number: 300481.

The door swung ajar. Emily reached in.

Hans Dunne the goldsmith took the card from my hand and glanced at it.

'Where did you get this?'

'A nobleman in Paris.' A vision of Jacques' broken face flashed before me. 'He said it came from here.'

Dunne laid the card on his counter. 'Not from me.'

Four months' pent-up hope tottered on its foundations. Before it could crash, Dunne continued, 'That was one of Kaspar Drach's. The painter.' A strange look crossed his face. 'Among other things.'

'Is he here?'

He saw me peering over his shoulders at the apprentices in the workshop behind him. 'Not now. Come back tomorrow if you still want to see him.'

'Where is he today?'

'At the crossroads of St Argobast.' He glanced at the sun. 'You'll struggle to get there and back before dusk.'

'How will I recognise him?' I persisted.

'Look for a man on a ladder.'

There are many days, perhaps most, when destiny eludes us, slipping from our grasp while we bump around like blind men. There are days, few and rare, when it runs to meet us like a mother gathering her children. And then there are days when it taunts and teases but holds out the promise of victory to the persistent. That day I would not be denied. I felt it in my soul, a trembling excitement that only grew as I wound my way back across the bridges and canals, past the mills and farms that lined the banks of the Ill. Canvas sails spun the sun into flashes of light. Yellow-downed ducklings teetered in the mud at the water's edge.

I reached the crossroads an hour before sunset. The labourers had left the fields and the road was empty. Haze filled the air. A few birds chirruped in the hedgerows, but otherwise all was still. A little beyond, I could see a few timber-framed houses that made the hamlet of St Argobast.

A copse of three rowans, just coming to bud, stood where the roads met. A panel showing the Virgin had been raised on a high pole in front of them, a shrine for travellers. A man with a palette in one hand and a brush in the other stood on a ladder against it, apparently careless of the height. Though he had his back to me, I knew at once he was the man I had come to find. I only had to look at the Madonna he had painted. The crown had been smudged into a halo, and instead of a deer there was a docile child sitting on her skirts, but otherwise she was the queen from the cards. The same abundant hair, one raised hand carelessly stroking it; the same full lips and coquettish eyes admiring her reflection in the hand mirror – which in this incarnation had become the face of her child. With her full hips, her swelling breasts and her legs spread wide open under the folds of her gown, she was the most brazen Virgin I had ever seen.

I walked to the foot of the ladder.

'Are you Drach?'

He looked down. The sun hung behind his head like a nimbus, hiding his face in its brightness.

'Did you make the cards? The deck of birds and beasts and flowers and wild men that miraculously duplicate themselves?' I held up the eight. The low sun shone through so that the paper glowed amber in my hand. The swirling outlines of the beasts traced themselves on the back of the card.

I heard the soft laughter that afterwards I came to know so well.

'I did.'

XXVII

Paris

The taxi drove past the tourists already gathering in front of Notre-Dame cathedral. It crossed the river on the Pont Neuf and turned into the block of tiny alleys that wound around the church of St Severin, near the Sorbonne. It stopped about halfway down the lane outside a hotel, an old building with an awning over the door advertising a brand of beer. A tabby cat jumped down from the receptionist's chair as Nick and Emily walked in and stalked away. A moment later, an elderly man appeared from the adjoining office. He answered Emily's question with a nod and a smirk, and produced a pair of keys from the drawer. He didn't ask for any paperwork.

They took the elevator up to the room. Nick looked at the double bed and tried to hide what he was thinking.

'I asked for a twin,' Emily apologised. 'I'll go down and ask them to change it.'

'I can sleep on the floor.' Just at that moment he could have slept anywhere. But not yet.

He dropped his bag and went to the small table by the

window. He pulled the stiff-backed envelope from his inside coat pocket. By unspoken agreement, they had waited until they got back to the hotel room.

Like a pair of clumsy lovers they both reached for the envelope at the same time. Their hands collided, withdrew. Nick took it. He forced his finger under the flap of the envelope and tore it open. Something firm and smooth to the touch waited inside. He slid it out onto the table. A flat oblong about the size of a postcard, wrapped in white tissue paper.

'Let me.'

This time he let her have her turn. Emily slid a nail under the tape and peeled back the folds of paper. They both stared.

After everything he had endured, Nick's overwhelming feeling was disappointment. The object of his quest was utterly familiar. Four bears and four lions, no longer on a screen but printed on stiff, fluted paper. Age made it grey, though the printed lines were still sharp.

Emily pulled on her gloves and picked it up by the edges.

'There isn't any stamp or insignia on it.'

'Should there be?'

'If it came from a library or a major collection.' She flicked on the table lamp and held the card against the shade so that it glowed. 'There are no outlines around the animals. This was printed from a single copper sheet – not one of the later cut-up composites. And there.' She pointed to the middle of the card. 'The watermark – a crown. That's the same as the other early cards.'

'What about those?' Nick pointed to a cluster of dark blots smeared on the bottom-right corner of the card. Some were black, others a reddish brown. 'They look like dried blood.'

'Maybe wine spilled during a game?' Emily laid the card back in its tissue paper and covered it reverentially, like a

181

corpse. Her lips were moist with excitement. 'This is genuine, Nick. The first of these cards to be discovered in a century.'

Nick didn't respond. If anything, her excitement only fuelled his resentment. He felt a sudden urge to tear the card into pieces.

'We're supposed to be finding Gillian.'

'Who wanted you to have the card.'

'And what am I supposed to do now? Put it in a museum with a sign? "Gift of Gillian Lockhart, shame she disappeared."' Nick knew his tiredness was running away with him but couldn't make himself care enough to stop.

'Did she leave anything else?'

Emily's question stopped him like a slap in the face. Nick picked up the envelope and shook it. Something rattled inside.

He turned it over. A credit-card-sized piece of plastic and a small gold microchip tumbled out onto the table.

He examined the plastic card first. It was red with 'BnF' next to an image of an open book. He turned it over and stared. There was Gillian, printed into a one-inch box in the corner, staring down the camera like the barrel of a gun. It took him a moment to recognise her. An overhead light glared off her forehead and drowned her face in an unflattering, office-issue shadow. She'd cut her hair since he last saw her and dyed it blonde. He remembered a line from a poem she'd liked to quote at him: 'Naught shall endure but mutability'.

'BnF is the Bibliothèque Nationale de France,' said Emily. 'The French national library. Forty of the original playing cards are there. This must be her pass.' She pointed to the gold microchip. 'What about that?'

Nick picked it up between his finger and thumb. 'It's a SIM card. For a cellphone.'

'Why would she leave that?'

'Maybe so we could see who she called.'

Nick pulled out his own phone and prised off the back cover. He slid the SIM out of its holder and replaced it with Gillian's. He was about to turn it on when suddenly he paused. His finger hovered over the power button. 'Or . . .'

'Or what?'

'Or because they could trace the signal to locate her.'

He put the phone in his pocket, grabbed his coat and headed for the door. Emily jumped up in alarm.

'Where are you going?'

'To the Métro station.'

The cold hit him the moment he stepped out of the hotel. A raft of bruising clouds hung low over Paris, and there was a bite in the air that promised snow. He hurried around the corner to the Saint-Michel station. Across the Seine, a flock of birds wheeled around the towers of Notre-Dame. He bought a ticket, pushed through the narrow turnstiles and down a flight of stairs to the crowded platform.

He switched on the phone. *Searching,* said the screen. When he was satisfied there was no reception, he went to work.

He started by scrolling through her phone book. A few of the names sounded familiar in a second-hand way; some were French, others looked American. Nothing leaped out. 'Museum, Natalie Cell, Paul Home . . .'

No 'Nick'. His stomach tightened. *She deleted me.* After everything else it was a petty disappointment, but it hurt like a bullet to the gut. Perhaps more because it was so banal: not a gesture or a message, just a piece of housekeeping.

Maybe she wanted to protect me, he tried. But he couldn't convince himself.

So why did she send me the card?

A red double-decker train pulled into the station. For half a minute everything was chaos as one group of shoppers and sightseers exchanged places with another. The train lumbered away.

He rummaged through the folders to check her text messages. They were empty – every message deleted. Except one.

I don't know what I've done but please please call me. Even if you don't want to talk, just call once. I still love you. Nick

The time stamp said six months ago. She'd never replied. Why had she kept it, leaving it to gather digital dust in this forgotten corner?

Nick closed the message. The platform was beginning to fill up again. At the far end, a dreadlocked guitar player was singing Pink Floyd in French. Without much hope, Nick went to the phone's call log.

There were three calls. Two of them to numbers that looked French and weren't in her phonebook, the third – and most recent – to someone called Simon. Nick clicked to view the number. That looked local too.

He scribbled down the three numbers with the time and duration of the calls, then switched off the phone.

He spent fifteen minutes in an Internet café, then went back to the hotel room. Emily was sitting on the bed examining the playing card again, her feet tucked under her like a schoolgirl.

'Did you find anything?' said Nick.

She shook her head. 'You?'

'Three numbers.' He pulled the scrap of paper out of his

pocket. 'The last three calls Gillian made from her cellphone.'

'If it was hers,' Emily cautioned. 'You don't know that.'

'It was hers.' Nick slumped into an armchair. His hands were still stiff from the cold outside. 'One of them was to a taxi firm. I've got the time and date of the call, so we could see if they have any records. Then there was one to a guy listed as Simon.'

'Does he have a surname?'

'Not even an initial.' *What did that imply?* He'd never heard Gillian talk about any friends called Simon. He pushed the thought out of his mind.

'But the third one I had more luck with. His name's Professor Jean-Baptiste Vandevelde. He's a particle physicist at the Institut Georges Sagnac, just outside Paris. He specialises in X-ray fluoroscopy, whatever that is.'

Emily raised an eyebrow. 'Her phone told you all that?'

'He's got a website.' Nick handed her the printout he'd taken from the Internet café. 'All his contact details. When I searched for the phone number, it came up.'

Emily squinted at it. 'Why would Gillian want to talk to a particle physicist?'

'Let's ask him.'

XXVIII

Strassburg, 1434

What can I say about Kaspar Drach? He was the most obscenely talented man I ever met – more so, I believe, than Nicholas Cusanus. While Cusanus tended his thoughts in walled gardens, Drach roamed freely across the earth; where Cusanus pruned, watered, shaped and cropped, Drach sprayed his seed without thought for where it would land. Tangled meadows of bright and fantastical flowers sprouted wherever he walked. Though among their twisted stems, serpents lurked.

None of which I knew that spring evening. I remember his bare feet slapping on the rungs as he descended the ladder. The crooked grin as he saw my surprise. I had expected someone like the goldsmith, wise and venerable, a man who had given his life to attain his new art. Instead, I saw a slight young man with a mop of unruly black curls, younger than me by several years. His skin was the colour of raw honey, his eyes like viscous oil – blue, green, grey or black by the changing whim of the light. A barbarian streak of blue paint creased his forehead.

He plucked the card from my hand and glanced at it. I looked for a sign of recognition, perhaps a glow of paternal pride that his prodigal child had been brought back to him. There was nothing. He handed it back to me.

'Did you lose?'

'What?' I had not been paying attention. His fingers had brushed mine as we exchanged the card. In that moment, I had felt the demon who inhabited me stir, a gust that brings a taste of the storm.

'The game. Did you lose it?'

I thought of Jacques' pulverised face, his blood on the stones. 'No.'

Drach gave me his crooked smile. 'A bad workman blames his tools. A bad gambler blames the man who made the cards.'

He suddenly turned his back on me and began walking towards the river. I could not tell if it was a dismissal or an invitation. I followed. He squatted on the bank and sluiced water over his palette. Threads of colour streamed off it into the river.

I stood at the top of the embankment and watched. 'How did you make them?' I shouted down. My voice seemed unnaturally loud in the evening stillness. 'How do you make them so perfect?'

He didn't look round. 'What is your trade?'

I hesitated. 'I used to be a goldsmith,' was the best I could say.

'And if I came into your shop and asked for the secret of enamelling, or the way to fire gold with copper to bring the engravings to life, would you tell me?'

'I—'

'I discovered something which no man ever did before. Do you think I would share that with every stranger who passed me at a crossroads?' He pulled the wooden palette out of the

187

river, shook the water off and tucked it under his arm. He marched up the riverbank, straight past me.

'I want to make something perfect,' I said, and something in my voice – desperation or desolation – must have rung true. Drach turned back.

'Only God is perfect.'

Written down now it looks a pompous rebuke. But writing cannot capture the way he said it: the overblown solemnity undercut by a twitch at the corner of his mouth, the mischievous cast in his eyes as they met mine in complicity.

'God – and your playing cards,' I said.

This answer pleased him very much. He spread his arms and took a bow. Everything was theatre to Drach.

'Even God could not make two men so exactly alike as my cards.' He considered this thought while I tried not to show my shock. 'Except twins. And they are unnatural.'

He looked at the sky. The sun had disappeared; the heavens were darkening to black.

'Are you hungry?'

We crossed the fields to the village. The path was narrow and broken by the plough; often we collided. I longed to take his hand and walk arm in arm, for I was already besotted, but of course I did not dare. I contented myself with the brush of his sleeve, the occasional bump of his shoulder.

He kept his paint jars in a sack, which tinkled like harness bells wherever he walked. His conversation was the same: flowing chatter that pleased my ear and never grated. He asked my name and where I came from; when I told him Paris, he fixed me with a look that made me think he knew everything.

'There is a story there,' he said. 'Someday I will force it out of you.'

I could not think of anyone I would more happily tell it to.

We came to an inn called L'Homme Sauvage, the Wild Man. On the sign, a man whose skin peeled off his body like foliage strummed a lute and looked over his shoulder. It was as if I had entered a different world; everywhere I looked, the cards seemed to come alive. Drach saw my gaze and nodded.

'I am always welcome here. They will give us a meal and a bed for the night.'

He said 'us' so casually I could not tell if he meant anything by it. To me it was like a button fallen unnoticed off his coat, to be picked up and cherished long after he had forgotten it.

We crossed the stableyard and entered the inn. The candles burned bright after the darkness outside, while the fire in the hearth dispelled the spring chill. Though the village was too close to Strassburg to detain many travellers, there was no shortage of custom. Three men-at-arms in fine cloaks sat in the middle of the room and bragged of their deeds. In a corner, two merchants from Vienna haggled and gossiped.

A girl with flaxen hair braided into pigtails brought wine. Drach drained his almost immediately and called her back for more. I waited for her to leave, trembling with the idea I had been nursing in all the months of my slow journey across France.

At last she left us.

'I have a proposal for you,' I said. I had meant to wait, to tease him in with hints and subtlety. But I could not contain myself: the words spilled out of me. 'You learned how to make perfect copies of your pictures. Did you ever think what else you could copy?'

He cocked an eyebrow, inviting me to go on. I drew a breath. 'Words.'

He took a moment to understand what I meant. When he

did, he laughed. 'Words? How much will men pay for *them*? I have illuminated manuscripts and seen how well the scribes were paid for *words*.'

'Some words are worth more.'

In my mind, I looked back to my father's mint, the stream of identical coins flowing into the scales. The principle of perfection had not turned lead into gold in Paris. I was convinced in Strassburg it would hold more sway with paper.

'The word of God, for example.'

Drach snorted so hard wine blew out of his nose. He gave me a keen look, wondering if he had misjudged me. 'Bibles?'

'Indulgences.'

That surprised him. He sat back in his chair and considered it. Even turned inwards in thought his face was more alive than most men's ever are.

'Indulgences are receipts,' he said at last. 'Chits the Church sells you to prove you have bought remission of your sins. There is no beauty in that.'

'No beauty in one,' I agreed. 'But in a thousand, all exactly the same . . .'

'A thousand,' he repeated, savouring the size of the number.

'Using your art.'

'It would be a single page.'

'A standard text.'

'We'd leave space for the names and the date.'

'And the price.' I was flushed with excitement; I felt like a key that had found its lock. I had never felt such a rush of understanding.

'God knows we'll never want for customers.'

'Though by God's grace, He will perfect us all some day.'

It was a reflexive comment, inescapable, but it broke the spell and drew another appraising stare from Drach.

'A perfect world would be a feeble place. And far less profitable.'

'Of course,' I stammered. All I wanted was to bring back the light of his countenance. 'I only meant—'

He cut me off with a gesture to the far corner of the room, where a woman was leaning over to pour a drink, displaying herself to the traders and field hands at the table. Her breasts sagged close to her waist, the neck of her dress almost as far. Thick red powder gave her cheeks the texture of a badly plastered wall.

'As long as there are women like her – and men like those – we will be rich.'

Still watching the prostitute, I shuddered in revulsion. The contrast with Drach – smooth, quick, aloof – was absolute. I realised he had been watching me, like a priest in confession. I composed my expression and tried to think of a remark that would cover me. Drach shook his head, as if he knew what I was going to say and wanted to keep me from embarrassing myself. He reached across the table and laid his hand over mine.

'Your secret is safe.'

He laughed at the confusion brimming in my eyes.

'Your proposal. It is a plan of genius.'

'The cards—' I demurred

'Were only a beginning. I sold them to rich gamblers with taste. They are a limited market. With these indulgences, all mankind is our market, and they will come back for more so long as men sin.'

Our knees brushed under the table. I knew then that as long as Kaspar Drach and I were together, there would be no lack of sin in the world.

XXIX

Paris

The Institut Georges Sagnac occupied a low concrete campus in a western suburb of Paris. Plastic blinds covered most of the windows; the few rooms with lights on shone like television screens. A group of teenagers skateboarded on one of the access ramps, but otherwise there was no one to be seen.

Nick and Emily stopped in front of one of the buildings and rang the bell marked VANDEVELDE. The plastic housing on the intercom was cracked, the speaker muffled by a collage of faded stickers advertising underground bands, radical politics, bleeding-edge art or simply proclaiming anarchy.

'*Oui?*'

Emily leaned closer to the wall. 'Professor Vandevelde? It's Dr Sutherland.'

A noise like a buzz saw ripped through the speaker. The door clicked open.

'*Venez.*'

The elevator was out of order; they took the stairs. Professor Vandevelde's office was on the fourth floor at the end of a long linoleum corridor that probably hadn't been refurbished since 1968. They knocked, and a brisk voice summoned them in.

It was a large office. To the left, a broad window offered bleak views of the tower blocks which barred the horizon. There was a wood-veneer desk littered with papers, a whiteboard scribbled with half-erased equations and two low chairs. Yellow foam poked out of holes in the seats. The only decoration was a poster taped to the wall, a page from an illuminated manuscript advertising a long-gone exhibition at the Louvre.

Professor Vandevelde stood and came around the desk to shake hands. He was a tall heavyset man, dressed in cord trousers and a blue sweater, his shirtsleeves rolled up over the arms. Apart from the silver-rimmed spectacles he wore, Nick thought he looked more like a fisherman than a physicist.

'Emily Sutherland,' said Emily. 'This is my assistant, Nick.'

Vandevelde flipped on a kettle balanced on top of a grey filing cabinet. He motioned them to sit.

Emily perched on a chair and crossed her legs. 'Thank you for seeing us at such short notice, and on a Saturday afternoon. I'm so sorry my email never arrived.'

Vandevelde wiped a spoon on his sweater and opened a jar of Nescafé. '*Ça ne fait rien.* I am here anyway. And you have come all the way from the Metropolitan Museum in New York.'

'I've read so many of your papers.' Pulled off the Internet in a smoky café and skimmed in the time it took to finish an espresso. 'But my colleague struggled to understand the process.'

Nick smiled apologetically as if to say he didn't blame Vandevelde.

'I wondered if you could explain for him.'

'Of course.' The professor stood and ushered them through a side door into a plain windowless room.

'This is where we have the proton milliprobe.'

The machine looked like something out of a dentist's surgery: white metal pipes sticking out of the wall and the ceiling, ending in a nozzle that pointed at a steel lectern. A bundle of thick cables snaked away from it to a computer on a desk against the wall.

'What we are doing, it is called PIXE technique. Particle-induced X-ray emissions.' He exaggerated each word so slowly that with his thick accent they became almost unintelligible. 'It has been developed in San Diego in the 1980s. What you are doing is to fire a beam of protons through the pipe – *ici* – into the object you analyse. In my experiments it is a page from a book. The protons, they pass through the page, they hit the atoms and they break them. This release the X-rays, who we measure with a fluoroscopy system.'

He tapped the nozzle suspended from the ceiling, then pointed to the computer. 'It analyse the emission and tell us what is inside the page.'

'Doesn't that damage the book?'

'*Non.* We scan only one millimetre of the page and the protons break only a few atoms. Except at the molecular level, there is no damage.'

Nick glanced at Emily. She seemed happy for him to continue with his questions. 'And this tells you what's in the paper?'

'It tell us what is in the ink. Every ink have a chemical signature we identify. We analyse the early printed texts so that we see who have made them.'

Nick took a deep breath and reached into his coat. 'So what did you find when you scanned this?' He held up the card, keeping his eyes fixed on Vandevelde's.

'I work only with books. I have not analysed this card.'

But Nick had seen it on his face – recognition, and something else. Fear? 'A woman called Gillian Lockhart brought this to you.'

'I have never seen this Gillian Lockhart.' He said it in the same laboured way he had explained the PIXE acronym earlier, something memorised.

'What did you find?'

'I have told you. I have not ever seen this before.' Vandevelde stood. 'I think perhaps you are not interested in my work. I am sorry, I cannot help you.' He put his hand on the door. '*S'il vous plaît . . .*'

Nick and Emily stayed where they were. 'When did Gillian come here?'

'Never.'

'She called you a month ago. Three weeks after that, she disappeared.'

Vandevelde sighed. 'I am sorry to hear this. Truly. But – I cannot help.'

'Do you remember her calling you?'

'What do you say is her name?'

'Gillian Lockhart.'

Vandevelde shook his head a fraction too soon. '*Non.*'

'We have her phone records. The conversation lasted almost fifteen minutes.'

'Perhaps my secretary have put her on hold while she look for me. Perhaps she does not give me her name – or not her actual name. Perhaps she pretend she is interested in my work because she want something else.'

He let go the door handle and walked back to his machine. 'You think I hide something from you? I hide nothing. I promise to you I have never seen your friend, or this card. But if you want for me to analyse it, if this makes you happy, I do it. *Oui?*

He held out his hand, his head cocked to one side. Nick glanced at Emily, who nodded cautiously.

The Frenchman laid the card flat on the lectern in front of the pipe, then fussed with the nozzle until it was aligned to his satisfaction. Nick leaned in and squinted.

'It's pointing at nothing.'

'We take two measurements. The ink is absorbed in the paper, yes? So first we measure the paper by itself, then with the ink. If we subtract the first measure from the second, we have left only what comes from the ink.'

He turned a handle to lock the nozzle in place, then crossed to the computer. Nick still crawled with misgivings. 'Do we have to leave the room or anything?'

'It is very safe. You absorb more protons standing fifteen minutes in the sun. If you do not trust me, you can be holding the card all the time I do the experiment.'

Nick took a step back. 'I'll watch from here.'

There was almost nothing to see. Vandevelde pressed a key on the computer; there was a rumbling sound from behind the wall, and a red light went on over the pipe. Seconds later, the light went off and the rumbling stopped. Vandevelde readjusted the nozzle so that it now pointed at a luxuriant part of a lion's mane, where the ink was thickest. The light blinked on again, then off. A jag-toothed graph appeared on the computer screen.

'What does that mean?'

'It shows the different elements we can detect.' Vandevelde traced one of the sharp peaks with his finger. 'This line shows the sodium content. This is the copper.'

'So . . . what? You can figure out what the ink was made of?'

196

'Not all of it. Some elements the X-ray fluoroscopy system cannot measure. Sometimes we do not know where it has come from. For example, we find lead. Perhaps it has come from massicot, which is an agent for the drying; or it has come from a heated lead oxide for the colour; or – if it is a book – it has rubbed off from the lead alloy types. All we can say with this machine is there is lead.'

'So what's the point?'

'Every ink have a signature, you understand? Every printer, he uses a different ink. We have a database.'

'Can you check this ink?'

'*Bien sûr.* I show you.'

He pressed a button on the computer. An hourglass spun lazily over the graph. A few seconds later a single line of text appeared at the bottom of the screen. Nick guessed what it meant even before Vandevelde gave his one-word summary.

'*Rien.*' He shrugged and edged away from the computer. There was a wariness in his movements, Nick thought, like a dog that has been kicked too often. He gave Nick and Emily a sad look. 'If your friend have come here – and I promise she did not – I would tell her the same.'

Nick took the card off the lectern, wrapped it in the tissue paper and put it in his bag. He stared at Vandevelde, certain that there was more but unable to think of anything to say.

Vandevelde opened the door and gave a sad smile. 'I hope you find your friend.'

Reluctantly, Nick stepped into the dark corridor. As Emily followed, Nick heard Vandevelde mutter something to her in French before he shut the door. They walked down the stairs in silence. Outside, the sun had set and the skateboarders had gone. The only light now came in orange pools under the street lamps. The air was bitterly cold.

'What did he say when you were leaving?' Nick asked.

'He said, "Not all the marks on the card are ink."'

Nick glanced back, wondering what it meant. But when he looked up, the room on the fourth floor was dark.

XXX

Near Strassburg, 1434

'Be careful. If you spill even a drop we'll burn like heretics.'

Drach speared an onion on a sharpened stick and grinned. That frightened me. He only smiled when he was serious.

Perhaps it was Drach's promise of danger, but all my senses sang at a high pitch that day. The sweetness of coal and the surly smell of flax-seed oil; the bright August sun that made pillars of light in the smoke; the viscous bubbles swelling and popping inside the cauldron that stood between us. I could feel every drop of sweat running down my naked back.

Drach crouched with his skewered onion beside the cauldron. I pulled on a pair of leather gloves and reached for the copper hat that covered the pot. Our eyes met through the oily steam.

'Remember. Not one drop.'

I was at one with the world. I had never been so happy.

Strange though it seems now, Drach made me respectable again. For that, I forgave him a lot of what came afterwards.

St Thomas Aquinas says that all creatures are born to a destiny in the world; fulfilment comes from achieving that purpose. I had always known my purpose, but for twenty years I had blundered about it like a blind bull. With Drach, I began at last to discern my path. Opportunity brought ambition; ambition begat hope; hope began to bring me back to the life I had fled ever since my father died.

I had assumed that that life had been obliterated long ago. Instead I found it had only been sleeping, like a bear waiting for spring. I wrote to my brother Friele at my father's house in Mainz, and received a guarded reply that welcomed me – cautiously – back into the family. Through Friele, I made several discoveries. First, that he still held certain annuities in my name which paid out a sum of gold every quarter. Being an honest man with a clerk's sensibilities, Friele could account for every penny that had accrued since my departure. He regretted to tell me that much of it had gone to Konrad Schmidt in Cologne, who had sued for the full value of my broken apprenticeship, but the rest he would transfer to Strassburg.

My brother made no mention of the reason I left Schmidt. From this I deduced a second fact: that Schmidt had preferred to protect his son's reputation rather than blacken mine, and had kept the scandal of my departure to himself. It was a secret he had now taken to his grave, for my brother reported he had died some years back. I never learned what became of little Pieter.

Friele's remittance provided me with a small amount of capital and an income to look forward to. By the strange alchemy of credit, whereby those who least need money attract it most, I was able to transmute this modest sum into a larger one by borrowing. It had quickly become obvious that I would be the one to fund our adventures. Drach, for all his genius, was spectacularly careless of money. When he told me how little he had sold the cards for I was appalled; when he admitted he could not make any new copies because he had sold the press to pay a debt, I wondered what nature of man I had yoked my fortunes to.

'Look at St Francis,' was all he said when I tried to discuss it. 'There is nothing more glorious than a life of poverty.'

'And humility,' I reminded him. That made him laugh, for vanity ran through his bones and he knew it. He tousled my hair and called me a disputatious old woman. After that, I rarely brought up the subject.

I took a house in St Argobast, the village by the crossroads where I first met Drach. It was a pleasant house: a low cottage with three rooms and a barn, and a stone outbuilding across the yard. A grove of poplars shielded it from the road, while across the water meadow I could watch the river Ill meander towards the city, some three miles distant. There were no neighbours to observe the irregular hours that Drach came and went, to notice the strange smells that often poured out of the stone shed late at night, or to complain of the noise when Drach accidentally set fire to a hen one evening. It was the first house I had ever been master of, and I loved the sensation of freedom it brought. I was thirty-five.

In short, with Drach's help, in a very brief space of time I hauled myself out of the pit I had inhabited and regained my place in the world.

I pulled back the copper lid, angling it so that the liquid did not boil over into the fire. Drach and I both had rags tied over our faces against the foul vapour that billowed out. He dipped the onion into the bubbling broth. The moment it touched the surface a brown scum erupted from the oil, frothing around the onion and racing up the sides of the cauldron.

'Don't let it over the rim!'

Drach pulled the onion away and I clamped the lid back down. 'Too hot,' he declared.

With a poker and tongs, I spread the coals beneath the trivet to burn cooler. When the boiling oil seemed less vigorous, we attempted the experiment with the onion again. This time the scum rose more slowly, blistering the skin of the vegetable but not threatening to spill over.

'Perfect,' Drach declared. While I held the lid open, he took a bowl of resin dust and sprinkled it over the surface of the oil with a ladle. Each time the dust touched the oil it provoked another belch of scum and foam, which needed rapid stirring to keep it from bubbling over into the fire and setting the whole cauldron ablaze. This was the most precarious part of the operation: not just because of the danger (which was considerable) but because of the way Drach wilfully courted it. Each ladleful of resin he added was more than the one before, prompting the foam to climb ever closer to the rim and me to stir with ever more desperation. Drach seemed to enjoy this hugely, like a child baiting a dog with a stick; I hated it. The fumes and exertion and fear all cloyed together to make me feel ill.

Gradually, the mixture thickened. When it was the consistency of soup and the colour of piss, we ladled it out of the cauldron into glass jars. While we waited for it to cool, we damped the fire and went down to the river.

I stripped off my trousers and dived in, kicking back so that I could watch Kaspar undress on the bank. The oil that had coated me drifted away in a foul-smelling slick; my anger went with it. I felt foolish for having allowed myself to become so irritated by his game.

Kaspar waded in and squatted in the shallows. For all his carelessness with fire, he had a strange fear of water. It was the one arena where I could outpace him, and I spent some minutes splashing about in the current, diving down and holding my breath to make him anxious. When I opened my eyes underwater, the sunlight shining through the reeds reminded me of days dredging gold out of the Rhine. I could not believe that had been my life.

I broke the surface and swam back to the bank. Kaspar had waded out so that the water almost reached his hips; he wore a petulant look that made me laugh with delight. Coquette that I was, I delighted in provoking his envy.

I swam round behind him and stood in the mud, sluicing water over his back and scrubbing away the soot and oil. His skin was taut, his shoulders beautifully firm from long hours of work. When he turned around, I sank beneath the water so he would not see my arousal.

We dressed and went back up to the house. We took the oil into the barn, where a pair of wooden tables had replaced the byres and straw, and spooned it out onto a stone slab. By now, the mixture had cooled to a greasy paste. An oyster shell beside it held a small mound of lamp soot, which we gradually stirred in. I watched the black swirl through the varnish, then dissolve into it.

Drach dipped a fingertip in and wiped it on a scrap of paper beside the slab. A black smear appeared on the paper, though as I watched the ink dry it faded to a duller grey. Despite all the effort we had lavished on it, I felt a grain of disappointment.

'It should be darker. Stronger. Like real ink.' I thought back to all my weeks in Tristan's tower in Paris, chasing every hue of the rainbow. 'Copper powder burns black if the flame is hot enough. If we mixed that with the lampblack, it might be more vivid. Perhaps red massicot too, to add depth.'

Drach looked peeved. He touched a finger to my lips to silence me. 'This will do. After all, we do not have a press yet.'

XXXI

Paris

'Why did he lie?'

The train rattled back towards Paris. Night cloaked the suburbs around them: when Nick looked out the window, all he saw was his own watery reflection and Emily opposite, ghosts in the darkness.

He rephrased his question. 'Why *would* he lie? Why pretend he never saw Gillian or the card?'

Emily shivered and pulled her coat closer around her. 'He was so eager to put the card through his machine. He knew he wouldn't get a match.'

'Because he'd already analysed it with Gillian.'

'But if he didn't find anything . . .'

'. . . why did he lie?'

The train shook as it crossed a set of points. A station flashed by.

'I wonder why Gillian took it there.'

Nick looked at her, confused. 'To analyse the ink.'

'All Vandevelde's work has been on printed type – books.

But the first book wasn't printed until about 1455. As far as we know, the cards date from about twenty years before. The cards are printed intaglio – the ink sits inside the grooves cut into a plate and is pressed into the paper. Type is printed in relief, with the ink on the raised surface of the letter. I don't know for sure, but I'd think they'd use very different kinds of ink.'

'So she went to a man who couldn't help her and didn't find anything – and that's so secret he has to lie about it?' The jet-lag headache throbbed in his temples.

'There must have been someone else,' said Emily quietly. 'Somebody was after Gillian – maybe they got to Vandevelde. Maybe that's why he was so frightened.'

They got off at the next station. Nick found a payphone on the empty platform and dialled the second number from Gillian's phone. His hands were shaking so badly he could barely get the coins in the slot. He told himself it was because of the cold.

The phone answered after three rings. 'Atheldene.'

Was it a person? A company? A hotel?

'Is Simon there?'

A guarded pause. 'This is Simon Atheldene.'

It was a British voice, foreign yet unexpectedly familiar. Nick took a leap in the dark. 'Do you work for Stevens Mathison? The auction house?'

'I do.'

'My name is Nick Ash. I'm a friend of Gillian Lockhart. I think I spoke to you a few days ago.'

Another pause. 'Are you here in Paris?'

The payphone number must have displayed on Atheldene's phone. 'Yes.'

'Then we should meet.'

206

Nick and Emily arrived at eight. For Nick, who had never been to Paris, the Auberge Nicolas Flamel was everything he might have imagined from a French restaurant. Stone pillars supported fat oak beams; more stonework framed the leaded windows, and a bull's head looked down on the room from above a vast fireplace. Most of the tables were full, and a warm hubbub filled the room. Nick was suddenly ravenously hungry.

Simon Atheldene wasn't hard to find: he was the only man in the restaurant wearing a double-breasted suit. He was sitting on his own at the back of the room, with a bottle of wine open in front of him. He stood as he saw them approaching and shook hands.

'Nice place,' said Nick.

Atheldene poured them each a glass of wine. 'It's the oldest house in Paris. Built in 1407 by Nicolas Flamel, the renowned alchemist.'

'I thought he was a fictional character,' Nick blurted out, then wished he hadn't.

To his relief, Atheldene laughed. 'Harry Potter has a lot to answer for.' He saw Nick's surprise and gave a modest smile. 'I have two daughters — when their mother lets me see them. They make sure I'm not completely stranded in the Middle Ages.'

Emily arranged her napkin on her lap. 'Flamel really existed. His tombstone's preserved in the Museum of Medieval Art here.'

'He was the first alchemist to turn base metal into gold. Taught himself from seven ancient allegorical pictures, which he then had copied onto the arch of St Innocent's churchyard. Allegedly.'

'The pictures were real,' said Emily. 'They're well attested.'

'Are they still there?' Nick asked.

'The cemetery of St Innocent was destroyed in the eighteenth century. All we have left of the pictures are copies.'

'Though I've never heard of anyone using them successfully to transmute lead into gold,' said Atheldene.

Nick looked around. 'He certainly could afford a nice house.'

A waiter approached and asked something in French. Atheldene waved him away with a smiled apology.

'Order whatever you like,' said Atheldene. 'My shout – or, rather, Stevens Mathison's.'

They studied the menus in silence. The social overtures had played out; even Atheldene looked unsure of what to say next. It was a relief when the waiter came back to break the deadlock.

Nick ordered, not certain which meal his jet-lagged body was expecting. Everything on the menu seemed to involve fish, cream or pâté – sometimes all three. When the waiter had taken the menus away, Atheldene got serious.

'I suppose you want to know about Gill.'

Nick had never heard anyone call her that before. He didn't like it.

Atheldene swirled the wine in his glass and contemplated it. 'Gill joined us about four months ago from New York. She'd come from the Met, as you know. Very quick, and an excellent eye. She knew what was valuable, and she also knew what would sell. You'd be surprised how many people in our trade can't manage both. She and I worked together on a number of sales. I found her impressive.

'A month ago, about a fortnight before Christmas, we were called in for a new assignment. Big estate job out near Rambouillet.' He pronounced it the English way, to rhyme with gooey. 'Extraordinary place. Great big crumbling chateau in the forest, probably hadn't been touched since the Revolution. Walls plastered with tapestries, a painting that looked suspiciously like an inferior Van Eyck, furniture so old it was probably made by Jesus. Even an honest-to-goodness suit of armour in the hall. None of which was our business – we had experts to tidy that up. Gill and I were there for the library.'

'What date was that?' Emily prompted.

'December the twelfth. It's my younger daughter's birthday and I was worried about getting home in time to phone her.'

Atheldene paused while the starters arrived. He spread a fat slice of foie gras on his toast and heaped onion marmalade over it.

'We drove out there together not knowing what to expect. We were dealing with the deceased chap's daughter who lives in Martinique. She just said there was a library and she thought a few of the books might be worth something. Not unusual – you'd be amazed how many children don't know what their parents own. Most of the time all they mean is that there are a few hardbacks on the shelves, or some good-looking freebie the old man got when he signed up for the book club. It's usually the ones who say there's nothing there who are sitting on the gold mine.

'Anyway, Gill and I picked our way through this ruin to the library. Pushed open the doors – which, by the way, were bronze and ten feet tall, probably recovered from a Renaissance church. Pulled open a few cupboards and couldn't believe what we found. Manuscripts. Folios. Incunabula.'

'What's an incunabula?' said Nick. He'd spoken to Emily, but Atheldene answered.

'Literally translated, *incunabulus* means "cradle book". It's a term we use for very early printed works, anything before 1500. As you'd expect, they don't exactly grow on trees. On the rare occasions that they come up for sale they can go for hundreds of thousands, if not millions. On our initial survey, we counted thirty of them in the collection. Plus at least as many illuminated manuscripts. Gill and I felt like Carter and Carnarvon in King Tut's tomb.'

He bit into his toast. 'We'd done our homework before we went out there, sales lists and auction records and so forth, to see if we could identify anything the old man had definitely owned. *None of what we found had ever come up for sale.*'

He looked around the table to impress the point. 'None of it. Which means they'd been sitting there for at least fifty years. Maybe centuries. Lost to the world. Never mind the financial implications, just in terms of scholarship this was pure gold.

'And then we looked up. Standard-issue Italian ceiling, blue sky filled with cherubs. Except there was rain falling from this cloudless sky. The roof had gone. The old man had been dying for months. Never left his bed. The daughter lives abroad, as I said, and the housekeeper wasn't allowed in the library. So no one noticed. You remember what a dreadful wet autumn we had? All that rain went straight through the chateau's roof and poured into the library.'

'What did you do?'

'Dialled the emergency services. An outfit that specialises in conservation and repair carted the books away. Two days later, Gill vanished. Never to be heard of again – until she emailed you.'

Atheldene slid his knife and fork together on the plate. He folded his hands and looked straight at Nick, who sipped his last few mouthfuls of soup in silence. The moment he put his spoon down the waiter appeared and started clearing the dishes. Had he been listening to them? He topped up their wine glasses, though Nick had barely touched his.

'Did any of the books go missing with her?'

Atheldene gave a good-natured sigh. 'I'm afraid that was our first thought too. *Honi soit qui mal y pense* – but the company gets very jumpy at the least whiff of scandal. Bad for business. The old man might have been gaga towards the end, but he was no fool. Had the entire collection catalogued. We went through the collection with a toothcomb. Everything was there.'

'So you called the police?'

'You know what Gill was like.' Atheldene leaned back so that the waiter could serve his main course. A leg of lamb thrust its bone into the air like a tower, surrounded by a moat of gravy and ravelins of boiled potatoes. 'One of life's free spirits. At first we assumed she'd turn up with some picaresque story of running away with Gypsies, or a forty-eight-hour bender on the Left Bank with a song of anarchists. But of course I worried. When she still hadn't turned up after three days I called the police. Who told me it was probably a love affair. I told them that was unlikely, but they just looked at me in that knowing French way.'

'Did you manage to search her apartment, her office?'

'Nothing there,' said Atheldene quickly. He dabbed a spot of gravy from his chin, then looked up. 'Gill was living at my place. Only until she found somewhere of her own. She was sent here at very short notice, and it's a bastard finding a flat in Paris.'

There was something defensive in his tone. Nick picked at the fish on his plate. His head felt swollen, as if he'd been injected with novocaine.

'I went back through the catalogue after you rang. Looked

211

for anything to do with the Master of the Playing Cards. Nothing turned up.'

He rested his hands on the table and fixed Nick with an expectant stare. Nick looked at his plate, resisting.

Atheldene sighed. 'Look – if you're serious about finding Gill then let me help you. You said she mentioned the cards in her email.'

'She sent a message for help,' said Emily. It was the first time she'd spoken since they arrived. 'A scan of one of the cards was attached to it. The eight of beasts.'

'The Paris copy or the Dresden?'

'Paris,' said Nick. 'You're obviously familiar with them.'

'Your phone call intrigued me. I went to the library and read up on them – even managed to get the curator to show me a few in the Bibliothèque Nationale. Extraordinary things. But nothing, as far as I can see, that connects to what Gill and I were working on. She didn't say anything else?'

Nick shook his head.

Atheldene leaned back in his chair. 'Gill's an extraordinary girl. I'd give a lot to know she's safe – or, God forbid, to find her if she's in any sort of trouble.'

XXXII

Strassburg

'This is too dark.'

'Nobody to spy on us.' Drach scooped a cobweb from one of the roof beams. A hapless spider dangled from his hand, its legs spinning silk in mid-air.

I peered around the dusty basement. In front of me, about head height, I could see cartwheels, hooves and feet trudging past through the windows that looked out at the street. Those would need covering with clouded glass to allow in light while leaving passers-by oblivious. It was not the place I would have chosen to produce finely detailed work, but Drach seemed delighted by it.

'And then there is the expense,' I cautioned. 'Why pay more for this basement when the house in St Argobast has all the space we need?'

In truth, the upkeep of my little household by the river was costing me more than I had expected – most of the income from my annuity. Meanwhile, the bulk of the loans had already gone on ingredients for the ink, tools for the workshop, copper sheets, coal, papers . . . The demands on my purse were bottomless. And now Drach insisted we needed a second workshop for the press – which we still did not have.

'Where do the leather tanners tan their hides?' Drach demanded.

'In the tanners' field outside the walls.'

'So the stench does not foul up the city. But where do the leather workers and saddlers manufacture their wares?'

'Here in Strassburg.'

'To be closer to their customers. We should do the same.' He pointed up and left, vaguely describing the direction of the cathedral. 'Here we are within pissing distance of the heart of the city. And where the heart is, there also will our riches be.'

A creak sounded from the stair. It was the landlord, a large man named Andreas Dritzehn, stooping low to clear the beams. On first acquaintance, other men often deferred to him on account of his size and rank; later they found that he craved nothing more than other people's good opinion and would endure much to avoid offence. Though judging by the size and solidity of his house, he was not so obliging as to pass up opportunities for profit.

'Is everything satisfactory?' He had a growth on his throat which made his voice perpetually husky.

'Perfect.' Drach spoke before I could say anything. 'It suits our business exactly.'

It is too dark, too expensive and redundant for our needs, I wanted to say. At least it might have got us a reduction on the rent. But I could not contradict Drach. I stood there awkwardly and said nothing.

Dritzehn peered at us. 'What did you say your business was?'

'Copying,' I said.

214

Dritzehn waited, hoping for more. I stared Drach into silence and said nothing.

'So long as you do not light fires or make too much of a smell.' Dritzehn flapped his hand in front of his nose. 'My last tenants here were furriers. They had not dried the skins properly and they stank like the dead.'

Outside, dung spattered onto the street from a passing horse. One of the balls rolled into the gutter, tumbled down through the window and landed on the floor.

We crossed the square to Hans Dunne's goldsmithing shop. I looked up at the cathedral, rising out of its scaffolding like a woman shedding her dress. I marvelled at it. To my mind, the intricacy of the scaffolding, its perfection in its humble purpose, was almost as beautiful as the stonework it supported. When I suggested this to Kaspar, he scoffed.

'Ropes and poles and ladders? Beauty comes from life: from lust, folly, laughter, misery.'

'How can misery be beautiful?'

Kaspar pointed out a cripple begging alms by the cathedral door. He had no legs; his right arm had been lost at the elbow. He sat on a low cart which he pushed along using a forked piece of wood lashed to his stump. A seizure had frozen half his face in a slack mask, while the other half was scratched and scarred where he had tried to shave himself.

'He's grotesque. Pitiful, not beautiful.'

Kaspar grabbed my shoulder. 'But you feel alive. Doesn't he make every limb in your body sing with gratitude simply for existing. How can that not be beautiful?'

It was the sort of strange, unsettling sentiment that Kaspar occasionally voiced when he wanted to be provocative. I had learned to ignore him, and hide my disquiet as best I could.

When we reached the shop, Kaspar bypassed the counter and let us in by the side door. Bolts and locks meant little to him. He possessed almost nothing except his talent, but treated the world as if all was his. He examined a sapphire ring while we waited for Hans to finish with his customer.

'I have found a man to build you a press,' said Dunne when he had completed his sale. 'Saspach the chest maker. He says it will cost six gulden with a wooden screw, or eight with iron.'

'It must be iron,' Kaspar insisted.

'Must it?' I asked, with a heavy heart and an ever-lighter purse.

'You know it must. The greater the pressure, the clearer the image. A wooden screw would grow loose – or snap altogether.'

Before I could argue further, Dunne had reached into his cabinet and pulled out a bundle wrapped in cloth. It was the size of a small book, though when he handed it to me the weight was considerable.

'This is the first batch.'

I unwrapped it. Insider were a dozen sheets of copper, rolled smooth and no thicker than a sword blade.

Dunne coughed – a polite sound that was becoming all too familiar to me. I sighed.

'Of course, you will have to be paid.'

XXXIII

Paris

It was dark when Nick woke, though his watch showed half past nine. The jet lag was playing havoc with his body. He lay on the floor for ten minutes failing to get back to sleep, his mind in overdrive, then stood up and almost fell over with fatigue.

Emily emerged from the tiny bathroom, already dressed and made up. There was something feline, unfathomable to Nick, about the way she managed to maintain her privacy in such close quarters. He'd spent the whole night in the same room as her and couldn't even say what colour her pyjamas were. Now she was wearing a thick cream sweater over a chocolate-brown skirt and black stockings.

Nick pulled off his T-shirt and threw it over a chair. Emily looked alarmed.

'There's a café around the corner. I'll wait for you there.'

A shower, a shave and a clean shirt made Nick feel more human. Half an hour later he braved the cold outside and walked the short distance to the café. Emily was sitting in a heated conservatory with a cup of black coffee, reading *Le Monde*. Unlike Gillian, who would have been looking around the restaurant, chatting up the waiters, checking the door every ten seconds, she looked completely at peace on her own.

Nick ordered the American breakfast and prayed the coffee would come quickly. Emily put down her paper.

'You're not in it.'

Nick didn't smile. He hadn't forgotten he was a fugitive. Every siren in the distance and traffic cop, every passer-by who stared, every tourist's camera he walked in front of was like water torture.

Emily gauged his moody silence. 'So what do we do today?'

'I don't know.' He felt empty. A pack of mopeds roared past the window, their drivers veering and swerving like birds as they raced each other. Regret gnawed at him. It was insanity to have come here. Better to have stayed in New York and let Seth defend him.

'Gillian left us three bits of information: the playing card, the mobile phone SIM and the library card.'

'Three cards.' Nick frowned and wondered if it meant anything. Even now, could it be some kind of bizarre joke on Gillian's part? *Gill's an extraordinary girl.* 'Two more and we'd have a full house.'

Emily's eyes narrowed as she puzzled at it for a few moments. 'We don't even know if she meant them to be found when she left them there.'

'But she sent me the code.'

'Afterwards.' Emily took out a pen and drew a line down the margin of her newspaper. She put a cross-stroke near the top. 'Gillian went to the chateau in Rambouillet two weeks before Christmas, December the twelfth.' Another stroke. 'Two days later she disappeared. December the fourteenth. Then no trace until she turned up online on January the sixth.' She looked up at Nick. 'Have you got the list you made of her phone calls?'

Nick produced it. 'She rang Vandevelde on the afternoon of December the thirteenth. The day before she vanished.'

'And the day after she'd visited the chateau.'

'That doesn't necessarily mean anything,' Nick cautioned. 'In Gillian's line of work she might have found the card anywhere. She could have been sitting on it for months – brought it with her from New York, even.'

Emily rolled her eyes. 'She found a card that's been lost for five hundred years, and she spent the day before she vanished in a library full of unknown fifteenth-century manuscripts. I know where I'd start looking.'

'Atheldene was talking about books. He didn't say anything about cards.'

'Most of the cards survived because they were pasted into other books. Often not long after they were printed. The library had been flooded and the books were damp. That would have loosened the glue – the card might have fallen out right into her lap.'

Nick watched the flush that came to her cheeks, the exaggerated hand gestures as she mimed the card falling out of the book. Thought uninhibited her like alcohol.

'OK. We'll assume she found the card in the dead guy's library.'

'The next day, she rang Vandevelde. She went out to visit him, he analysed the card and found . . . something.'

'Except that he says she never went there, and that even if she did there's nothing to find in the card.'

'He's lying.' Emily said it with sweet certainty. 'What was the next phone call?'

'The taxi company. December sixteenth.'

'And the call to Atheldene?'

'That was earlier. The night before she disappeared.'

'But after she found the card.' Emily stirred the foam on her coffee. 'Did she tell Atheldene about it?'

'I don't think so,' said Nick. 'He sounded pretty surprised when I asked him about the Master of the Playing Cards on the phone.'

He pushed a piece of waffle around his plate, soaking up the melted butter.

'We've looked at the playing card and the phone records. The one thing we haven't tried is the library card.' Emily sipped her coffee. 'The Bibliothèque Nationale is a research library. I spent some time there when I was doing my thesis. You have to order the books you want to be delivered to you.'

'So?'

'The library card logs you in to the catalogue. It keeps a record of what you've ordered. We can see what Gillian was reading.'

A bleak and paralysing despair washed over Nick. 'Would that help?'

'There isn't anything else.'

Nick drained the last of his coffee. 'I'm going to go back and check her home page. Maybe there's something there.'

Emily looked worried. 'Do you think it's safe to split up?'

'Safer for you than being together. I'm the fugitive, remember.' He stood. 'Anyway, hopefully we left all the bad guys in New York.'

XXXIV

Strassburg

The press stood on a solid table at the front of the room. It consisted of a base which held a slate bed, two upright legs which supported a crossbar, and a wooden board, the platen, suspended between them on an iron screw. It was little different from the presses the paper makers used to squeeze their sheets dry.

There were four of us in the room. I would have preferred it to be only Kaspar and me, but our enterprise had long since outgrown its beginnings. Dunne was there, of course; also Saspach the carpenter to tend the press he had built. Upstairs, I knew Dritzehn the landlord would be crouching by the cellar door, listening at the keyhole, but I had refused point-blank to allow him down. The more gold I spent, the more possessive I became of our secret.

Yet though I had strived so long towards this moment, I felt strangely detached from it. It was not that I had shirked the work. I had boiled the inks with Kaspar; measured timbers with Saspach; pored over copper sheets with Hans Dunne,

221

filing down the sharp edges left by the graving tools. I had written out the text of the indulgence, then spent countless hours staring at it in front of a mirror so that I could translate it in reverse for transfer onto the copper. Most of all, I had paid for it. Yet I did not feel it belonged to me.

Drach took the plate out of a felt bag and rubbed it clean with a cloth. He laid it on the end of the table and poured a pool of black ink onto it from one of the jars. He spread it with the flat of a birch-wood blade until all the copper was black, then scraped it away again with the sharp edge. Finally, he wiped the plate with a stiff cheesecloth. I marvelled at his touch. He could be so careless of some things, often gratuitously rough-handed, but he could also work with the most exquisite precision when he wanted. The cloth bloomed black as it soaked up the ink from the polished surface, yet in the incisions – only a few hairs' breadths deep – the ink remained untouched.

Drach arranged the plate on the stone bed of the press. I dampened a leaf of paper with a sponge and passed it to him. He laid it over the plate and stepped away.

Hand over hand, Saspach and Dunne turned the bar that drove the screw. It squeaked in its grooves. The wooden platen touched the paper and squeezed. I heard a tiny liquid belch – probably the water I had used to moisten the paper, but in my mind it was the sound of ink being drawn out of the copper into the paper.

Saspach and Dunne screwed down the platen as far as it would go, then spun back the lever to loose it. I stared at the paper, imagining I saw faint shadows on the underside. Drach peeled it away from the copper plate and raised it to show us. I held my breath.

It was hideous. In stark black and white, letters that had

looked neat and regular in the engraving were now as wild as a child's hand. On some of the words the ink had come out thin as cobwebs, on others, thick and heavy as tar. I wanted to weep, but with the other three men looking on I did not dare.

'Why has this happened?'

'Copper is like human flesh. The deeper the cut, the more the bleeding.' Drach traced his finger over a particularly obese A.

'But your cards – every line was perfect.' I knew I sounded like a petty child consumed by jealousy. That was how I felt.

'Yes.' Drach stroked his chin and affected to contemplate the paper. 'These are not as good.'

'It is easier to cut a long line than a short one,' said Dunne. He had engraved some of the text himself and had to defend himself. 'Each letter requires so many fine cuts it is inevitable some go too deep or shallow.'

'Inevitable in the wrong hands,' Drach muttered.

I pointed to a U, so deformed it looked like a B. 'And that?'

'The shape of the letters allows no room for error,' said Dunne. 'Any fool can make a picture. Change the shape of a deer's antler and it is still a deer. Change the shape of an A and it is meaningless. I think perhaps Drach's art is not suited to this purpose.'

'Perhaps you are not suited to this purpose,' said Kaspar.

'Perhaps the next one will be better.' Saspach tried to broker peace. His face showed none of the despair I felt, only irritation. For him, this was merely a job that had wasted his talents.

We repeated the procedure. When it was done, Drach took the paper from the press and laid it on a bench beside the first. We leaned over to examine them.

'The same,' grunted Dunne. He turned away in disgust. Yet I kept looking. Where he saw confirmation of our failure, I saw a spark of hope. They *were* the same. The same erratic script, the same malformed letters and drunken lines, the same place on the third sentence where *miserere* was misspelt *misere*. In their manifest imperfections, at least, they were perfect copies.

'The process is fine,' Drach declared. He thrived on perversity. 'All we need is to improve it.'

XXXV

Paris

A freezing wind whistled down the Seine. On an embankment above the river, four L-shaped towers jutted towards the grey sky. The architect had meant them to look like open books stood on end, but to Emily they looked more like the corners of a vast glass castle. Except there was no castle to be seen. The space between the towers – a slab of ground the size of several football fields – was empty. It was only when you looked down that you saw the inside-out heart of the complex: a glass pit, a deep rectangle dug sixty feet into the earth, with the different floors of the library looking out over a sunken courtyard. And instead of a castle in the forest, a forest in the castle, for the courtyard was filled with trees, so deep that their uppermost branches only just reached to ground level. It was like no other library Emily had ever seen.

The trees began to rise above her as she rode an outside escalator into the pit. It brought her halfway down, to a mezzanine level where a bored guard gave her bag a per-functory search. It was warm inside: a plush atmosphere of red carpets and polished wood, like a theatre foyer. Even the computers were housed in wooden cabinets. Emily crossed to one and laid Gillian's card on a flat metal scanner. An onscreen message in French welcomed Gillian Lockhart. Emily looked at the trail of cables snaking out of the computer into a duct in the floor, and wondered how far those tentacles stretched, which corners of the electronic world had just been alerted to the fact that Gillian Lockhart had apparently reappeared at the Bibliothèque Nationale.

Emily tapped a fingernail on the touchscreen. A list appeared:

Lost Books of the Bible
Studies on the Physiologus in the Middle Ages
Physiologus (Anonyme, XVème Siècle)

She frowned. A physiologus was a bestiary, a collection of fables masquerading as zoology. She'd studied plenty for her work on medieval animal motifs. Why had Gillian consulted them? Had she found something to do with the animals on the playing cards?

She tapped the screen again to order the books down from the towers where they were kept.

Merci, Gillian Lockhart

A twinge of discomfort ran up Emily's back. She didn't like being Gillian Lockhart. They'd never met, but Gillian had lurked in the Cloisters like a ghost brought over with the medieval stones, a name guaranteed to change the subject. All museums have their mysteries, and Emily – fresh from her doctorate, eager to please, her own secrets to hide – had let it lie. She wondered if Nick knew. There was something desperately innocent about the way he'd plunged headlong into the search for Gillian, a knight errant come to rescue his damsel. Emily had read enough medieval romances to know that women who drew knights onto quests weren't always what they seemed.

The books would come to the reading room on the courtyard level. She checked her bag into the cloakroom, then walked to the row of turnstiles and pressed the card against another reader. The barrier opened and she stepped through, trying not to shiver at the bar's cold touch through her stockings.

*

GILLIAN LOCKHART
is in mortal peril ☺
(last updated 02 January 11:54:56)

In an Internet café on the rue St Georges, Nick sighed. There had always been aspects of Gillian that remained a mystery to him. The way she would spread peanut butter on hamburgers. The way she sometimes turned off her phone and didn't come home at night. When he'd dared to ask if she was seeing someone else, she'd accused him of having no imagination and locked herself in the bedroom.

Why had she written 'mortal peril'? If she'd been in real danger she'd have called the police, or run, not logged on to the Web to update her profile. Unless it was a last gesture of defiance, a joke to belittle what was coming. That would fit.

Next to her name was a thumbnail photograph – different to the one on the library card. This was an older picture, Gillian with long black hair combed in a straight fringe, with panda-bear eyes like an art student.

He tried exploring the site. There was the billboard, where other users could post the usual banalities, rants and badly spelled insults that passed for wit on the Web. It was blank. He flipped to another part of the site, a photo album. There were a few pictures: Gillian swigging beer at a party wearing an enormous sombrero; Gillian sprawled over a rock in Central Park pretending to hug it while she smiled coyly at the camera; Gillian standing outside a *boulangerie* with baguette tucked under her arm. She'd gone blonde by then, the same face as on the library card. He wondered who'd taken the picture. Atheldene?

There were none of Gillian with Nick. He told himself he hadn't expected any, and wondered who he was really looking for.

Before he left he checked the news sites for anything about himself. He'd assumed it would have made headlines somewhere: SUSPECTED MURDERER FLEES COUNTRY. He found a couple of stories about Bret's murder, but nothing in the last forty-eight hours. Didn't they know he'd fled? Had they come to their senses and realised he was innocent? He thought of Detective Royce and decided it was unlikely.

It reminded him of something Gillian had said. He'd caught her one day looking out of the apartment window, peering between the blinds at the empty street. He'd pointed out there was nobody there; she'd answered in a fake-deep voice: 'Just because you can't see them, doesn't mean they can't see you.'

He'd thought it was a joke, a line from a movie, one of the personas she shrugged on and off all the time. He'd gone to fix a sandwich. But when he looked back through the kitchen door she'd still been on the windowsill, watching.

*

Once, the alarm had been a black Bakelite telephone connected to a switchboard, with black cables hanging off it like chains on a dungeon wall. Later, it had become a pager; later still, a succession of ever smaller and smarter cellphones. Through all those incarnations one thing had remained constant: it almost never rang. Months would pass in silence, sometimes whole years.

Now it was ringing for the second time in three weeks. Father Michel Renais, latest in a long line of men who had held that phone, stared at the screen. The last time it had rung he had broken out into a sweat and almost dropped it; this time he was ready.

'*Oui?*'

'One of our flags has come up. Bibliothèque Nationale, garden level, seat N48.'

'*Bien.*'

Technology made it too easy, Father Michel thought. Once they'd have had to sift through paper request slips, cross-reference university records, scramble to make even the most basic enquiries. Now they knew even before the readers found their seats.

He dialled the number the cardinal had given him.

'At the Bibliothèque Nationale. The same book as before. And the same name. Gillian Lockhart.'

He heard a dry laugh on the other end of the phone. 'I very much doubt it is Gillian Lockhart.'

It was like entering a spaceship, or a medieval dungeon reimagined by a future civilisation. Emily rode a long escalator down through the cavernous hall that formed the outer shell of the complex. An underground moat surrounding the underground castle. The outside walls were solid concrete, while the

229

inside was protected by huge curtains of steel rings like sheets of chain mail. At the bottom, another machine checked her card before admitting her through the final pair of doors. Here, she was back inside the castle: desks, carpets, polished wood.

Emily found the seat that the computer had assigned her and waited. She stared out of the windows at the forested courtyard. It was like something out of legend: thick evergreens bristling among the leafless birches and oaks, with thin icings of snow on the branches. Even in winter, she could hardly see the other side of the courtyard beyond the trees.

A red light above the desk summoned Emily to the issue counter. A bored librarian held out her hand.

'*Votre carte?*'

Emily smiled to hide her anxiety. She held up the card, keeping her thumb over the top half of Gillian's face to hide it. The librarian barely glanced at it before reaching into a cubby-hole behind her and depositing two books on the counter.

'I ordered three,' Emily said in French.

The librarian narrowed her heavily made-up eyes. Before Emily could protest, she swept the card out of her hand and slapped it down on the reader by her computer. She studied the monitor.

'Anonymous, *Physiologus*. This book is missing.' She scrolled down. 'You have requested this book before?'

'Um, yes. In December.'

'And it was missing then, also.'

Was that a question? Emily opted for what she hoped was a suitably French grunt, accompanied by a vague twitch of the shoulders.

'There is a note on the system that we could not find this book the last time you asked for it.'

Emily rested a hand on the counter to steady herself. 'I . . . I just wondered if it might have turned up.'

'*Non.*'

'The online catalogue still shows it as available,' Emily persisted.

'Then there is a mistake with the catalogue. I will make another note.' She lifted her gaze over Emily's shoulder to the person waiting in line behind her. Emily took the hint.

She went back to her desk with the two books that had come: *Studies on the Physiologus* and *Lost Books of the Bible*. Nothing to do with Gillian Lockhart was clear. All she ever saw were distant shadows flitting out of view, uncertain whether they were real or just tricks of the light. She almost felt sorry for Nick.

But she could only work with what she had. She started with *Studies on the Physiologus*, kneading new facts in with what she already knew. The term 'physiologus' had fallen out of use during the Middle Ages, but then revived when new-fangled printers wanted to give their books an old-fashioned stamp of authenticity. The book that hadn't come was listed in the online catalogue as fifteenth century. Emily flipped to the appendix. There were eleven printed editions of the *Physiologus* known before 1500. None of them was the one listed in the catalogue.

A dead end. She turned to the other book, the *Lost Books of the Bible*. This was more of a struggle: she found it hard to engage with the text without knowing what she was looking for. She turned through the pages looking for any pencil marks that Gillian might have made in the margins, any words she might have underlined. She scanned for references to animals, bestiaries or cards; all she got were prophets, ancient kings and angry gods.

She heard a cough behind her and looked round. It was the librarian.

Her heart beat faster. 'Have you found it?'

The librarian shook her head. 'There is a message. You must go to the information desk on the upper level. There is a man there to see you – Monsieur Ash. He says it is an emergency.'

The last number Gillian had called from her cellphone was a taxi company. Nick could have rung, but that would have been too quick. This was his last lead; once it was done, he'd have nothing left. So he got the address off the Internet and walked, trying to fool himself for a little while longer that he was achieving something.

He hated the feeling of not knowing what would happen next. Gillian used to tease him that he wanted all life to be like school. 'If God handed you a schedule for the rest of your life – three periods of work, a half-hour for lunch, forty minutes online, an hour extra-curricular sex – you'd be happy.' He hadn't denied it.

Gillian, on the other hand, was spontaneous. Sometimes, when he was too tired to keep up, Nick thought it was almost a neurosis. She'd find a flyer for a concert or an exhibition lying in the gutter and go that night; friends he'd never heard of would call at midnight, just arrived in New York, and she'd scoot out to Penn Station to bring them back to the apartment. She'd meet a guy on a train and be in his apartment at two the next morning playing canasta.

'People's lives go like clockwork,' she told him. 'They start out buzzing with energy, and by the time they hit thirty they've totally run down. If you don't act, you're doomed. You need to introduce some random chaos into your life.'

After she left him, he'd seen those flyers blowing down the street and wondered if that was what he'd been. Something she'd found, an impulse acted on to prove she still could. Random chaos.

The taxi office was a small kiosk that had somehow wormed itself into a crevice between two large buildings. There wasn't much inside: a wilting plastic pot plant, three plastic chairs scarred by cigarettes and two women sitting behind a window in front of a faded map of Paris. Their faces were so heavily made up that they too might have been plastic. Both wore coats, wool hats and fingerless gloves. Each time the phone rang the woman on the left would answer it, bellow a series of questions, then relay the answers to the woman beside her. She in turn would pick up a radio mike and repeat everything the first woman had just said. It looked like the sort of division of labour that only the French could have dreamed up.

Nick went to the window.

'Do you speak English?'

The radio woman was still shouting orders into her microphone. The telephone woman glanced at him, then jerked her head at her colleague. Nick waited for her to finish.

'*Anglais,*' the telephone woman barked.

The radio woman scowled. 'A little.'

'A friend of mine took a taxi on the fourteenth of December. I want to know where she went.' He looked around, losing confidence. There was no sign of a computer, not even a filing cabinet. 'Do you have any records?'

The woman stared at him from turquoise lagoons of eyeshadow. '*Non.*'

If he was honest, he hadn't expected any more. Hope was painful; he was almost grateful to her for killing it off. He turned away.

'*Nom*,' the woman said behind him again. '*Sa nom*. Her name.'

Nick looked back, sheepish as he realised he'd misunderstood.

'Gillian Lockhart.'

The ring of a telephone interrupted the exchange. The ritual played itself out between the two women. When it was dispatched, the radio woman looked back at him. Closing her eyes, she recited as if into a microphone, 'Gillian Lockhart. 14.30. From rue Saint Antoine, she comes here.'

Nick looked around the plastic office. 'Here? *Ici*?'

The receptionist pointed across the road to a grand neoclassical building. 'The station. The Gare de l'Est.'

It extended his quest by a few minutes, so Nick walked across the street and into the station. It smelled of diesel fumes and steel. He stared at the banks of monitors on stalks that sprouted from the walls, reading the destinations. He'd always loved European railway stations: the grandiose architecture dimmed with soot, the sleek trains, the destinations that stretched across a continent rather than just safe commuter suburbs. He read the names off the flickering screens. Bâle; Epernay; Frankfurt; Munich; Salzburg; Strasbourg; Vienna.

Where now?

The tongue of the turnstile rolled over and spat Emily out into the foyer. The information desk was ahead of her in the middle of the room. She searched for Nick but couldn't see him.

She glanced at the glass wall to her right, through onto the balcony that overlooked the forested courtyard. In summer it became a café, packed with tables and chairs; now it was all but deserted. A short man in a silver puffer jacket leaned against the balustrade smoking a cigarette. Was he looking at her?

He threw his cigarette butt onto the floor and ground it out with the toe of his shoe. Emily went up to the information desk.

'I had a message in the reading room. Is there a Nick Ash to see—'

'Right here.'

A hand clamped on her arm so tight she thought the bone would snap. It pulled her away from the nodding receptionist and spun her towards the door, pulling her along. Fear froze her into obedience. Was this what had happened to Gillian? She looked up and saw a heavyset man with a crooked nose and bristling black eyebrows. His left arm reached across his body to hold her; his right jabbed something round and blunt into the small of her back.

'I have a gun. Do not scream; do not try to run.'

She would never have run. Her legs were jelly; she could barely walk. Her captor almost had to drag her across the carpet. They were halfway to the door already. Outside, the man in the puffer jacket hurried to meet them.

The beep of an alarm cut through her panic. By the entrance, the security guard was patting down a long-haired student whose profusion of chains and studs had set off the metal detector. Emily stared at it. Could you really get a gun through that? Or was he bluffing?

'Please don't take me,' she whispered to her captor. They were almost at the exit. 'I know what you want. It's in my bag. You can have it. Just please let me go.'

He paused just shy of the velvet rope that marked the edge of the foyer. At least he was listening. He looked down at her empty hands.

'Where is your bag?'

She jerked her head at the cloakroom. 'I had to check it in before I went to the reading room.'

As abruptly as he'd grabbed her, he swivelled her back around and marched her towards the cloakroom. Just before they got there he let her go, pushing her off balance so that she stumbled headlong into the counter. She thrust her ticket at the startled attendant, who came back a moment later with her brown bucket bag. As soon as she had it in her hands she felt the grip back on her elbow.

'One euro,' said the attendant.

Emily snapped open the bag and rummaged in the bottom. The vice around her arm tightened; she felt faint with the pain. But she'd found what she was looking for. She pulled out a coin – but she was clumsy. It slipped out of her fingers and dropped onto the carpet.

She smiled a weak apology at the attendant and made to bend down and pick it up. Unsure whether to allow it or not, her captor loosened his grip.

It was enough. She came up faster than he'd expected, knocking him back off balance. That brought her room to turn around. She thrust her hand up towards his face and before he could respond, squeezed hard on the can wrapped in her fist.

A jet of pepper spray erupted from the nozzle, straight into his face. He reeled away clutching his eyes. An alarm bell started to screech; Emily wondered if the spray might have triggered a smoke detector. But it was coming from the door. The man in the puffer jacket had seen what was happening and had burst in, triggering the metal detector. He was reaching inside his bulky coat, then went down as a security guard tackled him to the floor.

Emily picked up her bag and fled.

236

XXXVI

Strassburg

A paw was taking shape. Just as the mother bear licks unformed flesh into the shape of her young, the chisel's tongue rasped against the stone to carve the image. I could already see the curve of a haunch bulging out of the block; a sloping back and a knob that would become an ear or a snout.

The stone carver stood over his bench in the square and chipped it out. Behind him loomed the cathedral, where the animal would eventually graze among pillared glades and vaulted branches.

This is how God forms us all, I thought: raining down blows to draw out shapes from the crude stone of our creation. A tap and a crack, a puff of dust, the rattle of fragments falling on the cobbles. Another piece of our imperfection cut away. The smoothest skin is scar tissue.

'The curve of the knee is too sharp.'

A shadow fell over the bench. Drach had arrived, stealing up behind me in silence. He glanced at the bear, emerging from

237

the stone as if from a forest, then at the drawing pinned to the tabletop.

The stone carver looked up. He was well-used to Drach's interruptions. 'The bear needs to fit the column. I made him crouch lower.'

Drach laughed and swung away. I followed him through the stone yard. It was like a cemetery: a field of stones in every stage of refinement, from boulders fresh out of the quarry to fluted sections of arches that only wanted a keystone to make them stand erect.

'That is the way to create copies,' Drach said. 'I make a picture and he copies it. What could be simpler?'

'You said yourself it isn't a true copy.'

'True enough.'

'Not for me.'

We sat down on a roughly dressed ashlar. On a stone capital opposite, a bearded man parted foliage like curtains and peered out. I squinted, but it was not one of Kaspar's.

'I have found a way we can raise the money,' he said, without preamble.

A season had passed since our experiment in Dritzehn's cellar. I had not meant it to, but sometimes time escapes all plan and reason. For three days afterwards I could not raise my spirits to even think about it. When the worst of my melancholy had passed, I no longer cared. I found other things to occupy me; I concentrated my energies on earning my living and maintaining my household. My stays in St Argobast became longer; Drach's visits less frequent. The passion that had run so full in my veins had eased. Yet when Drach sent a boy to call me to this meeting, it had flooded back unbidden, as high as ever.

'Tell me.'

'There is a widow in this town named Ellewibel. She lives by the wine market.'

He paused, playing up the suspense. I humoured him. 'Do you expect me to marry this widow for her fortune?'

'No. But she has a daughter, Ennelin. Twenty-five years old and not yet married. If Ellewibel could find a husband to take her, the dowry would be immense. All the money we need to advance our art.'

I stared at him. He smiled, nodding, encouraging me to follow his train of thought.

'That is the most preposterous idea you have ever suggested.'

'Why?'

'You know why.'

We had never spoken of the demon that possessed me. But from the moment we had shared our first drink in the Wild Man, he had surely known. He allowed me to wash his back in the river and watch him dress; when he stayed at my house we slept in the same bed wrapped together like an old married couple. Sometimes he allowed my hand to slide into the hollow of his hips, so I could lie awake and torment myself with possibilities. I never went any further. The demon had wormed itself into my soul so deep it had become a part of me, a tumour I could not remove without also destroying myself. Drach was different. I knew he did not desire me, but encouraged my cravings because he loved perversity, danger, the hair-thin ledge he walked along the cliffs of damnation. Perhaps, I begged God in the solitary hours of the night, because he loved me.

But now he was pitiless. 'You are a bachelor of thirty-some years. You have an income, a house, a good family behind you. Why should you not marry this girl?'

Because I love you, I wanted to scream. But I understood that to say it would destroy everything.

'If she is twenty-five with a substantial dowry, why is she still unmarried?'

He stroked my cheek with his finger, taunting me. 'So uncharitable, Johann. She is probably a rosebud who has not yet opened.'

'At twenty-five?'

'Then perhaps she is as ugly as a two-headed mule.' He shrugged. 'You shouldn't mind. When indulgences are pouring out of our press like wine, you can buy one to salve your conscience.'

He slid off the stone and paced around me. 'If every challenge was overcome at the first attempt, it would never have been a challenge. Do you know how many sheets of paper and copper I ruined to make the playing cards? How many three-legged bears and unicorns that looked like goats?'

'Your unicorn still looks like a goat.' I wanted to wound him, but he shrugged it off with rare modesty.

'Catch me one and I will draw it better.'

'At least a unicorn would be worth something.'

'But we are hunting a rarer beast. If – when – we make it right, a more *valuable* beast.'

He pulled a coin out of his pocket and flipped it towards me. He must have brought it with him precisely for this piece of theatre, for I never otherwise knew him to carry any money. I snatched it out of the air.

'Imagine *that* is your bride.'

The image on the coin was a man, John the Baptist, his head framed in a heart-shaped halo. I read the inscription around the border. IOHANNIS ARCHIEPISCOPVS MAGVNTINVS. John, Archbishop of Mainz.

'I saw Dunne the goldsmith yesterday,' Drach said. 'He has been carving a new plate which he says will make the lettering more even. But it takes hours to make. He cannot afford the time without extra payment.'

I was not listening. The lettering on the coin had transported me back to my childhood. Some colleagues of my father from the mint had lived in our house for a time. A die maker had been one. I remembered tiptoeing into his room one afternoon and watching him at work. He took the block of iron that he had engraved with the design, held a steel rod against it and struck it hard with a hammer. Sparks flew; I whimpered in surprise. He heard me and beckoned me over. He let me hold the steel rod and told me it was called a punch. He showed me the end, which had been carved away so that the letter A stood proud on its tip. When he struck it against the die, it left a perfect imprint in the iron. Later it would be filled with gold, and the impression of that letter hammered into the coin. Such was the unceasing cycle of creation and reproduction: punch and form, male and female, stroke and imprint.

Like all obvious ideas, the wonder afterwards is that it took so long to discover. Why had we wasted months trying to carve the words with a graving tool, when Dunne and I both knew that the best way to imprint letters in metal is with a punch-stamp? All I can say is that Drach had engraved his cards, and we were so bent on following his method we did not pause to think.

Drach was watching me impatiently. He hated to be ignored. I met his gaze and smiled. Of course I saw what he was doing. But I could not help myself.

'How much is Ennelin's dowry?'

XXXVII

Paris

'Could they have followed me?'

It had taken Emily three hours to get back. She'd changed trains, jumped indiscriminately on and off buses, browsed in the reflections of shop windows, made sudden detours – all the while looking over her shoulder for any sign of pursuit. Darkness had fallen by the time she sneaked back into the hotel. She'd shaken Nick awake from his jet-lagged sleep and dragged him to a café in a quiet backstreet near Montparnasse. She still didn't feel safe.

'If they'd followed you, they'd have come back to the hotel.' Nick sipped his beer and looked around the café for the dozenth time. He couldn't sit still. 'It was lucky you had that pepper spray.'

'I had a bad experience once.' Emily barely moved. Shock gripped her like stone. 'It must have been the book. It must have triggered some kind of alarm somewhere. A tripwire.'

Not so long ago it would have sounded ludicrously paranoid. Now, Nick just nodded. 'Maybe that's how they found

Gillian. That's why she left her library card in the bank vault.' The cards Gillian had left them were beginning to look more like a box of sharpened knives than a treasure trove. 'If only *we* could find her that easily.'

Emily cupped her palms around her mug of coffee in silence. Twice she looked as if she was going to say something, but held back. Nick could guess what it was.

'If you want to go home, I understand.' He said it quickly, knowing he'd regret it if he gave himself time to think about it. 'God knows what those guys would have done to you if you hadn't escaped. There's no reason for you to risk it for Gillian.'

Emily seemed to flinch. 'I'm not . . .' She trailed off, paused, began again. 'I'm not going home.'

He knew he ought to argue but he didn't have the will. She flicked him a tentative look and he held it, trying to reassure her. It was hard when he had so little to give.

'At least I got something for my troubles.' Warmth returned to Emily's face. 'Gillian was reading up on a physiologus – a book of beasts. I'll bet that was the book she found the card in. There must have been one in the chateau's library.'

Nick thought about it for a second.

'I know the man who'd know.'

'Atheldene.'

The familiar voice, so intimidating in its studied neutrality. 'It's Nick.'

A taxi drove past the phone box. The noise of its wheels on the slick cobbled street drowned out Atheldene's surprised silence. As it died away, Nick heard, 'Any news of our mutual friend?'

'Maybe – we're not sure. We need to check the list of books she recovered from the chateau. Can you do that?'

'Perhaps with a good enough reason.'

'Gillian's missing. Emily went to the Bibliothèque Nationale today and almost ended up the same way. How's that for a reason?'

'I'm very sorry to hear it.'

Nick glanced at Emily, watching through the phone-box door. She nodded.

'Gillian found a card. An old one.'

'The Master of the Playing Cards, I presume.' Atheldene didn't sound surprised. 'Have you got it?'

'We think she may have found it in some sort of bestiary, or . . .' Nick stumbled over the word. 'Physiologus.'

'Really?'

Nick could almost imagine the raised eyebrow, the searching stare. He was glad of the phone line between them. He waited out the silence.

'I'll check the inventory from Rambouillet. Can I call you back on this number?'

'It's a payphone.'

'I'll be quick.'

Atheldene hung up. Nick waited in the phone box, scanning the road through the cracked glass. A little way down the street, a homeless man sat hunched under a filthy quilt on a raft of cardboard boxes. Nick was amazed he hadn't already frozen. His hand dipped to his pocket to find some euros, but fear restrained him. What if the old man wasn't what he seemed? He was sure he'd read books where spies dressed as bums to conduct surveillance. Was the man looking at him? Nick watched him carefully and kept his hand in his pocket.

A shadow crossed his line of sight. He jumped, but it was only Emily. She walked across the empty street and crouched beside the homeless man. She dropped some coins into his styrofoam cup and exchanged a few words, then hurried back. Nick felt ashamed.

'What did he say?'

'He said you should stop staring at him.'

Before Nick could feel even more guilty, the phone rang. He seized the receiver gratefully.

'Yes?'

'Good news. There was a bestiary in the old man's collection. Just the one. Gillian catalogued it. Date, mid to late fifteenth century. Remarks: some stylistic similarities with the workshop of the *Bedford Hours* Master.'

'The who?'

'I'll tell you later. You'll like it.'

'When can we see the book?'

A dry laugh. 'I'm afraid it's not quite so straightforward.'

'What do you mean?'

'Well for one thing, the book's not in Paris any more. Remember it had been soaked through? The conservators took it away to their controlled storage facility.'

'Where's that?'

'Brussels.'

Nick swore. 'Can we get in there?'

'I *could* get you in there.' There was an implicit offer in the sentence, a stress that opened a negotiation. Nick's mind raced. He looked down the street and saw that the beggar had gone. Had he used Emily's gift to find a warm bed for the night – or was he even now telling a man with a broken nose where to find Nick and Emily?

'How soon can we leave?'

'Straight away, if you like. It's only about three hours' drive. But there's another problem.'

Nick waited.

'The book's frozen solid.'

XXXVIII

Strassburg

The house reminded me of my father's. That instantly
deepened my discomfort. It stood near the wharves, where the
streets echoed to the roll of barrels coming up from the barges.
The square opposite looked like a rabbit warren: holes yawned
outside every house where trapdoors stood open to the wine
cellars beneath.

There was a trapdoor outside the widow Ellewibel's house,
but it was bolted shut. So were the shutters over the ground-
floor windows. I knocked on the door and hoped no one
would answer.

The door swung in. A servant in black admitted me and led
me up to a room overlooking the square. My first impression
was that it looked well enough. Rich wine-coloured fabrics
draped the walls; a welcoming fire burned hot in the hearth.
Though it was not yet dark outside, candles were lit. Four large
chests positioned around the room announced they had no
shortage of possessions.

Yet on second glance, the picture diminished. The floor

around the chests was streaked with dust, as if they had only recently been dragged into place. The chandeliers had been scraped clean of old wax, but the candles within were little more than stubs. The cloths on the wall were scarred with many darnings; one of them looked like an old dress that had been recently pressed into service. Even I, who had spent half my life in hovels and attics, could see through the pretence. It was probably the first time in my life that anyone had tried to impress me.

A woman of about fifty rose as I entered. She wore a long black robe belted just below the breasts, with a white collar and a scarf carefully arranged to cover her thin grey hair. Her mouth turned down at the corners; her eyes were small and hard. But, like the room, she did what she could with what she had. She forced a smile and managed to hold it for as long as it took to usher me across the room. She put me in the place of honour, a high-backed chair that must have been her husband's, and told the servant to bring the best wine in the best silver cups.

'My daughter will join us presently,' she told me. 'I thought it best we acquainted ourselves first.'

The servant brought wine on a tray. I took the goblet and drank thirstily – far more than was respectable. Ellewibel looked surprised, but collected herself and sipped parsimoniously at her own.

'I am told you are a goldsmith, Herr Gensfleisch.'

'I served an apprenticeship.'

I did not volunteer any more information. I doubted the widow Ellewibel wanted to hear how it had ended.

'My late husband was a wine merchant.'

I did not dispute it.

'I have heard that Mainz is also renowned for its wines.' She peered at me hopefully. 'That is where you come from, is it not?'

'It is.'

'And your father: he was . . . ?'

A brute? A pig? 'He was in the cloth trade. He was also a companion of the mint.'

Hope rose in Ellewibel's drawn face. 'And your mother's family?'

'Grocers.'

She visibly deflated, as I knew she would. I enjoyed it. The wine and my misgivings put me in a cruel humour.

'Tell me of your work here in Strassburg.'

'Various ventures,' I said vaguely.

'Andreas Dritzehn tells me you instructed him in the art of gem polishing.'

'I owed him money.'

She did not flinch. 'But you have an income?'

'A little.'

'And a house?'

'Rented. In St Argobast. You probably do not know it – it is some miles from Strassburg.'

Her eyes narrowed. 'I know it well. A pretty village, and no distance from the city at all.'

I was about to embark on a disagreeable anecdote about a woman who had been surprised by bandits and abducted on the road to St Argobast, when a knock sounded at the door. Ellewibel stood.

'My daughter. She will be delighted to meet you.'

I had prepared myself for a monster. In fact, all that surprised me was her utter ordinariness. True, she was no beauty. Her face was flat and hard, like overbaked bread, its oval shape accentuated by her white wimple. Her nose was small, her teeth crooked (but no more than normal), her skin no longer smooth. With two hundred gulden attached to her name, there seemed no reason any man should not want to marry her. Except me.

She curtsied. We both stood there, neither knowing what to say. With a start, I realised she was examining me just as I had examined her. What did she see? A man in his middle age, sweating under the weight of the fur-trimmed hat and coat he had borrowed. My back was stooped, my face scarred by too many misadventures in the forge. Grey had begun to appear in my beard, though my fair hair disguised it. With a good name and an adequate income, why should she not want to marry me?

'Of course, there is the matter of the dowry,' I said.

'My late husband – bless him – was an honest and thrifty man. When he died, his estate was valued at two hundred gulden. I am willing to endow my entire claim on Ennelin.'

There was something evasive in her manner. 'That is very generous.'

'A mother's joy at seeing her daughter established in marriage is beyond price.'

I did not answer. My borrowed coat weighed on me like stone; the collar choked me. I could hardly bring myself to look at Ennelin. The worm twisted in my guts.

'I will have to consider . . .'

Ennelin was well schooled. She watched me modestly, without betraying the least doubt. Her mother was more direct.

'Herr Gensfleisch, do you want to marry my daughter?'

XXXIX

Paris

The Jaguar pulled away from the kerb and headed up the boulevard de Sebastopol towards the E19 highway and Belgium. Atheldene swung across two lanes of traffic and past the Gare du Nord, then gunned the throttle as the road opened in front of them. Nick sank back in the leather seat and wondered if Gillian had sat there, if she'd felt the same throb of the car's powerful engine and been impressed by it.

He glanced over his shoulder to see if anyone was following. The road behind was empty. All he saw was Emily, curled up in the corner of the back seat staring out of the window.

'What did you mean when you said the book was frozen?' Her voice was soft, barely audible over the engine noise.

'It's the latest thing in conservation. After fire, water's a book's worst enemy. You need to get rid of it as quickly as possible. But drying out a book – a valuable one – is a bugger of a job. If you've got a whole library on your hands you can't deal with the books individually. No time. So you flash-freeze them and keep them in a cold store until you're ready to thaw them out and conserve them properly. That's what this outfit in Belgium does.'

'How long does it take to defrost?'

'A few hours. They have all the kit there on site.' Atheldene guided the car past a line of trucks. 'Then we'll see what we find. Maybe your mysterious playing card?' He jammed on the brakes as a small Peugeot veered in front of them, then swung out to overtake. 'Unless, of course, you've already found it?'

Nick had expected the question, had debated at length with Emily what they'd do. He reached into the bag in the footwell and pulled the card out of its stiff-backed envelope. Atheldene's eyes flicked towards it.

'Where did you get that?'

'Gillian left it for me.' Nick knew it sounded defensive. He glanced down at the card, then across at the badge on the steering wheel, a snarling jaguar's head. Everywhere he looked he saw open jaws and sharp teeth.

'I don't suppose she left any clue where she'd disappeared to?'

'Nothing.'

'Pity.' Atheldene fixed his gaze back on the road. The speedometer needle edged slightly higher.

'Nick said you mentioned the *Bedford Hours* on the phone,' said Emily from the back. 'What's the connection?'

'As I'm sure you know, Emily, a book of hours is a prayer book that offered lay people a series of prayers to use through the different hours of the day. It's based on the idea of the monastic schedule. The *Bedford Hours* is one of these books, commissioned for the marriage in 1423 of the Duke of Bedford. The *Bedford Hours* is an enormously elaborate and richly decorated book produced in Paris. We don't know the name of the artist who commissioned it, so we call him the Master of the *Bedford Hours*.'

'Like the Master of the Playing Cards,' said Nick. 'Don't any of these guys have names?'

'Almost none,' said Atheldene. 'Not until the end of the fifteenth century. Until then, the medieval ethos of anonymity prevails. Art wasn't seen as a way to show off your own genius, but God's. All inspiration came from God, so the thinking went, and the artist or craftsman was merely a channel. It was only with the Renaissance that art becomes egocentric again. You can draw a straight line from da Vinci right through to Picasso, the ghastly Mr Hirst and all the rest of that gang.'

'It's an attractive way of thinking,' said Emily.

'But not terribly helpful when it comes to determining the origins of a piece. All we can do is try to identify work on stylistic grounds. Which is where the Bedford Master comes in. So far as we can tell, he must have kept a studio in Paris and employed a number of journeymen and assistants to execute the work. Various people have studied the books attributed to the workshop; what they noticed is that several of the motifs from your playing cards also occur in these books. Birds and animals that look very similar, sometimes absolutely identical, to the ones on the cards. I suspect the point Gillian was trying to make, ever so obliquely, is that the pictures in the bestiary she found are closely related to the images on the cards.'

Nick digested that. 'So you think the playing card Master might be the same as the Bedford Master?'

'Probably not.' Atheldene reminded Nick of one of the professors he'd had at college, a pompous man who'd loved nothing more than displaying his learning like a peacock – especially when it came to pretty female undergraduates. Had Gillian been impressed by it?

'He could have worked in the studio as an apprentice. He might just have seen the pictures and decided to copy them. Or there might have been a common model book.'

'A model book?'

Atheldene didn't let Nick's question divert him. 'Europe in the fifteenth century is really in the twilight of the medieval and the pre-dawn of the modern age. Everything's changing – and nowhere more so than in the diffusion of ideas. People are waking up to the fact that they need to communicate far more widely, but they don't have the tools. Model books are one response to this. You make up a book with examples of a whole set of different pictures, and then anyone who gets hold of the book can create a more-or-less exact copy of the picture. Some of them come with step-by-step instructions of exactly how to draw the picture and colour it in. Painting by numbers. The Master of the Playing Cards takes this to its logical conclusion by inventing copper-engraved printing: mass production.' He blew air through his nose. 'And a few years later, of course, Gutenberg blows the whole thing open with the printing press.'

The car roared on up the empty highway.

Heloise Duvalier was a smoker. That made it easier. 'Don't call from the office,' they'd warned her. 'Use the payphone down the street.' They'd even given her a phonecard so she wouldn't need change.

'If Monsieur Atheldene goes on a trip to Brussels, you must tell us at once,' the priest had said. And two days later, Atheldene had come striding out of his office, pulling on his overcoat and shouting to his secretary that he was off to the warehouse in Brussels. Heloise had been polishing the glass partition on the next-door office at the time – she'd been giving it a lot of attention that week.

How did the priest know Atheldene would go to Brussels?

He was a priest: he knew the mysteries of the world. He had promised her five hundred euros if she told him. It was more than she made in a month cleaning the Stevens Mathison offices, where men would pay that much for a bottle of wine over lunch.

She decided to wait fifteen minutes, just to be safe. After ten she decided it was enough. Delay might cost her. She had six sisters in Abidjan who relied on the money she sent back: with five hundred euros, she might even have a little left to spend on herself. She mimed a cigarette to her supervisor, who tapped his watch and held up three fingers. Three minutes. He was a real con about time. The security guard buzzed her out of the building.

A girl in a short skirt and a pink coat with fake-fur trim was using the phone. Heloise waited in the cold, shivering, listening to the little princess complain to whoever was listening. Probably a boyfriend. One minute ticked by, then two. She tapped the side of the phone booth and got a dismissive glare. She'd have to go soon: she couldn't afford to lose the job. Not even for five hundred euros.

The girl hung up. Heloise pushed in past her even before she'd left the booth. She picked up the phone and dialled the number she'd been given. The priest answered on the first ring.

'*Oui?*'

'He is en route.'

XL

Strassburg

What had I done?

I stumbled out of the house in a daze. Across the street, two porters used staves to manhandle a hogshead of wine into an open cellar. I wanted to throw myself in after it and break my neck, or drown head first in the barrel. To my right, the river flowed swiftly past the wharf at the end of the alley. That would serve. It would sweep me down to the Rhine; past Mainz, where my brother or my sister might look up from their work and notice a small piece of flotsam in the stream; then on out into the great ocean.

Gold was my undoing. From the moment my child's fist closed around the stolen coin, dreams of gold and perfection had possessed me as surely as the demon. They were inseparable. Gold was perfect. Perfection was expensive. I, with all my imperfections, had sold myself for two hundred gulden.

Madness held me like a fever. I wandered the streets of Strassburg not knowing where I went, not caring. Night fell; a filthy rage blossomed in my heart. The worm who possessed me swelled into a monstrous dragon; he took flight and scorched fire in my soul. For years I had held that desire in check; now I let it own me. I wanted flesh, to claw and scratch, to bite and squeeze. To dominate.

I knew there were places where such things could be had, as there are in every city. Ever since I came to Strassburg I had avoided them. Now I charged in. It was near the cathedral – for vice envies virtue and is never far away. Down a lane where tawdry women shouted offers of pleasures I did not want; along a backstreet where the propositions grew more outlandish; into an alley that was little more than an open sewer between the backs of houses.

I was surprised by how crowded it was. I had nursed the demon so close to me so long I thought it only existed in me. Here there was a whole congregation. Men dressed as women with red paint smeared on their stubbled cheeks; musclebound men with arms covered in scars; gaunt men with sharp faces who stared at me hungrily; scrawny boys in tunics that barely covered the soft skin of their thighs.

I suppose I might have felt a sense of kinship with them but I did not. I resented them: simply by their existence they diminished me. Jealousy fanned my anger and banished my doubts. I strode deeper into the lane. Hands pawed at me and tugged the sleeve of my borrowed coat; men whistled and shouted proposals, prices. I ignored them.

Near the end of the alley, where the shadows were deepest and the stench worst, I found what I wanted: a slight, olive-skinned man with a mop of black curls. He was not as beautiful as Kaspar – he had a slight hunch, and his face was twisted like old vines from years of sin – but he was like enough. He named a price and I paid it without argument. Ennelin's dowry.

He turned away and beckoned me to follow. The fire in my

soul was cooling. I did not know what to do; I was frightened. But I was determined to carry it through – if only to spite Drach, Ennelin, the world that had condemned me to misery and despair.

There was a kink in the wall, little wider than shoulder width. It was all the privacy we would get. My companion thrust me into it and spun me around; he squatted in front of me and parted the folds of my coat. I tried to relax, to enjoy it. I closed my eyes. All I could hear was the trickle of sewage down the alley.

And footsteps. I opened my eyes again. I thought that corner of the alley must be the blackest place on earth. Yet, impossibly, the darkness had deepened. A shadow blocked the entrance to our little niche. He pulled the prostitute off me and sent him sprawling into the gutter.

'Johann?'

Drach's voice.

'Are you mad? If the watchmen catch you here they will burn you alive.'

Over his shoulder I watched the prostitute pick himself out of the gutter. Effluent dripped from him; in his hand I saw the dim grey of steel.

'*Kaspar*,' I gasped.

Drach turned. He moved so fast I could not see what he did, but next instant the prostitute was rolling down the alley howling with pain. Drach picked up the fallen knife and hurled it after him, towards the hole where the sewage dropped into the canal. He looked at me.

'You're shivering.'

I collapsed forward. He caught me in his arms.

There was no thought of taking me back to St Argobast. I was limp as a blade of grass. Drach half-carried, half-dragged me

258

through the empty streets to his lodgings. Near St Peter's church two watchmen challenged us. Nightmare visions of flame seized my eyes, but Drach mimed drinking and told them I had fallen into a cellar. They let us go.

Drach's home was the attic of a house owned by Andreas Dritzehn. I had been angry when I first found out; I had wondered if Drach's insistence that I should rent the cellar had somehow been a conspiracy with his landlord. Now I was grateful I did not have to go a step further.

He manhandled me up the stairs and laid me down on his straw mattress. Apart from a chest of tools, it was his only furniture. He sat on the floor beside me and stroked my brow.

'What were you thinking?'

'Ennelin,' I mumbled. 'I agreed to marry her.'

He unbuttoned my coat and slid it off me.

'It was borrowed,' I croaked.

'I know.' He held it up and examined it. 'It could have been much worse. You were only ankle deep in shit.'

'Thanks to you.'

He came around behind me and pulled my shirt over my head. Sweat drenched it.

'Go to sleep.'

He pulled a blanket over me. I closed my eyes and let my body sink into the straw.

'I love you,' I whispered. But I could not tell if he had heard me, and I did not dare open my eyes to look.

I woke to the feel of something hard against my forehead. For a golden moment I imagined it was Drach's face pressed against mine, our bodies together. I reached an arm forward and felt nothing but straw. Reluctantly, I let the illusion go and opened my eyes.

A package lay on the mattress beside me, wrapped in an old shirt. I propped myself on my elbow and looked around. Sunlight streamed through the gable windows, but Drach was nowhere to be seen.

I pulled apart the wrapping. It came away easily; inside lay a small bundle of paper, the unclothed body of a book. The pages had been gathered and sewn together, but not yet closed in covers. I opened the first leaf.

'*Leo fortissimus bestiarum ad nullius pavebit occursum . . .*' I read. The lion is the bravest of all beasts and fears nothing.

It was a bestiary – I had copied one in Paris. This was far grander: a sumptuous edition written in a fine hand on vellum. At the head of the first line stood a magnificently illuminated capital L, spreading into a thicket of branches and leaves, beneath whose foliage a lion sprang after a defenceless ox. The lion resembled one of the animals from the cards; the ox was unfamiliar, but clearly from the same menagerie.

I turned through the pages, ignoring the text and savouring the illuminations. I had only ever seen Kaspar's pictures in black and white, or painted on signs where rain and sun had bleached their vitality. In the pages of this book they lived in a perfect state of nature. Lush foliage overflowed the margins like another Eden. Birds with brilliant plumage sang from the branches or swooped between columns of text. Fawns peered shyly from behind gilded initials. A hopeful bear clambered up the stem of a P to reach the honey cupped in its curve, while another squatted at the base and dug for grubs. The gold leaf shone like a new dawn; the colours as deep and pure as the ocean. It was the most beautiful object I had ever beheld.

I reached the last page with a pang of regret and read the colophon: 'Written by the hand of Libellus, and illuminated by Master Francis.'

Drach's head and shoulders popped up through the hole in the floor that led downstairs. He smiled to see the awe on my face.

'Master Francis, I presume.'

Balanced on the ladder, he executed a small bow.

'How did you come to have this? Surely it belongs in a king's library.'

Kaspar bounded up the ladder and sat down on the end of the mattress. 'A duke's library. The plague took him before he could pay for his commission. His widow would not honour the contract so I kept it. Now it is for you.'

'I cannot—'

He leaned towards me. 'I want you to have it.'

I hugged the book to my chest. In that moment, I would have done anything for him. But his next words were like a knife against my throat.

'Consider it your first wedding present.'

XLI

Near Brussels

When Atheldene said Brussels, Nick had imagined cobbled
streets, gabled roofs and baroque houses. Instead, he seemed
to have brought them to Belgium's version of New Jersey. The
Jaguar left the highway and entered an asphalt maze of
corrugated siding, chain-link fences and harsh floodlights. The
only traffic they passed was trucks.

They turned off the road and stopped at a barrier next to a
hut. Freezing air whipped inside the car as Atheldene lowered
the window to show a guard his pass. Nick heard Emily stir on
the back seat. She'd been asleep since the border.

He checked his watch: 1 a.m. 'Will they let us in?'

'They have clients all over the world,' said Atheldene.
'They're on call twenty-four hours a day.'

Sure enough, the guard handed back the card and the
barrier swung up. Atheldene nosed the car through and
stopped in front of an anonymous grey warehouse. He killed
the engine. After three hours on the highway, the sudden
silence was a relief.

They got out of the car. Nick winced as the cold hit him full blast and wondered if it would affect the playing card. He didn't dare leave it in Atheldene's car.

'I guess they don't need a warehouse to keep the books frozen,' said Nick. Nobody answered. They followed Atheldene up a short flight of concrete steps, their breath misting in the air, and through a door he opened with a keypad. It brought them into a bare room of unpainted breeze blocks. A guard in a brown uniform lounged behind a window in the wall reading a dirty magazine. It didn't look like much protection – until you saw how thick the glass was. When he buzzed the next door open, Nick saw it was four inches of steel.

'Are they expecting trouble?' he asked, as they stepped into an elevator.

'The books and manuscripts inside this place are worth millions,' Atheldene answered crisply. 'A little paranoia is very much in order.'

There were no buttons in the elevator. A synthesised voice said something curt in French; the doors closed; the elevator hummed into motion, descending. Nick glanced at Emily, still swaddled in her red coat. She looked frightened, but managed a tired smile.

The doors opened. Nick stared. His first thought was that he'd stepped into the bowels of a submarine. Everything was bathed in red light, reflecting off row upon row of high glass-fronted cabinets. A low electric hum filled the room.

'Good evening, Herr Atheldene.'

A man in a pinstriped suit with a white lab coat over it walked towards them between the cabinets. He had a round face, floppy hair and a wide moustache which dropped at the corners, giving him an earnest, eager-to-please look. He didn't

263

seem bothered by the strange hour. Perhaps in the constant half-light of this basement it made no difference.

'Dr Haltung.' He shook hands enthusiastically with Atheldene, Nick and Emily. 'Your visit is very, uh, surprising, no?'

'An urgent request from a client,' said Atheldene. 'The Morel collection.'

'Of course, no problem, of course.' The doctor bobbed up and down. 'Please, come.'

They followed him down a corridor between the cabinets. It was an eerie experience: with every step, motion-sensitive lights in the floor came on automatically to guide their way, then faded as they passed. In the cabinets, Nick saw books and piles of paper laid out on shelves like meat in a butcher's shop. Digital readouts above the doors confirmed the temperature inside: -25°C.

Dr Haltung stopped at a bank of cabinets near the middle of the room. He fumbled in his lab coat and pulled out a small hand-held computer. 'The Morel collection.'

'Has anyone been here to look at it since it arrived?' said Nick.

Haltung tapped the computer screen. 'Nobody has accessed this material except our staff. As per your instructions, Herr Atheldene.'

Nick felt the familiar ache of disappointment. Gillian hadn't been there.

'For which exact piece do you want to look, please?'

'Catalogue number 27D,' said Atheldene. 'Anonymous bestiary, fifteenth century.'

'Of course.' Haltung tapped the computer again, pursed his lips, then pressed a button on one of the cabinet doors. Nick heard the *smooch* of a seal being broken, then a hiss of air.

Haltung pulled on a pair of heavy mittens, counted down the shelves, then lifted the volume down and laid it on a wooden trolley.

Nick tried to make out the book in the dim light. It was smaller than he'd expected, about the size of a normal hardback, bound in frayed brown leather. A fur of frost had accumulated along its spine, like ice cream left too long in the freezer. Two bands of gauze strapped the cover shut.

Moving quickly, Haltung wheeled the cart to a glassed-in room at the end of the basement. A bank of overhead lights snapped on the moment he stepped through the door.

Nick rubbed his eyes, startled by the sudden brightness. A huge machine like a turbine or a jet engine stood bolted to the floor in the centre of the room: an enormous cylinder attached to a box, all gleaming stainless steel. Red and green lights glowed on the side, while cables and tubes fed into it from the walls and ceiling.

'The process actually is very simplistic,' Haltung said. 'Like for making instant coffee.' He swung open a door on the front of the machine, revealing another stack of racks like a baker's oven. He put the book inside, then went around the side and began pushing a series of buttons. Lights flickered on the panel.

'Right now, at this moment, the pressure in the chamber is like normal, one thousand millibar. We reduce this to six millibar. This is almost a perfect vacuum.'

He pressed the final button. All at once the machine began to hiss and vibrate; there was an enormous roar like a hairdryer on full blast.

'The vacuum turns the ice at once into gas, without it becoming water. Sublimation, yes? So, the book is dry. The ink does not run, and the cloths keep the pages in alignment. Perfect, no?'

'Can we have a look now?'

Haltung tutted. 'The book is still at negative twenty degrees Celsius. If you try to turn the page it snaps in your hand. Now we must restore the normal pressure and the normal temperature of plus twenty degrees.'

'How long will that take?'

'Maybe two hours.' Haltung stepped away from the machine. The gale-force blast died away, replaced with a low whirring. 'You want some coffee while you wait?'

'Do you make that in the machine too?' Nick asked.

Haltung missed the joke. 'We use Nescafé.' He picked up a phone on the wall and dialled a number. He waited.

'Perhaps the guard has gone to the toilet.' He put the phone down, looking vaguely puzzled. 'I go up. Please, wait here.'

He left the room. Nick followed his progress through the red-lit warehouse, watching the glow of the floor lights rippling ahead of him like a bow wave, then fading behind him. Haltung stepped into the elevator and vanished.

Nick wandered back over to the machine and peered through the porthole. The book lay on the shelf, inert. The crust of ice had vanished. A pair of gauges next to the door showed the temperature and the pressure creeping up.

'It's incredible, when you think about it,' said Emily behind him. 'Five or six hundred years ago, that same book was sheets of vellum and a pot of ink on a desk somewhere in Paris. It's survived who knows how many kings, wars, owners . . . It's been soaked through, frozen, freeze-dried with all the technology the twenty-first century can throw at it . . . and after all that, the original words the author wrote will still be there.'

'If we're lucky,' said Atheldene.

A wave of tiredness hit Nick hard. It was almost two in the morning – and the jet lag still hadn't finished messing with his body. There was no sign of Haltung and his coffee.

'I'm going for a walk,' he announced.

Atheldene looked as though he was going to argue, but made do with a grunted, 'Don't touch anything.'

The door opened automatically to let Nick through into the red cocoon of the warehouse. He let himself wander along the corridors of frozen books, hypnotised by the way the floor lights seemed to spill ahead of him. He peered through the doors as he passed, the bundled books on the shelves, and wondered what lay within the tattered covers. Could there be pages that no one had ever read, fossils locked in the permafrost waiting for discovery? Could that be what Gillian had found?

He came around a corner and saw solid concrete: he'd come to the far end of the warehouse. He ought to go back, he supposed. He turned.

Almost at the same moment, a pool of yellow light appeared halfway along the front wall as the elevator doors slid open. Haltung stepped out. He wasn't carrying any coffee – which was just as well, for he was trembling so badly he would surely have spilled it.

A black-gloved hand poked out of the elevator, holding a gun to his spine.

XLII

Strassburg

The screw tightened. The platen wheezed as it pressed the damp paper. We held it a moment then raised it back. Drach peeled the paper away from the plate and draped it over a rope strung between two beams.

'Twenty-eight.'

Twenty-eight. I let go the handle of the press and walked over to examine it. In a sense there was nothing to see: it was exactly the same as the previous twenty-seven. But to me, that was everything. I gazed on it like a parent on his child. Better than a child, for a son is only an imperfect copy of the father. This was flawless.

It was not beautiful. The text was monotonous, hard to read, for the steel punches had taken me so long to cut that we only had upper-case letters. There was none of the variation of size or weight that a scribe would have applied – except for one flamboyant initial that Kaspar had carved into the copper plate separately. For the twenty-eighth time I looked at it and sighed. My drab rows of words whose chief merit was their discipline, against the vivid curves and wild tendrils of his single letter. It captured something.

Kaspar loaded the next sheet of paper and we took up our positions on opposite sides of the screw handle. These were golden times for me: quiet afternoons locked away in our cellar, the two of us working as one in our common purpose. In these moments I could almost forget how it was paid for.

'I met an Italian once, a merchant who had travelled as far as Cathay,' said Kaspar. 'Do you know what he found there?'

'Men with the heads of dogs and feet like mushrooms?'

Kaspar didn't laugh. Like many quick-witted men, he was impatient with others' humour.

'Instead of gold and silver, they pay each other in paper.'

I laughed, and nodded to the back of the room. A ream of paper stood baled up on a workbench waiting for the press. 'We should go to Cathy. We would be rich men. We could use our paper to buy their silver, transport it back here to pay for more paper, use that to buy yet more silver in Cathay . . .' I looked at him suspiciously, wondering if this was another of his complicated jokes. 'Surely if it were that easy every paper merchant in Italy would be rich as the Pope by now.'

'Perhaps.' He shrugged. 'I think that their princes must mark their paper with some symbol, as our kings mint coins.'

'You can melt a king's head off the coin and it will still be gold. Scrub it off a piece of paper and it is only paper. Burn it and you have nothing at all.' I reversed the screw and pulled the sheet off. 'Twenty-nine. I think your merchant spun you a traveller's yarn.'

'Is it so hard to believe? What are we doing here if not the same? We take pieces of paper that cost us a penny a dozen, and sell them for three silver pennies each to the Church. They in turn will sell them for sixpence. Has the nature of the paper changed?'

This was facetious. 'Men are not paying for the paper. They are buying expiation of their sins. The paper is just a receipt which the Church provides.'

'Yet without the paper there is no transaction. Do you think that on the last day we will rise up clutching fistfuls of indulgences and present them to St Peter as if we were cashing an annuity?'

'Only God knows.'

'If God knows, why does He need a piece of paper to remind Him? Men need the paper because they are credulous fools.'

It always surprised me how Kaspar could speak of men thus, as a species apart from himself.

'The paper is blessed by the Church.'

'Because it knows men will pay more if they are given something in return. Even if it is worth no more than the so-called money of Cathay.' He gave me his peculiar smile, at once conspiratorial and condescending. 'You know this is true. This is the alchemy you hope will make you rich: taking something worthless and making it valuable.'

'If it succeeds.'

I turned back to the press. In the time we had been talking, we had run off three more indulgences. I pulled the fresh copy from the press and checked it, still in thrall to its perfection. How many times before I grew tired of it? A hundred? A thousand? Ten thousand?

Yet even as I savoured that delight, I felt it ebbing away. I examined the paper more closely. The letters were all there, each in its proper place. But they looked less defined than before, like stone worn smooth by many feet. I rubbed my eyes, wondering if too many hours in the basement had dulled my sight.

'What is it?'

I stood under the window. The stippled glass cast wispy shadows over the sheet, but the lettering was clear to see. I was not mistaken. The edges had blurred and spread, thickening each letter. Some had become almost indecipherable blots. Even Drach's capital flowed less smoothly.

I found the first page we had printed and compared it. Its text was crisp, far more legible than the other. I showed it to Kaspar.

'Perhaps we did not press hard enough.'

We printed another, then again. By the third attempt we could not doubt it. With each pressing the lines grew subtly less distinct. Eventually this gradual degeneration would render the text illegible.

I looked around the room, at thirty-odd indulgences hanging on ropes or stacked on our table. They taunted me with their illusory perfection.

But I had more urgent concerns.

'Why has this happened?'

Drach leaned over the press, pushing his fingers into the grooves of the copper plate. 'Copper is soft; the pressure we need to make the imprint is immense. Each copy we make squeezes the plate and deforms it.'

'Is there nothing we can do?'

'Make another plate.'

'It took Dunne a week to make that.' I did a rough calculation in my head. 'I paid him three gulden for the labour and the copper sheet. If a sheet can only produce forty or fifty indulgences for three pennies apiece, we would lose a full gulden on every batch. Even before we count the cost of ink, paper, rent . . .'

'You sound like a merchant.'

'One of us has to.' I rounded on him. 'Why didn't you tell me this would happen?'

'I never printed enough of the cards to find out.'

I slumped down onto the floor. The promise of Ennelin's dowry had been enough to convince Stoltz the moneylender to extend me more credit, but I had already drawn all that I could. Even when I married her I would need most of the capital simply to repay my current obligations.

I picked up one of the indulgences that had fallen to the floor beside me. Tears blurred the writing to nothing. I had mortgaged my life to pursue this project because I believed I could make something valuable.

Now all I had was paper.

XLIII

Near Brussels

The man pushed Haltung forward and stepped out of the elevator. Another man followed. Both were dressed in black leather jackets and black balaclavas that hid their faces. Both carried guns.

One of them leaned forward and muttered something to Haltung, who pointed a trembling arm towards the machine room at the end of the warehouse. The two gunmen exchanged a couple of words; one gestured the other to go around the side of the room. Instinctively, Nick took a step back.

That was his mistake. The floor lights by his feet had faded out while he stood still; now they sensed his movement and immediately came on – not bright, but enough to betray him in the red murk of the basement. The two gunmen spun round and saw Nick; one of them lifted his pistol, but in that moment Haltung wrestled free of his grip and started running towards the machine room. The gunman hesitated, just long enough for Nick to fling himself down the corridor to his left.

It was the same nightmare as on the roof of his apartment.

Shots rang out, though Nick had no way of knowing who they were aimed at. He ran down the corridor between the cabinets, reached a corner and turned right. A luminous path spread on the floor ahead of him. He swore, but there was nothing he could do. He made another left and another right, then stopped and waited for the lights to go out. He must be about halfway to the machine room. But what if the gunmen got there first?

The footlights faded and left Nick in half-darkness, leaning against the cold glass, breathing hard. He tried to twist around without moving his feet and scanned the space above the cabinets for the telltale glow of movement.

He was so busy looking up he almost didn't see it coming. Only a sixth sense – perhaps a reflection in the glass, or something in the corner of his eye – saved him. He glanced back the way he had come and froze. The lights were coming on, rippling forward one by one as the footsteps advanced. They spilled around the corner and lapped towards his feet like a rising tide. Then stopped.

The intruder must be just around the corner. Did he know Nick was there? Was he waiting to see if the lights came on again? Nick's body screamed at him to run, though he knew it would mean certain death. But he couldn't stand there.

The lights were still on. Nick could move without being detected, but only towards the danger. He fought back the fear.

Terrified that the lights would fade, he edged towards the corner of the cabinets, like a child shuffling towards the end of a high diving board. He crouched down, feeling the warmth of the lights on his face.

The lights flashed up again as the gunman stepped around the corner. Nick didn't wait: he pushed off on his feet and launched himself forward. The man fired, but too high. Nick crashed into him and brought him down, then rolled away. He wouldn't win any sort of fight. He kicked the gun out of the man's hand, then scrambled to his feet and ran.

Panic took over. Nick zigzagged through the cabinets, trying to work his way towards the machine room. He was trapped in a maze, unable to see more than an arm's-length ahead or behind. Three more shots came, three bolts of lightning, terrifyingly loud in the low-ceilinged room. The last one rang on in his ears; the flash echoed in the darkness. Had he been hit? Was this what it felt like to die?

It was an alarm. Perhaps one of the bullets had hit something sensitive. It was no help to Nick. The alarm lights strobed the room; the bells drowned any hope of hearing his enemies. At the far end of the aisle, steel shutters were descending from the ceiling, blocking out the glass walls of the machine room. They were already below head height and slithering down with ominous speed. Nick had no choice. He hurled himself forward and sprinted down the corridor, praying there was no one with a gun behind him. All the floor lights were on full blast now, while a recorded voice barked urgent instructions he could neither hear nor understand. The grinding shutters and trilling bells were all around him, while in the background rose an enormous whine like a jet engine revving for take-off.

The doors sensed him coming and parted automatically. With the shutter closing, the opening was little more than a foot high: he flung himself onto the floor and slid underneath it.

The shutter touched the floor and snapped taut. Nick looked around, shivering with shock. Atheldene and Emily were peering out from behind the machine. There was no sign of the gunmen.

He pushed himself to his knees. He didn't trust himself to

275

stand. 'What happened?' He had to shout to make himself heard above the roar coming from behind the shutters.

'The smoke from the gunshots set off the fire alarm,' said Atheldene. 'It's on a hair trigger – as you can imagine, given the contents of that vault.'

'Why didn't the sprinklers come on?'

'Don't have them. Spraying water all over those books would be almost as bad as burning them. They seal the storage room, then suck out all the air.' He rapped his fist on the freeze-drying machine. 'Much like an overblown version of this.'

Nick rubbed his head. 'Lucky I got out when I did.'

'Quite.'

'What happened to Haltung?'

'They killed him,' said Emily. Her face was drained. 'Those men, whoever they were. They shot him.'

On the far side of the shutter, the roar of air died away. The alarm bell had gone off – or perhaps, Nick thought, sound couldn't travel in a vacuum.

'What do we do now?'

Atheldene nodded to the steel shutters. 'Nothing. The shutters can only be released from upstairs. Even if we could open them, it would be a bad idea. It's like outer space on the other side.'

'Then how do we get out?' Nick looked around. There were no doors except the one to the main vault.

'We'll have to wait for the police to arrive. It shouldn't be long.'

That was no comfort to Nick. He might be in Belgium, but the moment the cops ran his name through a computer they'd surely find out everything about him. He stared wildly around the room. There had to be an air vent, an escape hatch, a service tunnel. Anything. All he saw was a concrete prison. The only hint of a break was behind the machine, where a two-foot pipe led into the wall.

Nick examined it. 'Almost a perfect vacuum', Haltung had said. So the air had to go somewhere. There was a steel coupling where the pipe joined the wall, studded with four wing nuts. Nick ran over and twisted one of them. It didn't budge.

He searched for something to hit it with and found a fire axe in a recess in the wall. He grabbed it, turned it round and hammered the nut with the flat end of the axe head. It shuddered, then shifted a few degrees. He kept going, bashing desperately until he had turned it a couple of rotations. The bolt itself must have been an inch thick, but now it was loose enough to be turned by hand.

'Over here,' he called to Emily. He pointed to the bolt. 'See if you can get that out.'

She understood at once. Three more to go. Nick looked back at the shutters and wondered what was going on behind them. Had the police arrived? Had the men in balaclavas been asphyxiated, or had they escaped like he had before the vault was sealed?

The fourth bolt was the hardest of all. By the time he had it unlocked, Emily had removed the other three. He knelt beside her, their hands fumbling over each other like children with a Christmas present. Despite the chill air, Nick was sweating.

The bolt came free. Nick leapt back, expecting the pipe to drop like a stone. It didn't move.

On the other side of the room, something banged against the shutters. In fury and frustration, Nick lifted his leg and slammed his foot against the pipe. It burst free of the coupling with a pop and fell to the ground, just missing his toes. A dark hole yawned in the wall. When he put his hand up to it, he felt a current of cold air.

'Better than nothing,' he muttered uncertainly. He looked back at the machine. 'Is the book done?'

Atheldene looked at the dials. 'It'll be at least another hour until it comes up to room temperature.'

'We don't have time.'

'What do you mean?' Atheldene grabbed his arm. 'That book's priceless. You can't yank it out halfway through the process.'

Nick shook him off and ran around to the control panel. He scanned the buttons until he found a large red knob labelled NOTAUSSCHALTUNG. Emergency shutdown. He slammed his palm against it. The whirring noise inside the machine died away. The lock clicked. He opened the door and slid out the book. It was cold to the touch, but not hard.

I don't even know why I'm taking it, he thought to himself. But someone thought it was worth killing for.

'It doesn't belong to you,' Atheldene protested. 'Just wait for the police.'

'I can't.'

Nick put the book in his backpack with the card and handed it to Emily. Then he pushed himself head first into the hole. He was in a narrow concrete tunnel, barely wide enough to fit his shoulders. It went straight back for a few yards, then stopped in a sheer wall.

'Air's still got to go somewhere.'

He flapped a hand above his head and felt emptiness. He squirmed around until he lay on his back and looked up. A few feet overhead, he saw a lattice of bars silhouetted against the city glow in the sky. He tucked up his knees and pushed off, wriggling up the shaft until he could touch the grille. It lifted free without resistance. He slid it back, hauled himself through the opening and flopped onto frozen grass.

He'd come out on the side of the building. While Emily pulled herself out after him, Nick got up and edged his way around to the front. A body lay sprawled on the asphalt beside the guard hut, another by the steps going up to the front door. A black Lexus 4x4 with Italian plates was parked diagonally across the car park, blocking in Atheldene's Jaguar.

Sirens wailed in the frozen night – distant, but racing ever closer. How was he going to get out of there? There were no other vehicles in the car park and no signs of life at any of the adjacent units. Deep in the heart of the sprawling industrial estate, they wouldn't get far on foot.

And that was when he heard the music.

At first he thought it was a hallucination, his ears still ringing from the noise in the basement. But it didn't go away, or start repeating itself the way snatches of songs usually did. He listened. It was Bob Marley, just about the most incongruous thing he could have imagined. It seemed to be coming from the Lexus.

One track ended and another began. Nick looked closer and saw there was exhaust coming from the Lexus' tailpipe, clouding the night. Was there someone inside? He crept closer, trying to see beyond the headrest. A floodlight on the wall beamed through the windscreen: if there had been anyone inside, it would have made a perfect silhouette. He couldn't see anyone. And the engine was running.

He slid alongside it, keeping below the windows, and reached for the handle of the driver's door. With a deep breath, he yanked it open.

Hot air spilled out of the warm interior. The car was empty. Nick jumped into the driver's seat and threw the gear lever into reverse. The accelerator was more sensitive than he was used to: the car jolted backwards with a squeal of tyres. In the rear-view mirror, he saw Emily running across the grass from the open air shaft carrying his bag. Then, suddenly, she seemed to trip. She pitched forward on her hands and knees and disappeared from view.

Nick looked around again. The front door to the warehouse had burst open; another man in a balaclava was standing on the steps with a gun in his hand. He looked around wildly; the sirens were getting louder.

Emily pulled open a back door and hurled herself onto the seat. The moment Nick saw she was in the car, he gunned the engine. In his panic and unfamiliarity, he almost rammed into a lamp post; swung away, only to veer towards the guard hut. His erratic driving probably saved him. The passenger window exploded as the gunman on the steps finally realised what was happening; a shower of glass sprayed through the car, slicing Nick's arms and face, but the bullet went wide. Nick barely noticed. He was through the gates. He swung the car onto the access road and hit the gas.

XLIV

Strassburg

'I feel honour bound to tell you, madam, that I am no longer as secure a prospect as I was. I have made certain investments which have not returned what I hoped. These have incurred debts which will divert most, if not all, of my income. Under the circumstances, I would not blame you if you preferred to break off my suit of marriage for your daughter.'

Ellewibel's face never changed as she listened to my rehearsed words.

'That is very good of you, Herr Gensfleisch. Such honesty does you credit. Indeed, it only confirms the good opinion I have formed of your character. For that reason alone I would never stand in the way of this match. My late husband was a merchant: I know how fortunes may rise and fall. It is faith and character that make a man what he is. In those I know my daughter will not be disappointed.'

I bowed deeply, like a man with a knife shoved in his belly. 'Thank you.'

I stood at the table in the barn of my house in St Argobast and looked at the wreckage of my endeavours. Kaspar was in Strassburg painting an altar panel; I was alone with my failures. The copper sheet that I had punch-stamped and three of the indulgences that came off it; a few bottles of ink; twenty-six steel rods tipped with the letters of the alphabet; a stack of unused paper weighted down with a stone. I felt an echo of that last morning in Paris. I had sealed all my hopes and labours into that crucible, heated it in the fire seven times. Yet when Tristan smashed it open with his sword the metals had become sludge. Nothing.

Deep in my soul, a familiar urge began to beat – the same instinct that a rabbit feels when it scents a fox, or a traveller when he hears a branch snap in the forest. It was the instinct that had carried me away from Mainz, from Cologne, from Basle, from Paris – wherever danger threatened. But now I was almost forty, and forty is not twenty. I had a house, a position. I could not live the life of a vagrant again. And I could not bear to leave Kaspar, the only friend I ever had.

I was trapped. Not by bars or walls, but by remorseless circumstance. A helpless rage welled inside me. I slammed my fist on the table. Glass and metal rattled; one of the ink bottles tipped over and spilled across the worktop. It lapped against the scattered punches coating the tips black.

I stared. As if in a dream, I lifted one of the punches, upended it and stabbed it onto the tabletop. The table shivered, as if the timber itself understood the import of that moment. I lifted the punch away. A single mark revealed itself, blazed on the wood. The letter A.

I dipped the punch in the pool of ink again and made another, then another. Soon I had dozens of them stamped across the table. Punch and form, male and female. One enters the other and reproduces.

I ran across the yard to the stone shed. The fire had been cold for weeks: I had plenty of coal but no kindling. I went back to the barn, gathered up the remaining indulgences and tore them into strips. I knelt before the hearth and scraped sparks over them with my steel. The edges began to smoulder. I blew, coaxing the fire into life, burning away my failures.

On a shelf by the window I found a bar of lead I had used to blacken the ink. When the fire burned hot, I set the lead over it in an iron bowl. It softened and buckled, melting like butter. I stirred it with a ladle and watched carefully: if it overheated, it would stick too much to the mould.

I laid the copper plate on the bench, among the pestles and vessels we had used for the ink. I dipped the ladle in the liquid lead and scooped a small amount over the copper. Steam hissed as the metals met, the molten lead channelling its way into the grooves cut by the letters. I tapped it to loose the air bubbles.

When the lead had cooled, I worked a knife under it and prised it out of the copper. My hands were trembling; I dared not apply much pressure for fear of bending the soft metal. At last I had it out, a flat slug about the size of my thumb. I carried it back to the barn, dipped it in the ink and pressed it against a fresh sheet of paper with the palm of my hand. I held it there, almost too frightened to see what I had made.

At last I pulled it away.

EGO TE ABSOLVO

It was written backwards, for it is the nature of such impressions that the child is the mirror of the parent. But I could read it easily enough. The words shouted into my soul.

I FREE YOU.

XLV

Near Brussels

Three police cars raced down the road towards the warehouse. They didn't see the black Lexus parked down a side alley in the shadow of an industrial gasses unit. Nick waited until they were well past, then pulled out cautiously.

'How did they find us?' asked Emily. Her voice sounded small and lost. 'We didn't even know we were going there until a few hours ago.'

Nick gripped the steering wheel tighter. Ice-cold air was blasting through the shattered window; the dashboard readout said the temperature outside was ten below. He turned the heater up as far as it would go and aimed the vents towards his body.

'What happened to Atheldene?'

'He stayed behind. He wanted to wait for the police.'

'Great,' said Nick. 'At least he can tell them that I didn't do it this time.'

An ambulance blazed past them in the opposite direction and he glanced down, trying to shield his face.

'So where are we going?'

'Somewhere we can examine that book. Do we need any special equipment or anything?'

'Books are robust. If it survived the defrosting, it should be OK to touch. Obviously a temperature-controlled, stable-humidity environment would be better than a moving car with the heating on full and an arctic gale coming through the window.'

Nick saw a gas station ahead. The lights were out, the pumps like standing stones in the darkness. He pulled into the forecourt and parked behind the kiosk, out of sight of the road. Emily came forward into the passenger seat.

'Let's find out.'

He was too nervous to touch the book himself: he gave it to Emily. She laid it on her lap and peeled open the cover. Nick stared at the creamy vellum, cast yellow by the car's map light.

The manuscript began on the first page.

' "*Et si contigerit ut queratur a venatoribus, venit ad eum odor venatorum, et cum cauda sua tetigit posttergum vestigia sua . . .*" ' read Emily. ' "And if it happens that the lion is pursued by hunters, he smells their scent and erases his tracks behind him with his tail. Then the hunters cannot trace him." '

She frowned. 'That's not how the bestiaries begin.'

But Nick was hardly listening. Halfway down the page a small illustration intruded on the text. Damp had smudged it so that the picture seemed to melt out into the writing, but it was still distinct. A lion sitting up on its haunches, one paw lifted in the air, staring across the page with teeth bared in an imperious glare.

'It's the same as the card,' he breathed.

Nick watched as Emily turned the pages, through the

fabulous menagerie of beasts that inhabited the book. Not every page was illustrated, and some had been damaged worse than others – by the damp, or by other ordeals in their long history. Many of the animals were creatures Nick had never imagined: birds that hatched from trees; a beast with a bull's head, a ram's horns and a horse's body; griffins, basilisks and unicorns. But not all were so fantastical. Two cats, a black and a tabby, chased a mouse across a kitchen floor while a buxom cook slurped wine by the fire. An ox pulled a plough across an autumnal field. A stag stood on a knoll in the forest, while a bear grubbed in the dirt.

Nick tried not to show his excitement. He knew the bear – and he was pretty sure he recognised the stag from one of the deer suit cards.

'What does it say about the bear?' he asked.

' "Bear cubs appear from the womb without form, as tiny white lumps of flesh without eyes, which their mothers lick into shape." ' Emily read the Latin effortlessly. ' "They crave nothing more than honey. If ever they attack bulls, they know the best areas to strike are the nose or the horns – usually the nose, for the pain is worst in the most sensitive place." '

Nick sat back in the driver's seat. With the engine off, the car had become icy cold again. 'I think the lion was closer to the mark, obliterating its traces so hunters can't track it. That's Gillian. We've got her book, we've got her card – and we've still got no idea what she found in them. And people keep trying to kill us.'

Emily went quiet. Nick gave her a sideways glance.

'What are you thinking?'

'There is someone who could help us. Someone who could analyse this book to see what Gillian might have found. Where it took her.'

'Who?'

Emily drummed her fingers on the door handle. 'His name's Brother Jerome. He's a Jesuit – or used to be. He's an expert in medieval books. He was . . . He taught me at the Sorbonne. He's retired now.'

'Does he live near here? Is he trustworthy?'

'Near the German border. Probably about an hour's drive from here. As for trustworthy . . . *You* can trust him, I suppose.'

Nick craned around and stared at her.

'If there's something you need to tell me, then tell me. If this guy's not above board, I'm not going anywhere near him.'

'You can trust him,' Emily repeated. She sounded close to tears. 'It's just . . . *awkward.* I was his student, once. He made a pass at me; I reported him. He lost his job.'

Now it was Nick's turn to stare at the dashboard in embarrassment. 'If you think—'

'No. He's the only man who can help us.'

Before they left, Nick found a tyre lever under the back seat and smashed out the remained shards of broken glass from the window. From a distance it made the car look a bit more reputable. Then he started the engine and pulled out of the gas station. He could see the highway ahead: trucks thundering across a bridge in the night. Blue signs pointed left and right. Nick slowed the car.

'Which way?'

Italy

Cesare Gemato sat behind his desk and stared through the windows of his eighth-floor office. Rain beaded on the bulletproof glass; beyond, the ships crossing the Bay of Naples were mere smears of grey against a grey sea.

'*Nessun dorma! Nessun dorma!*'

287

Pavarotti burst into life on his phone. Gemato saw the number flashing on the screen and grabbed it. He listened for a minute and said nothing, though his knuckles went white.

'OK,' he said, and hung up.

He spent five minutes delaying what he had to do next. There weren't many people he was afraid to call, but Nevado was one. Perhaps the only one.

He picked up the black phone on his desk – the secure line – and dialled the number from memory.

The voice was there at once. 'What happened?'

'My men followed them to the warehouse you told them. They . . .' He swallowed. 'They were caught by some security device. Two died; one managed to get away. The man and the woman escaped.'

He waited for a tirade of abuse. Instead, all he heard was a soft voice rasping, 'What are you going to do about it?'

'They stole a vehicle belonging to my men. Like all our vehicles, it is fitted with a tracking system. We have traced it to a suburb of Liège near the German border.'

'Did the American take the book?'

'The police came too soon for us to find out.'

Gemato waited.

'I will go myself,' said the voice. 'Have one of your men meet me there.'

One hundred miles to the north-west, the old man put down the phone and stared at the office wall. There were rooms in this building decorated by Raphael and Michelangelo; others that housed marvels from an art collection built up over almost two thousand years. Nevado could have had any of them to decorate his office. Yet he had chosen a small, spare room overlooking an obscure courtyard, and the only

288

decoration on the wall was an ivory crucifix. He contemplated it for a moment.

There were records he could have consulted, books and files – he did not trust his secrets to computers – but he did not need to. Somewhere in the Vatican's vast archive was an index card with Emily Sutherland's name on it. He had studied it only yesterday. It had referenced another file in another basement, this one much fatter. He had read that too. He knew who Emily Sutherland wanted to see near Liège.

He buzzed his secretary.

'I need to travel to Liège. At once, and in private.'

Near Liège, Belgium

Nick had never thought about monks retiring. If he ever had, he'd have assumed they just carried on until they died, like the pope. He certainly wouldn't have guessed the reality. Brother Jerome had swapped the Society of Jesus for the drab mortification of the suburbs: a cul-de-sac of brick and pebble-dashed bungalows on the edge of a small town. It felt like the end of the world.

Nick parked the car against a hedge to hide the broken window. Low clouds were holding back the dawn; the world was sunk in shadows, a thousand shades of grey. A woman in a quilted jacket walked a terrier along the opposite pavement; she shot them a suspicious glare as she passed. Otherwise, the street was empty.

Emily led them up a path to a white front door and rang the bell. Nick rubbed his hands together. The cold air was the only thing keeping him awake right now.

Emily rang the bell again. A second later, Nick saw movement behind the blurred glass panels in the door. A voice mumbled at them to be patient while keys jangled and locks clicked. The door cracked open on its chain and a gaunt face peered through the gap.

His eyes widened. 'Emily. Was I to expect you?' He noticed Nick. 'And a friend. Who is he, please?'

If Andy Warhol had ever taken holy orders and retired to Belgium, perhaps this was what he'd have looked like. Brother Jerome was a thin, bony man with a mop of white hair that almost touched his eyes. He wore a Chinese-patterned bathrobe, loosely knotted so that when he walked his bare legs were exposed right up to his thighs. Nick had the unpleasant suspicion he was naked underneath it.

He unchained the door and kissed Emily on both cheeks; she stiffened, but didn't pull away. Nick got a nod, but Jerome was already leading them into a room off the hall.

Nick looked around in amazement. The room was a mess. Books and papers overflowed from shelves that had been screwed to every available inch of wall. Mould frothed on the half-empty mugs that clustered around the battered easy chair in the middle of the room, which had several more towers of books wobbling uncertainly on the arms.

Jerome headed for the kitchen. 'You would like some coffee?'

No one else did. Through the door, Nick saw him boiling a kettle.

'So – Emily. It is a long time, yes? How have you been?'

'Fine.'

'I have thought perhaps I never see you again.'

'We've got a book we'd like you to look at.'

Jerome came out of the kitchen with a steaming mug. It looked as though it hadn't been washed up in weeks.

'You want to give this to me?'

'We want you to help us.'

The words had an extraordinary effect on Jerome. His bowed head suddenly snapped up with a furious stare; his body went rigid.

'Do you know why I am here?' He flung out an arm at the dilapidated living room. Hot coffee spilled over his fingers and dribbled onto the carpet, but he didn't notice. 'Do you know the reason of this exile? Do you?'

Emily bowed her head. A tear ran down her cheek. Nick moved closer to protect her, but neither she nor Jerome noticed. He had no part in their story.

'I'm sorry,' Emily whispered. 'If I could go back . . .'

'You would do the same. And so would I.'

As abruptly as it had flared up, his anger died away. He stepped forward and wrapped his arms around Emily. Her face was hidden from Nick, but she looked as though she was hugging a corpse.

Jerome stroked her hair. 'Let us no longer deceive ourselves with remembrance of our past pleasures. We only spoil our lives and sour the sweets of solitude.'

Emily pulled back – gently – and straightened her hair. 'I'm sorry to disturb you. But we need your help. And . . . I thought you would appreciate this.'

'Let me see.'

At a nod from Emily, Nick pulled the defrosted bestiary out of his bag. Jerome licked his lips and held out his hands. 'Please.'

Nick gave him the book. Jerome almost snatched it from him. He lifted it up like a priest reading the gospel and examined it.

'The binding is of the seventeenth century.' He turned it in his hands. 'Calfskin leather with blind stamping, possibly German workmanship.'

'I thought it was supposed to be fifteenth century,' Nick interrupted. Brother Jerome fixed him with a scornful look.

'It has been replaced. Bindings wear out faster than pages. As bodies fail before the soul.'

He carried the book to a wooden bureau in an adjoining room and sat down. From a drawer, he extracted a foam cushion and a pair of thin gloves. He pulled them on over his bony fingers, a pathologist preparing for an autopsy, and laid the book on the desk. He slipped a finger under the cover and gently tugged, peeling it away from the page beneath to rest open on the cushion.

The illuminated lion stared off the page. Nick glanced at Jerome to see if he recognised it, and caught the old man giving him a sly glance from under his white fringe. Neither said what the other was thinking.

Jerome thumbed the crease of the page. 'This book has not been well preserved.'

'It was in a library that got flooded.'

'Beyond the obvious. There is a gutter here.'

Nick stared, not sure what he was looking for. 'What's a gutter?'

'The bones of a missing page.' Jerome pushed the cover and the first page further apart. Nick saw the edge of a thin strip of parchment, barely protruding from the spine.

'A page has been cut out.'

'Is that normal?'

'Depressingly so. It is hard to steal a book but very easy to take a page. An individual leaf can fetch thousands of dollars. All these ancient manuscripts are worth far more in pieces than as a whole.'

'It's been going on for centuries,' Emily added.

'This one is not so long ago.' Jerome pointed to a series of dark smudgings on the topmost page. 'You see here the marks where the missing page has soaked through. It has only been taken after the flood.'

Emily and Nick looked at each other, daring each other to state the obvious. Jerome watched with a wicked smile, enjoying their discomfort.

'Gillian was a professional who loved books,' said Nick at last. 'She'd never have mutilated it like this. She worked in museums, for God's sake.'

Emily avoided his gaze. 'It would be nice to know what was on that first page,' was all she said.

'Maybe we find more.'

Jerome fumbled in a drawer of the desk and brought out a thin metal tube that looked like a pen. He twisted the end, and a pale beam of purplish light glowed from the tip.

'Ultraviolet,' he said. He shone it on the inside of the cover. To Nick's amazement, dark letters appeared on the stiff board, emerging under the light like hidden runes. Unlike the dense bestiary text, this was written in a thin, spidery hand.

'How did that get there?' Nick's voice was barely a whisper.

'It was written by the book's owner. When somebody else got it – by gift or purchase, or perhaps by stealing – he erased the mark of the first ownership. But the trace remains still.'

'What does it say?'

Still holding the light, Jerome picked up a magnifying glass to read it more closely.

' "*Cest livre est a moy, Armand Comte de Lorraine.*" '

'What does that mean?'

'It means it belonged to the Count of Lorraine. Once. The Count of Lorraine possessed one of the greatest libraries of early modernity.'

Nick didn't know what Jerome meant by 'modernity', but guessed it didn't fit with anything he thought of as modern.

'What happened to it?'

Jerome shrugged. 'It was lost. The Count's heirs sold his collection piece by piece, or allowed unscrupulous men to loot it. What was left, I think, passed to the city archives of Strasbourg in the nineteenth century.'

Page by page, Jerome's gloved fingers worked their way through the bestiary until he reached the end of the book. There was no illustration on the last page, only a couple of lines of text and a rectangular brown stain on the parchment about the size of a postcard. Nick swallowed hard and fought back the urge to pull out the playing card to overlay it. It looked as if it would fit perfectly.

'Something has been stuck in here,' said Jerome. He flicked another suspicious glance at them.

Emily leaned closer, holding her body very deliberately away from Jerome's. 'Is there an explicit? Any indication of who wrote this book, or whom for?'

'It says, "Written by the hand of Libellus, and illuminated by Master Francis. He also made another book of beasts using a new art of writing."'

'What does that mean?'

'Libellus and Francis are pseudonyms that the scribe and the illuminator used,' said Emily. '*Libellus* is Latin for "little book"; Francis is probably a reference to St Francis, playing on the fact that he's mastered the animals.'

'But there have been two hands,' said Jerome. 'The first sentence and the second have been written by different men with different inks.'

Nick studied the aged writing. He was pleasantly surprised to find he could see what Jerome meant. He could even pick out some of the words: *Libellus – Franciscus – illuminatus.* The first line was written in the same black script as the rest of the book; the second sentence appeared to have been added in more ragged writing in brown ink. Was it the same hand that had pasted in the card, he wondered?

Jerome picked up the ultraviolet penlight again and scanned the back cover. Nick watched closely and saw nothing – but something seemed to catch Emily's eye.

'What's that?'

'Nothing.' Jerome put the light down and looked round defiantly. 'I thought perhaps there was another *ex libris*, but there is nothing.'

'On the page,' Emily insisted. Before Jerome could react, she snatched up the penlight. She held it almost parallel to the page, so that the beam barely touched the surface.

'Hard point.'

Nick squinted. For the second time that morning, he was looking at letters that had not been there a moment before. But these were not faded ink brought out of a dark background; instead, they seemed to be written inside the parchment itself.

'What do they say?'

XLVI

Strassburg

'Written by the hand of Libellus, and illuminated by Master Francis.'

I sat on the floor, resting against a timber post, and read the inscription for the hundredth time. I held the book like a chalice, a talisman. I could have sold it and paid off half my debts at once, but I would never do that.

Kaspar, fiddling with the press, glanced over. I knew he liked to watch me reading his book. I angled it down.

'What is that?'

His eyes were sharp as ever. I turned the book around and raised it so he could see what I had done. The blank space underneath the explicit was now filled by the card I had pasted in: the eight of beasts, the map that led me to Kaspar.

He smiled. 'You are a collector.'

'A devotee.'

'You're right to hang on to the card. There will not be any others.'

A confused look.

'The plate is gone. I melted it down and sold it.'

I was aghast that something so beautiful should have been lost for ever. 'All of them? The whole deck?'

'About half.' He laughed at the expression on my face, though I did not find it funny.

'Johann, you saw what happened to our own plate. Even in a few dozen pressings it decayed. The same would have happened to the cards. Nothing endures.'

'You shouldn't have done it,' I insisted.

He clapped me on the shoulder. 'Some survive in Dunne's workshop. Speaking of whom, I must go. He has some work for me.'

I wrapped the bestiary in its cloth and followed Kaspar out. My joy in the book had gone. *Nothing endures.* Except failure, I thought – and my engagement to Ennelin.

I made my way through Strassburg to an apothecary's shop where my credit was still tolerated. The lead cast I had made of Dunne's plate barely survived my experiment: the metal was so soft it blurred the moment it touched the paper. But, like the first print I ever saw from Konrad Schmidt's ring in Cologne, I had recognised something in it. I knew I could make it stronger. Already, by alloying it with tin and antimony I found I could make a good clean cast. The hope was just enough to hold off the full weight of my dread whenever I thought of Ennelin.

She was still lurking in my thoughts when I passed the *Rathaus*, the city hall. I almost missed her. The court was in session, and crowds thronged the street outside waiting for verdicts. I glimpsed her coming down the steps and almost dismissed it as a manifestation of my imagination. But it was enough to make me look again, just in time to confirm it was indeed her. Her mother was behind her. They stepped into the crowd and vanished before I could reach them.

I found someone who knew her, a member of the wine merchant's guild, and asked why they had been in court.

'They have just heard the suit regarding her late husband's estate. He had a son by his first wife who challenged her inheritance.'

'And?'

'The son won. The widow – his stepmother – is left with nothing but a room to live in and food to eat.'

Before I could react, a heavy hand clamped down on my shoulder and spun me around. I looked down into the last face I wanted to see. Stoltz, the moneylender, a regular acquaintance of mine.

'Were you in court this morning?'

I shook my head, too numb to speak.

'The widow Ellewibel's estate is worthless.'

'I have just heard.'

He grabbed me by the collar. 'I loaned you fifty gulden against that inheritance.'

'And I can repay it.'

He was a small man, lean and cunning. Even so, for a moment I thought he might try to shake the money out of me. Then something behind me caught his eye – no doubt another debtor of doubtful means. He let me go.

'I will come and visit you to discuss it presently.'

I left him and ran down the street. The two women had disappeared, but I could guess where they had gone. I overtook them just outside their front door. Ellewibel's eyes narrowed as she saw me; her face was grim. Her daughter kept her eyes downcast and said nothing.

'Herr Gensfleisch. I am sorry – this is not a good time for us.'

'I know.'

She drew herself up and fixed me with her sternest stare. 'A few days ago you came to my house and confessed your prospects were not as promising as you had led me to believe. I admired your honesty and treated you generously, though I was under no obligation to do so. I hope that now you will extend me the same courtesy.'

'There will be no marriage.' The words were sweet in my mouth.

'You have agreed the contract. You cannot break it off.'

'You have broken it. You promised me your husband's estate, two hundred gulden.'

'I promised nothing of the sort,' she said quickly, a gambler who had been waiting to play her top card. 'I promised you my *claim* on the inheritance. In good faith, I believed it was worth what I told you. I could not foresee that the court would side with my stepson.'

'Perhaps if you had mentioned the suit I could have judged its prospects for myself.' I drew myself up with a shiver of righteous glee. 'Perhaps if you had paid me the courtesy of fair dealing I would be more inclined now to forgive the deficiency of Ennelin's dowry.' That was a lie. 'As it is, you have tricked me twice over. The contract is void.'

The pleasure must have told in my voice. It only added to her fury.

'This is not the end of the matter, Herr Gensfleisch. I will take you to the courts for breach of contract, if I must, and this time they *will* side with me.'

I turned to Ennelin. 'Goodbye, Fräulein. I am sorry it has ended this way.'

Ego absolvo te. I free you. I did not need to buy an indulgence: I had never felt freer.

XLVII

Belgium

Nick stared at the letters that had appeared on the page. 'What is that?'

'Hard point,' said Emily. 'You press the words into the parchment with a blunt nib, a pen with no ink. It only shows up if you look at it in the right light, and know where to look. It's simple but very effective. Did you ever read a mystery story where the detective looks on a pad of paper for the impression of what was written on the sheet above?'

'I guess.'

'This is the same thing, only deliberate. Medieval scribes often used hard point to rule their lines. Some of them adapted the technique to write hidden messages.'

'So what does it say?'

Emily read the words slowly, tracing them out with the light. Jerome watched her with a look somewhere between fury and grudging respect.

' "*Occultum in sermonibus regum Israel.*" ' She looked up. 'It means, "Which is hidden in the sayings of the kings of Israel." '

'And what does that mean?'

'It's a continuation of the previous line. He – Master Francis, the illuminator – also made another book of beasts using this new form of writing, which is hidden in the sayings of the kings of Israel.'

Nick's head throbbed. 'Great. You know, I'm surprised they bothered to hide it. It makes absolutely no sense. There's no way Gillian could have found it.'

'I think she did.' In her tiredness, Emily spoke so quietly that Nick struggled to hear her. She said it again. 'I think she found it. The *Sayings of the Kings of Israel* is a lost book of the Bible.'

She watched their reactions. Nick confused; Brother Jerome with his strange, ill-concealed irritation. 'I'm right, aren't I?'

Jerome played with the hem of his dressing gown and said nothing.

'I saw it in that book in the Bibliothèque Nationale. *Lost Books of the Bible.*' She pointed to the bestiary splayed open on the desk. 'Gillian got it out the day after she found this. I'd be pretty sure she saw the inscription. But where that gets us . . .'

'What do you mean by a lost book of the Bible?' said Nick. 'Do you mean a lost book as in a missing copy, or as in a piece of text like the Gospel according to Mary Magdalen or whatever?'

'I don't know.' Emily slumped back against the wall. 'I didn't read that carefully. I suppose it's more likely to be a book as in text, like the Book of Revelation or the Book of Job. Though how that's supposed to get us closer to Gillian . . .'

'Gillian must have been searching for something when she left Paris,' said Nick. 'It wasn't the card, and it wasn't this book – she had both of those already. There must have been something else.'

Emily turned back to the book on the table and stared at the

301

illuminations. 'This book alone is priceless. A bestiary that we can attribute with near certainty to the Master of the Playing Cards – practically signed by him. Just discovering it would have made Gillian's professional reputation for life. What would make her abandon this to go chasing after something else?'

They wrapped the book in newspaper, made their excuses and left. For all his hostility, Jerome seemed reluctant to see them go. He followed them to the car, standing on the pavement in his bathrobe until they were out of sight. Nick wished they hadn't spoken so freely in front of him. Only when they'd left him well behind did he voice the obvious question.

'Where now?'

'Strasbourg,' said Emily confidently.

They were still driving through the suburbs: grey, four-square houses built in four-square grids. The heating was losing its battle against the cold air blowing through the glassless window, but even that was barely keeping Nick awake any more. He felt numb, his eyes like concrete.

'Because that's where the bestiary came from?'

'And therefore where Gillian's most likely to have gone.'

'You don't know that. She was probably way ahead of us. If she figured out what the *Sayings of the Kings of Israel* meant, she could have gone anywhere.'

'True. But the only place we *know* she could have gone is Strasbourg. And before that, I suggest we find alternative transportation. Driving around in a car we've stolen from a gang of murderous thugs seems a sure way of guaranteeing a short trip.'

'We can't just walk into Avis,' said Nick sourly. 'The police know all about me already – and now they've got that bloodbath in the warehouse to pin on us as well. Atheldene's probably told them everything. Pretty soon, we're going to be the hottest property in Europe. We—'

'*For God's sake look out!*'

Emily grabbed Nick's arm. His eyes jerked open – he hadn't even felt them close. Adrenalin ripped through him as he saw he'd drifted halfway across the street – straight into the path of an oncoming Volkswagen. Nick jerked the wheel and tried to hit the brakes. Instead, he slammed his foot on the accelerator. The big car leaped forward and right, just missing the swerving Volkswagen. Nick turned the wheel back. The car straightened abruptly – but kept going round as the tyres lost all grip on the frozen road. Emily screamed. Nick spun the wheel and jammed on the brakes; the car shuddered as the ABS kicked in but didn't stop.

It was all over in an instant. The car spun across the road, round 180 degrees, and banged into the kerb. They both sat there in stunned silence. From an adjacent garden, a little girl in a woollen hat looked over the fence in astonishment.

'I think we'll take the train,' said Emily.

XLVIII

Strassburg

Andreas Dritzehn wanted me to like him. He had spread his
table with venison, capons, jellies and sweetmeats. He flattered
my new coat, which was second hand, and laughed if he even
suspected a joke. He pressed me with wine, which he served
himself, though there were many servants on hand to pour. I
was quite willing to oblige him. He wanted to give me a great
deal of money.

I made him wait. I refilled my plate and my glass often. I
discoursed energetically on the weather, the harvest, progress
on the cathedral, Paris. I was a delightful guest. Kaspar, across
the table, said little. His spirits burned like a candle: they could
be snuffed out in an instant. If my attention was deflected even
a degree away from him, he became sullen and withdrawn.

At last the plates were cleared, the servants dismissed, the
women dispatched to their chambers. Dritzehn threw another
log on the fire and leaned closer.

'Tell my about your mirrors.'

*

Like many ideas, it had been born of necessity. In this case, necessity took the guise of two men who one afternoon visited my house in St Argobast. Working in the forge, I did not see them arrive, or notice anything until one announced himself by rapping his cudgel on my shoulder. It was not a friendly tap, but a heavy blow that left my arm numb. I dropped the ladle with a howl. Boiling metal slopped into the fire, setting off a noxious steam that stung my eyes. I almost tipped the entire crucible over my legs. Weeping and choking, I turned around to meet my visitors.

One was the man who had hit me. If ever a man's face bespoke his character this was it. His right eye, left earlobe and left arm were missing – though to judge by the knock he had given me, enough strength remained in his right arm for two. His nose had been broken so many times it looked like a sack of rocks; his lips, bared in a sneer, looked permanently bruised.

The other man stepped out from his considerable shadow. It was Stoltz, the moneylender.

'We were supposed to meet yesterday to discuss your debts. You did not come.'

'I forgot.'

The one-armed man made another movement. Still blinking back tears from the pain and fumes, I did not see it clearly. All I felt was another explosion of agony, this time in my knee. I dropped to the floor.

Stoltz stood over me. 'You would be astonished, in my line of work, how forgetful men become. It is as if lending a man gold instantly addles his wits. Fortunately, my memory does not suffer this defect.'

He reached into the bag on his belt and pulled out a small notebook. I remembered the clerk in the Mainz mint with his enormous ledger, the all-knowing book from which my theft could not be hidden. I trembled.

'Three months ago I loaned you fifty gulden.'

This was worth another blow, this time to my arm. I rolled over on my side. Stoltz stood over me.

'Some men find money a strange abstraction. It flows from man to man and from country to country and knows no boundaries. In a single day it can go from the hands of a king to the hands of a beggar and back again. But in truth, money is very simple. It is a tool, just as a pair of bellows or a plough are tools. And within that tool lies an inherent utility. This we call value.'

A kick in the ribs. I covered my face with my hands. Nothing destroys a man's credit so quickly as a mask of bruises on his face.

'If I lend you a plough, its value is that it can improve your field to make it more fruitful. For that, you pay me. Likewise if I lend you fifty gulden, you pay me for the use of it. For the use of *this* money, you were to pay me five shillings a month.'

Two swats from the cudgel contorted my back in agony.

'You have already failed to deliver the last month's payment. Now I hear that the surety you gave me for the loan – the dowry of the girl Ennelin – turns out to be worthless. You have broken off your engagement to her.'

'Her mother tricked me,' I pleaded.

'Then more fool you. I will not be left with the bill. By breaking the engagement you have forfeited your collateral. Under the terms of our agreement, I am entitled to claim back the entire loan immediately.'

'I cannot pay.' The money had barely touched my hands as it passed through them – some to Dunne and various suppliers, but most to pay off other loans that had fallen due.

306

'Then I shall ruin you.' Stoltz nodded to his henchman, who swung the cudgel underarm against the sole of my foot. I screamed. 'When Karl has finished with you I will set the courts on you.'

'Please. Please God.' I scrabbled to get away from the brute. He let me, like a bear handler letting out the leash. I could not go far.

Desperation loosened my tongue. 'I have invested it in a great labour. One that, God willing, will make me rich. If you ruin me now you will get nothing, pennies for gulden. If you wait I can repay you everything.'

Stoltz said nothing – but there was no movement from Karl. I took this as an invitation to continue.

'I am devising a new art, one that will make me rich.'

'What is it?'

'You spoke of ploughs and fields. Imagine this is a plough which could make fields give up ten times as much wheat.'

'Explain.' Stoltz had no time for riddles. Karl stepped closer and stroked my ribs with the tip of his cudgel.

But I could not say it. Even then – bleeding, bruised and with the promise of worse to come – I could not. It was my secret, incomplete though it was. If every man knew it, there would be no advantage. I had to cling on.

I stared up at the thin, bloodless face looming over me. A wink of light behind him caught my eye: a pilgrim's mirror that Aeneas had given me by the Rhine. I gazed at it, praying for salvation.

Stoltz swept a glass jar off the table. It shattered on the floor, jolting me back to him. 'Pay attention.'

He glared down. Karl tapped the club against the side of his leg and licked his puffy lips. And that was when it flashed into my mind.

'The mirrors,' I croaked.

'What?'

I pointed. He stepped back, fearing a trick, and eyed the mirror on the wall. A ring of light played over his face where the mirror reflected it onto him.

'That will not save you.'

'Not in the way you think. But perhaps . . .' I stood. Karl lifted the club to knock me down again, but Stoltz raised a hand to still him. I pulled the mirror off its nail and examined it. My mind raced.

'This has been cast from an alloy of lead and tin. I have worked with this alloy: it shrinks as it cools and tightens around the mould.' I ran my finger around the interlocking circles. 'For a design so intricate, the only way to free it is to shatter the mould. Every mirror requires a new mould to be carved. It is slow and expensive.'

I did not know absolutely that this was true, but just as some physicians can diagnose a man's sickness by looking at his face, I could read it in the shape and flow of the metal.

I pointed to the figures sculpted on the medallions inside the rings. 'You see how flat and featureless these faces are? You cannot achieve the quality of detail from casting in this way. I can make them better than that – and cheaper.'

'How?'

'A new alloy. One that does not shrink as it cools. I can use the moulds again and again, and each time produce a truer copy than this.'

I pressed the mirror into his hand. He took it, scraping a fingernail over the rough carvings.

'How many would you make?'

'A thousand. At twelve shillings each, that would be five

hundred gulden. I could repay your loan with double the interest.'

'Lending money at interest is a venal sin,' Stoltz admonished me. Karl glanced at him to see if this merited another blow. Thankfully, it did not. 'You pay me for the *use* of the money.'

'Then I would pay you double. For it would be twice as useful.' I did not know where this extravagance sprang from, or how I would ever honour it; I did not care. My mind glowed hot with the sudden promise of this new idea. All I wanted was to begin it.

Andreas Dritzehn laid the mirror I had given him on the table. 'And these are to be sold to pilgrims in Aachen?'

'Do you know the Aachen relics?'

'I have heard of them.'

'They are the holiest relics in the empire. The blue dress of the Blessed Virgin Mary. The bands that swaddled Christ in the manger, and the cloth that covered his modesty on the cross. Also a piece of fabric which is said to have wrapped the head of John the Baptist after Herod cut it off.'

'A complete wardrobe,' said Kaspar.

'Once every seven years, they are taken out of their chests and displayed. So great is the number of pilgrims that the whole city can barely contain them. The priests mount a scaffold between the cathedral towers: every street, every square, every rooftop and window becomes an observatory.'

Andreas frowned. 'It must be hard to see anything.'

'Exactly.' I leaned forward, brimming with excitement. 'The pilgrims carry mirrors – like this – to capture the light of heaven which radiates from the relics.'

'Is it visible?'

'Only to God,' said Kaspar piously.

309

'But the holy mirrors capture it. The pilgrims wrap the mirrors in cloths and take them home. Then, when they are in need, they can unveil the mirrors and let the holy light cure their afflictions.'

'How many do you intend to make?'

The idea had settled since I blurted out the first number that entered my head to Stoltz. I had done some research, ascertained the facts and established a more realistic basis for my estimate.

'Thirty-two thousand.'

Dritzehn almost dropped the mirror on the floor.

'There must be over a hundred thousand pilgrims in Aachen when the relics are shown. All of them need mirrors, or the pilgrimage is in vain. Ours will be better quality than our rivals', and cheaper. As I said, this happens only every seven years. The next pilgrimage will take place in some twenty months. Time enough for our work.'

'But what of the Aachen goldsmiths? Surely their guild will not allow you to flood their market with your wares, at their expense?'

'The Aachen goldsmiths forfeited their rights long ago. They cannot make enough of the mirrors to meet the demand. Some years ago there were riots: pilgrims who could not obtain mirrors fought in the streets with those who had. Several died. Since then, the privileges of the Aachen guilds have been suspended for six months each year that the relics are shown.'

Dritzehn clasped the mirror to his chest and murmured something indistinct. I waited for him to repeat it.

'How can I be part of this enterprise?'

'The housing and the mirrors will be manufactured separately. We need someone to polish the mirrors.'

'I can do that.' He furrowed his face. 'But not as a servant. If

I am to be part of this, it must be for a share of the profits.'

'The profits will be very great,' I agreed, almost as if it were cause for concern. 'For that reason, this endeavour must be a close secret. If knowledge of our art spreads, there will be no advantage.'

'I can keep the secret.'

I glanced at Drach, who played his part and looked doubtful.

'I am sure of it,' I said. 'But we must keep the circle small – no more than half a dozen men. Half the profits will accrue to me and Kaspar, as the inventors of this art. It follows that any man who invests must buy at least a quarter share of the remainder.'

'How much is that?'

'Eighty gulden.'

Dritzehn was a merchant: he could do his sums. 'Thirty-two thousand mirrors – you will sell for how much?'

'Half a gulden.'

'Sixteen thousand gulden. Half to you, eight thousand. A quarter of the remainder to me: two thousand.'

He whispered the number like a man who has beheld God. I knew how he felt. Even now, the magnitude of the project awed me.

'Can this be true?'

'We have the art and – you behold – the ambition. All we want is capital.'

'Nothing can go wrong,' Drach assured him.

'Is this what you have been concocting in my basement all these months?'

'A part of it.' I changed the subject. 'But you must decide quickly. There are many others who would happily take your place.'

Dritzehn wiped his brow and stared into the fire. Kaspar looked as though he was about to say something, but I tapped him under the table to stay quiet.

'I will take the share you offer.'

'It cannot be yours until we have the money,' Kaspar warned.

'You can have fifty gulden tonight. The rest I will fetch tomorrow.' He thought for a moment. 'You will sign a contract that this is to be used only for the good of the enterprise?'

'Of course. But I must have absolute control.'

Dritzehn went to a chest by the wall. He fetched paper, a writing box and a heavy bag that clinked when he set it on the table. I tried not to stare.

He uncorked the bottle of ink and dipped in the pen. In the firelight, the ink dripped off the nib like drops of gold.

The fire had burned low and the servants were asleep. Dritzehn ushered us downstairs to the door himself.

'Be careful on your way home,' he warned me. 'It is not safe carrying bags of gold through the streets.'

'Nothing will happen to it.'

We crossed the road and walked around the corner. At that hour the streets were almost empty – but not quite. Two men stood in the shadows under a baker's sign. They stepped out to block our path as we approached. One was tall and stocky and leaned on a thick staff; the other short and thin.

'Did he agree?' Stoltz asked.

I handed over the bag Dritzehn had given me. Stoltz hefted it in his hands, then passed it to Karl. The one-armed man struggled to hold it and the staff at the same time.

'It's all there,' I said.

'If it isn't, you will soon know.'

The two men disappeared down an alley. We watched them until they were out of sight.

'Is that for the good of the enterprise?' Drach asked.

My conscience was clear. 'If it keeps me from having my legs broken, it is certainly for the good of the enterprise.'

Stoltz had been wrong about money. It was not like a plough or a pair of bellows, to be hired out and returned. It was water driving the mill of endeavour. It did not matter where it came from or where it went. So long as it kept flowing.

XLIX

France

They abandoned the car in a car park. Nick left the windows open and the keys on the front seat. Hopefully someone would steal it before the authorities found it. Then they went to the rail station.

Nick slept most of the way to Strasbourg, clutching his hand across his chest where he had the book tucked under his coat. When he woke, he saw the day had got darker. Flakes of snow whirled past the windows, while the sky promised more to come. On the opposite seat he saw Emily watching him.

'What time is it?'

'Almost noon.'

A hunger pang ripped through his stomach. 'I'm starving.'

Emily reached in her purse and pulled out a paper bag. 'I got you a croissant.'

Nick ripped off the end and stuffed it in his mouth. It felt like he hadn't eaten in a week. 'You're a godsend. I don't suppose you've got a cup of coffee in there as well?'

Emily slid a paper cup across the table between them, together with a pile of sweeteners and creams. He emptied three of each into the cup and swirled it with a plastic spoon while he devoured the rest of the croissant.

'Did you sleep at all?'

'A little. I couldn't stop thinking.' She stared out the window. 'Gillian must have known something we don't.'

Nick waited for her to go on.

'She found the bestiary, and the card inside it – either of which would be a major discovery. But she didn't tell anyone, not even Atheldene.'

'So he says,' Nick interrupted.

She acknowledged the point. 'Then she locked the card in a bank vault and the book in the deep freeze, and disappeared. I assume to look for the "other" bestiary. Why?'

Nick sipped his coffee and let Emily continue.

'She knew something. Something that made the other book even more valuable than the one she had.'

'What?'

Emily screwed up her face. 'I don't know. But she must have found it quickly. She was only in Paris for a day after she saw the book.'

'The day she went out to see Vandevelde.' Nick thought back to the physicist, his evasions, his eagerness to prove he had nothing to hide. He wanted to pull out the card again, to see what Gillian might have seen on it. In the train carriage, even half empty, he didn't dare.

'Whatever it is, someone's excited about it,' he said. 'It's unreal. The speed they turned up at the book warehouse – and before that at the library. But if they know all about the book, why are they chasing after us to find it?'

Emily looked out the window, where the snow flurries were

gathering force. 'Maybe they don't want to find it at all. Maybe they want to make sure it stays hidden.'

Near Liège, Belgium

Brother Jerome pored over the desk and rubbed his bloodshot eyes. Seeing Emily again had left him with a splitting headache. He reached for the plastic jar that was never far from his desk and popped two pills. As a younger man he'd prided himself on keeping his body pure. A temple, a fortress of God. Now the temple lay in ruins: flooded with caffeine to keep him alert, sedatives so he could sleep, codeine for the headaches and some pills his doctor had given him for his heart. And some stronger drugs, powders that couldn't be prescribed, for the memories.

He looked over the notes he'd written.

> *bestiary*
> *nova forma scribendi*
> *Armand, Comte de Lorraine (Strasbourg??)*

A new form of writing. Emily had always had a brilliant mind, a sort of academic cunning that knew when to look deeper. But there were some things she didn't know. That was what she'd recognised in him: a depth of experience without equal. It had been an intoxicating mix.

Why did you come here? Jerome asked for the hundredth time. He was pleased he had managed to stay so outwardly calm – a lifetime of religious self-discipline still had some hold – but it had been an immense effort. The feelings she still aroused, anger and longing.

Forget her. He tried to focus his thoughts on the book again. Another bestiary in a new form of writing, illustrated by the

316

Master of the Playing Cards. It was incredible. The discredited theories and baseless speculations would turn out to be correct. And maybe other, deeper secrets that prudent men only whispered.

A tentative knock sounded from the front of the house; his heart leaped. It was shameful, but he didn't care. She'd come back. He jumped to his feet and ran to the door, gathering the dressing gown around his thin waist. Without even bothering with the peephole, he unlatched the door and pulled it open.

Two men stood on the doorstep. Both wore heavy black coats with the hoods raised against the cold. They pushed inside before he could react. Jerome stumbled back and fell against the wall. The shorter of the two men unzipped his jacket and rested his hand inside the lapel; the other man pulled back his hood to reveal a craggy face with a patrician crest of white hair, and coal-black eyes that seemed to bore into Jerome's soul.

Jerome stared. '*You.*'

He had only met him once, thirty years ago: a Spanish priest from an obscure office of the Vatican, visiting a promising young researcher who had just begun to make a name for himself. Even then, menace surrounded him. He had spent half an hour asking about Jerome's work – always stiffly formal, but lethal, poised like a fencer probing his opponent's guard. At the end he had said, 'There are many undiscovered books in this world. Some are treasures undeservedly lost; others vanished for a reason and should remain forgotten. If you ever find one of these latter books, you must tell me at once.'

In the years afterwards, Jerome had occasionally seen photographs of the priest – at first only in Church bulletins, then in newspapers and finally even on television. In the whispered gossip of his order he heard rumours about the methods the priest had used in his rise to power, and believed them.

And now he was standing in Jerome's living room, beside a squat thug with a broken nose and a livid scar across his chin. A cardinal's jewelled ring gleamed on his finger. He looked around the dishevelled room, at the half-empty coffee mugs clustered around the chair.

'You have had visitors today?'

'Only memories.'

Behind Nevado, the thug pulled his arm out of his coat. A black pistol had appeared in his hand. He squinted down the barrel as he pulled back the slide and snapped it home. The sound made Jerome wince.

'Sometimes memories come to life.' Nevado moved forward; Jerome cringed, pressing his bony shoulders against the wall. 'You, Brother, have good reason to fear them.'

Jerome looked into those pitiless eyes. He didn't even try to hold their gaze. His spirit had been broken long ago. He couldn't resist: they would find out everything.

'She came here,' said Nevado. 'Emily Sutherland – your little Héloïse. Did she bring you a book?'

'No one came here.'

Jerome's head snapped against the wall as Nevado struck him, a stinging blow. Blood dribbled from his lip where the cardinal's ring had cut him.

'Liar. She was here. Did she bring her new boyfriend to flaunt him? To taunt you? Did she offer you her body again if you would help them?'

Jerome's dressing gown sagged open. His naked body seemed to shrivel under Nevado's glare. He imagined Nevado's hands on Emily's throat, that cold smile never wavering.

There was only one way to protect her. Jerome launched

himself forward, pushing off the wall as he lunged past Nevado for the pistol. He knew he wouldn't make it. The gun came up and fired three times into Jerome's chest. The first bullet went straight through his heart. He collapsed on the floor, his blood pumping into the carpet.

'*Idiot*,' hissed Nevado. 'We needed him to talk.' He gazed around the room. So many books, so much chaos. It would take hours to search the house. He had an audience in Rome in three hours: people would talk if he missed it. Gossip didn't matter to him, but if anyone looked into where he'd been there might be trouble. He couldn't risk being discovered here.

But Nevado had built his career on seeing what other men could not. He stood very still in the centre of the room and slowly scanned it, dismantling it with his eyes. Ugo, the guard, waited behind him.

He looked through an open door to the study beyond. He saw a desk whose jumble of books and papers had been pushed back to clear an open space. A magnifier, a UV penlight, a foam cushion and a pair of white gloves filled the space.

In an instant, Nevado had crossed into the study and was examining the desk. Ugo came up behind him, surprised by how quickly the old man moved.

It didn't take Nevado long to find everything he needed. Crumbs of worn leather littered the cushion, and a book beside it was weighted open to a page showing the queen of wild men. The notepad beside it displayed the list Jerome had made just before he died.

Nevado read over it.

Armand, Comte de Lorraine (Strasbourg??)

A shiver ran down his spine. *They'd found it.* His life's work, now almost complete.

He turned to Ugo.

'You go to Strasbourg. I will meet you there as soon as I can. Find the American and his friend, and find the book they have. That is all that matters.'

He reached in his coat and pulled out a folded sheet of paper.

'If you find the book, tell me at once if the first page is the same as this. You understand?'

Ugo nodded. He took the paper – but Nevado had not let go. The black eyes locked on his.

'If anything happens, if you are arrested or compromised, you destroy this paper immediately. No one can be allowed to see it. If you fail me in this, your wife, your children and all your family will suffer torments even you cannot imagine.'

His gloved fingers released the paper. Ugo stumbled back a step.

Almost to himself, Nevado murmured, 'They have no idea what they have found.'

Strasbourg, France

Nick had never seen Strasbourg before. If he'd had an idea of how it would look, it probably involved great blocks of European concrete filled with parliaments, courts and commissions. Instead, he felt he'd stepped back a thousand years. The centre of the town was built on an island, the river a natural moat. Half-timbered houses hung over the narrow streets and alleys, funnelling the freezing wind so that it whipped snow in their faces. Many houses had fanciful creatures carved into their beams: grotesque faces sticking their tongues out at him in mockery.

A tram whistled past. Nick stuck out an arm to hold back Emily, who had been about to step out into the street.

'Thanks.' She gave him a sheepish smile. 'I should have slept more on the train. I'm a wreck.'

Nick looked at her. She had piled her hair under her beret and turned up the collar on her coat. Her cheeks had flushed pink, and her eyes were bright in the cold. 'You look pretty good for a wreck.'

Again, Emily seemed to flinch from the compliment. This time the smile was purely defensive. 'I'll feel better once I've had a shower and a hot meal.'

'After we've been to the archives.'

They reached the cathedral, which dominated the heart of the city. Even with his mind on Gillian, Nick had to admire it. The facade was a vertiginous tangle of Gothic tracery: spires and pinnacles, a rose window, peaked arches and statues. A single tower stretched high above it, the pink sandstone spun to a lacy thinness that seemed incapable of supporting such a height.

Emily followed Nick's gaze up the tower. 'It's almost exactly the same age as the playing cards. If the Master ever came here, he'd have seen it just the same way as we do.'

'I'm more interested in if Gillian saw it three weeks ago.'

They carried on around the square, past rows of shops offering ice creams and souvenirs. Nick imagined that in summer tourists would swarm like wasps around their sticky offerings, but on a wintry day in January there was nobody. Half-empty wire racks of postcards sat forlornly on the pavement where they had been pushed out by hopeful shopkeepers, draped in polythene shrouds to keep off the snow. The plastic whipped and crackled in the wind, scaring the pigeons who scavenged on the cobbles.

The archives were housed in a gloomy stone building at the back of the square. They entered by a gate in a stone wall, and walked up a gravel path to the main door, past beds of rose bushes that had long since ceased to flower. Only the thorns remained.

Nick turned a heavy iron ring on the door and was admitted to the reception area. Nothing in the exterior had prepared him for it: instead of oak floors and ancient furniture, he found himself in a corridor with a linoleum floor and strip-lighting. A woman in a severe black skirt-suit sat behind a desk, underneath a poster in a plastic clip-frame.

'*Bonjour*,' said Nick. He turned to Emily. 'Do you want to explain?'

'I speak English,' the archivist announced without looking up. She kept writing. 'Can I help you?'

'We're interested in the library of the Count of Lorraine,' Emily said. 'We were told that it became part of your archive.'

A look of surprise broke the archivist's scowl. She put down her pen. 'You are the second person in a month to ask me about the Comte de Lorraine. *Etrange.*'

'Who was it?' Nick demanded. The archivist gave him a blank look. 'Was it a woman, tall and thin with red hair?' He pulled out his wallet and fumbled among the cards for the battered, passport-size photograph that he'd never got round to removing. *Just in case*. Next to him, he caught a sideways glance from Emily.

'Was this her?'

The archivist pursed her lips in confusion. '*Oui. C'est elle.* But blonde.'

'Do you remember when she came? The date?'

The archivist watched him through narrowed eyes. 'Do you have her name?'

'Gillian Lockhart.'

She flipped through a ledger that lay open on the desk, a

register of names and dates and scribbled signatures. There hadn't been many. Two pages back, Nick spotted it. The familiar shape, the bold G and the brisk lines that followed. A very masculine signature, he'd always thought.

He read the date in the left-hand column beside her name: '*December 16*'. She must have come here almost straight from Paris. Nick's heart raced with more hope than he'd felt in a week.

'And did she find it? The book she was looking for?'

A sigh. 'I tell you the same as I have told her. The books of the Comte de Lorraine came here in the century of the eighteen hundreds. You know the history of Strasbourg?'

Nick shook his head.

'In 1871, we are attacked by the army of Prussia. They surround the city and they bombard it. Much of the city burns – including the great library. Some books survive – but of the Comte de Lorraine, there is not.'

L

Strassburg

Often the fates drag us down like ocean waves and all our toils count for nothing. But sometimes, rarely, they rush us aloft on currents so quick even angels would struggle to keep pace. Such was my experience in those golden months in Strassburg. With Dritzehn's money, I paid off my old loans and restored my credit. That allowed me to take out new loans, on better terms, to buy metals for our project – which in turn stood as collateral for another round of loans. Those bought more metals, which funded more loans – and so again, a virtuous circle. Of course there was little income in those months to repay the loans, but I had allowed for that. I had agreed that the interest would be added to the principal and none of it fall due until October of the following year, once the mirrors were sold in Aachen. Then, armed with the profits, I could turn my efforts back to the indulgences.

Some nights I dreamed that I sat atop a giant tower of mirrors stacked halfway to the sky, swaying and bending like a rope end in the breeze. The height made me dizzy; I knew that a single gust of wind might topple the whole tower and shatter it in ruin. But it never did.

Manufacturing the mirrors required two separate processes. The latticework frames had to be cast from the alloy, and the steel mirrors polished to a high reflective sheen. Eventually, the one would be attached to the other by means of clips, but we agreed this should be done as late as possible. When spring came we would hire a barge to carry our cargo down the Rhine to Aachen, and we did not want the mirrors scratched in transit. None of us knew how that might affect their holy properties. So we cast the frames at St Argobast, where I had the forge, and used Dritzehn's house for the mirrors.

Late that September, the fates moved again. I had spent the day in Strassburg, arranging delivery of the next batch of metals and assuring my creditors that all was proceeding apace. The sun was edging towards the horizon, but I did not have to hurry. I made the journey between my house and the city so often in those months that I had acquired a horse, a docile mare I named Mercury. So I decided to visit Dritzehn.

I was just approaching the house, picking my way around two dogs squabbling over a piece of offal that had fallen from a butcher's cart, when I heard a loud voice behind me.

'Johann?'

It was not uncommon to be hailed on the streets. I had been in Strassburg almost four years and my name was well known, if only because I owed so many of its citizens money. What struck me was the surprise in the voice, the force of long-lost recognition. I had no long-lost friends I wanted to see again.

I turned, dreading who might be there. At first I did not recognise him. The last time I saw him he had been young and fit, overflowing with energy. Now his face was lined, his hair

325

greyed far more than mine. He walked with a cane, dragging one leg behind him. Yet whatever misfortunes had blighted his life, they had not dimmed the essential fire that animated him.

'Aeneas?'

He beamed. 'It *is* you. I was certain of it. You look as if the years have treated you well. Unlike me.'

I glanced at his withered leg.

'What happened?'

'I went to Scotland.' He grimaced. 'A barbarous place. I almost died. Then my ship sank and I had to walk home.'

It must have been terrible, but he said it with such relish that I had to laugh. 'You almost died the day I met you,' I reminded him. 'You should take more care of yourself. But why are you in Strassburg?'

'I am supposed to be meeting some priests from Heidelberg. I think they want me to spy on the Pope.' He winked. 'But I am Italian; they will expect me to be late. The last time I saw you we agreed to meet in a tavern. I did not think it would take six years to get there, but I am happy I have found you at last. Will you share a drink with me?'

I had been wrong. There were faces from my past I was happy to see.

I led him to a wine cellar near the river, one I had never visited before. I wanted to avoid any place that Drach might see us together, Somehow, he and Aeneas belonged to separate parts of my life. I did not want them to meet.

Aeneas raised his glass and toasted me. 'You are an extraordinary man, Johann. You emerged from that river mud fully formed, and vanished like a ghost. Now here you are, by your attire apparently a prosperous merchant. "*Varium et mutabile semper*," as the poet says. Always changeable and surprising.'

326

He fixed me with his familiar gaze, eternally hopeful and inquisitive.

'I'm sorry I abandoned you so suddenly,' I said. 'I had to go.'

Aeneas waited for more. When he saw he would get none, he nodded. 'I suppose even men who emerge from the mud have pasts. Perhaps some day you will tell me how you came to be there.'

I changed the subject. 'And Nicholas? How is he?'

Aeneas looked sad. 'We do not speak so much now. You know that the Pope has just dissolved the council of Basle?'

I did not, though I knew that it had continued until recently. Every few months I heard some news of it in church or in the marketplace, and was astonished that the council I had briefly participated in six years earlier still ground on.

'The council was finally beginning to achieve something. There is so much rotten with the Church, and it all starts at the top. The council had taken some sensible measures to reform the worst abuses. Naturally, this involved curtailing the Pope's power. We – the council – needed to assert that the Pope is a servant of the community of the Church, not its master.'

He spoke animatedly, rocking on his stool as he talked and catching my eye often to be sure I agreed. I tried to look non-committal; that only stoked his enthusiasm.

'The Pope, jealous of his position, dissolved the council in Basle and ordered it to reconvene in Italy. By having it closer to Rome, he hoped to bring it to heel. Many members obeyed: but those of us who see how the Church must be reformed refused. We stayed in Basle and voted to suspend the Pope, who has at last shown his true colours.'

'Nicholas went to Italy,' I guessed.

'He has his reasons. I cannot agree with them. He wants the Church unified; I want it perfected.' Aeneas stared at the

327

table dejectedly. Then, suddenly, a smile flashed across his face. 'More to the point, it is the men in Basle who pay my wages.'

I do not know what ever happened to the priests from Heidelberg who hoped to meet him. We sat in the tavern some hours, emptying cups of wine and plates of food. As always, Aeneas talked most, but I was happy to listen. He was easy company. Conversation with Kaspar was a field of swords: no statement went unargued, no compromise or trivial hypocrisy unwithered by his sarcasm. I never knew when the idlest comment might be hurled back at me – or wound him so unexpectedly that he would spend the entire evening sulking. It was exhilarating, but also exhausting.

Aeneas, by contrast, prided himself on neither giving nor taking offence. In this he was only intermittently successful: his love of speech was so great that words often outpaced tact. But he always recognised his mistakes, with such sincere contrition that it was impossible not to forgive him.

'It is good to see you looking so well,' he told me. I believed it: he always took genuine pleasure from those around him. 'Are you married?'

Some memory of the disaster with Ennelin must have shown on my face. Even before I could demur he hurried on. 'For myself, I am lately in love. Smitten. There is a woman at the inn where I am staying – Agnes is her name – from Biscarosse. The most sublime creature.'

Despite myself, I was drawn into his story. 'Is she travelling alone?'

'Her husband is a merchant. He leaves her there while he travels up and down the river to contract his business. I saw him at breakfast two days ago. He is a fool. He does not deserve her.'

'Is this how you plan to reform the Church? By seducing other men's wives?'

Aeneas gazed on me with a soulful look. 'I could never take the vows of a priest. She ravished my heart with a single glimpse. Do you see these bags under my eyes? I cannot sleep because of her. Every night I go to her door and plead with her, but she is cool and steadfast as marble. She does not admit me – yet she gives me reason to hope. Perhaps tonight I shall finally conquer. I must, for tomorrow I return to Basle.'

He dropped his head like a dog. 'I know this love is ruinous. But I would rather this agony than a lifetime of numb comfort. Can you understand that?'

'I understand,' I murmured, and the longing in my voice must have penetrated Aeneas' self-pity. It drew a swift glance.

'I will not ask,' he said. 'You never tell me anyway. But I hope we both win our hearts' desires.'

I raised my glass to that.

'And now I must go.' He stood abruptly. In another man it would have been discourteous; with Aeneas, it signified only that his busy mind had leaped forward again. 'I must sleep now if I am to woo my Agnes tonight.'

I was sad to part. He had reminded me of a simpler age in my life, a humble time when all that mattered was faithfully copying what Nicholas said. Also how wretched I had been before he rescued me. All I had repaid him with were sudden disappearances and evasions. I owed him more; I wanted him to know my gratitude.

'I am sorry about Basle.' I pulled the mirror out of the pouch on my belt. It had become a talisman for me in those golden months, proof of our good fortune. I carried it everywhere. 'I never forgot your generosity.'

His face lit up with delight. He embraced me. 'I am glad I

found you. I hope you do not disappear again.' He took the mirror from my hand and examined it, smiling. 'My Aachen mirror. I had almost forgotten it. I do not know that it ever brought me good fortune, but perhaps it averted some great misfortune that would otherwise have befallen me. Perhaps I stood too far away to feel the full effects of the rays.'

He handed the mirror back. 'I have just returned from Aachen, actually, on an errand for the council.'

'Is all well there?' I asked, feigning carelessness. I had not told him the secret of the mirrors. 'Is all in hand for next year's pilgrimage?'

'It is a disaster.' Aeneas began to turn away, eager to be back to his inn. 'Has the news not reached here yet? An outbreak of the plague has swept the north. No one knows when it will end or how many souls it will claim. The authorities in Aachen have had no choice but to postpone the pilgrimage for a full year.'

He peered at me through the deepening gloom. 'What is wrong, Johann? You look as though you are about to disappear again.'

LI

Strasbourg

They checked into a hotel near the cathedral. Nick felt deflated, utterly empty. Once again he had caught a glimpse of Gillian; once again she had vanished.

'I'm going to look around the town,' Emily announced. 'Would you like to come?'

'I'm not interested in sightseeing,' Nick growled. But when he threw himself down on the hotel bed, he found he couldn't sleep. After two minutes he hurried downstairs and caught Emily in the lobby, just about to leave.

'Changed my mind.'

They stepped out. Although it was early afternoon, the sky was dark. The yellow lights in the hotel windows glowed warm behind them. A thin layer of snow already dusted the street, and looking at the pregnant clouds Nick guessed there was more to come. When he looked back at their footprints they seemed small and lonely, like two children lost in the woods.

He pulled his coat around him. 'Where are we going?'

'The cathedral,' said Emily. 'There's something I want to see.'

They walked up between black and white rows of half-timbered houses and passed through the cathedral's west door. It was so dark inside that Nick thought for a moment it must be closed – darker even than the day outside. All he could see was glass, spectral-coloured images floating above him, dizzyingly high. For a moment, he shared the awe the medieval congregation must have felt as they entered the sanctuary, the sense of a half-glimpsed heaven above.

The darkness disoriented him. He reached out in the gloom and touched Emily's arm to reassure himself she was still there. She moved closer, as if glad of a human connection in the face of the medieval God's icy grandeur.

Nick pointed up to the north wall, where a line of larger-than-life men stood proudly in the glass. 'Who are they?'

'The Holy Roman emperors. It's one of the most famous compositions in medieval glass.' She made a little harrumphing sound. Nick couldn't see her, but he knew the frown of concentration that went with it.

'What are you thinking?'

'The kings of Israel.' Nick wasn't sure if she was speaking to him or the darkness.

'I thought you said they were the Holy Roman emperors.'

'The kings of Israel were another popular motif in medieval art. The facade of Notre-Dame in Paris was decorated with twenty-four statues of them. There's also the Dom in Cologne, which has forty-eight kings in the stained glass of the choir, I think. They're assumed to be the twenty-four kings of Israel and the twenty-four kings from the Book of Revelation.'

'Thought to be?' Nick echoed. 'Doesn't anyone know?'

'Medieval cathedral builders didn't necessarily spell out what

332

they meant by their decoration. There are clues in the symbolism, but it's in the nature of symbols that they're ambiguous. The kings on the front of Notre-Dame, for example: they're an unimpeachable biblical theme. But it's no coincidence that they were put on a building which the kings of France wanted to use as a symbol of their own power. The medieval mind was much more sophisticated than we give it credit for. Semiotics, symbology, whatever you want to call it: they were profoundly alive to the overlapping meanings of the world. If you were a layman walking past Notre-Dame in the fourteenth or fifteenth century, you'd see the statues as the kings of Israel, but you'd also see them as the kings of France. One king becomes another, depending on how you look at it.'

'It sounds like Gillian you're describing.' Nick was surprised he'd said it. 'The same person, but so different in different contexts.'

'Everyone's like that, a bit.' It could have sounded dismissive, but she said it so gently it sounded like agreement. 'You mustn't give up hope.'

Nick wondered if she was thinking of the picture in his wallet. 'I just want to find her.'

'Rescue the damsel in distress.' Again, it might have sounded snide but didn't. To Nick, it felt almost wistful. He smiled in the darkness.

'I hadn't thought of it like that.' His mind wandered back to all the late nights in Gothic Lair killing monsters and storming castles; and before that, Friday nights in high school, sitting around with his friends rolling dice in the basement, totting up the numbers that would decide whether their fellowship lived or died. Perilous quests had been so safe then, something to look forward to through the dreary week at school. A far cry from the lonely, terrifying reality.

333

'What was it you wanted here?' he asked, changing the subject. 'Did you find it?'

'Oh – it was the kings. They reminded me of the kings of Israel, that's all. I thought perhaps it might trigger some sort of insight.' She shook her had. 'But – nothing.'

They finished their tour of the cathedral, Emily pointing out different features as they walked up and down the dark aisles. The way the architecture became more elaborate as you moved from east to west, the shift in style from Romanesque to Gothic which had happened over the centuries of its construction recorded in stone. She showed him the pillar where angels blew the trumpets of the Resurrection, and numerous stone carvings tucked away on buttresses and bosses. At first Nick paid attention out of politeness, but gradually he found himself becoming drawn into the intricacy of the art. By the time he emerged from the darkness into the gloomy day, he had a whole new vocabulary.

'I'm going to go and buy some new clothes before the shops shut,' said Emily. Snow was still falling, frosting the ridges of the cathedral. 'I'll see you back at the hotel.'

'Be careful,' Nick warned.

LII

Strassburg

Twenty-seven kings stared down from their glass thrones: proud and solemn, elevated above the cares of the world. Beneath their vitrified gazes, the world they had left moved apace. The cathedral echoed with the ring of hammers, the shouts of masons, the creak of pulleys and the squall of infants. Somewhere in all the din, the choir was trying to sing a litany. And at the back of the church, two men stood in an alcove whispering furiously.

'You promised me nothing could go wrong.' Andreas Dritzehn was neither proud nor solemn. His cheeks were flushed with anger, his fists balled tight as if poised to strike someone. Probably me. That was why I had insisted on meeting in the cathedral.

'Do you think you are the only one who has put money into this venture?' I felt sick just thinking of it, though I did not expect Dritzehn to sympathise.

'We must melt down the mirrors we have made and sell the metal.'

'No. What we bought was lead and tin and antimony. What we have now is alloy. We cannot unmix it, any more than we could melt those windows to make sand and lime.'

'Then sell the alloy.'

'That metal is the key to our enterprise – and our fortunes. If we sell it, other men will realise its power and teach themselves to copy it. If one of them happens to be an Aachen goldsmith, then he will cast the mirrors and take all the profits of our labours.'

'Let him.' Dritzhen's face puffed with anger. 'I need my money back.'

'The pilgrimage has been postponed, not cancelled. All we need is to hold our nerve and sit out one extra year. Then we will be as rich as we ever dreamed.'

'*I cannot sit out an extra year!*' He bellowed it like a gelded colt. I looked to see if anyone had heard, but the sawing of carpenters hid it.

'I should have listened to my brother Jörg,' he moaned. 'He told me you were a vagabond, a conjurer. That you would be the ruin of my family.'

It was then I realised, perhaps for the first time in my life, that I was responsible. I was too old to run. I owed too many men too much to be able to disappear. One-armed Karl would find me, or someone like him, and my crushed body would be dragged off one of the canal weirs, snagged among the scum and branches.

I had to free myself. And like a drunk who finds release in one more draught, I reached for the only cure I knew.

'There is another art I know. Less advanced than the mirrors, though with rewards that might dwarf them. All it needs is patience.'

He shook his head. 'I have had enough of your secret arts.'

'Did you never wonder what Kaspar and I were doing in your basement? The mirrors were never more than a sideshow, sowing the seeds for our greater work.'

Even in his despair I could see he was interested. 'You never spoke of this.'

'Of course not. The mirrors are already secret enough. But this new art is ten times greater. Only four men know of its existence.'

'Can it be carried off before next year?'

'Difficult to say. As I told you, its progress is less advanced than the mirrors. But once it is ready there will be no delay. No waiting for pilgrimages, no shipping it down the river. Even the plague could not stop it. All it will require is a little investment.'

He grabbed my coat and thrust me against the cathedral wall. 'Are you deaf? Have you listened to a word I say? *I have no more money.* How can I spend my way out of bankruptcy?'

With a calmness I did not feel, I pulled his hand off my collar and stepped away. Light sparkled on a gold pin he wore on the shoulder of his coat, Christ on his cross with a verse of scripture scrolled around it.

'What about that?'

He cupped his hand over it. 'It was a gift from my wife.'

It was beautifully made. Every sinew in Christ's body strained against death, as if his flesh tried to fight back the spirit from breaking free. The lettering underneath was perfectly even, punched into the thin metal with impossible finesse. It reminded me of the task at hand.

'You can borrow the money we need. I will be at my house in St Argobast if you change your mind.'

*

Sometimes I believed that borrowing money was my true business, and all my work with ink and metal existed merely to provide a pretext for the loans. The mirrors had become a monster devouring itself; when nothing remained, I needed a new idea to borrow against. In those days I no longer thought of the arts in terms of profit, or even if they would work. All that mattered was that they kept the stream of money flowing.

Three days after our meeting in the cathedral, Dritzehn came to my house. I met him in the yard between the barn and the forge. Hens pecked around our feet; my pig rooted for apples fallen from the tree behind the barn.

'How much?' Dritzehn asked without preamble.

I had thought of little else in the intervening days. 'One hundred and twenty-five gulden.'

He spluttered in indignation, which rapidly exploded into a violent fit of coughing. I watched him anxiously. I did not want him to die before I had his money.

'That is more than I have loaned you already – and that has almost bankrupted me.'

'Sometimes the only way across the river is to go deeper. What about your house?'

He wiped spittle from his mouth with his sleeve. 'What about it?'

'You can borrow against it.'

'I already have.'

'Borrow more,' I urged him. 'If your debts fall due and you cannot pay, they will take your house however much you owe. Better to risk everything on success than fail with half measures.'

I knew he would agree. Otherwise, he would never have come. It took a few minutes for him to come to terms with himself. He scuffed his boot in the dirt; he swung his shoulders and kicked his feet like a straw man on a stick.

'I can give you forty gulden now. The rest, I can raise in a few weeks.'

'Are you sure? Once I have taught you this art you cannot leave our partnership. If you have any doubts, go home now.'

He wanted reassurance. 'This money is to be used only for the good of the enterprise?'

'Of course,' I said, already calculating how best to distribute it among my creditors. 'And we will share the profits in the same proportion as before.'

'And if any of us dies before the venture is complete, all the investment will revert to his heirs?'

I looked at him sharply. 'Are you expecting to die?'

'No.' Another fit of coughing overtook him; he tried to swallow it and only made himself choke. 'But I am older than my father was when he died. Life is short; death stalks all our shadows.'

I crossed myself. 'This secret is too great to hazard to inheritance. If any of us dies, he will take it to his grave.'

This agitated him. 'What of my wife? She must get something if I die. Am I to mortgage her widowhood?'

'A merchant who invests in a voyage cannot reclaim his capital while the ship is at sea. Any money you put in must remain with the partnership until it is completed.'

He sighed, his face grey with defeat. I clapped him on the shoulder and tried to feign enthusiasm. 'Forget this talk of death. In two years' time you will laugh that you ever doubted me.'

I stood at the gate and watched him wander down the road, a sad and haggard man. Had I reduced him to this state? Lost in the labyrinth of my schemes and my debts, I could no longer tell if I was his benefactor or his nemesis.

'Did he bite?'

Kaspar walked out of the barn. His sleeves were pulled up, and a round welt shone on his palm from pushing the engraving tool into the metal.

'He'll pay.'

'Then why so sad?'

Kaspar reached out to stroke my cheek. But my dealing with Dritzehn had left me in a solitary mood. I turned away.

'What has come over you? You are so morose: you trudge around as if all the world was piled on your shoulders.'

'Perhaps it is the weight of the gold I owe.'

'Do you remember the old times? You were a much more interesting man then. Before this obsession with gold and loans and debt. You were an artist; now you are a money-changer.'

'Finance is as much part of this art as lead or ink or copper,' I snapped. 'It is the size of this enterprise which justifies it. You want to create things of rare and novel beauty – and no man is better at it. But for this art, the beauty comes from its scale. A drop of water is nothing, but a river is majestic. An ocean is unfathomable.'

'Have you ever looked at a drop of water? Suspended from a branch on a sunlit morning, the whole world reflected in its orb – stretching as the bough shakes, not knowing if it will cling on or fall and disappear into the earth. That is beautiful.'

'If I could do this work for nothing and give it away for free, I would. But you have seen how the costs pile up on each other – and we are not nearly finished yet.'

'Either beauty is present or it is not.' Kaspar and I were in different conversations. 'If you print one indulgence, or cast

340

one mirror, it is what it is. Whether it is unique or there are a thousand others the same, it does not matter.'

'What about gold? Are a thousand gulden more beautiful than a single coin?'

'They are to you.'

Two months later, Andreas Dritzehn died.

LIII

Strasbourg

The hotel provided free Internet access in the room. Nick spent ten minutes lying on the bed and staring at the wall socket, fighting the temptation like a saint. After a week offline he felt as though he'd lost a limb; he was desperate to reconnect. But the men who were chasing him seemed to have an almost telepathic ability to trace his movements. Could he risk it?

The Internet was a vast and deafening conversation; Nick's presence would be a whisper in comparison. And he knew a few tricks. Tingling with doubt, he swung himself off the bed and plugged in his laptop.

Working in digital forensics had made him paranoid about safety. First he cleared all the stored history in his web browser – anything that might inadvertently check in with a site he'd used before and betray him. Then he made his computer a citadel. He threw up a firewall around it and closed all the ports except one, so that all traffic had to pass through a single well-guarded gateway. Like all walls, it was as much about what was kept in as what was kept out. Inside, his antivirus patrolled the corridors and courtyards of the fortress, vigilant to any hint of suspicious activity. It wasn't a frontal attack he feared but spies.

Now to venture out. He connected to the Internet and immediately went to a website which styled itself an anonymiser. It was the sort of thing popular with perverts, criminals and conspiracy nuts, but it had its legitimate uses. Borrowing a metaphor, Nick thought of it as an invisibility cloak, a way of sneaking around the Web without leaving any trace of who you were or where you'd come from.

Even with all his defences up he still felt nervous – like sneaking down to the living room in the middle of the night to explore his father's liquor cabinet. Every page he loaded felt like a floorboard waiting to squeak. Gradually, though, the flow of information closed around him. He forgot the dangers and was swept along on currents of knowledge, following connections as they branched all around him.

He began with the kings of Israel and found little beyond a series of names that were at first familiar and quickly became obscure: David, Solomon, Rehoboam, Abijam, all the way through to Zedekiah. The online encyclopedias provided a lot of regurgitated Bible history, but nothing that looked relevant.

Next he moved on to the *Sayings of the Kings of Israel*. That brought a run of information that quickened his pulse. The *Sayings of the Kings of Israel* was a work casually referenced in the Book of Chronicles. *Click*. 2 Chronicles 33:18: 'The rest of the acts of King Manasses, his prayer to his God, and the words of the seers who spoke to him, these are recorded in the Sayings of the Kings of Israel.' *Click*. These sorts of references were scattered through the Old Testament, throwaway clues to other books that might once have existed but now only remained as ghosts to taunt scholars. *Click*. Like Sherlock Holmes adventures alluded to by Dr Watson but never written by Conan Doyle. *Click*. The case of the politician, the lighthouse and the trained cormorant.

Nick realised he'd reached a dead end. He backtracked and went down a different path, picking up on another keyword, Manasses. Sixteenth king of Israel. Apostate who was captured and taken to Babylon, but who was restored to his kingdom when he repented and returned to God. *Click*. Prayer of. Although the *Sayings of the Kings of Israel* had been lost (if it ever existed), someone around the first century AD had taken it on themselves to invent Manasses' prayer of repentance and pass it off as the original. A sort of fan fiction. It was a fake, but a fake so old it had acquired its own value. It was now included in the Bible as part of the Apocrypha.

Click back to the Bible. 'I am weighted down with many an iron fetter, so that I am rejected by my sins and I have no relief.'

I know how you feel, Nick thought.

Finally, he went back to Gillian's homepage. He knew it was risky, but he had to look.

GILLIAN LOCKHART
is in mortal peril ☺
(last updated 02 January 11:54:56)

It hadn't changed; she hadn't been back. He looked at the images again, his own absence, and cringed as he thought of the photo in his wallet. He went back to the billboard, just in case.

There was one new comment.

344

Are you safe? Did you find it? Please call me. I have a
new number: www.jerseypaints.co.nz
(posted by Olaf, 11 January 17:18:44)

Nick read the message three times over. He checked the date
on his watch. Two days ago. Caution told him he shouldn't go
further; it was a trap. He shouldn't even be online. But he
couldn't resist.

A new page appeared on screen: a picture of a rainbow-
striped cow standing on a ladder, wielding a paintbrush and
grinning. 'Home and industrial paint solutions.' There was a
phone number prefaced by what Nick assumed was a New
Zealand area code, and a couple of testimonials from satisfied
customers. There was no mention of anyone called Olaf.

Nick checked his online security. Everything showed green.
The website didn't seem to be trying to download any kind of
malware.

He had to risk it. He lifted up the hotel phone and dialled
the number shown on the website. There was a delay, then the
foreign bleep of a distant telephone.

'Jersey Paints,' said a New Zealand-accented voice.

'Uh, hi. Is Olaf there?'

An exasperated silence. 'Is this some kind of joke? I've told
you three times already there's no Olaf here. Would you please
stop calling?'

'Sorry,' said Nick.

The moment he hung up a wave of guilt overwhelmed him.
He shouldn't have called, shouldn't even have looked at the
website. Certainly shouldn't have rung from the hotel. *I've told
you three times already.* Somebody else had read the message
and acted on it.

There was a noise at the door. He froze. Had they come

already; had they traced him that easily? From the corridor, he heard the rasp of a key card sliding into the lock. He looked wildly to the window – but it was screwed shut.

The light on the lock went green. With a click, the handle began to turn.

There was nowhere to hide: even the bathroom was down the hall. Nick grabbed his bag with the book and the card inside it. Maybe he could push past the intruder, knock him down and escape.

What if there was more than one of them?

The door swung open. Emily stood in the dimly lit corridor carrying two shopping bags, her hair damp from melting snow. She looked at the bag in his hands.

'Were you going out?'

Nick slumped on the bed in relief. 'I thought . . . I was just making sure the book was still safe.' He looked at her again, noticing something different. 'You've changed.'

She put down the shopping bags and hung her coat on the back of the door. The skirt she'd been wearing since Paris was gone, replaced by a tight rollneck sweater and figure-hugging jeans. It was the first time he'd seen her not wearing a skirt, let alone in jeans. Part of him was almost embarrassed by it, like running into your teacher in the grocery store at the weekend. Part of him was struck by how good she looked.

'I thought trousers would be better if we need to run away again,' she said coolly.

She pulled off her ankle boots and flopped down on the bed next to Nick. Once again, the hotel staff had given them a double when they'd asked for a twin. They lay there side by side, like a married couple in an old movie. To Nick's surprise, it was strangely comfortable.

'The snow's getting heavier outside,' she said after a

moment. 'We might struggle to get out of Strasbourg.'

'If we had anywhere to go.' Nick leaned over and found the TV remote on the bedside table. He turned it on and flipped through the line-up of French game shows and chat shows until he found an English-language news channel. A reporter in a flak jacket was standing in a scorched landscape, while soldiers in hues of brown and tan searched a mud-brick house behind him. It looked like a godforsaken place, but at least it was hot. Nick felt he'd been stumbling around in the cold for half a lifetime.

He muted the TV, letting the images play out in dumbshow in the background.

'I went back on Gillian's web page,' he said. 'Someone left a message for her.'

Emily didn't reply. He looked down and saw that she'd fallen asleep. Her eyes were closed, her pale skin framed by the dark hair fanned out on the pillow. He pulled the blanket at the foot of the bed over her shoulders. She murmured something in her sleep and rolled over, burying herself against his side.

Her body was warm against him. Nick felt the heat spreading through his skin, melting the sheet ice that had been encasing him since Gillian's message first appeared on his desktop. He knew it was a mistake; that when she woke up she'd be embarrassed and he'd be ashamed. But he didn't want to disturb her. He'd let her stay, for a while.

He turned his eyes back to the television, reading the captions and watching the silent parade of spokesmen, sportsmen, apologists and starlets on the far side of the glass wall. Not so long ago they'd seemed so important to him, heroes and villains and storylines played out in the media. Now they seemed a world away.

The picture cut back to the news anchor in the studio. A

new caption had appeared on screen: DISGRACED JESUIT FOUND MURDERED.

Nick reached for the remote and turned up the volume. Emily stirred at the sudden movement. The anchor disappeared, replaced by a grainy mugshot. Nick stared. The man standing too close to the camera, holding the letter-board . . .

'That's Brother Jerome.' Emily sat up, brushing the hair back from her face.

The reporter's voiceover droned on through his shock. 'Neighbours heard gunshots . . . Police called to the house . . . Mafia-style execution . . . Suspicious car reported early this morning . . . Brilliant scholar . . . Sex-abuse scandal . . .'

Nick looked at Emily. Tears were streaming down her cheeks. He wanted to comfort her but she looked so fragile, like she'd shatter if he touched her.

'I killed him,' she whispered.

Back on the television, the story had finished and a new one begun, Brother Jerome's face replaced with a boatload of shivering refugees. Nick muted it again.

'You had no way of knowing,' he murmured.

'I destroyed him.'

'I know how you feel,' Nick tried. 'It's like Bret. If it wasn't for me, he'd be alive. It's like poison inside me. But you can't think that way. It's the guys who killed him who are responsible.'

'I'm responsible,' she insisted. 'He wouldn't have been there if it wasn't for me.'

'Because he tried to take advantage of you when you were a student?'

Emily gulped back some tears and stared at the bedspread. Then, just when he thought she hadn't heard, she said very

348

quickly, 'It wasn't his fault. Jerome and I – we had – we were lovers. He didn't just make a pass at me; we had an affair. When the university found out they fired him, and he was expelled from his order. It destroyed him. Academia was his life.'

Nick thought of the old man with his mop of white hair and tried not to imagine his scrawny hands crawling over Emily's skin. 'He still should never have touched you.'

'He should never have touched me,' she repeated. 'That's right. But not the way you think. *I* fell in love with *him*. I seduced him, if that's the right word. I was infatuated, relentless; I wouldn't take no for an answer. I didn't realise what I was doing.' She wiped a tear from her face. 'Eventually the guilt got too much for him and he broke it off. I was so angry with him, all I wanted was revenge. I reported him out of sheer spite. I destroyed his life. And now this.'

LIV

Strassburg

I examined the paper with the familiar ache of broken hopes. Some of the letters had barely registered; others had pressed so hard that blots of ink drowned the characters. In several places the paper had torn where we had not smoothed the edges of the cast metal forms. The whole sheet had smudged badly when we removed it from the press. Drach had been right: I could press ten thousand copies of this and it would still be ugly.

I picked up a file, resigned to another afternoon of thankless labour. Casting the metal form from the engraved copper plate had been easy, but I had not anticipated the fine accuracy that would be needed. If any letter stood even a hair's breadth lower than the others it would hardly touch the page. The same amount too high and it would crush the paper with ink. As the letters were created by hammering a steel punch into the copper, it was all but impossible to make them a uniform height except by the most meticulous filing.

'Where are the forms?'

Kaspar looked up. 'In the bag?'

I looked in the bag that Kaspar had brought from Dritzehn's house. Apart from a few lumps of cast-off lead, it was empty.

'Perhaps you put them on the workbench.'

I rummaged through the debris of paper, tools, copper plates and miscast forms that littered the bench. I could not find them.

'Are you sure you brought them back?'

He shrugged. 'I thought so.'

This was when I hated working with Kaspar. If he did not care about something he thought nothing of ignoring it, and no rebuke could reach him.

'You must have left them in the press.'

'Perhaps I did,' he agreed.

'I told you to bring them back.' Dritzhen had been on his sickbed a week now, and the house had become a thoroughfare for concerned family, prying friends and creditors who feared they might never see their money again. 'If anybody sees them our secret is lost.'

'I locked the door.'

I did not want to quarrel with Kaspar – we had already argued too much that year. I turned my back on him and looked out the barn door, breathing the December air to cool my temper.

A boy was standing in the yard. At first I thought he might be a vagabond or a thief but he did not run away when I stepped out of the barn to challenge him. I looked closer and realised I knew him, an errand boy of Hans Dunne. He looked as though he had run all the way from Strassburg.

'Did Dunne send you?' I called out the door.

He nodded. 'He said to tell you Herr Dritzehn is dead.'

*

351

With its bowed-out walls and blunt gable, the house already looked like a coffin. The shutters were closed, and no light emerged from within. We stood on the doorstep a long time before a servant admitted us. Inside it stank of vinegar and resin where they had burned pine dust in the fires.

'Go downstairs and rescue the forms,' I told Kaspar. I handed him the key we used to lock the cellar. 'Take the screws out as well.' To reduce the effects of a single mistake, our latest innovation with this press was to divide the text into four separately cast strips, one for each paragraph, screwed together to make the plate.

'Where will you go?'

'To pay my last respects.'

I took a candle from the wall and climbed the creaking stairs. Shadows flitted across the walls. A dozen pairs of eyes fixed on me as I entered the room: mourners and servants gathered outside the bedroom door. All seemed united in some silent accusation. Most were clustered around a stout woman in a white veil – Dritzehn's wife, now widow – and the man she clung to, his brother Jörg.

I removed my hat. 'Frau Dritzehn, I have come to say how sorry—'

The moment she saw me she detached herself from the throng and flew at me.

'You have done this,' she shrieked. 'You and your friend. He was a good man, an honest man, until you seduced him with your magic. If any good can come of this day, it is that you will no longer have a claim on him. When Andreas is buried you will give me back every penny he paid you.'

She rained down blows upon me. Her brother-in-law flung his arms around her and pulled her off me.

'Go to your husband,' he ordered her. 'I will deal with this.'

He almost pushed her into the bedroom. Through the open door, I saw the dim shape of Dritzehn's body lying flat on his bed under a shroud.

Jörg closed the door and gave me a crafty look. I had met him once or twice before in my visits to that house and never liked him. He was a small, hunched man with swollen cheeks and a stubby chin like a club foot.

'She is hysterical,' he said, no trace of sympathy. 'Understandably. At times like this, business is better left with cooler heads.'

'Your brother is dead,' I answered. 'Business can wait.'

'I spoke to Andreas before he passed on. He told me of your venture, that his only regret dying now was that he would not live to see the vast riches he knew would come of it. He said that I should have his share of the partnership.'

'If he said that then the disease must already have claimed his mind,' I said. 'But we can talk of this another day. I came here to mourn Andreas.'

It was true. I did not deny that I had played on his greed and encouraged him into ventures that would profit me more than him. But Dritzehn had been a merchant: he speculated as he saw fit. How he financed it was his affair. As one man to another, I mourned him.

'I will go. I did not mean to upset his family in their hour of grief.'

'You will upset me much more if you do not listen to me,' Jörg warned. 'I know how much money Andreas sank into your little scheme, though he could never tell me why you deserved it.'

'Then you will never know. His money and his secrets stay in the partnership.'

'Then I must take his place.'

353

'I have a contract signed by him that in the event of his death his heirs will receive nothing until the venture is finished. Even then, he died owing me money.' I could not believe I was having to say this before his corpse was cold.

'Would you leave his wife destitute?'

'She is your responsibility, not mine. She will only go destitute if you let her.'

'Then I will go to the courts.' Jörg had started shouting. 'Whatever it is that you and Andreas kept so secret will be exposed to the whole city. You cannot keep me out.'

I met Kaspar outside. 'Did you get the forms?'

He handed me a heavy bag. 'I also took the screw out of the press. No one who sees it will guess what it was for.'

'They may learn anyway. Dritzehn's brother threatened to drag me through the courts.'

'Let him. There are only four men alive who know the full secret. Saspach and Dunne will not betray us.'

I took little comfort from that. 'We must get home. Jörg Dritzehn is wild for our art. I would not be surprised if he broke into our workshop to sniff it out.'

We borrowed a horse for Kaspar and rode back to St Argobast in the dark. All I remember of that ride is cold air and horse sweat. As soon as we arrived I stoked up the fire in the forge and lit all the lamps and candles I could find. With Drach's help, I scoured the barn for every casting we had ever made: every form, every fragment of lead, any piece of metal with letters cast in it. I gathered them in an iron crucible and set it over the fire. The only ones I spared were the engraved copper plates. I wrapped them in a sack and buried them under a stone in the yard. They were too expensive to waste.

I added coals to the fire and coaxed it to a blazing heat. The forms began to soften. The tiny letters blurred and melted away, running down the face of the metal like tears.

'Is this the end of our enterprise?'

I looked at Kaspar. Beads of sweat ran down his cheeks from standing too close to the fire. I jabbed a poker into the crucible to break up a stubborn lump of metal.

'Even if we see off Jörg Dritzehn, what do we have? An art that does not work and a venture that has no capital, only debts. Ennelin, the mirrors, now Dritzehn: everything we attempt ends in disaster.'

I stared into the crucible and watched the last crumbs of metal dissolve into the slurry. I remembered Dritzehn's widow. *You have done this.*

I glanced up. Drach was gone.

Panic overwhelmed me. Had he abandoned me? Had I driven him away with my failures? I left the forge and ran to the barn.

Kaspar was there, bending over the press in the corner. I sagged against the door frame in relief. With his back to me, he extracted a copper plate and fixed it in a vice on the bench. He took a fine-toothed metal saw from a rack of tools on the wall.

'I told you to gather all the plates so I could bury them.'

He didn't look up. 'This is not yours.'

I crossed the barn and looked closer. The lamps shone into the grooves cut into the surface, a herd of lions and bears incised in copper.

'This was the plate for the ten of beasts.' Drach lined up the saw blade on the edge of the plate and drew it slowly across the metal. Sparks flew.

'What are you doing? There is no need to destroy these. This is your art.'

The saw bit. A jagged gash appeared in the copper.

'I am not destroying it; I am remaking it. We will need more money to continue with your art. I can make more cards and sell them. It will not be much, but it may tide us through.'

'But you told me half the plates were gone. And now you are breaking this one too.'

'This card is the sum of all the others. He put his palms against the plate so that he masked off different portions of it. 'Here is one, and two, and three . . . I can break it into its parts and combine them to make any number I like.'

I wrapped my arms around him and hugged him close to me. His body was warm against mine, a perfect fit. I loved him.

And in that moment, an angel began to sing inside me. What Kaspar had done with the card, I could do with the indulgences.

We would tear it up and start again.

LV

Strasbourg

On the dresser, the television played silent images of war and grief. Nick watched, hypnotised. The shock of Brother Jerome's death left him numb.

He had to break the spell. He grabbed the remote and turned off the TV. 'We need to leave.'

There was an unusual firmness in his voice, an urgency he'd never felt before. It snapped Emily out of her daze.

'Where? There's nowhere to go.'

'Let's start by getting out of here. The TV said the neighbours heard the shots this afternoon. Whoever did it was only a few hours behind us.'

'Could they have followed us?'

'Jerome was the one who suggested Strasbourg. He showed us the *ex libris*, told us the whole story of the Count of Lorraine. He must have guessed we'd come here. If he told them . . .'

They took the stairs down to the lobby, out into the street. He didn't notice the black Audi parked opposite the hotel. The snow seemed to be coming down less heavily now, though there were still flakes whirling in the cones of light under the street lamps. Plenty had fallen already. They crunched deep footprints as they walked around the cathedral and down one of the side streets. Nick looked back but saw no one. The shops were shut, the workers gone home.

A few streets away, they found a small bistro that was open for dinner. It was only half full, but after the wintry solitude outside it felt cosy and welcoming, filled with candlelight and smoky smells of herbs, roasted meat and wine. They took a table behind a wooden pillar, hidden from the windows but with a view of the door, and ordered *vin chaud* and *tartiflettes*. In other circumstances it would have been a perfect romantic evening: candlelight, hot wine, knees bumping under the small table. Now the intimacy just seemed another rebuke, a taunt from a world that had abandoned him.

He swirled his glass and stared at the dregs. 'Atheldene was right. I don't know what any of this means but it's crazy.'

'It means something to somebody,' Emily countered. 'If we weren't on the right track, they wouldn't keep trying to stop us.'

'We're not going to find Gillian.' The words were bitter in his mouth. 'All I've done is get people killed. Bret, Dr Haltung, now Brother Jerome.'

'Brother Jerome was my fault,' said Emily quietly. 'If I hadn't taken you there he'd never have been involved.'

'If I hadn't brought you here *you'd* never have been involved.' Nick squeezed the stem of his wine glass, so hard he thought it would shatter.

He glanced up. Emily seemed not to have heard him; her face was fixed in an emotionless stare over his shoulder. He began to turn to follow, but she grabbed his hand and pulled him back.

'Keep looking at me. There's a man three tables behind you who's been watching us for the last five minutes.'

Nick felt a familiar surge of dread. 'What does he look like?'

'Dark, heavy build. A crooked nose. Italian, maybe. He hasn't taken off his coat since he came in.'

Nick flicked his eyes to the gilded mirror on the wall but couldn't pick him out. His mind raced.

'I've got an idea.' His whole body was tensed, half expecting to feel a gun in his back any second. He locked his eyes on Emily's to steady himself. 'In a moment, we'll have a blazing row. You'll run off in tears to the bathroom. I'll storm out the door. We'll leave the bag on the table and see what he does.'

'What if he comes after you?'

'Then you come after him.'

'And if he comes after me?'

'Scream the place down. I'll be right there.' Nick gripped her wrist. 'Are you ready?'

She nodded – then suddenly pushed back her chair and leaped to her feet.

'How dare you say that?' she shouted. Around the restaurant, the rattle of cutlery and conversation went still. Even Nick was shocked. 'You don't have a clue what I'm feeling.'

She looked wildly around, then threw up her hands and ran out to the toilets. Nick sat stunned for a moment, then pushed back his chair so that the bag hanging on the arm was clearly visible. He slammed a twenty-euro note down on the table and stalked to the exit, keeping his eyes glued to the floor.

Even before the door shut, he heard the scrape of a chair being hurriedly vacated. He ran along the well-trampled pavement to the nearest corner, ducked behind it and looked back.

Almost at once, the restaurant door banged open again. A

thickset man in a long black coat strode out. The lantern over the door bathed him in yellow light. Nick glimpsed dark hair, dark skin, a boxer's nose and his own backpack dangling from the man's fist. There was something familiar about him – from the Belgian warehouse, perhaps? He looked briskly up and down the street, then pulled his keys out of his pocket. The man pressed whatever was in his hand. Orange lights blinked on a black Audi across the street. No snow had settled on the roof: it couldn't have been there long. Nick tried to look inside, wondering if there was anyone else behind the dark windows.

The man crossed the street and opened the driver-side door. Nick made up his mind. The snow was silent underfoot. The man had his back to Nick and was fumbling with the backpack, perhaps making sure that the book was inside. He didn't hear Nick coming until he was almost on top of him. Nick dropped his shoulder and drove his fists into the man's stomach. All the anger, fear and frustration he'd endured in the last week released itself in that one moment of contact, a perfect spear of rage. The man doubled over; the keys fell out of his hand into the snow. Nick kicked them under the car, then kneed his adversary in the face. He grabbed for the bag.

But Nick was an amateur. The other man was a pro. Nick's knee had unbalanced his opponent but not knocked him over. As Nick stretched out for the bag, the man's big hand whipped out and closed around his arm. He twisted; Nick felt his arm almost torn off its elbow. His whole body was wrenched around. His feet skidded on the snow, lost their grip and slid from underneath him. The man threw him back onto the ground.

Nick gasped as the breath was forced out of him. Looming above, the man took a step back. For a split second Nick thought he might just turn and run. But he was only giving himself more space. He reached inside his coat and pulled out a pistol. It looked tiny in his hoof-like fist.

This was how it would end. Lying in the road, his blood melting into the snow around him until it cooled and froze. He'd never know what had happened to Gillian, never understand why he'd come to this icy corner of France to die. He raged at the injustice of it.

With a scream, Emily flew out of the night and hurled herself against the man. She was too slight to have much effect, but she wrapped herself around his arm and dragged it down, away from Nick.

Nick sprang to his feet and grabbed for the gun. His hand closed around the cold barrel and clung on for his life. For a moment the three of them were caught in a heaving tangle of limbs and steel, swaying and staggering in the snow. Then something gave. Nick lost his balance; the next thing he knew his cheek was planted in the snow, pinned down by somebody on top of him.

'Are you OK?'

Emily pushed herself off him and stood. Nick scrambled up after her. He still had the gun, holding it by its muzzle like a club. Where was their opponent?

Halfway down the street, a large shadow flitted across the snow under a street lamp. Nick looked around.

'He's still got the bag.'

'Wait,' Emily called. But Nick was already running. His feet crunched in the snow; his arms pumped so fast he barely noticed the weight of the gun. The man might be strong but he wasn't quick on his feet. Nick had little trouble keeping him in sight as they sprinted along the empty streets. The black and white frames of the half-timbered houses were skeletal in the gloom, their shuttered windows blind to the frantic chase.

The man glanced over his shoulder, then ducked down an unlit side street. His heavy tracks were printed clearly in the snow – especially here, where few other feet had disturbed it. Nick followed, gaining. He glimpsed the black gleam of water below as he crossed a bridge and turned again.

The houses thinned, giving way to a strip of grass and trees. To his right, he saw a jumble of wooden battlements and turrets – a children's playground. The chill air rasped in Nick's lungs. But he could see his quarry clearly now, barely twenty yards ahead of him. He swallowed the pain and kept going.

Between the trees, Nick saw water on all sides. They must have come onto some sort of island in the river. Ahead, a row of high stone towers stood floodlit against the darkness where the island ended.

The man was trapped. He slowed to a walk, then stopped. Nick skidded to a halt on the icy path, keeping well back. He raised the gun as his quarry turned to face him. They stood there among the trees and snow in silence, a dozen paces apart like duellists. But only one of them had a gun.

'Who are you?' Nick shouted. The night seemed to swallow his words.

The man didn't answer. He looked down at the bag still dangling from his hand, then let it drop. It landed in the snow at his feet. The movement drew Nick's attention; in that moment, the Italian's hand dipped inside his pocket. Nick's gaze snapped back. With the sickening knowledge that he'd made a fatal mistake, he raised the pistol. But his finger hesitated on the trigger.

The man hadn't pulled another gun. Instead, he'd extracted a sheet of paper. His hands scrabbled with it as he folded it over and over, then began tearing it into pieces.

'Stop!' Nick shouted. Tiny fragments fluttered to the

ground like a shower of snow. Nick jerked the gun – but he couldn't shoot a man in cold blood.

A brilliant beam of light swept across the park behind him. A barge was coming up the river, its captain taking no chances in the darkness. In a second, Nick would be picked out like an actor on stage. He lowered the gun to his side, into the shadows. Like deer caught on a road, neither he nor the man dared move.

The barge drew level with them. The river was so narrow here that the boat's hull almost touched the embankment, its deck only a foot or so below Nick's feet. Floodlights bathed the park in light, blinding Nick. In that moment, the Italian jumped. He heaved himself over the railing and dropped like a stone onto the barge. Nick ran to the rail, but all he saw was a wall of dazzling light blazing back at him.

Footsteps crunched behind him; he swung around. Emily was running across the park, her breath fogging the night.

'Where is he?'

Nick pointed to the barge, now disappearing around a bend in the river. 'He got away.'

He walked over to where the bag lay and scanned the ground. As his eyes readjusted to the darkness he found he could pick out a few of the scraps of paper lying limp in the snow. He picked one up. It seemed to be normal office paper, with a fragment of a word on it.

'What's that?'

'Something important. When I had the guy cornered, the one thing he cared about was destroying it.'

They knelt together in the snow, sweeping the ground and gathering the fragments in shivering hands. Nick thanked God there was no wind. When they had collected as many as they could find, they shook the snow off them and bagged them in a pocket of Nick's backpack. Emily looked doubtfully at the pile of sodden scraps, not much bigger than confetti.

'Do you think we'll make any sense of that?'

Nick grimaced. The city glow reflected off the snow and gave his face a ghoulish cast. *I piece things together.*

'We have the technology. We can fix it.'

LVI

We would tear it up and piece it back together.

By liberating the beasts from the flat cage of their copper plates, Drach could make any card he wanted. Even if only one animal remained, he could print and reprint it as often as he wanted onto the same card. The system was not only perfect, it was infinitely variable.

It was not a new idea. We had started down this road when we divided the indulgence plate into four paragraphs. But we had not gone nearly far enough. One afternoon I counted three thousand and seventy-four individual characters in the indulgence. We would cast each one individually and bring them together to form a single page, as thousand of souls form a single Church.

Hans Dunne disliked the plan. 'Each time you encounter a problem, you find an answer that creates ten new problems and does not solve the first,' he warned me. But he had earned more than a hundred gulden from me for creating the copper plates which had proved so troublesome, so I ignored him.

Kaspar did not like it either. 'You are turning in on yourself.

You are trying to climb a mountain by counting pebbles. You will spend the rest of your life making this art so intricate that nothing can be done with it.'

We were journeying through a forest in late October. It was like walking through fire: all around us the leaves burned vivid shades of scarlet, ochre, yellow and orange, shimmering in the breeze. It was a dangerous time to be abroad.

'And even if you succeed, it will just turn out like the mirrors,' Kaspar prodded me.

Much had happened since the night Andreas Dritzehn died. His brother Jörg had sued me to be admitted to our partnership – and lost. The judge awarded him fifteen gulden. The Aachen pilgrimage had come and gone, the relics put away for another seven years. Some of the mirrors waved aloft to capture the holy rays had been mine, but not many. First, a good portion of our metals had been sold to pay the interest on my debts. Then we had been swindled by our barge captain and decimated by tolls along the river, before being opposed at every turn by the Aachen guilds. By the time we were finished, the torrent of tin and lead I had prepared to pour down the Rhine had dwindled to a trickle. The torrent of gold I had hoped would flow back to me suffered a similar fate. Once I had paid our costs, paid the investors, paid my debts, including the fifteen gulden to Jörg Dritzehn, only the thinnest residue remained.

Kaspar hated it when his comments drew no reaction. He tried a third time. 'And it is madness to be on the road now. I heard that a week ago Breisgau was razed to the ground. They made a bonfire of the village and roasted its livestock on the coals. Some say they also roasted the inhabitants and ate them too.'

I shuddered. For months now the country around

Strassburg had been infested with a plague of wild men, the *Armagnaken* or 'poor fools', the remnants of a great army which had been marauding around Europe in the service of one duke or another for years. An unholy cabal of the French king, the German emperor and the Italian pope had schemed to send them to Switzerland to sack Basle: the king because he wanted them out of France, the emperor because he aimed to annex Switzerland to the empire; the pope because he wanted to put a stop once and for all to the council which Aeneas and his friends had conducted now for over ten years. The Swiss had defied the *Armagnaken* and defeated them at terrible cost. The survivors had fled, rampaging down the Rhine in a storm of fire and blood that – men said – only the Apocalypse would equal. They had arrived near Strassburg in the spring. Many thousands had died.

The forest was no longer beautiful. I peered into its depths, trying to see what lurked behind the blaze of foliage.

'Nick? What the hell happened to you? I've been hearing some bad things.'

Urthred the Necromancer paced his chamber in front of a roaring fire. A unicorn stood tethered obediently in the corner.

'Long story. I need some help.'

'Where are you?'

'Strasbourg.'

'Is that Kentucky?'

'France.'

'Right.' A waxwork scowl was fixed on Urthred's face. 'Um, I'm kind of a long way from France right now.'

'I need a high-res scanner and a fat data pipe. As fast as possible. I thought you might know someone.'

Urthred tapped his staff on the stone floor. Blue sparks

fizzed from its tip. 'Sheesh, Nick, you don't make it easy. What time is it with you?'

Nick checked his watch. 'Nine at night.'

'You know, this is not cool Nick.' A pause, then a grumpy sigh. 'OK. I'll check my contacts for insomniac French data-centre managers with a hard-on for fugitives from justice. Stick around.'

Urthred disappeared in a puff of smoke. Nick unhooked the headset from his ear and looked up from the laptop. The cobwebbed walls and swirling mists of the Necromancer's tower were replaced with thick red paint and cigarette smoke, an underground bar off the Quai Saint Jean. To Nick, the other customers seemed as outlandish as anything in Gothic Lair: piercings through every permeable patch of skin, hair dyed red or purple or green, steel chains around their necks and waists. None of them looked as if they'd come to take advantage of the free wireless Internet.

'Are you sure this is the time to be playing computer games?' asked Emily. She sat next to him on the threadbare banquette, sipping a Jack Daniel's and Coke.

'You know the slogan, "The network is the computer"?' She shook her head. 'Well, in human terms the network is Randall. Urthred. If there's anyone who can help us, Randall probably knows him somehow.'

'I don't understand. We've got an Internet connection here.'

'Nowhere near fast enough. And we need to scan the pictures. You can't do that with a mobile-phone camera.'

On the laptop screen, Urthred reappeared out of nowhere. Nick put the headset back on and tried to ignore the sneering looks he drew.

'I got it,' Urthred bragged. 'You heard of a place called Karlsruhe?'

'No.'

'It's in Germany – about an hour away from you, according to the Interweb. *Hochschule für Gestaltung.* It's some kind of technical college. There's a chick in the computer science department there, Sabine Friman. She can hook you up.'

Nick hesitated. 'Can we get there without a car?'

'What am I, a fricking concierge service?' Urthred crossed to the large book spread on the wings of an eagle-shaped lectern and consulted it. 'Says there's a train from Strasbourg to Frankfurt at 21.50 that stops at Karlsruhe. You want me to tell you where the restaurant car is too?'

'We'll find it.' Nick reached for the lid of the computer, ready to shut it down. 'But there's one other thing I need you to arrange.'

Whatever dangers lurked in the forest, we reached our destination without harm. Schlettstadt was an unremarkable town some twenty miles up the Ill from Strassburg. Like every town in those days, it existed in a state of siege. Guards manned the walls, and its gates only opened when we had proved we carried no weapons. Suspicious gazes followed our progress along the winding alleys inside, up the hill towards the church.

'Have you noticed how goldsmiths always keep their shops near churches?' Drach muttered. 'Jesus preached poverty and forsaking worldly goods.'

'Keep your voice down,' I warned him. 'It's bad enough that everyone here thinks we must be an advance party of *Armagnaken*, without you sounding like a Free Spirit heretic as well.'

We found what we had come to see in a steep-gabled house plastered red between its branching beams. Much of it was familiar from all goldsmiths' shops: the tools on the walls; the boxes of beads and wire; the plate glinting behind the bars of the show cabinet; the residues of quicksilver and hot metal.

But they were not fresh. No smoke rose from the furnace at the back of the house, and the anvils were silent. These were lean times for goldsmiths – they could not work gold when it was all buried under mattresses and floorboards.

I leaned on the empty counter and peered inside. A man sat on a stool, pulling rings off a spindle and polishing them one by one.

'Are you Götz?' I asked.

He nodded. He must have been about thirty, with bushy brown hair and a thin face. I introduced myself.

'I am associated with the goldsmiths' guild in Strassburg. I have seen your work there. A brooch of Christ on his cross.' It had been Andreas Dritzehn's. His brother had brought it into Dunne's shop to sell after Andreas' death. Through discreet enquiry, I had found out who had made it. 'The lettering on the inscription was exquisite. So precise.'

He accepted the compliment in silence.

'I assume you cut the letters with punches.'

A suspicious look. I sympathised. 'I do not want to steal your secret. I want to buy it.'

I put a purse of coins on the counter.

'I want you to make me a set of punches, exactly as you made your own.'

Götz eyed the purse but did not touch it.

'I can cut your punches.' He hesitated. 'But not *exactly* as I made my own.'

'What do you mean?'

He chose his words cautiously. 'You want punches that will stamp each letter in metal. I do not have any.'

370

'But the brooch . . .'

'You could scour my workshop from top to bottom and you would not find a single alphabetical punch.'

I tried to remember everything I could about the writing on the brooch. 'Surely you did not engrave it freehand?'

He pushed the purse back towards me. 'I would rather not say.'

Frustrated and perplexed, I was about to turn away. But the wink of gold in his cabinet delayed me. I peered through the leaded glass.

'May I examine that cup?'

I could see his doubts – but the purse still lay on the counter, and I might be the only customer he would have that week. He unlocked the cabinet and handed me the cup. It was about six inches tall, with a bowed stem and garnets set into the bowl. Around the base was written a verse from St John's Gospel.

I studied it a few moments, pressing my fingertips into the sharp incisions. The lines were too straight, too clean to have been carved by hand. They must have been stamped. Yet Götz claimed he had no letter punches.

I put down the cup and picked up the purse.

'Thank you.'

The taxi dropped them off outside the *Hochschule für Gestaltung*. In the dark, Nick couldn't see much more than a cluster of square, practical buildings surrounded by trees. Sabine Friman was standing by the front door waiting for them. She was a lithe woman with short blonde hair that poked around her ears in elfin spikes, blue eyes and a tanned face. In spite of the cold, she wore nothing more than an olive-green tank top and cargo pants.

'The Wanderer arrives,' she said. Her English was perfect, with a Scandinavian crispness. 'Did you have a good journey?'

She led them in. Even at that time of night, there were plenty of students in the corridors. Everything was warm, bright and clean; it was the safest he'd felt in ages.

'Randall told me what you need.' She unlocked a door from the ring of keys clipped to her belt. Inside was a small, windowless room with a computer monitor and a scanner set up on a plastic folding table. 'The scanner is 2,400dpi, and we have a direct connection to the i-21 data network.'

'Great. Can we start with the scanner?'

Sabine lifted the lid and held out her hand. To her obvious surprise, Nick reached in his coat and handed her what looked like a pile of greetings cards.

'Did you forget someone's birthday?'

Nick flipped one round so she could see the back. Tiny scraps of paper made a mosaic on the glossy red card. 'We needed a high-contrast reflective background. This was all they sold at the rail station.' Thankfully the train had been pretty empty, not too many passengers to wonder why he and Emily spent the journey gluing the fragments on. 'It'll make scanning easier.'

Sabine laid the greetings cards on the scanner and closed the lid. It hummed into life; a bar of green light slowly traversed the platen. A vastly magnified picture of the back of the card slid down the screen.

'Now to upload them,' said Nick. He sat down on the metal chair. 'This is where it gets interesting.'

Sabine leaned over his shoulder and studied the screen. 'How does it work, exactly?'

'We upload these pictures to the server that hosts my program. That picks out the fragments of paper and turns them into individual images. Then it analyses them for edge shape, fragments of letters or words and tries to piece them back together. Like doing a jigsaw.'

Emily looked at the computer as if it were an alien object. 'Can't you just do it on your laptop?'

'The raw number crunching you need for this thing is way too intensive for a home computer.' Nick opened a web browser and typed in an address. 'It's like trying to solve all the possible outcomes of a chess game, but with thousands of pieces that are all different shapes. The processing has to be done on massive central servers – in this case, belonging to the people who fund my research.'

'Who's that?'

'The FBI.'

Even Sabine's ice-cool composure took a knock. 'You want to hack into the FBI's computer system? From here?'

'I'm not going to hack in anywhere. I'm going to walk up to the front door and use a valid user name and password.'

Sabine shot him a crooked look. 'Randall said you were maybe not so happy with the police right now.'

'That was the NYPD. The parts of the Bureau that fund me are a long way away from the parts that hunt bad guys. If we're very lucky, the right hand might not have gotten round to telling the left hand what's been going on. After all, it's the last place they'd expect me to go.'

'Maybe they've got a point.' Emily folded her arms and walked to the back of the room. Sabine glanced between her and Nick.

'Can I get you a drink?'

'Something with caffeine. It's going to be a long night.'

Sabine went out. After a moment, Emily turned back to see what Nick was doing. To her surprise, she saw that the scanned picture had given way to a thick forest, through which Nick seemed to be navigating a one-eyed man in a grey cloak and a bronze helmet.

'Gothic Lair?'

Nick didn't look up. 'Whoever's after us, they've tracked every move we've made.' Emily noticed how white his knuckles were as they gripped the computer mouse. 'I don't want Sabine to end up like Brother Jerome if they trace us back here. So I'm taking the long way round.'

On screen, the Wanderer came out into a clearing that surrounded a giant oak tree. It looked ancient. Its branches sagged low and its wizened bark was pocked with disease. A mess of gnarled roots tangled the earth around its base like cables.

'You came.' Urthred the Necromancer stepped out from behind the tree. He sounded disappointed.

'Did you manage to do it?' Nick asked.

'Did I ever tell you about the time the FBI came to visit me when I was sixteen?' Urthred examined the leaves on one of the low-hanging branches. 'Not a good time in my life.'

'All you have to do is get me to the front door.'

'It's all set up.' Urthred pointed to the bottom of the tree, where a fat root split in two like a cloven hoof. It forced the earth apart, leaving a triangular hole in the fork. 'Down you go.'

The Wanderer jumped. The screen went black as the hole swallowed him. Nick waited for something to happen. The green light on the computer's network card blinked furiously, but the screen stayed blank. Had Randall screwed up?

'Should something be happening?' said Emily.

'I got him to set up a secure connection to the FBI servers in Washington. Hopefully it'll make us untraceable.' Nick drummed his fingers on the desk and stared at the screen. All he saw was his own reflection. 'If we get there.'

A blue screen appeared with a government seal and the words FEDERAL BUREAU OF INVESTIGATION emblazoned across the top. Nick had never thought he'd be so glad to see it. He typed in his password and held his breath.

Password accepted

The screen changed again, a plain list of files and folders. Nick clicked one and entered a file name. The lights on the network connection went into overdrive; a green bar began crawling across the screen as the file started to transfer.

'How long do we have to wait?' Emily asked.

'Maybe half an hour for the upload. After that . . .' Nick shrugged. 'The program's written to deal with bags of shredded material at a time, so one sheet should be quicker. On the other hand, we don't know if we have all the pieces, and we don't know how wet they got in the snow. And there's the question of what was actually on the original sheet of paper. The more detail, particularly words, the easier it is for the algorithm to figure it out.'

'Nick – you there?' Randall's disembodied voice jumped out of the computer speakers. Nick leaned towards the microphone he'd plugged in.

'Worked perfectly.'

'That's what I'm telling you: it didn't. Somebody's sniffing all over that connection. You must have triggered some kind of alarm when you logged in.'

'Is it coming from the Washington end?'

'Doesn't look like it. How much longer do you need?'

Nick looked at the status bar.

'It's going to be a while.'

'That was a wasted errand,' Kaspar complained. But I saw his eyes dart towards me as soon as he'd said it, always probing.

I played along. 'I found it useful.'

A brief silence followed, while he pretended he did not want to know and I pretended I did not want to tell him.

'How?'

'Every letter has a different shape. But each is composed of a much smaller number of basic shapes. A stroke, a dot, a curve. I would guess that with a set of six punches, maybe ten, you could strike almost any letter.'

Drach snorted. 'So reductive. You reduce the page to words and the words to letters; now the letters to lines. Next you will want to form each line from individual grains of metal. And you still don't know how to make any of it work.'

'Götz does.'

'Then why don't you hire him?'

'Maybe I will.' I was fed up with Dunne. I suspected he had stopped believing in the enterprise long ago, and now saw me only as a tap of easy money to be left dripping as long as possible. 'But first I must know what I want Götz to do.'

I sighed. Trying to comprehend the project on every level, from the finished plate to the tiniest stroke of each letter, turned my mind inside out. Every level depended on the others, and the least change to one caused changes to all. It was like trying to imagine the design of a cathedral while simultaneously knowing every stone within it. Sometimes I glimpsed the harmony of the whole, or felt its resonance. More often, it made my head hurt.

'We should start back.'

Kaspar looked back at the clock tower. 'It will be dark before we're halfway there.'

'We'll find an inn.'

We ducked out of the town gate and joined the road back to Strassburg. High clouds had covered the sky. Without the sun the leaves no longer seemed so vibrant, merely old. They put me in a melancholy mood. I looked at their withered faces, the waxy green of youth dulled to dry brown, and saw my own face mirrored back to me. The purse of gold weighed like lead in my pocket.

We had not gone far when a new noise intruded on the rustle of leaves and flowing water. The staccato clop of hooves, soon swelled by a murmuring chatter of voices. Kaspar and I glanced at each other, then scurried off the road and crouched behind a pair of thick oaks. I clutched the purse tied under my shirt and tried to see who was coming.

LVII

Karlsruhe

TRANSFER COMPLETE

'Now for the hard part.'

Nick took a deep breath and hammered out a few commands on the keyboard. The file icons disappeared; the screen turned a hazy purple. One by one, white blots appeared like raindrops on a window. Some faded back to nothing; others beaded together in clusters and spread across the screen. The effect was hypnotic.

'It's beautiful,' said Emily. 'Is that what the program's doing?'

Nick hit a key. The screen blinked out of existence.

'That's just the visualiser. The people who write the cheques like to see it. It keeps the grants coming in, but it slows everything down.'

Emily looked anxiously at her watch. 'Then do we have to wait here? Can't you leave the program running and pick up the results somewhere else?'

'It's not designed for that. The Feds get antsy if confidential information is left unattended. Even on a machine. If you log out, it pulls the plug.'

'So we just sit here?'

Nick pushed back the chair and punched the tab on a can of Coke. 'You can explore the wide world of Gothic Lair if you like.'

He pressed another key. Suddenly, they were back in the forest. By the edge of the clearing, Urthred was scratching himself with jerky, repetitive motions that meant Randall had gone somewhere else.

Emily looked at the shimmering forest. 'Do all video games provide back doors to the FBI?'

'Randall's a seventy-first-level mage.' Nick saw that didn't explain much to Emily. 'He's also done some work for the guys who publish Gothic Lair. He has a lot of access.'

'And a whole lot of pain.'

The Wanderer turned around. Urthred had come up behind him, apparently repossessed by Randall.

'It's a shitstorm. Someone was tooled up and ready for you to go back to that account. They're trying to take it down. Massive botnet DoS.'

'What does that mean?' said Emily.

Nick covered his mouthpiece. 'It means they've got a network of zombie computers – machines they've infected with a virus – that they can get to all try to make connections to the FBI server at the same time.' He thought for a second. 'Imagine you've got a water fountain where people go and get a drink. As long as everyone takes his turn, no problem. Now imagine that a hysterical mob converges on it, all fighting to get a few drops of water at once. Eventually there are so many that they actually block up the pipe and no water can even get

379

out. The pipe backs up, or breaks open, and the whole thing's wrecked. That's what they're trying to do here.'

'Will it work?'

'It's already pissed off the Feds,' Randall's voice said from the speakers. 'Now they're on to us as well.'

'Do you think they can shut down the program?'

'I doubt it. They need you to stay logged in.'

'How come?'

'So they can find out where you are.'

Two horses came around the bend in the road. Both riders wore chain-mail hauberks and carried lances. I could not see any insignia, though that would have meant little. Plenty of knights had lost their standards to the *Armagnaken*. I crouched lower in the undergrowth.

But the riders were only the vanguard. Behind them came a group on foot – men and women, walking together, laughing and talking. About two dozen of them. Many carried stout walking staffs and wore short capes, with pointed hoods raised against the autumn chill. It was a company of pilgrims, probably bound for the shrine of St Theobald near Strassburg.

With a breath of relief, I stepped out into the road. One of the riders saw us and spurred forward. I stood my ground and made the sign of the cross. He reined in just in front of me.

'Who are you?'

'Travellers on our way to Strassburg. Can we join your company?'

A fat priest with an officious face stepped out from among the pilgrims. 'Can you pay?'

I paused, taken aback.

'The road is dangerous.' He pointed to the two riders. 'We have hired these guards from our own pocket. If you wish to share their protection, you should contribute.'

Fear outweighed my sense of injustice. 'I can contribute.'

He held out his hand. 'Now.'

I reached inside my shirt and fumbled in the purse, trying by touch to find copper rather than gold. The pilgrim grabbed the coin that emerged, sniffed it, then pointed to Kaspar. 'And one for him.'

'When we arrive safely.'

The door banged open. Nick, who had been dozing, almost fell off his chair in surprise. Sabine stepped into the room with two more cans of Coke. On screen, Urthred and the Wanderer meandered in eccentric circles around the clearing, bathed in the silver light of an improbably bright moon.

'Getting far?'

Nick rubbed his eyes. 'I don't know. What time is it?'

'Four a.m.'

'Damn.' He snapped open the can, trying to remember something. Something he'd been thinking before he fell asleep. He was sure it had seemed urgent.

'Once we're done on the server, we're going to have to get out of here pretty fast. You too. There are bad guys after us and you don't want to be around when they show up.'

Sabine nodded. 'I have a car here.'

'Great.'

'Nick?' Randall's voice barked out of the computer. 'We've got a problem. They've figured out our weak link.'

Nick snatched up the headset and snagged it over his ear. 'What do you mean, *weak link*?'

'Gothic Lair. The way I set it up, this is the cut-out. They can't penetrate the connection between DC and the game, or between the game and where you are. But there's nothing to stop them coming inside.'

A rumble of hooves welled up through the speakers. In the clearing, the Wanderer looked around. Something was moving in the forest.

'Oh, cute.'

A mounted knight galloped out of the forest on a monstrous horse. Moonlight glinted on the wicked spikes that bristled from his black armour, each bedecked with a ragged ribbon that fluttered in the rushing wind. Nick, who had seen that sort of thing before, suspected they were shreds of the flesh of vanquished enemies. A small armoury of morningstars, swords and axes hung from his belt, while his right arm held an obscenely long lance.

The Wanderer drew his sword. 'The Death Knight's not a novice character. They must have been here before.'

'They probably bought it off some Korean kid on eBay.' Urthred the Necromancer clenched his fist. A cloudy haze came out of his staff and spread into a dome of light that wrapped itself around him.

'They won't have a clue how to use it.'

The knight circled his horse round. Suddenly, it kicked up on its hind legs. A gout of fire erupted from its mouth and hosed the clearing with flame. The ground turned black; a shrub burst alight.

'Maybe they bought the kid as well,' said Nick.

'Does it matter?' Emily slid into the chair next to him. 'What happens if you die in the game?'

'You drop out; you can't get back in for forty-eight hours.'

'Is that so bad?'

'Our connection to the FBI mainframe's being routed

through the game. If we die in Gothic Lair, we'll be logged off and the program will shut down.'

'It's worse than that.' Randall was backing towards the tree, crab-walking slowly so that the magic shield came with him. 'I didn't have time to secure the connection at this end. If they get into it, they can trace you right back to where you are.'

'So what do we do?' asked Emily.

'Don't die. And don't let them get in the hole by the tree.'

The knight lowered his lance and charged.

We halted at a crossroads in the forest. Night was coming: for the past hour the pilgrims had fallen silent, anxiously peering around every corner for any hope of lodging. The riders at the head of the column conferred with the fat priest. I heard fragments of an ill-tempered discussion. One remembered an inn another mile towards Strassburg; the other did not, but was certain that the side road led to a village where we could find shelter. The pilgrims grew restive. The sun dipped below the trees.

Eventually they decided we would make for the village. We turned down a rough track that led through the forest towards the river. Soon the warm smell of woodsmoke reached us, promising hearths and fires and roasting meat. We hastened on, desperate to outpace the darkness and the monsters it might bring.

'Listen,' said Kaspar.

'What?' I strained my ears. All I could hear was the babble of the river, and the wind shivering the trees. 'I hear nothing.'

'It's sunset. Why are the cocks not crowing? Where are the barking dogs and the screaming children? The church bells?'

Shouts suddenly shattered the silence. The riders spurred their horses forward; the pilgrims rushed after them, desperate not to be left behind. Kaspar and I, bringing up the rear, followed. We rounded a corner and there was the village.

It was not large: a dozen houses and barns, set around a small church in a clearing. Beyond the church, on the river-bank, a stone mill stood over the water on pilings. The village was deserted. The creak of the wheel turning in the current was the only sound.

As my eyes adjusted to the hazy dusk I saw why. The village had been devastated. Splintered doors dangled on broken hinges. The ground outside the mill was white as snow where a sack of flour had been cut open and spilled. In several places it was stained with blood. The smoke we had smelled was not a kitchen fire or a baker's oven; it was the ashes of houses.

The guards rode around the village, swords out, peering through smashed windows and open doors. Most of the pilgrims knotted together in the open ground outside the church, though a few dared to explore. One, a woman in a white dress, made for the church. Perhaps she wanted to pray; perhaps she thought we could shelter there, for – alone among the buildings – its roof was still intact.

'Where are the villagers?' Kaspar wondered.

'Perhaps they'd already fled.'

Kaspar pointed to the dark stains on the carpet of flour. 'Someone hadn't.'

One of the riders trotted over. Twilight hid his face under the brim of his helmet, but his voice was grim. 'We must leave.'

'Leave?' Even in that awful place, the fat priest sounded outraged. 'It is almost dark. Who knows where the men who did this are? If we take to the road now, we may blunder into them in the dark and all will be lost.'

'The ashes are still warm. They cannot have gone far – and

384

they may come back. We found three mules tethered behind a stable.'

'I would rather—'

A shriek shrilled through the village. The priest cried out and fell to his knees; the pilgrims clutched each other and stared around wildly. But it was a lament, not a war cry. It came from the church. The woman who had gone to investigate it stood in the doorway. The skirts of her dress were spattered with blood, her face a mask of anguish.

'Do not come here,' she cried. 'Do not look on this.'

Ignoring her warning, several pilgrims rushed towards the church. Kaspar tugged my arm. 'How much money is in your purse?'

'Enough to make me worth killing.'

'Perhaps we can bribe the guards to take us to Strassburg. If they carried one of us each . . .'

The knot of pilgrims had begun to drift apart: some to gaze at the horror in the church; some to the empty houses; some sidling towards the barn, perhaps thinking they might commandeer the mules for themselves. Above all this confusion, the two riders sat on their horses and talked urgently.

They broke off their conversation as they saw us approach.

'What do you want?'

'To help,' said Drach.

'Do you have a sword?'

'A plan. This rabble cannot defend itself with pilgrim staffs and clasp knives. Our only hope is to ride for help.'

The guards exchanged impenetrable looks.

'Happily, my friend here has a purse full of gold. If you brought us to the nearest town, we could hire a company of men-at-arms and bring them back. But we would have to hurry, before the *Armagnaken* get wind that we are here.'

385

'A sound plan,' said one of the riders. 'Shall we explain it to the priest?'

'There's no time.'

'Then let's go. We— *Christ in Hell!*'

Without warning, his horse reared up with a terrible scream. Blood streamed down its breast, black in the twilight. A crossbow bolt jutted out below the neck. Kaspar and I leaped back, just avoiding the flailing hooves as it crashed to the ground. Its screams mingled with its rider's as it crushed him.

From out of the forest, we heard the screech of devils as the *Armagnaken* burst into the village.

The horse spat another burst of fire down over them. The shield dome dimmed and flickered – but held. As soon as the flames stopped, Nick charged. Smoke from the charred landscape obscured his approach. He saw the giant hooves in front of him and jumped. The horse reared up to protect itself; hooves flailed, but it hadn't yet recharged its fire-breathing ability.

Nick hung in the air. He raised the broadsword over his head, then brought it down in a hammer blow on the black knight's helm. The force of the impact threw Nick back up, giving him time for another hacking swing at the knight's neck before he dropped to the ground. The knight reeled.

Nick's eyes flicked to the bottom corner of the screen where a colour-coded bar displayed his enemy's life force. He swore. He'd barely scratched him.

'Watch out for the horse!' Urthred shouted.

Nick sprang to his left and rolled away, just in time. A curtain of fire pursued him along the ground, so vivid he could almost feel the heat on his cheek. It raced up behind him; in a second he would be swallowed.

With a flash of blue light, he rolled inside the umbrella of Urthred's shield. The flames beat against it like waves but could not get through.

'You need to get him away from here,' said Randall. 'I can't hold the shield much longer. It's draining my power.'

'I can't get to him while he's on that horse.'

'Remember the dragonsteed at the Tower of Charn?'

'Uh, kind of.' With all that was happening, Nick found he could still feel embarrassed at having this sort of conversation in front of Emily. It was almost impossible to reconcile the stark room, the strip lighting and metal chairs, with the desperate fantasy battle on screen. But each was real enough in its way.

The Wanderer scrambled to his feet. He reached into the folds of his cloak and pulled out an iron shield almost as large as he was. He raised it and crouched to spring. Urthred staggered and swayed behind him, jerked like a puppet on the end of the beam of light flowing from his staff. He was losing control, exhausted by the effort. The black knight saw his weakness and wheeled around to charge again. Smoke flared from the horse's nostrils; sparks drooled from its mouth.

Urthred spun around, lost control and fell. His staff clattered to the ground beside him. The knight charged. All that stood in his way was Nick. Dust flew up under the horse's iron-clad hooves. The earth seemed to shake. In seconds he'd be trampled, or impaled on the end of the knight's black lance.

He raised his sword towards the onrushing horse. The knight saw him; Nick could have sworn he heard him laugh. Against the bulk of the horse and the length of the lance, his blade was little better than a needle.

Tingling, Nick's fingers danced over the keyboard, tapping

out an intricate pattern. The sword in the Wanderer's hand began to glow molten red, then white hot. A shaft of light sprang from the tip of the blade; it pulsed, then hardened to steel in an instant. The sword had become a spear. The Wanderer dug the butt into the ground and angled it up.

It impaled the onrushing horse, sinking deep in its chest. The constraints of the game made it an incongruously bloodless wound. The horse's momentum carried it into the Wanderer's shield and bowled him over; he flew back across the ground.

With a ghastly scream, the horse sank to its knees. The black knight leaped down from the saddle. He'd dropped his lance in the collision; in its place he now wielded an enormous mace.

The Wanderer had been thrown so far back he was now beyond Urthred, who still lay in a heap. The black knight advanced; the mace made eerie noises as he whirled it over his head. Nick reached for his spear, but it was still embedded in the horse.

And suddenly Urthred was on his feet, lightning crackling from his fingertips. The knight leaped back, but too slow. Urthred's spell caught him clean on the chest and blasted him away, almost to the edge of the clearing.

Urthred took a step after him as Nick got up and ran to retrieve his sword-spear. 'He's not so tough.'

The bar in the corner of Nick's screen had dropped by about half, and now showed orange. The black knight had taken a hit, but he wasn't beaten.

'How much more time do you need?' Randall asked.

Nick didn't answer. A sound was rising out of the forest, like a swarm of insects accelerated to a blood-curdling scream. The woods quivered with movement within.

The Wanderer picked up his sword and rolled it in his wrists. He knew that sound. He dropped into a crouch, as the vanguard of a goblin army poured out of the trees.

The *Armagnaken* rushed out of the forest like a battlefield giving up its dead. Half naked, streaked with mud, clad in an outlandish array of mismatched armour and carrying stolen swords, spears, bows and rusting farm implements. They fell upon the pilgrims with howls of glee. The fat priest died pinned to a barn wall with a spear through his belly. One of his companions tried to defend himself with his staff but was beaten down. The *Armagnak* chopped of his head like a chicken's, held it aloft by the hair, then kicked it down the street after a group of fleeing women. It struck one on the back of the leg. She stumbled, tripped and fell. Before she could get up the *Armagnaken* were ripping into her.

It had happened so fast. The second rider, who a moment ago had been beside me, had vanished. All I saw was a flash of armour disappearing into the forest, pursued by half a dozen *Armagnaken* hurling curses and stones. Near my feet the first guard's horse flailed in a froth of blood and mud. The dying hooves still had enough power that there could be no thought of rescuing the rider trapped under the mount. We probably could not save ourselves.

With a final whimper, the horse rolled over and lay still. I darted forward. Ignoring the guard's pleas, I grabbed the sword he had dropped and ran back. I had never wielded one before: I had no idea it could be so heavy. I dragged it along the ground like a plough and offered it to Kaspar.

'Don't waste your time.' He pulled a dagger from a fold of his cloak and threw the scabbard away. 'Have you got a knife?'

'Only a penknife.' In all the hours patiently trimming reeds

389

and quills with that knife, I had never imagined my life might depend on it.

Many of the pilgrims already lay dead, but a few had managed to form a line across a narrow gap between two houses. They jabbed the *Armagnaken* back with their staffs: one had managed to find a billhook, which he swung with lethal effect. It only served to draw more of the wild men onto him.

'The mill,' I said. 'It's stone: they can't burn it. Maybe we can find a storeroom to hide in.'

'We'll be trapped against the river.'

I remembered Kaspar's fear of water. But we would not get far in the dark forest. Before Kaspar could argue, I started across the square.

The fighting was desperate. Nick sat hunched over the keyboard, firing off sequences of buttons that launched the Wanderer in a blizzard of dizzying lunges and parries. He hadn't played the game in months, but somehow the commands had written themselves into his subconscious. Hordes of goblins pressed all around him, while the black knight paced in the background, directing the battle.

The Wanderer tripped one goblin and stabbed him through the back, blocked an incoming sword and leapfrogged his next opponent's spear thrust. He landed behind, spun round and sliced off the goblin's head with a single cut. To his right, he saw Urthred wheeling and leaping like a dancer as he fended off the enemies who pressed around him. The tip of his staff smouldered with magic fire: any goblin who touched it reeled back with a burning scar seared into him.

'Keep close to the tree.' Randall's voice was calm and concentrated. On screen, he somersaulted into the air and swept his staff around full circle. A shock wave of green fire rippled out around him, throwing back a whole cohort of the goblins who ringed him. The bodies lay there for a second, then faded away. But more rushed in to take their places almost immediately, pressing hard to drive him back from the oak tree.

Nick tried to advance. Goblins hemmed him in, jabbing and stabbing from all sides. Their computer-generated attacks never tired, while fatigue was beginning to take its toll on Nick. A goblin charged; Nick moved to duck and come up under his guard but nothing happened. The Wanderer just stood there, unnaturally still, utterly vulnerable.

He must have pressed the wrong key. He stabbed at the keyboard to get it right, but too late. The goblin's spear struck the Wanderer clean in the stomach. He staggered back, arms flailing; Nick tried to bring up his sword in defence but the game wouldn't respond to his desperate commands. His health status flashed red. The goblin raised the spear over his shoulder for the killing blow.

A bolt of lightning crackled across the clearing from the end of Urthred's staff; it lifted the goblin off the ground and sent him spinning into oblivion. The Wanderer jumped back, stabbed the next attacker and turned to thank—

'Urthred!'

Seeing his chance, the black knight had waded back into the battle. The goblin army were like dogs at his feet. He towered over Urthred, whirling his mace over his head. Urthred turned; he flung out his staff and shouted an incantation.

But the lightning strike had drained the last of his magic. The spiked mace head struck the staff and splintered it in two. The surrounding goblins edged back obediently, forming a

391

circle around the two combatants as Urthred wearily drew his sword.

'Get to the tree.'

On screen, Urthred was swaying like a drunkard, ducking and rolling to avoid the thundering sweeps of the mace. Through the speakers, Randall sounded close to exhaustion. Nick glanced at the oak. Above its tangled roots a glowing sphere had appeared, a ball of light hovering among the branches like forbidden fruit.

The black knight must have known what it was. With a roar of fury he swung the mace and struck Urthred on the side of his head. He crumpled to the ground. The goblins shrieked in triumph as they poured in to finish him.

'Randall?'

There was no answer. The black knight strode towards the tree, kicking goblins out of his way as he walked. Nick checked his health. His avatar was bruised and bloody, his robes torn. One more blow would finish him. There must be fifty goblins between him and the tree, and the black knight was almost there.

We slipped between two houses and crouched behind a wattle fence. Night had almost fallen: the battle had become a fog of blurred shapes and sharp sounds. Some of the *Armagnaken* had kindled torches, windows in the darkness revealing ghastly tableaux of savagery.

I heard footsteps to my left and ducked down. Through the gnarled weave of the fence I saw a woman run past, closely followed by two *Armagnaken*. One carried an enormous club which he swiped merrily as he pursued her. It looked too huge to wield, until I saw it was actually a lute held by its neck. He must have plundered it from one of the houses. He swung it again, missing the woman and smashing into a post he had not seen in the dark. With a twang and a groan, the lute shattered. He tossed it aside and carried on.

The way was clear. We vaulted over the fence and sprinted over the open ground to the mill door. My foot snagged on something; I almost tripped, but fear drove me on. Grey clouds puffed up like spectres around our feet as we crossed the spilled flour. Then we were inside.

The mill smelled like a stable. Straw crackled underfoot, and dust in the air coated my tongue. I heard the toil of stone, the creak of axles, the rush of water under my feet. Oblivious to the horror outside, the mill grumbled on. I found it strangely comforting.

I put out my hand and steadied myself on Kaspar's shoulder. We felt our way forward through the cluttered room, careful lest we catch ourselves in some piece of the mechanism.

We reached a wall and edged along it. I felt a door, pulled it open. Cold air rushed over my face together with a blast of noise: the rattles, splashes and squeaks of the wheel turning in the mill race. Looking down, I could see silver foam where the paddles churned the water.

'Not that way,' I whispered. I left the door open to admit what light there was and carried on.

All of a sudden the room lit up like a lantern. I spun around, blinking. Two *Armagnaken* stood in the door. One was a hunched ogre of a man, with a hooked nose and bulging cheeks; he carried a burning brand in one hand and an axe in the other. His companion was very different: an angel, with soft fair hair gone gold in the torchlight, buttery skin and slender shoulders. It was a strange beauty to behold in that awful moment.

They saw us at once. The ogre whooped with delight; the

angel smiled. He lifted his arms into the light, and I saw they were drenched in blood up to the elbow. He carried a sickle.

The ogre went to his right, picking his way over the debris of fallen rafters and broken furniture that littered the floor. The angel stayed by the door, watching. The smile never left his face.

Kaspar raised his dagger and moved towards the ogre. He ducked under the shaft of the mill wheel, which was still spinning, and skirted the stone in the middle of the room. I should have gone to help but I held back, paralysed by terror. The knife in my hand felt feeble as a reed.

The ogre let Kaspar approach. He was in no hurry. The millers must have been making some repairs when the *Armagnaken* found them. A wide plank stood across two sawhorses, the saw blade still wedged into the cut it had begun. It formed a natural barricade between the two men. They eyed each other like two cats across a wall. Kaspar crouched. He looked quicker than his opponent, though doubtless the ogre was more practised.

But perhaps he had killed enough. With a look of disdain, he lowered his guard. Kaspar saw his chance and moved forward. At the same time, almost as if he was too weary to carry it, the ogre let his torch slip from his hands.

Everything after that was a nightmare of fire and horror. As Kaspar sprang forward, he kicked up a plume of sawdust from the floor. It swirled and caught the flame from the torch. In an instant, the dust exploded in a cloud of flame. Kaspar landed in the inferno with a scream, stumbled back, caught himself on the upraised plank and was knocked back into the flames. I ran to him.

But I had forgotten the other *Armagnak*. He came the moment he saw me move, dancing across the spinning stone wheel. Monstrous shadows swayed behind him. He swung his sickle at my head and I jerked back. Almost far enough. The back of the blade caught my cheek: it should have been blunt, but he had honed the tool so that both edges were razor sharp, tapering to a wicked point that could have flicked out my eye with a single prick.

Blood streamed from my cheek. The angel advanced towards me. Silhouetted against the fire, he looked like Death himself. I scrambled back on my hands. To my left, Kaspar writhed in flames. Even above the roar of the fire I could hear his screams.

As I scuttled back, my palm pressed against something hard and thin on the wooden floor. A long nail, probably dropped by the carpenters. I balled it in my fist, the point just protruding between my knuckles, and struggled to my knees as the angel approached. He thought I was praying and laughed, delighted. His left hand made a blood-soaked sign of the cross, while his right raised the sickle for the sacrifice.

I toppled forward, stretching my arm towards his boot. Perhaps he thought I was beseeching him for mercy, for he hesitated with his blow. The nail sank in with all my weight behind it: it pierced his bare foot and went clean through into the floor.

He howled and swung the sickle wildly, but I had already rolled clear. He tried to follow but could not: for a moment he was nailed to the spot.

I ran to Kaspar. Half his clothes had burned away: beneath the charred cloth I could no longer tell what was skin, ash or bone. I turned him over to smother the flames, but each time I moved him they seemed to creep around to the other side.

The fire had spread across the middle of the room now – an impenetrable rampart. The only way out was into the river. I picked up Kaspar in my arms and dragged him towards the high door. The moment I stood smoke rushed into my lungs. My head swam; dizzy with lack of air I almost fell on top of poor Kaspar. He was barely conscious.

I looked back. The angel was still there: he had ripped himself free, leaving a hunk of bloody flesh nailed to the floor. He came limping towards me through the smoke. The blade he held burned with reflected fire. Below me, through the open door, water spilled over the giant wheel.

I stood and confronted the angel, putting myself between him and Kaspar. I had dropped my knife in the fire and was defenceless. He swung his sickle at me and I retreated – tripped on Kaspar's limp body and stumbled back. I spread my arms to catch myself on the wall.

All I felt was the emptiness of open space, the awful horror of nothingness. I was falling. My arm struck the wheel with a sickening crack. I bounced off it like a stone and landed in the churning black water.

The screen dimmed. In the windowless office, Nick almost screamed in frustration. Had a goblin stabbed him? His health bar still showed life. He looked around. It wasn't the slow fade of death, but a giant shadow crossing the sky. As the sun returned he saw an enormous fish eagle swooping down towards the black knight. Its outstretched talons tore into his armour, carving deep rents in the steel.

The goblins abandoned Urthred's dissolving corpse and charged. A beat of the fish eagle's giant wings swept them off their feet and hurled them back, bowling over the ranks behind.

Nick saw his opening. With the goblins programmed to rally against the biggest threat, a way had opened to the tree. He ran forward, hurdling the few spears that still stabbed at him, knocking others out of the way before they could strike. At the corner of the screen, he saw the fish eagle batting its wings to fend off the goblins, who had at last managed to get within range. The black knight picked up his lance and aimed it like a javelin, right at the fish eagle's heart.

The bird rose into the air, a couple of goblins screaming and writhing in its claws. The knight hurled the lance. The fish eagle twisted to avoid it, but its very size impeded it. The spear pierced its beating wing. It lurched, swooped and plunged back to the ground.

The black knight was already running, back to the tree and the prize floating in its branches. But the Wanderer was closer. He bounced over the tangled roots, leaped up and snatched the ball of light. Branches rushed past his face, though they could not scratch him. With a cry of fury, the black knight whirled his mace and flung it like a hammer, straight at the Wanderer's head. At the bottom of the screen, a message in a Gothic font announced:

𝔉ile acquired

Nick hit ESCAPE.

The river was strong, far stronger than my exhausted limbs. It took all my power just to keep my head afloat. I shouted to keep myself awake, to prove to the darkness I still lived. I shouted to my father and cursed him for bringing me into the world. I shouted to Kaspar. I told him I was sorry. I told him I loved him.

The current carried me far downriver until I came to a place where it eased into a broad bend. There, on the near shore, I saw the glow of lamplight. It was almost too late. I had sunk into a cold stupor: I might never have roused myself. But I owed it to Kaspar to stay alive. With the last of my strength I splashed to the shore and waded through the shallows until I found a place where cattle had trodden a ramp in the riverbank. I crawled up it and sprawled in the mud.

'Is there somewhere we can print this out?'

Nick's fingers felt arthritic, the sinews in his wrists knotted from the battle. He looked up from the computer. Sabine was standing in the door, breathing hard.

'Your machine's already connected to the printer in my office.'

Nick clicked the button. He pushed back the chair, but Emily was already standing.

'I'll go.'

Sabine pointed to an office across the hall. She let Emily past and leaned against the door frame, her arms folded across her chest.

'Who was that guy – the black knight?'

'You saw him?' Nick's head was pounding like a drum; the merest twitch of his eyes drew stabs of pain in his temples.

Sabine turned her body and lifted her right arm slightly. For the first time, Nick noticed the tattoo on her bare shoulder. A giant fish eagle, wings back and talons bared.

'Randall told me to look out for you.'

'Thanks.' He pushed his memory stick into the computer and copied the file across. He hadn't even looked at it yet. 'If you hadn't saved me we'd have lost everything. Whatever it is we got.'

'Nick?' Emily pushed past Sabine back into the room. She looked dazed. Her hand trembled as she put down the printout.

'I know what Gillian found.'

LVIII

Near Strassburg

I knelt in the chapel and prayed. Candles burned in every alcove, flickering off the painted ranks of saints and prophets on the walls. In the dome of the apse, above the altar, Christ stared down at me clutching an enormous open book against his chest. I could not look at him without weeping.

Miracles had occurred that night, though more would be needed before dawn. The cattle who trod the path to the river belonged to a monastery whose light I had seen from the river. Somehow in the dark I had staggered across the field to the gates. At first they would not open them: they thought it was an *Armagnak* ruse – and certainly I must have seemed a wretched, crazed creature to appear before them so late. At last my desperation convinced them. All their cells were full, so they brought me to the chapel.

Incense lingered in the air from the previous night's vespers. Soon it would be dawn and the monks would return for matins. For now, I was alone.

I prayed. I prayed as I had not prayed since I was a boy,

when I still thought I had a soul worth saving. I prayed with every ounce of my being. I emptied my self and made it a vessel for God. I despised every sin I had ever committed. I begged forgiveness. I renounced all evil. Henceforth I would live a blameless life. If only God would rescue Kaspar.

But I was a feeble vessel, cracked and riddled with holes. As hard as I poured in my prayers they spilled out. In the stillness of the chapel, other thoughts seeped in. My past flowed through me.

A blind man in Paris. *Do you know what the Stone really is? It is medicine, a tonic for all the diseased matter of this world.*

Nicholas, sitting at his desk in a bare room. *You do not desert me, but guard me at every turn with the most tender care.*

At the front of the church stood a lectern. The panoply of creation was carved into its stem, striving to ascend it: from flowers and beasts at the base, through men to the four angels who supported the great Bible spread open on their shoulders.

I walked around to look at it. Each page was the size of a gravestone, written in an outsized hand that even the blindest monk could read by candlelight. There were few of the ornaments and embellishments that would have delighted Kaspar. This was an austere beauty.

I screwed my eyes shut and touched my finger to a random part of the page. I prayed God would speak to me, show me words of comfort and hope. I looked to see what I had chosen.

'I came to bring fire to the earth, and how I wish it were already were kindled.'

The words offered no comfort. But in my despair, what enraged me most was not the cruelty of the words but the error in the text: '*were already were*'. It mocked me. How I could I find solace in God's perfection, when a mere slip of the scribe's pen could corrupt it? I stared at the writing, so clean and bold and neat and *wrong*. I thought of the impressions from my copper plates: messy and ragged, sometimes barely legible, but pure in meaning.

I gazed up at the Christ and wondered what was written in *His* book. More memories spoke inside me.

The mint master, earnestly trying to impress my father. *Each must be exactly the same, or all would be worthless.*

Nicholas again: *Diversity leads to error, and error to sin.*

Kaspar: *You were an artist; now you are a moneychanger.*

I knew why the mistake in the Bible offended me. It *was* me. My soul was a book, dictated by God but so corrupted by copyists' errors as to be meaningless.

In the beginning was the Word, and the Word was with God and the Word was God.

The Word was God; the Word was perfect. I was a miserable creature, as far from the Word as the stars from the sea.

The full compass of my wickedness overwhelmed me. I had never felt so wretched. I felt every one of my sins like hard pustules erupting from my skin. I fell prostrate on the floor. The poison rushed out of me and I vomited; even when my stomach was empty I could not stop, but convulsed with dry heaves until the last drop was squeezed out of my bones.

I lay on the floor, gasping and moaning. Out of the depths I called to God. He answered. In that chapel, with Christ looking down, I comprehended the eternal. My whole body trembled with the resonance. The book of my being broke into the words that formed it; the words into letters; the letters into the impressions of the sharp chisel that first made them. In an instant, I was transported back from the farthest wastes of the world and reconciled to God.

Glowing threads stretched out from the candles and spiralled around me. They wrapped me in bands of light. They whispered warm words in my soul. I was forgiven. The worm, the demon who had inhabited me so long, was banished. His shrivelled corpse lay on the floor amid the bile and poison.

I had always been with God, but in my sin I had not known Him. I had sensed him my whole life, had pursued Him even when I did not know it. The principle of perfection, the unity of all things. One God. One faith. One perfect substance in the universe.

God is perfect form in which all differences are united.

I would take lead and change it. I would melt it, stir it and reshape it. I would coat it with oils and squeeze it out. I would transform it from base metal into the very word of God.

You alloy it with the Stone, so that the seeds imprisoned in the metal blossom, until in the unity of perfection it can take any shape you command.

I would redeem the gross imperfections of my soul.

Not for wealth or riches, but to perfect the universe.

LIX

Karlsruhe

The night still hadn't broken. The darkness was absolute as they hurried outside and crossed the car park. The car was an old Volkswagen Golf, the side panels bashed and dented, the roof hooded in two inches of snow. They waited while Sabine scraped the windscreen, then longer still while she nursed the cold engine into life. The tailpipe spluttered and belched fumes. Sabine hopped out of the driver's seat and gestured Nick to get in.

'Take it.'

Nick started. 'What about you?'

'I can have a ride with my boyfriend. For now, it's better for me to stay here – make sure they cannot trace you.'

Nick thought of Brother Jerome and shook his head. 'You've done enough for us already. If you think the black knight was scary online, you really don't want to meet him in person. These guys are vicious. Half the people who've helped us in the last week have ended up dead.'

'Now you tell me.' Sabine gave a tight smile. 'My boyfriend's parents have a cabin in the Black Forest. I can stay there a while maybe.'

'Be careful,' said Nick.

'You too. And bring back the car, OK?'

'I'll even give you a full tank of gas.'

Nick slid behind the wheel. Emily got in the other side, then leaned over from the passenger seat. 'Is there a library on campus?'

Sabine pointed to a round building on the far side of a soccer field. 'It's open all the time.'

'Thanks for everything.'

Nick put the car in gear. He almost stalled twice on his way out of the car park, fishtailed on a patch of ice at the gate and regained control just in time to avoid smacking into a lamp post. He checked the rear-view mirror and hoped Sabine hadn't thought better of her offer.

'What was that about the library?' he asked.

'I need to check something out.' The hard edge in Emily's voice discouraged Nick from arguing. He was too tired anyway – almost too tired to drive. He pulled up on the kerb outside the library.

'Keep the engine running,' Emily said.

Nick sat behind the wheel and waited while Emily ran up the steps into the building. He rubbed his hands together and wished he had some gloves. The old car's feeble heating was no match for the bitter pre-dawn cold outside.

His eyes drifted down. A blurred white shape stood out against the darkness, a sheet of paper lying on the passenger seat. The printout. Emily must have left it there in her haste. He flicked on the map light and studied it. In the rush to be away from the computer lab he hadn't even looked at it; when he asked Emily what she'd found, she'd only put a finger to her lips.

404

The image in his hand looked like a half-finished jigsaw, one that had been put together impatiently by someone who didn't have the attention span for the fiddly background bits. Nick had told the program to ignore any fragments which had no marks on them, so as to speed up the assembly process. The result was an hourglass portion of the torn-up page. Whatever Emily had seen certainly wasn't obvious to Nick. Half the page was taken up with a picture that looked like an ox with an unusually long tail. The digital reconstruction wasn't perfect: false overlaps and subtle distortions gave the picture an impressionistic blur that wasn't helped by the dim light in the car. Even so, Nick was pretty confident he could identify the artist by his style. He'd seen enough of the Master of the Playing Cards' work in the last few days to become an expert.

Underneath the picture were a few lines of writing. This was sharper – Nick's algorithms were tuned to pick out text – but he still struggled to decipher it. The letters were thick, densely packed into their lines and irregularly shaped: the upright strokes had a vertical solidity like the pillars of a cathedral, while the vaulting curves and cross-strokes bridged them with thread-like delicacy.

He delved in his bag for the bestiary they'd rescued from the warehouse in Brussels and opened its first page to compare. They were different. The book's pictures were pushed to the side of the text, while on the printout it sat proudly centred in its own space. The handwriting looked neater on the printout too, though when Nick actually tried to read it he found it harder to make out the letters.'

A vivid white flash split the night open. Nick turned in absolute terror. Had he been seen? Photographed? Shot at?

It flashed again – not a camera or a gun, but a strobe light mounted on the front of the library. Nick realised that the sound he'd thought was the panic of his own subconscious was actually the muffled ringing of an alarm bell.

The alarm got suddenly more frantic as the library door burst open. Emily ran out down the steps. She threw herself into the car and slammed the door.

Nick looked at the book in her hands, a tall slim volume bound in red and black cloth.

'Did you just steal a library book?'

'Borrowed.' She shoved it into the pocket in the door. 'Just drive.'

The car lurched off the kerb and down the road. Nick checked his mirrors but didn't see anyone coming after them.

'Now will you tell me what this is all about?'

LX

Mainz, 1448

Two old men stood on a hillside. A passing observer might
have taken them for brothers. They were a similar age, near
fifty, both with grey beards and lean bodies wrapped in furs
against the autumn chill. Their features differed in detail, but
beneath the aged skin and crooked bones both faces bore the
hunger of men who still had business with the world.

They were not brothers. One was Johann Fust. The other
was me. All around us, labourers turned the soil in the sloping
field. They pulled up rocks and deposited them in piles to be
fitted into walls. In the middle of the field, a group of
carpenters raised timbers for a watchtower. When spring
came, the derelict land would be planted with vines and
blossom into a vineyard. In the same way, I hoped Fust's seeds
would make my own venture flourish.

I had not spoken to him in fifteen years, not since our
chance encounter in Olivier's workshop in Paris. In some ways
it was surprising we had not spoken sooner. I had been there a
year, and Mainz was not so big that two men engaged in the

work of books and papers should not cross paths. But I had avoided him. Until now.

I cannot count the disappointments of those intervening years. Kaspar once told me that the mystery of pressing copies of the playing cards was not one great secret but a dozen – the ink, the metal, the press, the paper – each element in its correct form and proportion. In that I suppose it resembled alchemy, though he produced more than my efforts in Paris ever had. But if his art was a dozen secrets, each to be unravelled and understood, mine comprehended a hundred, or a thousand. Every one of them eluded me. And, as Dunne once told me, every time I solved one problem I created ten new ones.

Yet unlike earlier setbacks, they did not make me despair. I was an overenthusiastic pilgrim who had embarked without knowing his route. Thinking the journey would be short, I had blundered blind in the thickets of the forest. Now I had found my road, though my destination proved to be further than I could have imagined when I set out. And that gave me confidence which stones and blisters could not break.

But though faith sustains a pilgrim, he makes his way in the world of men. I still needed money. And that was why I had come home to Mainz. I had left the city of roads and returned to the city of my birth, like an old bear returning to its cave. When I set out, almost thirty years previous, I had left behind a home, a mother, two siblings and a half-sister who had stolen my inheritance. Now all were gone except the old house, which had finally passed to me.

Fust's vineyard stood on the hill that rose out of the river valley behind the city. Below, I could see all the walls and spires of Mainz, dominated by the great red dome of the cathedral, stretching forward to the banks of the Rhine. A brown haze smudged the air above it, smoke of countless fires. The autumn sun had reached its zenith, but no bells tolled noon. Every church stood silent. The effect was eerie, as indeed it was meant to be.

'You chose a strange time to return after so long,' Fust said. 'Golden Mainz has lost its lustre.'

I knew. For decades, the patricians who ran the city council – men like my father – had operated an elaborate system of annuities which diverted the tax revenues into their own pockets. The interest they paid themselves had spiralled, much like my own debts, until at last the city was forced to declare bankruptcy. Among its angry creditors was the Church, which promptly suspended all services in the city. Masses went unsung, babies were not baptised and the dead suffered without Christian burial.

'There must be some wealth still in Mainz.' Beyond the distant walls, craft of all sizes clustered at the riverbank, while cranes and stevedores loaded bales onto barges. Three milling boats swung at their moorings, grinding the last of the harvest.

'This vineyard, for example. It will take years of careful nurturing to bear fruit. You would not be reclaiming it if you thought the city's prospects were tarnished for ever.'

'There will always be a demand for wine. The worse things get, the greater it will be.'

Fust looked at the rough earth around him a moment longer, then switched to me. *Why have you come here?* his sharp eyes said. But he would make me go first.

'Wine is not all that can flow out of a press,' I said.

He waited. From the bag I was carrying, I handed him a sheet of paper.

'I have discovered an art. A new form of writing without a pen.'

He unfolded the paper and studied it. 'Indulgences?'

409

'That is just the beginning.' I reached in my bag again and pulled out a small booklet, four leaves folded inside each other to give sixteen pages.

'The Latin primer of Aelius Donatus. Every student in every school needs one.'

He gave me an impatient look: he knew what it was. 'I must have sold three hundred of these. They sell as fast as the scribes can copy them.'

'I can copy them faster and more cheaply than any scribe. In a month, I could produce all the copies you have ever sold – and more.'

Fust watched the work of the vineyard around him and said nothing. He had bargained his way from Paris to Vienna and back; he knew how to control his emotions. But he could not hide all his surprise.

He glanced down and read through the first few lines of the book.

'No corrections,' he commented. It was true. Unlike other manuscripts there were no crossings-out, no scrawls in the margin.

'With this new form of writing, we can proofread and correct before we put a word on the page.'

That cracked his composure, drawing a sharp look to see if he was being made a fool of.

'Customers like to see corrections,' was all he said.

'They are scabs on the page. They disfigure it.'

'They prove that the author has taken care to examine his work.'

'But if he has taken the ultimate care there will be no mistake to correct.'

'Only God is perfect.'

'Then I will be as nearly perfect as possible.'

Fust examined the page again. 'You still have work to do. There is more to writing than spelling. However these pages were written, it was not with a steady hand.'

'That is why I need capital. To perfect the invention. I thought that with your interests in bookselling, you might be interested.' I put out my hand to take back the grammar book. 'Perhaps I was wrong.'

Fust held on to the book.

'A new form of writing that can be read before it is written and produce more copies in a month than a scribe in his lifetime,' I repeated. 'How much would that be worth to you?'

Fust gave a thin smile. 'I think you are about to tell me.'

I had had enough of scrabbling for piecemeal loans that barely paid the interest on the last. Nor did I want a syndicate of investors whose squabbles devoured my time more than the work itself. I had determined to settle in Mainz. That meant a single creditor, so indebted to the project that he could not let it fail.

'A thousand gulden.'

Fust lifted his hands and blew on them.

'That is a fabulous sum. How will you spend it in such a way that you can repay me?'

'Come and see.'

LXI

Near Mannheim, Germany
'What you're potentially looking at is the first or second book ever printed.'

They were parked in a lay-by. Emily spread the reassembled printout and the bestiary on her lap while Nick checked over his shoulder to make sure no one could see them. There was nothing in front of them except a dark stand of pines sagging under the weight of snow. Behind them, traffic thundered past on the A5 autobahn.

'The first book ever printed where?'

'Ever printed ever. To be precise, ever printed from movable type.'

'Movable type' was a phrase Nick recognised, though more as a face in the crowd than an intimate friend. The sort of thing name-checked in magazine lists of the Hundred Greatest Inventions or Men Who Changed the World. Usually closely associated with a name:

'Gutenberg?'

'Exactly.' Emily's skin was grey and tired; without lipstick and mascara, her bold lips and dark eyes seemed to fade back into her face. But when she looked at the pages in front of her, the energy was unmistakable. 'How much do you know about him?'

'How much is there to know?'

'Not much. So little that until the eighteenth century he was almost forgotten. He made some powerful enemies in his lifetime; after his death they did everything they could to obscure his legacy. It was only when scholars analysed the records hundreds of years later that they worked it out.'

'What, exactly?'

'He pieced things together.' She shot Nick a shy grin to see if he'd got the joke. 'Movable type. He worked out a technique to cast individual letters on blocks of metal, then put them together into words, sentences, eventually an entire Bible – and print it out.'

Nick tried to imagine assembling a whole Bible letter by letter. 'Must have taken a long time.'

'Years, probably. But the only alternative was handwriting. Once he had the page set up he could print off as many copies as he wanted. Then he'd take it apart and reuse the letters to create a whole different page. Infinitely flexible, while at the same time creating a product that was completely standardised and could be replicated as often as people wanted it. It was probably the greatest step forward in the communication of information between the alphabet and the Internet.'

'And when was this?'

'The mid-fifteenth century.'

'The same time as the Master of the Playing Cards.'

Emily held up the book from the library. There was nothing on the front cover except a grazing stag embossed in gold. Nick recognised it at once from the suit of deer. Emily turned the book spine on.

'*Gutenberg and the Master of the Playing Cards*,' Nick read.

'I came across it when I was looking into Gillian's card, back in New York. You're not the first one to wonder about a connection. There's an illuminated copy of the Gutenberg Bible at Princeton whose illustrations look like copies of the playing cards. The author of this book suggested that perhaps there was a partnership between Gutenberg and the Master to produce illustrations for the Bibles. The man who perfected printing text and the man who perfected printing engravings. It's a seductive idea.'

'Is there any evidence for it?'

'Only circumstantial. Most of the arguments in this book have been picked apart.' Emily stared at the printout as if she couldn't quite believe it. 'Until this.'

A siren howled in the distance. Nick tried to concentrate.

'Isn't it pretty similar to the bestiary we found in Brussels?'

'The bestiary is handwritten; this is printed. You can see how regular the type is, how perfectly straight the lines are. The same with the illustrations. The pictures in the bestiary have been hand-painted. It's hard to be certain with the reconstruction, but it looks as if the one here has been printed like the cards.'

The siren was getting louder. Nick wiped the window and looked out. The only other car in the lay-by was a silver Opel parked at the far end. Its driver stood with his back to them, relieving himself into the snow under the trees.

'So we've got a printed picture that we know dates from the mid-fifteenth century and some printed text. How do you make the leap to Gutenberg?'

Emily pointed to the letters. 'Gutenberg was the first. He

didn't just invent the printing press; he had to invent, or perfect, everything. The alloys used to cast the types and the tools for making them. The processes for putting together the pages and then holding them in place. The inks.' She suddenly trailed off.

'The inks . . .?'

The siren had swelled to an ear-splitting *whoop*. An ambulance sped past behind them, blasting its horn to clear the traffic. Nick exhaled a deep breath that promptly crystallised on the windscreen. Emily didn't seem to have noticed.

'That must be what alerted Gillian.' She pulled out the playing card and scrutinised it. 'Here.'

She pointed to a cluster of dark spots in the lower corner of the card.

'Gutenberg's ink is famous for its lustre. It doesn't fade; it's as dark and deep now as the day he pulled it off the press.'

'How come?'

'No one knows. Even among early printed books it's unique. People have tried everything to unravel his recipe – even analysing it with spectrometers.'

'PIXE,' said Nick. 'Vandevelde.'

'Gillian must have noticed the ink and guessed what it was. Vandevelde would have confirmed it.'

'Before they got to him. But how did you figure it out?'

'The font. Gutenberg invented that too. It wasn't a question of selecting Times New Roman or Arial; he had to design every letter and then cut it into blocks of metal for casting. In early printed books, each typeface is as unique as handwriting.'

She ran a finger over the reassembled letters. 'This is the grandfather of them all. The type he used for his masterpiece, the Gutenberg Bible. So far as we've ever known, that was the only major book he printed.' She caressed the printout like an infant. 'This is like finding an autographed copy of a lost Shakespeare play with illustrations by Rembrandt.'

'We haven't found it yet,' Nick reminded her. 'All we've got is a printout of a reconstruction of one page that a guy tore up in Strasbourg. I don't think that was original either, unless Gutenberg printed it off on office paper.'

'You pointed a gun at him and the only thing he cared about was destroying that piece of paper. It's a true copy of something. Somewhere.'

LXII

Mainz

For such a large building, the Hof zum Gutenberg was surprisingly unassuming: the narrow street offered no position where you could take in its full size. At ground level it blended unnoticed into its neighbour, while the greater part slipped around a corner into an alley. You would have had to crane your head far back to see the peaked gable overhead: most people were too occupied dodging livestock, dung and the pelts hanging from hooks outside the furrier's shop opposite to look much higher than their own feet. It was a perfect home for what went on within.

'I hear you have taken a new name since you returned,' Fust said.

'Gutenberg.' I had jettisoned my father's name and assumed that of my first and last home. It announced me as a man of property, which proved useful in some of my dealings; but more than that it anchored me. I belonged here.

As we stepped over the threshold I looked up, as I always did, at the crest carved into the keystone of the arch. It showed a hunched pilgrim in a high conical cap, bent almost double under the weight of the load he carried hidden beneath his cloak. What was that burden, I wondered? He leaned on a stick, while the other hand held out a begging bowl for alms. I did not know how it had become our family emblem – even my father could not say. But I felt, as always, a kinship – a weary pilgrim still begging alms to finish his journey.

I had been busy since my return. The front rooms which my father had used to display his cloths and wares had been boarded up. Now they were crowded with furniture, pushed against walls or piled high as if readied for a move. Dust had already begun to settle.

I led Fust into another room, then down a short corridor past the pantry. We paused outside an iron-bound door that led into the rear wing.

'What you see and what you hear – you swear by Mary and the saints you will not reveal it to anyone?'

Fust nodded. I opened the door.

In the middle of the room, three men sat at a table that had been moved there for the purpose. They were sipping wine, though none looked as if he was enjoying it. They knew what was at stake.

I introduced them.

'Konrad Saspach of Strassburg, chest maker and carpenter. He makes our presses, which you will see presently.'

Saspach was one of the few men who had grown in my estimation since I'd known him. His beard was now white and bushy as a prophet's, his hands so wizened it seemed impossible they could turn a lathe or make a saw cut so straight. He had always been on the periphery of our enterprise, but when I asked him to come from Strassburg he had agreed willingly.

'Götz von Schlettstadt, the goldsmith who engraves the dies and forms we use.' Not long after I met him the *Armagnaken* had sacked his town and looted his shop. A goldsmith with no gold cannot maintain a business. Soon afterwards he had come to Strassburg and offered to work for me. I accepted gladly, for he was the most meticulous goldsmith I ever knew. All metals were like clay in his hands.

'Father Heinrich Günther.' A younger man with a grave face and staring eyes. Günther had been vicar of St Christoph's church around the corner until – in a dispute between the archbishop and the Pope – he had committed the sin of siding with his superior's superior. The archbishop had stripped him of his benefice and left him penniless.

I looked at them all, watching Fust or studying their cups as their moods dictated. These orphans and outcasts were my guild, a brotherhood of craftsmen. If only Kaspar could have been among them my happiness would have been complete.

'And what do you all have in common? It sounds like the beginning of a joke: a carpenter, a goldsmith, a priest and . . .' He looked at me. 'Whatever you are, Hans Gutenberg?'

A copyist? An imprinter of paper? A beggar? A fool?

'A pilgrim.' I could see the answer displeased him. I hurried on. 'First, we will demonstrate the power of this art.'

I handed him a piece of paper. Four pinholes had been pricked in the corners, and a pencil line ruled apparently at random in the middle.

'Write your name here.'

With the reluctance of a man who thinks he is being made a fool of, he took a pen from the table and signed his name on the line.

'The paper is damp,' he commented.

'It takes the ink better.'

419

Saspach took the signed paper and disappeared through a door into the next room. From behind the door came a long creak of protest, like a ship straining on its hawser. Then a thud, a rasp and a clang. Fust's eyes narrowed, while the others affected not to notice anything.

Saspach returned and laid the sheet triumphantly in front of Fust.

'*Liebe Gott*,' he murmured.

His name was still there, just as he had written it. But where before it had been a solitary bloom on a barren page, now it sat in the midst of a garden, hundreds of words that had blossomed around it in an instant and drawn it into their web. His name was now part of a sentence:

> 𝔚herefore 𝔴e 𝔡ecree that 𝔍𝔒𝔥𝔄𝔑𝔑 𝔉𝔘𝔖𝔗 is truly forgiven of these sins and that the stain of them is removed.

'No pens. No desks. No mind to wander or hand to slip. A perfect copy every time. And, as you see, completed in an instant.'

Fust looked like a man who had fallen down a hole and found a cave of gold. He pointed to the grammar book I had shown him in the vineyard. 'And this came out of that room also?'

'Every page.'

'It is indistinguishable from the real thing.'

'Perhaps it *is* the real thing – as gold is to lead or the sun is to the moon.'

But Fust's merchant mind could not be dazzled for long. Already I could see the calculation in his eyes, measuring and counting. 'Why do you need a thousand gulden from me? Everything here seems complete.'

'This is just the beginning. This proves it is possible. To take advantage of the art I need more presses and equipment, more men to work them, more paper and vellum.'

'To print indulgences and grammar books?'

I shook my head and leaned over the table. I had sworn beforehand that I would not touch the wine lest it cloud my thoughts. Now I found I had already drained my cup. It rushed in my veins.

'A new venture. Bolder than anything we have attempted. For all our achievements, we are still apprentices in this new art. Now we will make our master-piece.'

LXIII

Rhineland-Palatinate, Germany

Nick took a random exit off the autobahn and drove until he found a motel. Emily slept in the seat next to him. He felt empty, his body a hollow tank trembling from the last drops of adrenalin and caffeine sloshing around inside. He had to force his eyes to stay open. He shivered with relief when they pulled into the car park at the back of the motel, and almost wept when he saw the plain room with its solid brown bed.

Emily threw back the bedspread and sat on the edge of the bed to take off her shoes and socks. She looked at him for a moment, a strange look that Nick didn't understand.

With a self-conscious shrug she stood, pulled her sweater over her head and wriggled out of her jeans. All she was wearing underneath was a thin white camisole and her underwear. She stood there on the carpet in the middle of the room, blushing slightly, like a virgin on her wedding night not certain what to do. Nick tried not to stare.

'I just want you to hold me.'

Nick nodded. He was too tired to feel awkward. He stripped

down to his boxer shorts and clambered into the bed after Emily. He lay down beside her, cupping his knees inside hers, pressing his chest against her shoulder blades. She shivered; he pulled back, but she reached round and pulled his arm firmly around her waist.

'It's nice. It's just it's been a long time.' She sighed. 'Not *that*. Just . . . warmth.'

'I think I know what you mean.'

She nestled back into him. Nick laid his palm flat against her stomach, terrified of touching her where he should not, and at the same time longing to. He remembered lying like this with Gillian, the same confusion, so close and so aware of the distance. Always the distance.

He fell asleep.

LXIV

Mainz

When Fust had gone I wandered through the house. The day was fading; soon it would be too dark to work. For the moment, the labours that were the life and breath of the house continued. When I stepped outside into the yard I could smell the heavy perfume of boiling oil, sharpened by the tang of coal smoke. My father's kitchen had become our type foundry, and the adjacent scouring house the room where we cooked up our inks. Inside the foundry I could see sparks where the fresh types were ground smooth on a wheel.

I climbed the stairs by an outbuilding and crossed a walkway back to the main house. Here, an outside gallery ran around the internal courtyard. I peered through the barred windows as I walked past. In the room where the die maker had once cut coin moulds for my father, Götz now chiselled letters out of copper squares. In the next room, Father Günther sat at a writing desk and pored over a small Bible. He had a sheet of paper beside him and a pen in his hand, which never stopped moving as he read. For anyone used to watching copyists it was an unnatural motion: the pen danced up and down the page, line to line, apparently at random; it never stayed still enough to form even one letter, but left a trail of dots and dashes like bird prints in snow. If he resembled anything it was not a scribe but a merchant clerk taking inventory of his stock. In fact, he was taking inventory of every letter in every word of the Book of Genesis.

He saw me pass and called through the open door, 'Did you get what you wanted?'

'He will give us eight hundred gulden now, and more later.' It was less than I had asked for, more than I'd expected. 'The equipment will be its own collateral. In return for exclusive rights to sell what we produce, he has also agreed he will not collect the interest. And he has ordered fifty copies of the Donatus grammar book for delivery in three months' time.' I laughed. 'You should have seen the look on his face. He could not believe such a thing was possible.'

'So he didn't notice the grammar book was a fake?'

'It was flawless.' Though the indulgence had been genuine, the grammar book I showed Fust was the product of two nights' desperate work by Father Günther and a quill pen when it became clear we could not produce enough types to set all sixteen pages in time.

'In three months, it will not matter,' I told him.

The next room was dark, though as I passed I caught a stale whiff of damp from the moist paper stacked inside. At the end of the gallery, another flight of stairs climbed to the topmost floor. I was about to go up, when a mournful knocking sounded in the twilight. Someone at the front gate.

I paused. No one called at the Gutenberghof, certainly not at this hour. Could it be Fust, rethinking his promises? Or the city watch? It was more than twenty-five years since I had fled

425

from my crime at Konrad Schmidt's house, but a knock at the door still had the power to chill my blood. I waited.

Beildeck, my servant, answered it. I heard him challenge the visitor, though the replies were so soft I could not make them out. The door creaked as it opened.

I leaned over and stared down. A figure emerged from the deep shadow under the arch into the lesser gloom of the courtyard. He moved slowly, hunched over a stick which rapped on the cobblestones as he walked. He stopped in the centre of the yard. Then, as if he had known I was there all along, he looked straight up at me.

My legs sagged; I groped for the rail.

'Kaspar?'

A bitter, brittle laugh like the chattering of crows.

'*Hier bin ich.*' Here I am.

LXV

Rhineland-Palatinate, Germany

Nick didn't know when he woke. The dark day and coarse curtains held the room in twilight. He'd been living in that sickly gloom for the last week, the light of railway carriages, street lamps, car headlights and bare bulbs. A fly drowning in amber.

But amber was cold; Nick was warm, radiantly so, wrapped in blankets and sheets and Emily. Her camisole had ridden up in her sleep so that her naked back pressed against his stomach, their bodies locked together in a single curve.

The heat of her body against his filled him with the glow of desire. He parted her hair so he could kiss the back of her neck; he caressed her bare arm where it clamped over the blankets. She turned her head towards him, her lips seeking his. He saw that her eyes were closed and held back, but she put her hand behind his head and brought his mouth down.

Desire billowed into lust. He ran his hand down over her thigh, then clamped his palm over her hip and held her against him, pulsing against her. She gasped; she pulled his hand away and dragged it up her body, so that he could feel her breasts through the tight cotton of her camisole.

She rolled onto her back and pulled him on top of her. He came willingly.

The next time he woke he was alone in the bed. His headache had gone but he was ravenous. Emily had dressed and was sitting by the chest of drawers, which she'd turned into an makeshift desk. She had the stolen library book spread in front of her, together with a poster-sized chart which she was annotating with a pencil.

Nick sat up. A tangle of memories that might be dreams, and dreams he hoped were memories, rushed through him. He blushed.

Emily looked over and gave a shy smile. 'Sleep well?'

'Mmm.' He scanned her face for traces of regret, until he realised she was doing the same to him.

'I don't want you to think . . .' she began. 'I know I shouldn't—'

'No.' That sounded wrong. 'I mean, yes, you should have. Not *should . . .*'

'I don't want to get between you and Gillian.'

Nick's tumbling thoughts stopped abruptly. 'Gillian?'

'I know what she means to you.'

'You don't.' Nick threw back the covers and stood, naked. Embarrassed, Emily looked away. 'Do you think when we find her I'm going to sweep her into my arms and ride off into the sunset.'

She jerked her head back and looked him straight in the eye. 'Then why are you doing this?'

Nick held her gaze and realised he no longer knew the answer.

'I'm going to take a shower.'

There was no shower; only a bath. He splashed himself in the lukewarm water as best he could, then dressed. When he came out, Emily was sitting cross-legged on the newly made bed, books and papers spread around her.

'What have you got?'

'I'm trying to pin down the links between Gutenberg and the Master of the Playing Cards.'

The exchange seemed to cement an unspoken agreement. Emily relaxed; Nick sat himself on the corner of the bed.

'We have to assume Gillian didn't see the page we pieced together. She must have followed a different trail.'

'Right.' Nick examined the large sheet of paper spread on the bed. It was covered in an irregular grid creased by folds; most of the squares were empty, those that weren't held cryptic snatches of writing: 'f.212r Bottom centre, similar.' Characters from the playing cards in miniature line drawings ran down the left-hand column.

'What is that?'

'It's a chart of books and manuscripts with illustrations that look like the playing cards. It lists which images appear where. One of them's the Gutenberg Bible from Princeton I told you about.'

Nick slid off the bed and crossed to a low table by the door which held a kettle and a box of teas. 'I don't get it. If the whole point of Gutenberg is that all the copies are the same, shouldn't they all have the same illustrations?'

Emily shook her head. 'Like a lot of revolutionaries, Gutenberg dressed up his invention in very conservative clothes. People distrust change. He wasn't selling novelty; he was trying to persuade people he had a better way of producing something very familiar. In this case, manuscripts.

The same way that the first motorcars looked like horse carts.'

Nick filled the kettle.

'In the Middle Ages, you didn't buy a book like you do now. They were all part-works. First you found the text you wanted and got a scribe to copy it. He'd write it out on quires of eight or ten pages, which you'd then take to a bookbinder to have bound together and put between covers. Finally, you got a rubricator to write in the rubric, the chapter headings, in red or blue, and an illuminator to add the pictures. Just black, thanks.'

Nick took two tea bags out of the box and tossed them into the mugs.

'Some of the early pages of the Gutenberg Bible show that he actually experimented with two-colour printing, so he could include the chapter headings as well as the body text. But he abandoned that very quickly – probably because it was too difficult and time-consuming. Gutenberg didn't want to change the way *books* were produced – just the way the *text* was reproduced.'

Nick remembered a phrase from the back of the bestiary: 'a new form of writing'.

'I should have realised what it meant much sooner. But the answer to your question is that although the texts of the Gutenberg Bibles are all pretty much identical, every surviving copy is unique. Each was bound and illuminated by different hands.'

'And the Princeton copy was done by the Master of the Playing Cards?'

'Some of the pictures in the Princeton edition are close copies of the figures on the playing cards,' she corrected him. 'It could be that an illuminator saw the playing cards and copied them or that both of them drew from yet another source.'

'Except that now we've got a piece of paper that puts Gutenberg and the Master on the same page of another book.' Nick poured steaming water into the mugs. 'Let's assume it's more than coincidence. Gillian must have.'

'Agreed. Which is why I wanted to look at the illustrations from the Princeton copy. Maybe there's some sort of pattern, a clue Gillian found.'

'Any luck?'

'Not yet. This chart only gives the page numbers. I need to see the text that goes with them.'

Nick stared at her. 'I hope you're not planning on stealing another library book.'

LXVI

Mainz

I took him into the parlour and gave him wine. The evening was cold, but Kaspar kept his distance from the fire, as if the scars from that night in the mill still recoiled from heat. His clothes smelled of damp and mud; dried blood laced his cheek where it had been scraped by brambles or branches.

'The *Armagnaken* dragged me out of the flames,' he told me. 'Half dead – more. I don't know why. They should have left me to burn. Instead, they took me as their captive. Their plaything.'

I shuddered. Drach kept perfectly still, so stiff I feared the least movement would snap him.

'They did things to me you would not believe. Could not imagine. Their cruelty was infinitely inventive. The things they taught me . . .'

'If I had known,' I said quickly. 'If I had known you were alive I would have moved heaven and earth to rescue you.'

'You would have been looking in the wrong place.'

I stared at him in the firelight. He was a dim impression of the man I had loved, sunken where he had once been proud.

432

In the lamplight, the right half of his face resembled one of his copper plates, criss-crossed with scars etched deep into his skin. Fire had burned away half his hair, and the rest was shaved away so that his skull had the mottled look of an animal hide. His eyes, which had shimmered with ever-changing colour when I met him, were fixed black.

'How long . . . ?'

'Months? Years?' Kaspar shrugged. 'I didn't count. At last I escaped. I went to Strassburg but you had gone. I asked after you; I heard you had gone back to Mainz. I have been making my way here ever since.'

I leaned forward awkwardly and touched his shoulder. 'I'm glad you came. I pray for you every night.'

Kaspar curled up in his chair like a coiled serpent. 'You should have saved your breath. God has no power over the *Armagnaken*.'

The ferocity of his gaze terrified me. I said nothing.

'But you've prospered.' In Drach's rasping voice it sounded like an accusation. 'A fur collar, gold stitching on your sleeves. A respectable burgher in your father's house.'

'Still in more debt than I can afford.'

'Still chasing your dreams of perfection?'

'Our dreams.'

Kaspar clenched and unclenched his hand. The fingers looked hard as talons. 'I have not dreamed in years.'

I stood, desperate for a distraction. 'Let me show you what we are doing.'

He padded after me down the gallery. I brought him to the press room, where silver shafts of moonlight bathed the machinery in their glow.

'We set each letter separately,' I gabbled. I was trembling. 'You would not believe how true—'

A cold hand gripped my neck and forced me down, squeezing my face against the inky bed of the press. I bent double, gasping for breath. Kaspar held me down with one hand, while the other fumbled with his belt.

'What are you doing?' I cried. 'In Christ's name, Kaspar . . .'

He was smothering me, thrusting himself against me from behind. The coffin smell of wet earth was all around me.

'Do you know what they did to me?' he hissed in my ear. 'What I suffered while you were playing with your toys?'

'*I thought you were dead.*'

His hands were tearing at my clothes, scratching my skin.

'*Please,*' I begged. '*Not like this.*'

'What is this?'

Tongues of light flickered around the room. In an instant, Kaspar was away from me. The shadows seemed to draw around him like a cloak. I pushed myself up and looked round.

Father Günther stood in the doorway holding a lamp, straining to see in. 'Johann?'

I stammered something unintelligible.

'I heard a scream.'

'The press squeaked. I was demonstrating it to . . . to my friend.'

Günther moved the lamp so that Kaspar's face swam out of the darkness. He gave him a searching stare but said nothing.

'If all is well . . .' he said doubtfully.

'I will be fine.'

Kaspar had come back, but he was not the same. The darkness in his nature, which I had once accepted as the inevitable shadows of a brilliant sun, had consumed him. After that first, terrible night, he did not talk about what he had suffered; nor, thank God, did he attack me. I forgave him that – what I could not accept were the small changes. The tiny cruelties, the savagery in his eyes. Like a ghost, he could chill a room the moment he entered it. I resisted the idea as long as I could, but in the end I was forced to admit it. I did not love him any more.

Yet his talent remained. Even the demons that ravaged him could not quench his interest in the work of the book. I encouraged it: I hoped it might draw out some of the poison and fix his mind on purer things. I gave him a room at the top of the house: ink, pens, brushes, paper, whatever he needed. And he repaid me.

He showed me one evening, when I climbed to the attic after the rest of the press crew had gone. Kaspar sat at a sloping desk at the far end of the room. He was writing intently and did not look up as I entered.

I leaned over to see what was on the desk. A single leaf of paper, twice the size of the indulgences, criss-crossed with faint pencil lines and sweeping arcs like the blueprint for a cathedral. A heavier line roughed out a rectangle in the middle of the paper, subdivided into two weighty columns like pillars on the page. Kaspar had shaded them with the flat of the pencil, except on the first line of the first column where he had written in a bold, meticulous hand, '*In principio creavit deus celi et terram.*' In the beginning God created heaven and earth.

'This is how it should look,' Kaspar said. He traced one of the arcs with his finger. 'The most harmonious proportions. Your perfect book.'

I rested my hand gently on his shoulder, imagining the columns filled with rows of words. 'It's beautiful.'

He seemed to be waiting for something more. When I said nothing, he sighed.

'You see how I have written the letters so they fill the column exactly, edge to edge? No scribe could do that except by luck. It took me a dozen attempts to do it just for this one line. But with your types, you can control the exact position of every word, every letter. Like a god.'

I knew at once that he was right. I could feel the familiar resonance, the echo of angels singing. I had been so busy staring down, getting each letter to print evenly, I had not raised my gaze to consider the broader scheme. We could arrange the words so that each line was as solid as carved stone: massy columns of text supporting the weight of the word of God. Something no human hand could do.

In the fading light, my old eyes blurred. For a second, I focused not on the shaded columns on the page but at the wide, white surrounds. Background and foreground reversed themselves: the blank paper became a window framing the misty darkness beyond its panes. The scribbled pencil marks seemed to swirl like ink drops in water, threading themselves into words that spoke of God.

It was the last, best gift Kaspar gave me.

LXVII

Rhineland-Palatinate, Germany

The battered Volkswagen crawled along the street. No one noticed it, except maybe the snowmen standing sentinel on the suburban lawns. If anyone had been watching, they would have been struck by the car's erratic progress. It nosed forward a few yards, braked suddenly, paused, then lurched into gear again. A few moments later it repeated the manoeuvre. Perhaps the driver was afraid of ice – except that the road had been ploughed and salted only that afternoon. Perhaps he was lost, or drunk. That might explain why the car always stopped in the shadows.

'In a different neighbourhood we'd be arrested for soliciting,' Nick complained.

They'd slept through the brief day; now it was evening. Nick advanced the car three more driveways and halted. Emily sat beside him with the laptop open on her knees. The glow of the screen was the only light in the car.

'Here's one.' She tapped the trackpad twice. 'Oh – encrypted. No good.'

Nick tapped the accelerator again. They'd set out from the motel an hour ago to find an Internet café, but the sleepy commuter town had no provision for tourists. They'd tried the public library, but that was closed. In the end the best they could come up with was trundling down residential streets trying to piggyback an unwitting family's airwaves.

Nick turned a corner and stopped beside a cluster of snow-covered trash cans. Emily leaned closer to the screen. 'How about this? "Hauser Family Network – unsecured wireless connection."'

'That's what we want.'

Nick took the laptop from her and clicked the new connection.

CONNECTING TO HOST 190.168.0.1

A green icon shaped like a radio tower appeared. He passed the laptop back to Emily, who opened a web browser and typed in an address. Mottled parchment lit up the screen.

'Is that it?'

'The British Library have two Gutenberg Bibles. They've scanned both of them and put them online.'

Emily turned the computer so he could see better. Dense text stood in two columns on the page, each as straight as a knife. Time had browned the parchment but the ink remained vividly black, defying the centuries. Despite the Gothic typeface and its obvious age, the design was startlingly clean.

'I can see why people get excited about it.'

'Those straight margins were his calling card. Scribes couldn't get the right-hand margins to line up so cleanly; you can only do it if you have the freedom to move the type around and space it exactly.'

'Guy must have been a perfectionist.'

Emily extracted the printout of the reassembled page. On the back she'd written a series of letters and numbers next to brief descriptions of the card figures.

'Read me the page numbers.'

Nick tried – and failed – to find them. Emily pointed to a column.

'f.117r?'

'F stands for folio – the physical, double-sided leaf. Medieval books didn't have page numbering like we do, so historians number from the first leaf. The final letter stands for recto or verso – the front side of the leaf, which appears as the right-hand page when you open the book, or the reverse side. So what we would count as page three would actually be—'

'f.2r,' said Nick. 'Top side of the second leaf. Got it.'

One by one, he read out the page numbers. There were about a dozen of them, starting from f.117r – about page 233, he figured – and ending at f.280r, some 325 pages later. It was a time-consuming process. For each reference, Emily had to find the scanned page, read the Latin text, then work out which book of the Bible it came from. At that point she read it out to Nick, who jotted the reference down next to the page and the description of the image.

But his thoughts were elsewhere. Somehow, the arcane system of page numbering had prompted a thought, an irritation at the back of his mind like a pebble in his shoe. He worried at it while Emily tapped out her searches on the computer.

'What's next?'

He consulted the list. 'f.226r.'

'Got it.' She stared at the screen for a moment. 'The sins I have committed outnumber the sands of the sea. I am not worthy to look up and see the height of Heaven because of the multitude of my iniquities.'

Nick waited for her to read out the chapter and verse. When she didn't say anything, he glanced across. Emily was staring at the screen.

'What is it?'

'What picture goes with that page?'

Nick consulted the chart. 'A digging bear.'

'The same one that's on the card?'

He didn't even need to check. 'Why?'

'That page is the prayer of Manasses.' She turned, her face glowing with discovery. 'The prayer that's supposed to be part of the lost book of the Bible, the *Sayings of the Kings of Israel*.'

'*He also made another book of beasts using a new art of writing . . .*'

'. . . *which is hidden in the* Sayings of the Kings of Israel. And here it is, with an illustration from the card on that same page.'

They sat there for a moment in silence.

'I don't get it,' Nick said at last. 'All these clues join up, but they just go round in a circle. The Bible with the illustrations by the Master of the Playing Cards is in Princeton, right? That can't be what Gillian was after. So there must be another book that connects with the card, with the Bible, and with the bestiary Gillian found in Paris.'

'Another book of beasts.'

'So where is it?'

Emily stared at the windscreen. Condensation made the outside world invisible. It was too apt, Nick thought: stuck in a fogged-up car going nowhere.

'There must be another piece of the jigsaw,' said Emily.

'Maybe it was on the first page of the bestiary. The one that got cut out.'

'Maybe there's more here. We haven't looked at all the Master's pictures yet.'

Emily leaned over the computer again and began typing, her keystrokes erratic with nervous haste. Nick glanced at the display. Printed page on web page, the fifteenth-century cowskin rewritten in the liquid crystals of the screen. For all the gulf of technology, it struck him how similar they were in essence: vehicles for information. However you wrote a page number – or for that matter, a biblical chapter and verse – it was nothing more than an address for looking up data.

Page 233, f.117r, Judges 5:4: ultimately they were all shorthand for (Emily said), 'The earth trembled and the heavens poured out water.' The same way that 190.168.0.1 was a convenient equivalence for the Hauser family's home broadband.

But what if you reversed it? What if the information pointed back to its number?

Nick flipped over the piece of paper in his hands. Recto and verso, front and back. He looked at the ox in the fuzzy engraving and thought of a smiling cow standing on a ladder with a paintbrush in its hoof.

I have a new number: www.jerseypaints.co.nz

Emily had stopped typing and was staring through the window, lost in thought. Nick grabbed the laptop.

'I haven't finished,' she protested.

'I won't be a minute.'

His fingers skidded on the keyboard in his excitement; he had to type the address three times before he got it right. The rainbow-striped cow grinned from the top of her ladder.

He pressed a button. The written address resolved itself into a string of digits which he scribbled on the sheet of paper.

Emily leaned over, still looking cross. 'What's that?'

'Every web address translates to a number.' He opened the car door. Fifty yards up the street, a payphone huddled under a blanket of snow. 'Maybe another kind of number.'

He ran to the payphone. Fresh snowflakes were beginning to spiral down in the light from street lamps; his fingers almost froze to the metal buttons as he dialled the number and waited.

The space between each ring felt like an eternity. Every crackle on the line sounded like a receiver being lifted off the hook. Then: '*Ja*?'

'Is that Olaf?' Nick said in German.

A pause. 'Who is calling?'

'It's about Gillian Lockhart,'

The man said nothing.

'Have I got the wrong number?'

'Who are you?'

'A friend of hers from America. She's missing; I'm trying to find her.'

'Ha.' Another long silence. 'I don't know where she is.'

Nick gripped the receiver tighter. His breath frosted the glass of the phone booth.

'But I know where she was going.'

Now it was Nick's turn to keep silent, frozen by the fear that the wrong word would ruin everything.

'Come to Mainz and I will tell you.'

LXVIII

Mainz

I stepped out of the front door, under the carved pilgrim, and turned towards the cathedral and the market square. It was not far, but in that meagre distance the street expanded and contracted many times. Sometimes it was so narrow even a dog cart could barely pass; in other places it spread wide enough to become a small *platz*, where gossips lingered and hucksters sold pies and hot wine from barrows. It made even the shortest journey a tale of many chapters.

One of these places where the road opened was outside St Quintin's church, where women came to gather water from a fountain in the church wall. A tall house stood on the corner opposite. The plaster between its timbers was coloured a lusty red, which had in turn been painted with garlands swagged along the dark timber ribs. Its name was Humbrechthof; it belonged to my third cousin Salman, who had lived there until a committee of guildsmen took over the administration of Mainz some years previously. Thinking these new men meant to beggar the ancient families into bankruptcy, Salman fled to

Frankfurt. The house had stood empty since then. I had written to him, giving him to understand that the situation in Mainz was worse than his most outraged imaginings, and declining fast. When I offered to take his empty house off his hands for a token rent, to protect it from the mob who would otherwise surely make it a brothel or a church of the black mass, he could not agree fast enough.

I entered by a gate, passed through a passage under the main house, and entered the courtyard within. Fust and the others were already there: Saspach, Father Günther, Götz, Kaspar and a young man I did not know. Fust nodded to him.

'My adoped son, Peter Schoeffer.'

He was a thin, earnest-looking youth, with pimpled skin and fair hair that flapped in the November breeze. I thought him diffident enough, but when he shook my hand it was with a look of extraordinary intensity.

'An honour, Herr Gutenberg.' His eyes were pale, icy with purpose. 'Father has told me about your art. You may rely on me absolutely. I thank God I will be part of it.'

'Writing makes his hands sore,' joked Fust. He stood a little further from his son than affection would have permitted, an old dog wary of his pup.

'So this is where we will make our workshop,' Götz said. The house suited our purpose well: it was not tall, but wide, with large windows onto the yard. Over time, my cousin Salman and his forebears had closed in what had once been an ample garden, joined the outbuildings together and extended them upwards until they stood almost as high as the house. They enclosed the courtyard completely, like an inn or a trading hall, so that nothing overlooked it.

I unrolled the sheet of paper I carried and hung it on a nail on the storeroom door. The others gathered around. Most of them had seen some part of it, but only Kaspar had seen it in its entirety.

'This is why we are here.'

Two columns of text ran down the page, perfectly aligned, exactly as Kaspar had sketched them. The grey cloud of pencil shading had become words, painstakingly set and carefully imprinted in the Gutenberghof. The text was black, save for the incipit on the first line, which was written blood red.

here begins the book of Bresith which we call Genesis

A long 'I' hung off the next line and dropped down the margin until its stem became a spiral tendril creeping around the edge of the page. 'In the beginning . . .'

The page flapped and snapped in the breeze; I had to hold it down for fear it would tear.

'Everything you see was pressed onto the paper by Saspach's machine.' This time it was true: there was no craft or trickery on the page. We had set and reset the text until every line filled its row exactly, stuffing parchment strips between the words to create the exact spacing. We had inked the incipit red and pressed it again. Finally we had run the whole page through another press to add Kaspar's engraved initial.

Schoeffer was the first to respond. Unless Fust had shown him the indulgence, he had never seen our work before. I had expected he would be awestruck. He stepped forward and examined the page closely.

'The words look faded.'

'We used the old types,' I explained. 'Some are uneven; others not the exact height. Götz is preparing a new set which will improve the impression.'

'And the alignment. It is almost perfect.'

'Better than you could do,' Kaspar growled from the back.

'Absolutely perfect,' I insisted. 'If you rule a line down the margin, it touches the outer edge of every final character.' God knew how much wasted paper had fed our fire to achieve it.

'It *is* perfect,' Schoeffer conceded. 'But it does not seem it.' He considered it a moment. Despite his youth and his presumption, everybody waited. 'Some lines end with minor characters – hyphens and commas. They are so small they make the line look shorter than it is.'

He pointed to a section of text halfway down the page.

𝕲𝔬𝔡 𝔠𝔞𝔩𝔩𝔢𝔡 𝔱𝔥𝔢 𝔡𝔯𝔶 𝔩𝔞𝔫𝔡 𝕰𝔞𝔯𝔱𝔥, 𝔞𝔫𝔡
𝔱𝔥𝔢 𝔴𝔞𝔱𝔢𝔯𝔰 𝔱𝔥𝔞𝔱 𝔴𝔢𝔯𝔢 𝔤𝔞𝔱𝔥𝔢𝔯𝔢𝔡 𝔱𝔬𝔤𝔢-
𝔱𝔥𝔢𝔯𝔢 𝔥𝔢 𝔠𝔞𝔩𝔩𝔢𝔡 𝕾𝔢𝔞𝔰. 𝕬𝔫𝔡 𝕲𝔬𝔡 𝔰𝔞𝔴
𝔱𝔥𝔞𝔱 𝔦𝔱 𝔴𝔞𝔰 𝔤𝔬𝔬𝔡.

'If you put the hyphen in the margin, the weight of the text will be more evenly spread. More pleasing to the eye.'

I glanced at Kaspar. The mesh of scars on his face puckered as anger took hold of him. Before he could react, I said, 'We will have to see. It is not like taking a pen and simply adding a stroke to the end of the line.'

Kaspar threw the boy a murderous look. Günther the priest prudently changed the subject. 'How many Bibles will we be making?'

'One hundred and fifty. Thirty on vellum, the rest on paper. I calculate we can manage two pages of the whole edition each day. Less in winter. We will have two presses, which Saspach will build there.' I pointed across the courtyard, to the first floor of the house. 'We will put them in the hall and the parlour.'

'We will need to strengthen the floors,' Saspach noted.

'Brick pillars in the rooms below. We will use these as our

paper store. Once you're done with the presses, you can build a hoist to bring the paper directly up to the press rooms.'

'What about the press in the Gutenberghof?' Götz asked.

'Too small. We will keep that to produce indulgences, grammar books, whatever else we can sell. There will be plenty of offcuts and scraps from the Bible we can reuse.'

Fust raised a stern hand. 'There will not. Whatever is bought for the Bible goes to the Bible.' He swung his stick in an arc around the courtyard, indicating the house while fixing each man there with a severe look. 'Do you understand? *This* is our joint venture. I do not want my investment entering by one door only to steal out through another. I know many of you will often have cause to be at the Gutenberghof; some of you live there. What you do with your own time or your own materials is your concern. But every penny that is paid into this project will stay in it. Not one scrap of paper, not one letter of type, not one drop of ink.'

'Nothing will be taken away from your investment in the project,' I assured him quickly. 'Everything will be accounted for, down to the last comma. As surely as they count every coin in the mint.'

'As you know, I would prefer that you concentrated all your energies on this business.'

'I have given you my word that nothing will delay it. But it will be months, God willing, before we are ready even to start pressing here, and a year until we reach full capacity. Even if all goes well, it will need two more years for the Bibles to be complete. Running the Gutenberghof press will provide income through these lean years, and a good place to train new apprentices.'

I walked across the courtyard to the stairs.

'Let me show you where it will happen.'

LXIX

Rhineland-Palatinate, Germany

They spent the night in the motel. They'd paid in advance, and their hoard of euros was running out. When bedtime came they undressed and crept under the blankets together without discussion. They slept wrapped around each other, their naked skin the only warmth in the room. At seven, they rose and left.

A thick fog had come down on the heels of the snow, leaving the world a damp and lonely place. They crossed the Rhine at dawn and barely saw it, then turned north. Emily had the laptop out on her knees but didn't open it; the white silence seemed to possess her completely. The only cars they passed were ghostly wrecks abandoned at the side of the road.

'Mainz was Gutenberg's home.' Emily's voice was hardly audible over the ineffectual clatter of the heater. 'I wonder if that's why Olaf chose it.'

Olaf had set the meeting for eleven o'clock at St Stephan's church, a whitewashed building trimmed in red sandstone, capped by a bullet-nosed dome. It stood at the top of the hill behind the city: looking back from the terrace outside, Nick

448

saw a snowy forest of roofs and aerials sloping down into the fog. For a moment he felt a powerful sense of dread, of unseen enemies sniffing for his trail in the snow. He shook it off and went inside.

It was like stepping into a fish tank. A soft blue light filled the church like water, so thick it was almost tangible. It came from the windows, a nebula of swirling blues speckled with white: birds in a cloudless sky, a starcloth, souls flitting into heaven.

Only at the back of the church, behind the altar, did the blue become a canvas for more literal illustrations. Nick walked up to examine them. An angel with fairy wings carried up a body that had swooned into its arms. A naked Adam and Eve considered an apple, while a blue serpent twined through the tree. A golden angel reading a book turned somersaults over a lighted menorah.

'The windows are new. The church burned in the war.'

Nick turned sharply. A straight-backed old man wrapped in a moth-eaten blanket had rolled up behind him in a wheel-chair. His hooded eyes looked old enough to have seen the church's devastation first hand. His lips curled in and hid whatever teeth he had left, while tufts of grey hair poked from under his battered hat.

'The new windows are by Chagall,' the old man continued. His tone was precise, unhurried. Nick guessed he didn't have much to do other than collar unsuspecting tourists. Nick and Emily might be his only catch that day. 'We were very proud in Mainz when so great an artist agreed to devote his work to our little church.'

'They're good.' Nick tried to steal a glance over the old man's shoulder. Olaf had refused to say how they would recognise him. Nick was terrified of missing him.

'But I liked the medieval windows too. I saw them in my childhood, before the war. Very beautiful – and so exotic. Stags, lions and bears, birds . . .'

'Flowers.' Nick stared at him and tried to remember. 'Wild men.'

'Indeed. The medieval symbolism, so dense, you know? If you start to look close you never know where you go. '

Emily took the plunge. 'Are you Olaf?'

The old man coughed loudly. A nun kneeling in the front pew looked up from her prayers and frowned. 'My name is most certainly not Olaf. But it serves. Let us find somewhere to talk.'

He waved away Nick's offer to push him and led them to a pew at the back of the church.

'I'm glad we found you,' Nick said. 'It was a clever trick, the way you hid your phone number.'

Olaf gave him a shrewd look. 'You mean you are surprised a man of my age can even read email, let alone have heard of an IP address. But I have always sought knowledge. Many ways of finding it have come and gone in my lifetime.'

He manoeuvred his wheelchair against the end of a pew, leaning forward as if about to launch into prayer. Nick and Emily slid onto the bench beside him. He pointed to the wall, where a mounted photograph showed pyramids of flame leaping out of the burning church. All that could be seen of the building was a row of steep gable ends standing tall and black like witches' hats.

'God's beauty is infinite,' he said inscrutably. 'Churches can be rebuilt, maybe more beautiful than before. But *history*. You cannot hire Chagall to restore that.' He gave a heavy sigh. 'Are you believers? Christians?'

'Not really,' said Nick.

'I was, once. Then I decided I knew better. Now I am not so sure.'

A mournful silence gripped him as he stared at the windows, into some painful corner of the distant past.

'You said you had something to tell us about Gillian,' Nick prompted. Olaf didn't seem to hear.

'I was fourteen when the war ended.'

Nick did a quick calculation and was surprised by the result. It must have shown on his face.

'You think I look older than I am.' Olaf coughed again. 'I *feel* older than I am. But I will come to that. For now, imagine me as I was. Old enough to have had a rifle pushed in my hands when Zhukov crossed the Oder; young enough to still have pride in Germany. Even when they told us the truth, all the things that make Germans ashamed today, I had pride. Those things were done by *Nazis*. I was a German.

'That is why I became a historian. I wished to reclaim our history from the monsters and foreigners who took it away from us. I went back further and further into the past, trying to escape the poison that had infected us. While my generation built a new future with the *Wirtschaftswunder*, I wanted to dig its foundation. A new past. A clean past.'

He sighed. 'You must understand, to be a historian in Germany is to be in thrall to a beautiful woman who has shared herself with everyone but you. There is hardly an archive or a library that has not been looted, burned, destroyed or lost at some point in its history. Sometimes facsimiles of original documents survive; sometimes even the copies have been destroyed. This has always been so – but after the war it was intolerable. A young researcher who wants to make a career needs documents, discoveries he can publish. But all our archives were only smoke and ashes. Until one day, in a convent library looking through old books of receipts, I found what I sought. A treasure.'

'What was it?' Emily asked.

'A letter. A single sheet of paper written in a fifteenth-century hand. In the corner was a device: two shields blazoned with the Greek letters chi and lamda, joined by a noose that yoked the neck of a raven. I knew at once whose it was.'

He glanced up to see he still had their attention.

'Johann Fust. You know Fust?' Olaf was too far into the past to wait for their answers. 'Fust was Johann Gutenberg's business partner. You know Gutenberg, of course. Everyone knows Gutenberg. *Time* magazine says he was the Man of the Millennium. But if you came to Mainz five hundred years ago, everyone knew Fust and no one knew Gutenberg. Gutenberg printed one book; Fust and his son Peter Schoeffer printed one hundred and thirty. A letter from Fust is like a letter from St Paul. And I found it.'

'What did it say?'

The knot of veins pulsed under Olaf's knuckles as he fretted with the frayed blanket. 'I should have published it. I should have told the librarian what I found. It would have stopped everything. But I did not.'

He took a furtive look around the church. 'I stole it. Almost before I knew it, I slipped it into my pocket. At last I had found my princess sleeping in her tower. She would not give herself to me, so I took her. The archive had no security: they thought they had nothing worth taking.'

'But you didn't publish?'

'The letter was just the beginning. It hinted at things much greater. I could have published, of course; I would go back to the archive, pretend to find it again, announce my discovery. But then I risked being left with the hook while someone else walked off with the fish. And I was jealous. I was like an old man with a young wife – except I was twenty-four and she was five hundred years old. I hid her away. My secret.'

While he spoke, he spun one of the threads of his blanket around the knuckle of his index finger, so tight the tip went white. He didn't seem to notice.

'I guarded my privacy. But not well enough. I was a young man: I had women to impress, rival scholars – who sometimes were also rivals in love – to outshine. I hinted; I made remarks; I allowed speculation. I was careless. I thought I was very clever.

'Then one day a man came to see me. A young priest, Father Nevado. He came to my house. He was thin – we all were then, but he was thinner; he had red lips, like a vampire. He told me he had come from Italy, though he was obviously Spanish. From this I deduced he worked for the Vatican. 'He told me, "I have heard rumours you have made a remarkable discovery."'

'"A letter from a man who complains that the Church has stolen something from him," I said. I was arrogant. "Have you come to give it back?"

'The priest's eyes were like black ice. "The letter is the property of the Holy Church."

'He looked at me then. I tell you, I had watched dead-eyed Russian soldiers march into our guns until they choked them with their own blood. I had watched them shoot children and rape girls in the street. They had not frightened me as much as this priest did when he looked at me.

'"You will give me the letter," he said. "You will give me all the copies you have made, including translations. You will give me the name of every person you have told about it. You will never mention it again; you will forget it ever existed."

'He broke me right there. I was a medieval historian; I knew what the Church could do to its enemies. Even in the twentieth century. It was in his voice. His eyes. I gave him the letter and all my notes.

' "If you ever tell anyone of this, you will surely suffer the torments of the damned," he told me.

'And so I kept silent. For ten years I devoted myself to my work. I completed my thesis and found a position at a provincial university. I attended seminars and workshops; I invited colleagues to dinner and flattered their wives; I reviewed obsequiously. I married. But my wound never healed.

'I wrote a book. A small book, interesting only to scholars, if anyone. But I was proud of it. To me, it was vindication. The priest had taken the treasure that would have elevated my career to Olympian heights, but I had clawed myself up nonetheless. And I could not resist a small crow of triumph.

'It was a footnote. Nothing more: a passing reference, so obscure no reader would even notice it. Just for my own pride.

'Two weeks before the book was to be published, my editor called me to his office. He polished his spectacles; he was very regretful. He said that very serious allegations of plagiarism had been made against my work.

' "But there is no plagiarism in my book," I protested. You must understand, to an academic it is like being accused of harming your children. I had sweated five years of blood to make that book.

' "Surely there is not," said my editor. "But they are suing us for a large sum of money and if we lose we will be bankrupt. Your book is important, but I cannot risk all our other authors for you."

' "Then what do we do?"

' "They require that we recall all copies and pulp them. They are not vindictive men; they have even offered to help pay for the costs of destruction."

' "Who?" I demanded. "Who are these men who say what will or will not be published?" I guessed, of course. "Was it the priest?"

'My editor played with his pen. "Make sure you bring in the advance copies you have at your house. We must account for every one."

'Three days later, I drove home from a dinner party with my wife. It was late, an icy night. Perhaps I had had a little too much schnapps – but in those days, everybody did. I came around a corner. Some fool had skidded and abandoned his car in the middle of the road. I had no chance.'

Olaf folded his hands. 'My wife died at once. I spent six months in hospital and came out in a wheelchair I have never left.'

'Did they catch the people who did it?' said Emily.

'The car was stolen. The police said it was youths, joyriders who panicked when the car skidded. I did not believe them.

'After that I abandoned my history. It was too dangerous. I wrote some tourist guides to Mainz; I volunteered at the museum. Those people took away my past, my present, my future. I lived forty years waiting to die. I never spoke of it.'

'But you told Gillian,' said Nick.

The old man rocked back in his wheelchair. 'My second wife died five years ago – from the cancer. I was almost glad: at least I could not blame myself. We have no children. There is nothing more they can take from me. When Gillian Lockhart contacted me, I thought it was my last chance. My wound still has not healed.'

'How did she find you?'

Olaf chuckled. 'Do you know the Hawking paradox?'

'As in Stephen Hawking?' said Nick. 'His calculations showed that when matter enters a black hole all information about it is destroyed. But that contradicts a fundamental law of physics: that information cannot be destroyed.'

'Dr Hawking was proved wrong. Even in a black hole, some information survives. So also with my little book. Somewhere, somehow, a few copies leaked out of the black hole Father Nevado made for them. One sat on a library shelf – who knows where – fifty years. Waiting. Until, it seems, an Internet company started digitising this library's collection as part of a project to accumulate all knowledge. If Father Nevado knew about it, he would probably tear down all the World Wide Web to get rid of it. But even he cannot police everything. Gillian found it first. Then she found me. I sat in this same church and told her what I have told you. Like me fifty years ago, she was too stubborn to hear the warnings.'

'You told her about the letter?'

'About the letter – yes. But for her it was more important to learn about the library.'

'Which library?' Nick felt like a drunk wandering across a frozen lake: slipping and skidding, with only the faintest idea of the airless depths beneath.

'The *Bibliotheca Diabolorum*. The Library of Devils.'

The blue light seemed to wrap Nick closer. Emily slid along the bench, pressing against him. By the altar, a young priest was reciting a litany.

'You know of it?'

Nick and Emily shook their heads.

'Few people have even heard its name. It is a construction, a myth. A hell for condemned books. The last curse of the thwarted scholar when all his efforts to find a book have failed: it must have gone to the Devils' Library.'

'Does it exist?'

'It must.' Olaf's hands were trembling. He knitted his fingers together. 'They almost killed me to protect it. That was the footnote in my book: "We should consider the possibility that some books from Johann Fust's collection may have been confiscated, perhaps to the so-called Devils' Library." That was why they killed my wife.'

'Was that what Fust's letter said?'

'Not precisely. You can see yourself.'

Olaf twisted in his seat and began fiddling with his wheelchair. It was an old contraption, with wooden armrests screwed to a metal frame. One of the screws was loose. Olaf scrabbled underneath and slid out a piece of paper folded over and over, concertina-style, so as to be no wider than the armrest.

He handed it to Nick. 'Even in the blackest hole, information survives.'

'To the Most Reverend Father in Christ, Cardinal Aeneas Silvio Piccolomini:

I am writing in order that I may humbly acquaint your most exalted person with the injustice which diverse blackguards and vagabonds have caused to be perpetrated in the name of the Church; which deeds, if you knew of them, you would surely deplore, as I do, to the depths of your soul. Yesterday, in the afternoon, two men came to my house by the church of St Quintin, the Humbrechthof. They interrupted various works my son was undertaking there, the nature of which need not detain Your Grace, and ransacked the workshop until they had found a certain book they sought. Though small and unremarkable in every way, this book had come into my possession from a particular gentleman known to Your Grace.

Despite my heated protestations, these men took the book away with them. Wherefore I pray Your Grace, if you know anything of this outrage, to bend your authority to seeking out the evil-doers and restoring to me my rightful property.

Johann Fust

Humbrechthof, Mainz

Emily stared at the piece of paper, as wrinkled as Olaf's skin. 'You remember it word for word?'

'The priest took all my papers, but he could not take my memory. Even after the accident. Since then, not a day has gone by when I have not recited it.'

'Who was Piccolomini?' said Nick.

'A man who rose from a farmer's son to be a cardinal, and eventually pope. He was also a novelist, a poet, a travel writer and a keen horseman.'

'A real Renaissance man.'

'Some decades in advance of the Renaissance itself. It is from him, incidentally, that we have the only eyewitness account of Gutenberg's famous Bible. He saw it at a fair in Frankfurt and wrote to describe it to a fellow cardinal.'

' "A particular gentleman known to your Grace," Emily read off the page. 'You think it was Gutenberg?'

'Gillian thought so.'

Olaf looked up. His eyes were pale, the colour dried up long ago. He fixed them on Emily, then Nick, stretching forward, trying to discern something distant.

'She was right.' Emily took the reconstruction out of her bag and gave it to him. The paper shivered in his hands.

458

He sighed deeply and settled forward in his chair. The wrinkles on his face seemed to sag, as if something inside him was slowly deflating. He murmured to himself in German: to Nick it sounded like, 'Only the spear that made the wound can heal it.'

'Thank you.'

'Did Gillian say where she found the reference to this Devils' Library?' Emily asked.

'Here in Mainz – at the Stadtarchiv, the state archive.'

'I bet it's gone now,' said Nick. 'The men who took your book seem to be pretty good at clearing up after themselves.'

'By the time she came here, your friend had started to realise this too. So she hid her discovery.'

'Did she tell you where?'

'She hid it where she found it,' said Olaf. For a moment, Nick wondered if his mind had started to wander. 'The clue – she did not say what it was – she found in an inventory of books from the Benedictine monastery in Eltville. This inventory came in a box which has a bar code for the catalogue. Gillian replaced this with a different bar code. If you look for the Eltville monastery inventory, you will find nothing. If, however, you look for a seventeenth-century treatise on agronomy, you may be surprised.' He wrote the reference on their paper.

'Did you go and have a look at it.'

Olaf shook his head. 'It would have been too dangerous. Even now.'

He reached across the pew and grabbed Nick's arm. Nick flinched, though there was no strength in the withered fingers.

'I said this library – if it exists – is a hell for condemned books. But books cannot endure torment as humans can. Be careful.'

LXX

Mainz

A sultry day in June. The sun streamed through every crack in the close-packed houses, steaming the limp-hanging laundry and baking the dung on the streets into bricks. Children played in the fountain outside St Christoph's church, screaming with delight as they splashed each other. Butchers put down their cleavers and wielded horsehair whisks in vain efforts to keep the flies away. The city slumped in a daze, stupefied by the smell and the heat.

I walked down the street from the Gutenberghof towards the Humbrechthof. Behind me, two apprentices hauled a hand cart loaded with small casks. Whatever the neighbours thought we transacted behind the Humbrechthof's doors and shuttered windows, they knew it was thirsty work. How else to explain all the barrels that rolled down that street?

This was my life's journey, I thought: a matter of a hundred yards. Past the baker where I had bought sweet pies as a child, the stationer who had sold me my schoolbooks, the sword master who tried to teach me fencing when my father still believed I might become a worthy heir. If I had walked past the Humbrechthof, the same distance would have taken me to the mint where I first glimpsed perfection. I walked more slowly now. The page of my soul bore the imprint of many pressings, some indelible, others written in hard point, invisible to all but the author. The ink was dense, heavy with crossings-out and corrections, new words overwritten on washed-out texts still visible beneath. In places, the nib had nicked tears in the paper. Water had stained it, fire curled the edges.

Today I would start a new page.

In seven months, the Humbrechthof had been transformed. All the walls had been whitewashed against damp. The thatch on the outbuildings had been stripped and replaced with tiles. The weeds in the courtyard had been trampled to dust by the criss-crossing of many feet, and a saw pit dug beside the old pastry kitchen. Stout timbers lay beside it. All the doors brandished new locks, and a heavy block and tackle sprouted from a dormer in the roof. Empty barrels like those that had just arrived stood stacked in a corner waiting to return up the road.

The apprentices unloaded the barrels and prised them open. Inside, large jars of ink lay nestled in straw like eggs. They began to unload, but I gestured them to follow me quickly into the house. Others had seen us arrive and emerged from the outbuildings: the paper shop, the ink store, the tool shed and the refectory. They followed me up the stairs, along the corridor and into the press room.

Everyone was there. Fust, with the haunted look of a soul approaching judgement; Götz, still wearing a leather apron from the forge; Father Günther, whose inky fingers played with the cross around his neck; Saspach, a hammer in his hand ready for any last-minute adjustment; and around them all our assistants and apprentices from both houses, almost twenty men in total. Even Sarum, the ginger cat who kept rats out of the paper store, had wandered in and crouched behind one of the table legs. And in the middle of them all, the press.

It stood like a gate in the centre of the room: two thick uprights, joined at the top and again halfway down by heavy crosspieces. The posts had been nailed into the ceiling and bolted to the floor, so that the whole instrument was knitted into the fabric of the house. A screw descended through the middle and held the platen over a long table that stuck out like an apron between the posts. That supported a flat carriage on runners, which could be slid under the press or pulled out to change the paper and the type. It was far removed from the wobbly device we had first erected in Andreas Dritzehn's cellar a dozen years earlier.

I stood beside the press and addressed the assembled team. I do not remember what I said, and I doubt they paid much attention. The only words that mattered that day lay set in lead on the press bed. I concluded with a prayer that God would cast his blessing on our humble enterprise, which we offered in His name and to His purpose.

As soon as I was done, Kaspar stepped forward. He did not look at his audience. He had always been capable of great concentration, in starts, but since his injury he had acquired an almost ferocious power to ignore all around him. I suppose he needed armour against the stares and mockery his deformity drew in the streets.

He uncorked two ink bottles, a large one of black and a small of red. First, he dipped a brush in the red and carefully painted it onto the head line, the rubrication. Then he poured the black into a pool on the block beside the press. It came out thick and sticky as naphtha.

He swirled the ink around the slab with a knife until it was evenly spread, then picked up two leather balls on sticks. He dipped one in the ink and rubbed the two together. When the brown leather was a uniform black, he rubbed them on the metal type in the press, using short round motions like kneading dough. A thin film of ink spread across the form.

He stepped back. I breathed a sigh of relief. I had wanted Kaspar to be a part of this moment – because his painter's hands were more deft than anyone's with the ink balls, but also because it was right. He was my lodestar, the beginning of all that followed. Yet – as ever – I felt a drift of unease. There was something about an audience that made him unpredictable, that stoked dangerous fires inside him.

Two young men flanked the press, an apprentice called Keffer I had brought from Strassburg, and Peter Schoeffer. Kaspar had complained about Schoeffer being accorded this honour, but I had overruled him. It was politic, with Fust watching – and deserved. Schoeffer had already proved himself the most promising of my apprentices. He had an instinct for books that none other of our crew of goldsmiths, carpenters, priests and painters could feel.

Schoeffer laid a sheet of vellum onto a board hinged to the bed of the press. Six pins held it in place. He folded it back so that the vellum was held suspended over the inked type, then slid the tray back. It slotted home underneath the platen. He and Ruppel took the handle that drove the screw and pushed it around.

I would have liked to pull it myself, but I was an old man and it wanted strength. The screw creaked and popped as it tightened; the platen pushed down. They held it there a moment, then turned the screw back.

Keffer slid out the tray and folded out the flap, revealing the underside of the vellum. He loosed the pins and pulled it free, made to hold it up then handed it to me instead. The knot of men around me tightened as all vied for a view.

Thousands of tiny letters glistened on the page, wet and black as tar.

n the beginning God created heaven and earth. But the earth was void and empty: shadow covered the earth, and the spirit of God swept over the waters.

It was not complete. The initial 'I' would be added later with Kaspar's copper plate. Tomorrow the leaf would be printed on the reverse. Later it would be brought back for the conjugate pages, two more days, then folded, stitched, eventually bound with all the others. But in itself, it was flawless. Every letter of Götz's new type had imprinted sharp and whole, more even than any mortal scribe could have made.

I looked to Kaspar, wanting to share the triumph with him. He would not catch my eye. He was staring at the vellum, his face screwed up as if he had bitten a sour apple. I knew what he was looking at: the punctuation in the margin. Peter Schoeffer had been right. The image of perfection was greater if the reality was less so. I could not understand why that should be, but it was.

I was about to go over and embrace Kaspar, to remind him that this was his victory as much as mine, when Fust appeared in front of me. His cheeks were flushed; he was holding a glass of wine. He clapped me on the shoulder.

'You have done it, Johann. We will run every scribe and rubricator in Mainz out of business.'

I forced myself to smile at him. 'God willing, this is just the

464

first page of the first copy. We still have almost two hundred thousand to go.'

The true test came ten minutes later, when Schoeffer and Keffer put the second sheet of vellum through the press. Schoeffer pulled it out and hung it on a rack beside the first. I stared between one and the other, scanning every letter for the least deviation.

They were indistinguishable. Perfect copies.

Sunlight shone through a bubble in the windowpane, splaying a fan of colour across the opposite wall. A new covenant. I remembered an old man in Paris.

In the moment of perfection it casts a light like a rainbow. That is the sign.

I drank in my moment of perfection and wished it would never end.

LXXI

Mainz

He was too famous to be doing this. Not that he'd sought it. He despised his colleagues who preened themselves on television, publicising arguments that should have stayed behind the doors of Mother Church. Those men often returned from the studios to find Nevado waiting for them, informing them they had found new vocations in remote dioceses in far-off continents. He enjoyed breaking them, like a gardener pruning branches that disfigured the shape of a tree.

But now he was near the summit of his profession. At such heights, the glare made it impossible to lurk in shadows completely. He became visible. When the last pope died newspapers had printed photographs of Nevado, among others. Ignorant commentators wrote ignorant articles for their ignorant readers, breathlessly speculating whether or not he might be *papabile*. He had read the articles, then used them to light the fire in his Vatican apartments. He'd been burning that sort of waste all his life. It was no more than it deserved.

But error, once it escaped into the world, could not be uprooted entirely. Perhaps fifty years earlier, when he began: not now. Even so, he knew he had to do this. Some men would have called it fate, or destiny; to Cardinal Nevado it was simply God's purpose.

He pulled the scarf up so that it covered his mouth, and stepped into the church.

They turned down the hill, towards the old town and the river. The houses in Mainz seemed to have been built to a different scale: their high walls dwarfed Nick and Emily as they walked hand in hand down the snowbound street.

The archives were housed in a modern building overlooking a main road, with a park and the Rhine beyond. A passenger ferry sat docked at a wharf opposite.

They were just in time. The archives were about to close for the day, the archivist evidently hoping to get home early in the snow. But she let them in with a scowl, and led them down to the basement, a maze of sagging shelves lit by naked bulbs. In a far corner, she extracted a flat cardboard box from under a pile of files. She put it down on a table shoved against the wall under a heating duct.

'The reading room is closed already. You can work here.' She looked at her watch. 'We give you one hour. Then we lock you in.'

Olaf sat in the church contemplating the angels. Sometimes, when his old eyes blurred out of focus, he enjoyed the illusion that the angels had escaped their glass prison and soared free through the blue heaven above. He imagined Trudi, his first wife, playing among them, and hoped she was happier now than he had ever made her.

467

The wheelchair jolted forward. Someone had knocked into it from behind. Olaf lifted his wrinkled hand to anticipate the apology – he was used to such things – but none came.

He turned, and looked up into the face from his nightmares.

There were twelve pages, single columns of closely spaced writing. Over the centuries the catalogue had been subject to many revisions. Ruled lines eliminated many of the entries, while the margins had become a parallel narrative of names, dates and scribbled numbers.

'What are we looking for?'

'Whatever Gillian was looking for when she found the reference to the Devils' Library. Probably something from the fifteenth century. Maybe a bestiary, or a title we haven't heard of before.'

Nick tried deciphering the first line of the catalogue. Medieval handwriting and Latin defeated him.

'How's it organised?'

'Chronologically.'

'It shouldn't be too hard to find the fifteenth-century books, then.'

'Chronologically by the date that the monastery acquired the books,' Emily corrected him.

Nick stared at her incredulously. 'What sort of way to organise information is that?'

Emily laid a protective hand on the page. 'Card catalogues weren't invented until the eighteenth century. Until then, all they could do was write down the books as they came into the library. When they were sold, or lost, they crossed them out. You can see why librarians were so important to monasteries.'

She leaned over to examine the first page. 'A lot of these

books will have been Bibles or prayer books. We can probably discount those.'

'Unless the monks pulled the same trick Gillian did here,' Nick muttered. 'If the book was so controversial, maybe they misfiled it.' He pointed to an entry in the middle of the page. 'What's that?'

'ITEM: DE NATURA RERUM.'

'When does that date from?'

'Originally? Probably about 300 BC.' Emily couldn't help smiling. 'It's Aristotle.'

Olaf hadn't properly believed in God since he was fifteen. But he believed in destiny, and at his age he had seen enough to recognise it when it arrived. He didn't resist Cardinal Nevado taking the handles of his wheelchair and wheeling him out. After the blue womb of the church, a foul yellow light drenched the world outside.

'You hid yourself well,' said the voice in his ear. 'We have been trying to find you for a week.'

'I always assumed you would.'

'But you did not really believe it.' The wheels skidded as he turned a corner. 'For such a cunning race, humanity is badly adapted for deceit. We trust too much to experience. If we have got away with something once, we assume it will always be so. But the more often we risk something, the more likely we are to fail. You betrayed us once with the American girl and escaped. You should not have met in the same place a second time.'

Olaf stared ahead. 'I like to look at the angels.'

'I hope you enjoyed them. They will be the last you see for some time.'

Olaf suddenly became agitated. He craned around, but all

469

he could see of his captor was a long black coat, a wall of darkness billowing behind him.

'What do you want me to tell you?'

'Nothing. We know everything.'

Cardinal Nevado reached in his pocket and pulled out a heavy fisherman's knife. He hooked it around the wheelchair's brake cord. With a twitch of his wrist, the blade severed it.

'God pardon you whatever sins or faults you have committed,' he murmured. He placed a gloved hand benevolently on Olaf's head and held it there for a moment in blessing. Then he pushed.

The hill was steep and smooth as glass. Olaf flapped his arms and tried to grab the wheel rims, but on the hard snow it made no difference. It careered down the street and skidded out onto the road at the bottom – a two-lane stretch of ring road.

From the top of the hill, Nevado actually saw the wheelchair pop into the air as a truck hit it front on. It flew into the next lane, bounced, and disappeared under the wheels of an oncoming car.

There wasn't much Nick could do. He paced the basement reading labels on boxes, wondering what other secrets they might hide. When that got boring, he turned on his laptop to play solitaire. When he'd lost three games in a row, he went back to Emily at the table.

'Any luck?'

Emily frowned. 'It's hard to tell. A lot of these titles are unfamiliar. I can't pin down dates at all.'

The clock on the computer showed half an hour had passed already. Without much hope, Nick activated the laptop's wireless card. To his surprise, it found a network almost at once.

'Maybe I can help.'

He dragged a cardboard box to the table and used it as a makeshift stool. As Emily read out titles he ran them through a search engine, gradually circling in on the section of the catalogue that seemed to have been written in the mid-fifteenth century. In the bottom corner of the screen, minutes ticked past.

'Here's one,' she said. 'No details at all, just a title. *Liber Bonasi*.'

Nick typed 'Bonasi' into the search engine.

Did you mean: ***Bonsai***?

Underneath, a list of links offered him various services to do with bonsai trees.

'Nothing coming up.'

'Strange.' She pored over the catalogue. 'Try "*Bonasus*". That might be a more common form.'

Japanese nurseries disappeared. Nick scrolled through the new results and tried to make sense of them.

'*Bonasus* seems to be the Latin name for some kind of Polish bison. Apparently they piss on wild grass which they use to flavour vodka. Gross, huh?'

He looked up from the screen, wondering why she'd gone so still. 'That's what it says here.'

'Try "Bonnacon".'

She spelled it out for him. Nick entered it and clicked on the first result that came up. Emily stood and walked round the table to look.

'That's it.'

A new picture filled the screen: a strange beast with muscular flanks, curled horns and cloven hoofs. Three knights were pursuing it with spears, but had been thrown back by a forked blast that shot out from the beast's rear end like lightning.

Nick read the caption. 'Bonnacon, also known as Bonasus. A fabulous beast with a horse's mane, a bull's body and horns that curve back and so are useless for fighting. When attacked, it runs away, while emitting a trail of dung that can cover two miles. Contact with the dung burns its attackers like fire.'

Half-listening, Emily pulled the reassembled printout from the bag and laid it next to the computer. Nick looked between them: screen to paper, paper to screen.

The animals were the same. Not identical, but clearly the same fantastical species. What Nick had taken for a bushy tail was actually a cloud of fiery excrement spraying behind it.

'Napalm shit,' said Nick. 'Glad I never walked behind one.'

'*Liber Bonasi* means the Book of Bonasus. It could be a pseudonym, like Libellus or Master Francis.'

Nick moved around the cluttered table to look at the catalogue again. 'So does it mention the Devils' Library there?'

'No.' Emily pointed to the entry. The title had been ruled through, struck out, but unlike the other books there was no date or description of where it had gone. The margin was empty.

'Olaf said Gillian found the reference here.'

'If you were going to send a dangerous book to a secret library, you probably wouldn't record it in the catalogue.'

'Not so people could see.' Nick pulled out his cellphone and turned it on – the first time he'd touched it since he left Paris. Blue-white light glowed from the screen.

'It's not ultraviolet, but it might give us an idea.'

He laid the phone flat against the medieval catalogue. Light spilled across the page. With tiny movements, he angled the phone back and forth, trying to catch any sign of hard-point writing.

'What's that?'

He just caught it: a faint scar in the paper, almost invisible in the weak light. He turned up the brightness on the screen, tracing the indentations like an archaeologist sifting through sand. He had to spell it out letter by letter; several times he realised he'd got one wrong and had to go back.

Bib Diab. Portus Gelidus.

Footsteps rang on the steel stairs. Nick jumped, but it was only the archivist. Emily swept up the catalogue and put it back in the box.

The archivist tapped her watch. 'Time you must go.'

They followed her back up. On the stairs Nick asked, 'Does the name Portus Gelidus mean anything to you?'

The archivist frowned, surprised.

'Portus Gelidus is the name in historical times for Oberwinter. It is a village on the Rhine, in the mountains.' She pushed through the door into the lobby and pointed through the front windows. Across the busy road, limp flags hung over a gangway on the pier. 'You can go by the ferry.'

Nevado checked the street – still empty. His hat would have hidden his face from anyone watching from the windows above, and any CCTV cameras. He doubted the police would even bother to check: it was plain enough what had happened. An old man had lost control of his wheelchair on the ice, skidded and died. A tragedy. He walked briskly away until he found a street down the hill where the pavements had been shovelled clear. In the distance, he could hear sirens.

A vibration in his coat pocket reminded him his work wasn't finished yet. He snapped open the phone and listened for a moment.

'Do nothing. Wait for me.'

473

*

Once, Mainz had been protected by stone; now its walls were ramparts of snow, ploughed to the sides of the two-lane highway that divided the riverfront from the rest of the city. Traffic was at a standstill, the cars pulled over so that an ambulance could nose its way through. Someone must have skidded – easy enough, in this weather. Nick looked for the accident but couldn't see anything.

They weaved between the stationary cars and came out on a wide concrete promenade over the Rhine. A biting wind hit them; out on the river it whipped the water into serrated white-capped teeth. By the flagpoles, a sailor in a blue boiler suit unwound a rope from the gangway. They hurried over.

'Does this boat go to Oberwinter?' Nick asked.

A roar drowned whatever answer he got as the ferry revved its engines to depart. Clouds of diesel smoke filled the air. The sailor pulled two tickets off a ring and shoved them in Nick's hand.

'You pay on board. Maybe we get you there.' He looked at the sky. 'Maybe not.'

They tottered down the gangplank and went inside out of the cold. They didn't look back, so they didn't see a man run across the road, dodging between the cars that had finally started moving, and examine the ferry timetable posted on a noticeboard on the pier. Nor did they see the man in the dark overcoat and low-brimmed hat who strode up a minute later.

Ugo heard Nevado coming and turned. 'The first stop is Rüdesheim – not far. Maybe with the car we can beat it.'

The cardinal shook his head. Out in the river, the ferry was passing between two huge coal barges.

'We know where they are going.'

474

LXXII

Mainz

The ferry pulled away from the pier, navigating carefully between two barges loaded with timber from the forests upriver. It had been a wet August: a powerful current struck the small craft side on as it emerged from the lee of the larger ships. A brown wave slopped over the side; the waterman paddled furiously, while the passengers gripped each other and crossed themselves. I watched their huddled faces from the safety of the riverbank. I had sat on that ferry once, a whey-faced youth setting out into the world. How far I had come.

Fust came out from a warehouse, passed behind a group of travelling players who had just disembarked, and approached. He greeted me as he always did.

'How many pages?'

'Nine.'

'Where should we be?'

'Twenty-one.'

'So far behind already.' He frowned. 'Why?'

'In a project of this magnitude, certain problems only

emerge with time. The types wear out faster than we had anticipated. We are using more ink than we allowed for – I do not know why. And we still cannot get the initials to align properly.'

'The second press?'

'Saspach promises it will be ready in two weeks.'

'He said that two weeks ago.'

'One of the posts wasn't seasoned properly. He insisted we pull it apart and start again.'

Fust rolled his eyes. 'Perfectionist.'

'That is not what is delaying us. It is taking the compositors longer to compose the text than it takes the printers to print it. I have set them to work in two teams on different parts of the Bible, but Günther still finds too many errors. He sent one page back fifteen times yesterday before it was ready. Even then, mistakes slip through. We had pressed nine copies of one page yesterday before we noticed that two lines were the wrong way round.'

'Paper or vellum?'

'Vellum.'

'You should press the paper copies first,' he rebuked me. 'It will make our mistakes cheaper. And you should be more relaxed about trivial errors. If we redo every page for each spelling mistake, we will still be pressing at doomsday.'

My face prickled. Any thought of a flaw in the book was like sores under my skin.

Fust turned away. 'Walk with me.'

I hurried after him, skirting the puddles that soaked the waterfront. I glanced at the overcast sky; there would be more puddles by nightfall. I would have to check the roof on the paper store before bed.

'The work you are doing is extraordinary, Johann.'

I kept silent. I did not trust it when he called me by name. Overhead, a crane squeaked as it winched sacks of quicklime off a barge. Some of the powder seeped through a tear in the sackcloth, hissing and boiling as it landed in the water.

'I know that with any new art there will be difficulties. Problems we did not anticipate. But we cannot be complacent. We must respond vigorously, or we store up troubles to come. And there are other considerations.'

While he spoke, we had come to a warehouse set back a little from the quay. It was built like a castle, with slit windows and a crenellated rampart around its roof. He presented a clay tablet to the watchman, who waved us in. Inside, it smelled of sawdust and wine. Bales of cloth, jars of oils and, in one bay, a pile of boxes sealed with wax and painted with the symbol of a bunch of grapes.

Fust took a clasp knife from the pouch on his belt and prised up the lid of the topmost box. He slit open the oilcloth which wrapped the contents. I knew what would be inside: I had opened a dozen myself in the store at the Humbrechthof. A bale of paper, brittle and shiny from the sizing glue.

'I did not order any more paper,' I said.

'I did.'

I counted nine more boxes. Each held two reams, almost a thousand sheets. A quarter as much again as we had already laid in.

'How much has this cost? Even with the wastage, we have plenty for our needs.'

'I have been speaking with my customers.' A reassuring hand on my arm. 'Discreetly. I have performed some calculations. You said yourself, the greater part of the labour is composing the page. That is a fixed cost – whether we press one copy or one thousand. Once that is done, putting it through the press is comparatively quick. So the more copies we press, the more we spread the costs of composition. The cost of the extra time, paper and ink almost pays for itself.'

'How many more?'

He pulled me away from the pile of boxes, back to the wharf outside. 'Thirty copies. All on paper. By my reckoning it will add ninety gulden to our costs – I will pay it – and nine *hundred* gulden to our profit.'

'If we sell them,' I cautioned. 'And it will put us even further behind our schedule.'

'We cannot let our deadline slip. The money I have invested in the work of the books is borrowed at interest and it must be repaid in two years.'

'Debts can be rearranged,' I said easily. Perhaps too easily. He spun around and fixed me with a hard look.

'The book *will* be finished on time. We must redouble our efforts. Perhaps some aspects of the process can be rethought.'

'What aspects?'

'The rubrication, for one. I have been in the press room – I have seen how much time we lose inking the form in two different colours. Sometimes I have seen black ink spill over into the red, and then the whole form must be removed, wiped off and inked again.'

'It is time-consuming,' I admitted. 'But we will not be able to charge so much if we sell the books without rubrication.' In truth, I hated the thought of another man's hand in my book, marring the unity of the whole.

'Nonsense. The customers will not know what they are missing. Anyone who buys a Bible expects he will have to pay a rubricator, just as he expects to pay the binder and the illuminator.'

'Not the illuminator. They will have Kaspar's plates.'

We stopped by the embankment. The river lapped against the wall below; a flock of swans pecked at the weed that trailed from the stones.

'Those must go too.'

Without looking, Fust must have known the expression on my face.

'I know he is your dear friend. But we have invested too much in this to allow mere friendship to threaten it.'

Mere friendship. 'He is more than my friend. He was the root and stem of all that we have done. He had already pressed his cards while I was still copying schoolbooks in Paris.'

'Then he will understand that a new art requires compromises.'

I doubted that very much.

'Is there anything else?' I asked.

'You should look at the composition of the pages. Peter thinks that you could fit two more lines on every page without changing its appearance. More lines on the page means fewer pages in the book. Less paper and time, more money. That alone would account for almost half the time we spend pressing the extra copies.'

'I will consider it,' I said stiffly. For all my age, I felt like a child denied the toy he was promised. I wanted to weep.

Fust slipped a rosary from his wrist. He flipped the beads around in short, precise movements, like counters on an abacus.

'You cannot do everything, Johann. This book is already a miracle. In two years we will produce more books than one man could in two lifetimes. We must not overreach ourselves.'

'This was my dream,' I whispered. 'God's word as God intended it.'

'The words do not change. It is only the ornament. For God's sake let it go. We have invested too much to fail because of it.'

'I am not doing this for profit.'

'No? I saw your face when I told you how much we will earn from the extra copies. But even if you are not – I am. And you are working for me.'

'A partnership.'

'If you do not like the terms I am happy to dissolve it.' He slapped the rosary into his palm and closed his fist around it. 'I did not mean that. I know how much this means to you. But you, of all men, must be *practical*.'

He watched me for a moment, then rattled the rosary back over his wrist. He sighed, made to leave, then remembered something.

'I made an inventory of our vellum stocks yesterday. Three skins were missing.' He peered at me closely. 'I heard that you pressed a batch of grammar books in the Gutenberghof last week.'

'The parchment we were going to use got wet. It would have crumbled like pastry when it dried. I had promised the books would be delivered on time, so I borrowed some from the store at the Humbrechthof. I will replace it as soon as I get a new batch.'

His eyes blazed. 'Do you remember what I told you? Everything that goes into our venture stays in it. You cannot *borrow*, like a labourer in the vineyard stuffing his face with his master's grapes. I will allow it this time, but never let it happen again.'

He left me on the quayside. Out in the stream, the wheels on the mill ships turned on. It suddenly occurred to me that my mother must have stood here, decades earlier, watching her

480

youngest son embark on a barge to Cologne with little more than a clean shirt to his name. Did she weep? Did she feel her life torn away from her: first her husband, then her child? Did she think on what might have been?

Fresh raindrops dashed against my face, mingling with the tears.

LXXIII

River Rhine

Nick stood in the bow of the boat. Spray spattered his cheeks, but he would rather endure that than the suffocating, tobacco-laden fug inside. He felt as if he was sailing into a fairy tale. Not the modern sort, with wisecracking animals and songs written to sound good as ringtones; the old-fashioned kind, tangled tales woven out of the fabric of the land, dark forests and hard mountains. Here, the Rhine flowed through steep-sided valleys covered in snow, under great cliffs where sirens once lured sailors to their doom. Stark castles guarded every hilltop, watching the boat as it crept downriver. Some were tumble-down ruins; others looked as though they only wanted a trumpet call to rouse their defenders to battle.

'It's just as well we came by boat.' Emily pointed a gloved hand to the shore. A single road wound along the riverbank, tucked into the slope. It was almost invisible under the snow. 'No cars. They must have shut it.'

'Good,' said Nick. 'Harder for anyone to follow us. Unless there's another ferry?'

'The bartender said this is the last boat today. He said there might not be any tomorrow either if the ice gets worse.'

'Good.' Nick repeated it, trying to convince himself. He was afraid. Not the sudden pulse of adrenalin that came with being chased – he'd had plenty of that in the last ten days. This was a deeper dread, cold fingers slowly choking him as he sank into a void. A feeling that there was no way back.

Emily pulled out a rumpled paper tissue and began shredding it between gloved fingers, letting the fragments fall into the water. 'Do you think we'll find it?'

'Do you mean *her*?'

'Sorry.' She watched a piece of tissue flutter down. The river soaked it up.

Nick didn't speak, but shuffled sideways so that he squeezed against her. She tipped her head so that it rested on his shoulder.

'I wonder how the prayer of Manasses fits into this,' she said.

'What do you mean?'

'We're following Gillian. But what was she following? If she went to Oberwinter, it was because of what she found in the Mainz archives. Nothing to do with the prayer of Manasses or the digging bear.'

'Maybe we were on the wrong track with the pictures,' said Nick. '*The Sayings of the Kings of Israel* is supposed to be a lost book of the Bible, right? Maybe that was the writer's way of saying that his book's gone to this place where lost books go. The Devils' Library.'

'But the bear. Do you think it's a coincidence that the picture from the card was right there in the prayer of Manasses?'

Bear is the key.

483

'You said yourself that medieval artists copied each other all the time.'

'It feels as if we're following a trail that someone laid down for us five hundred years ago. The hard-point inscriptions, the hidden books, the recurring images . . . But I'm not sure it points to Oberwinter.'

'Gillian was.'

Nick pulled away slightly, but only so he could stick his hand in his pocket to warm it. His fingers touched the slim bar of his cellphone, tingling as the blood returned.

No. It wasn't his blood, he realised, but the phone vibrating. It was ringing as well, though with the engines throbbing through the boat and the hiss of the water he hadn't heard it. He must have forgotten to turn it off when he'd used it to read the hard point.

He pulled it out, staring at it like a relic of some alien civilisation. And then, because he was tired and it was a ringing telephone, he answered.

'Nick? It's Simon.'

Nick almost dropped the phone. Emily looked at him and made an O with her mouth. *Who?*

'Atheldene,' Nick whispered. Then, into the phone, 'How did you get this number?'

'You rang me from your phone in New York. I've been calling for the last twenty-four hours. Didn't you get my messages?'

'Where are you?'

'Mainz. It's on the Rhine, near Frankfurt.'

Was there something too casual about the way he said it? Too confident, too knowing? Or was Nick just paranoid?

'Is Mainz nice?' he asked, trying to sound cool.

'There's a lovely Romanesque cathedral and a shop selling

484

chocolate busts of Gutenberg.' The sarcasm sounded right. 'But that's not why I'm here. I rang the office in Paris, found out a package arrived for me the day after we left. Postmarked Mainz. My secretary recognised Gill's handwriting.'

'What was in it?'

'Something you should see. Can you get to Mainz?'

'Not right now. Can you tell me what it says?'

'It would be easier to show you.'

Nick's head began to throb. 'For God's sakes, Atheldene, we're trying to find Gillian. This isn't a time to be playing games.'

'I quite agree. Why don't you tell me where you are?'

Nick hesitated. Atheldene gave an exasperated sigh.

'Have you heard of the prisoners' dilemma? Two men in a cell. If they trust each other, they go free. If they don't, they both hang. That's where we are.'

Still Nick didn't say anything. He was jammed, frozen by the uncertainties clogging his mind.

'Gill was definitely in Mainz two weeks ago. I've been to the archives here: they remembered her. We're near, Nick.'

'What was in the parcel Gillian sent?'

Atheldene paused. Then: 'Fine. You want my quid pro quo? It was the first page of the bestiary you ran off with from Brussels. Somebody had cut it out – I suppose Gillian must have found it. I've taken a photo of it on my phone and I'm sending it to you now. Hold on.'

Nick waited. Was this another trap? Every second he was on the line he felt his anxiety rising.

A background chime announced that a message had arrived. Atheldene must have heard it on his end.

'Now – where are you?'

Perhaps it was because he was tired. Perhaps it was because

Atheldene's voice, however patronising and unhelpful, was a rare touch of something familiar. Perhaps it was the desperation in his plea. *If we don't trust each other, we both hang.*

'We're heading to a place on the Rhine called Oberwinter. I'll call you when we arrive and we'll figure something out.'

'I'll see if I can get there. Travel's pretty grim at the moment.' He cleared his throat. 'Look, I'm sorry we parted ways in Brussels. We should have stuck together. For Gill.'

'I'd better go.'

'Wait. There's . . .'

Atheldene's voice broke up, his words crushed into staccato blocks of static. A few seconds later he came back.

'. . . what she is.'

'What was that?'

Nick looked around. They'd come round a bend between two mountains that trapped the river between them, blocking out the signal.

'I'm losing you.'

More static. Then nothing.

Nick hung up. In his anxiety he almost switched off the phone at once, until a blinking icon on the screen reminded him of the picture Atheldene had sent.

'I guess if there's no signal there's not much way of tracing the phone.'

He opened the image and gave the handset to Emily. It was hard to see much on the small screen. She fumbled with the buttons to zoom in.

'It's the standard opening of the bestiary. "The lion is the bravest of all beasts and fears nothing . . ." There's the picture.' A lion with its back arched, roaring so loudly it seemed to send shivers through the adjoining words.

Nick took the phone back and scrolled around the picture.

His hands were so numb he almost dropped it in the water.

'What's that?'

A mark in the margin near the bottom of the page, too faint to be part of the illumination.

'Maybe a smudge?'

Nick zoomed in. The pixels blurred, then sharpened themselves. It was a doodle – there was no other word for it – a crude sketch of a rectangular tower with three doors, and a large cross beside it.

'The cross must mean it's a church, or maybe a monastery. That would make sense. If the Devils' Library did exist, a monastery would have been the safest place to keep it.'

Nick stared at the picture a moment longer, then switched off the phone.

'I hope I did the right thing, telling Atheldene where we're going.'

Emily wrapped her hand in his and squeezed it.

'There's nothing you can do about it now.'

He stared into the water. Off the bow, black-backed rocks lurked beneath the surface like circling sharks.

If we don't trust each other, we both hang.

LXXIV

Mainz

All that winter we worked like dogs. While October rains flooded the fields and turned the roads to bog, we were stuck in our own mire of ink and lead. I watched carters bruise their shoulders trying to heave their heavy wagons out of the mud, and felt a kinship.

Snow fell in December. As Fust would not allow fires in the Humbrechthof, we froze. I had to send the crews back to the Gutenberghof in shifts, to thaw beside the forge where we boiled ink and recast the old types. It made the short, dark days shorter still. One morning we found the piles of damp paper frozen solid. The presses jammed, and ink would not to stick to the page.

Yet even more fragile was the human machinery. I was making more books than perhaps any man in history, but my fingers rarely touched paper or ink. The whole house had become a mechanism, as intricate as anything Saspach ever built. I was the screw that drove it. Too much pressure and the mechanism would snap; too little, and we would not make an impression. I had to know how many pages the compositors should set each hour, each day, each week, and how many men the task would need, so that the press men neither sat idle nor rushed their work. I had to see which apprentices were quarrelsome or placid, sloppy or over-meticulous, and match them accordingly. I had to make sure that it was impossible for a form to reach the press unless it had been approved, and I had to decide how to order the finished quires in the store-room so that we could divide them correctly when we assembled them into books. These were invisible mechanisms – systems of thought, order and imagination – but they were as necessary to our art as any invention of wood or iron.

And there was Kaspar. At first I tried to put him in charge of a press, but after three days he disappeared. The press sat idle all morning while we searched for him, and Fust was furious. When we found him, in an alehouse, he told me he did not want the job. I told him I would give it to Schoeffer, which angered him so much he agreed to stay on. But I quickly regretted it. He arrived late, quarrelled with his assistants and in short order offended half the men in the Humbrechthof. Sometimes he insisted on re-pressing for the least blemish; at other times, he waved through the most horrendous errors, and I would spend an afternoon digging through the store house to locate them.

Too late, I admitted he was not suited to the work. He delighted in novelty, in the wild freedom of invention. But our task was a discipline as much as an art, novel only in its absolute routine.

One evening, I tried to explain it to him. 'In this house we are a brotherhood, serving God, our art and each other. The books we make are not mine or yours or Fust's. They are of God. The more perfect they are, the closer to God they advance.'

'And will God take the profits when you sell them?'

I shook my head in frustration. 'You've missed the point. The work is boring and repetitive –'

'Like a hammer banging nails.'

'– but what matters is that we do it. Like monks saying their services, the unchanging cycle holds a mirror to God.'

'And a fine monk you'd have made, no doubt,' said Kaspar cruelly. 'If I wanted to live a flat and repetitious life I'd have become a farmer: plough, sow, reap; plough, sow, reap; ploughing the same old rut until it furrowed my grave.' The scars on his face throbbed. 'But I can do more, and so can you. More than pulling a lever to make another copy of your book, like a miller grinding flour.'

The next time he quit his post, as inevitably he did, I let him go. To avoid making the situation worse I gave the job to Keffer, but this only embarrassed him and offended Schoeffer, for both knew that Schoeffer was the better candidate. I paid Kaspar's wages, but he had no place in the Humbrechthof. Sometimes – rarely – he would visit, drifting around the house and setting me on edge until he left. I think he enjoyed inflicting disorder on our work. The rest of the time he stayed in the Gutenberghof, taking work as an illuminator to occupy himself.

I was sad, though it had become inevitable. Somewhere in our journey, it had stopped being our art and become mine.

In April, things began to change. Longer days relieved the pressure to use every scrap of daylight; men saw their tasks with fresh eyes not wearied from squinting through the gloom. Shivering hands that had flinched to pick up the icy metal types now plucked them nimbly and set them in their rows. A rhythm established itself, beaten out every day by the clack of

490

types in their racks, the creak of the press, the rattle of hand-carts bringing fresh ink. When Fust greeted me with, 'How many pages?' the answers no longer made him scowl.

I had told Kaspar we were like monks, and it was true. Like a monastery, we were locked away from the world. Men in the street could hear the sounds from within and wonder, but they never saw what passed behind our gates. The work of the books was our monastic rule. The fetching of paper and ink in the morning was our prime; the morning assembly, where we gathered in the print room to allocate the day's tasks, our chapter – and so through to vespers, when we washed the ink off the forms and the presses, unscrewed the frames and returned the letters to the type room, to be sorted for the next day. We worked together, we ate together, we argued and laughed together: we were a brotherhood.

Most of my days were occupied far from the press: answering questions, solving disputes, settling payments and accounts. But there were moments of peace, times when the whole house turned in ordered motion, like the orbit of the planets around the earth. Those were the hours I was most happy. I walked through the house, observing the world I had brought into being and marvelling at the daily acts of creation under its roof.

Of course it was not all sunshine. Men quarrelled; presses broke; errors emerged, usually just after we had broken apart the offending page and scattered its type. Stores went missing, occasioning furious arguments with Fust. As time passed, the burden of our enterprise began to tell on me. I lay awake in my bed, alone, obsessively counting the pages printed, pages set, pages yet to come. No longer flush with the adventure's promise, instead I longed for it to end. Each time I crossed the threshold of the Gutenberghof I glanced up at the stone pilgrim, bent double under his invisible burden, and felt a twinge of sympathy.

But I cannot complain. After all that had come before, and what happened after, these were good days.

LXXV

Oberwinter

Nobody disembarked at Oberwinter except Nick and Emily. The boat barely paused: by the time they reached the end of the pier, all they could see were running lights receding up the river. They crossed the empty highway, walked through a culvert under the railway tracks and entered the village through a stone gateway. Crooked houses leaned over them, as if the timbers within still preserved some vestigial memory of the trees they had once been. There were no cars, no people, not even footprints in the snow. If not for the wilting Christmas lights still draped between the houses, they could have been back in the Middle Ages.

They passed several guesthouses along the riverfront walls, but all were shuttered and dark. Paper notices pinned on doors said most wouldn't reopen until Easter. Nick's feet ached with the cold; he began to worry they wouldn't find anywhere, but wander this deserted town until they froze to death.

The high street ended in an irregular town square. A wide three-storey building with a roof like a gingerbread house towered over it, and a legend painted on the plasterwork in tangled Gothic letters announced the Drei Könige Hotel. To Nick's unbounded relief, the lights were on.

The hotel was almost as cold inside as out. They rang a bell and waited. Nick eyed the rows of keys on hooks behind the desk.

'Looks like they should be able to give us a room.'

Emily shivered. 'I'll take a cupboard as long as it's got hot water and a duvet.'

The back door opened and a man came out. He was wearing a dressing gown and smoking a filterless cigarette so low Nick worried it would set his moustache on fire. He was the only living soul they'd seen in Oberwinter, but he didn't seem the least surprised to see them.

He took a key from the wall and pointed upstairs. 'Room seven, second floor.'

It wasn't much: a few pieces of heavily varnished furniture marked with cigarette burns, a threadbare rug slung across the floorboards. When Nick touched the desk his finger came away damp from condensation. A freezing draught blew against his shoulder from the open bathroom door. He glanced in. Snow gathered on the sill where one of the windowpanes was missing. Perhaps he could stop it up with a towel.

The moment he stepped inside the bathroom he felt a dizzy wave of recognition. Reality blurred and the room seemed to darken. Instead of a bathroom, he was staring at a pixellated window in a living room thousands of miles away. A scene he had replayed in his head every day since. There was the mirror, the same shower curtain with the Christmas-tree stencils. But the wall was white. In the video it had been brown – he was certain.

He rushed out of the room onto the landing.

494

'Where are you going?' Emily called after him. He ignored her. There were five rooms on this floor, all with their doors cracked ajar in the forlorn hopes of welcoming a guest, and a door marked PRIVAT. One by one, he tiptoed into the rooms and examined the bathrooms. None of them was brown.

He went back out on the landing. On a hunch, he examined the door with the sign more closely. The frame was new, bare wood, while the lock must have been about the shiniest thing in the hotel. In the middle of the door, four dimples showed where screw holes had been filled in with putty. When Nick stepped back, he could see the ghost of the number 14 preserved in the faded paint.

He tried the handle. Locked. He looked back. Emily was standing on the landing outside their room, looking at him in confusion.

'What are you doing?'

Nick crept down to the lobby and counted the keys behind the desk. Thirteen plus a gap where theirs had come from. He listened a moment. All he heard was the distant roar of a soccer match coming out of a television in the back room.

Heart racing, he darted round and lifted the last key off its hook. There was no number on the fob, but the brass was shiny as a new penny, no scratches on its smooth surface. He palmed it against his leg so it didn't jangle and tiptoed back up the stairs.

'If anyone comes, stop them,' he told a by-now utterly bewildered Emily.

He approached the door. Nightmarish visions taunted his imagination. The key slotted into the lock and turned with a whisper. As the door creaked open he felt a shiver, as if a ghost had just passed through him.

He knew at once it must be the right room. The light from

the landing that spilled through the door illuminated a scene of utter destruction. The whole place had been torn apart. Floorboards prised off the joists, wainscoting pulled away from the walls, the bed dismantled and the mattress sliced open. His stomach turned over when he saw that. But there was no trace of blood, and the cuts looked too straight and efficient to have been aimed at someone lying on it.

He flicked the light switch but nothing happened. When he looked up, all he saw was a bundle of wires spilling out of the ceiling where the lamp had been unscrewed and taken away.

'What happened here?'

Nick almost jumped out of his skin. Emily had come up behind him and was peering over his shoulder at the vandalised room. She looked frightened.

'You were supposed to be keeping a lookout.'

'You're supposed to tell me what's going on.'

'When Gillian called me, the day she went missing, she left her webcam on.'

He stepped carefully across the room, balancing on the joists like railway sleepers. The bathroom door stood open, cracked from the impact of heavy blows, while the frame around the latch hung loose in splinters. A glance inside confirmed his suspicions.

'This is where she was. I remember the brown tiles on the walls. The curtain.' The side panel of the bath had been ripped off, but the Christmas-tree shower curtain still hung from the ceiling. He pulled it back. A small ledge was set in the tiled wall, about shoulder high, with a window behind overlooking a snowy roof.

'That must have been where she put the laptop.'

He looked around, trying to silence the scream that was echoing in his memory. The linoleum floor had been rolled back to the skirting board, the mirror unscrewed and leaned against the towel rail. A half-used toilet roll had been placed on top of the radiator, still clipped into the plastic holder that had been removed from the wall. Almost as if someone might need a pit stop amid all the destruction.

'This isn't random. They were looking for something.'

Emily surveyed the wreckage. 'They probably found it. If it was here.'

'Maybe.'

'Well there's no point waiting for them to come back and find us instead.' Emily headed for the door. 'Seriously, Nick. Everything's gone.'

But Nick didn't hear her. He was staring at the radiator, remembering.

Valentine's Day. Waking up, Gillian snuggled against him, the best Valentine's morning he'd ever had. He'd brought her waffles and Bloody Marys in bed, nervous in case she thought it was too cheesy. He suspected she'd have no time for Valentine's Day; wouldn't have been surprised if she'd suggested visiting a war memorial or a soup kitchen instead. But she'd smiled and rubbed herself against him like a kitten, though when he tried to kiss her she pulled away, spilling tomato juice on the bedclothes.

'First you have to find my present to you,' she told him, with a gleam in her eye that said he'd have his work cut out.

He'd turned the apartment upside down. Even Bret had been shocked by the mess. Gillian watched, goading him with hints that seemed completely arbitrary. The waffles went cold. Several times he begged her to tell him, but she just laughed and said love would find a way. Eventually he got so mad he pulled on his clothes and stormed out to the park.

She never told him.

Bret found it four days later. He was sitting on the toilet reading a dirty magazine when he came to the end of the toilet tissue. He came blundering out of the bathroom with his pants around his ankles, a tiny envelope in one hand and a cardboard tube in the other.

'I think it's for you.'

Bret had already opened the envelope. There was a card inside with a plastic gold key on the front, under the legend 'Key to my heart'. Over the flap Gillian had written three words.

'*You got me.*'

'Gillian used to have a trick.'

He went over to the radiator and pulled the toilet roll off its holder. He slid his finger in the cardboard tube. *Don't expect anything*, he told himself.

There was a crack. He squeezed his fingernail into it and teased it apart. The cardboard tube coiled back. Instead of a flimsy wad of toilet tissue, he felt the crisp crackle of writing paper. He pulled it out. Two pages, ragged at the top where they'd been torn from a spiral notebook.

A creak sounded from the stair.

LXXVI

Mainz

Devils haunted our house. So many of our crew believed. Over the next autumn and winter, a sullen joylessness overtook our works. They did not speak of their fears in front of me; they knew I did not like it. But I caught snatches in conversations heard through open doors: nervous comments muttered under their breath. I knew some of the men still distrusted the press. They found its power unnatural, felt discomfited by its casual surpassing of human ability. Some ascribed its powers to black magic. I thought these notions must have come from the townsfolk, anxious and ignorant of the goings-on behind our walls, but clearly many who should have known better thought so too.

And – I had to admit – strange things did happen. Sometimes at night I could have sworn I heard the creak and clank of the press in the room below. I thought it must be my cares creeping into my dreams, but gradually I discovered that others heard it too. One night the whole house woke to the sound of a great crash. We rushed to the press and found a

499

fresh ink jar smashed open on the floor. We blamed the cat, or swallows who had come in the window.

Eventually it became something of a joke. When a compositor reached into his case and found an x in place of an e; when a ream of paper was found to be two sheets short; when Götz's tools went blunt overnight; when a form left in the press was backwards next morning, men crossed themselves and blamed the press devils.

One morning, I found the compositors gathered in a high state of excitement. It was unusual to see them thus: by their nature most were sober and quiet men. They were examining a composing stick filled with type. When they had calmed enough for me to understand, Günther explained that they had found it on the desk when they arrived for work. None knew where it had come from.

I took it through to the proofing room and rubbed ink on the type. I used my thumbs to press a scrap of paper against it. A crude line of text appeared.

tifex is a most curious beast with mouths at

'That is no verse from the Bible,' said Günther.

I shot him a cautioning look. I did not want him frightening the others.

'It's nonsense – obviously. One of the apprentices must have crept in last night thinking to make himself a compositor.'

'The room was locked,' said Günther's assistant.

'Then you must have forgotten to take the key out of the door.'

'Or Kaspar Drach unlocked it.'

I rounded on him in a fury. 'Drach had nothing to do with this. He is never even in this house.'

'I saw him skulking by the paper store yesterday afternoon.'

'You were mistaken.' I looked for a ruler or a stick to beat him for his insolence, but all I could reach was the composing stick. I overturned it so that the letters scattered over the table. The sentence was broken.

'You see – gone.'

But I could not scatter my thoughts so easily. When at last they were settled back at their work, I left the house and hurried up the street to the Gutenberghof. I looked in on the press room, where a fresh batch of indulgences were being made, then climbed the stairs to Drach's attic.

I had not been in there for months. The room was a mess – though, typically for Kaspar, even then there remained something austere about it. All the surfaces, from the floorboards to the desk in the corner, were draped white with sheets of vellum and paper. Some bore snatches of writing; others were painted, or filled with charcoal sketches. Some looked like book pages ready for the binder; some were blank as snow.

I stood in the doorway. 'Where did all this come from?'

'Goats,' said Kaspar. He was wearing the silk smock he used for painting. 'And rags. You should have knocked.'

He scrambled off his stool and knelt on the floor, gathering the papers to his chest and piling them on the straw mattress in the corner. I stepped around him and crossed to the desk to see what he was working on.

It was a quire from a Bible. For a second my eyes tricked me, convincing me it must be one of mine. Before I could embarrass myself, sense returned. It was enormous – a quarter larger than mine at least, so big that even when folded it overflowed Kaspar's desk and relegated his paints to the floor. The gall-brown letters were neat enough but – after months of staring at the pressed Bible – crooked as an old man's teeth. Strange to relate, I looked at it and felt a stir of something like loathing.

'Not yours,' said Kaspar. 'It was commissioned by a curate at the cathedral.'

I admired the illumination. The page was framed by a riotous border of twisting columbines, in whose tendrils lurked the usual creatures who inhabited Kaspar's world. An affronted stag recoiling as a wild man brandished a forked spear at him; two old lions squatting on a flower stem with mournful expressions, beneath a rose that concealed a demon's face. A bear crouched in the corner and tried to dig up the roots of the plant.

'You have surpassed yourself.'

Kaspar stroked the vellum page, supple and soft. 'If you have your way, there will be no more like it. You know Reissman, the scribe who lives above the Three Crowns? It took him a year and three months to write this. In almost the same time, you can make a hundred times as many, and double again. How will he survive?'

'Your cards have existed for twenty years now. There is no shortage of artists.' I shrugged. 'What difference can one man make in the world?'

I turned away from the desk and scanned the other papers around the room. Most lay bundled under a blanket on Kaspar's bed, but a few had escaped his sweep. One I noticed showed sketches of an ox with curved back horns; another a serpent with a face like a man.

'Have you taken any other commissions? Another bestiary, perhaps?'

He didn't respond.

'We found a curious fragment of type in the composing room this morning. It looked like words from a bestiary.' I tried to look in his eyes, but his gaze was slippery as an eel.

'It must have been the press devil.' A sly look. 'Or perhaps

Peter Schoeffer. He is an ambitious young man. He does not want to spend his life pressing Bibles. I overheard him the other day in the type foundry: he thinks you should use the second press to begin a new work.'

'One of the men said he had seen you snooping around the Humbrechthof yesterday,' I persisted.

Kaspar turned back to the giant Bible on his desk. He picked up a brush. 'He must have confused me with Herr Fust. How is he, by the way?'

'He'd be happier if paper didn't go missing from our stores.' I stared hard at the piles of paper on the bed. Kaspar, as ever, ignored me.

'And his daughter Christina?'

I stared at him in astonishment. 'How should I know? I have only ever met her twice, when Fust had me to dine at his house. She cannot be more than fifteen.'

'Old enough to marry.'

I laughed: an old man's laugh awash with bile.

'Are you still trying to arrange me a marriage? Thank God, I already have Fust's money. I do not need his daughter's dowry.'

Kaspar dipped the brush in an oyster shell brimming with pink paint. 'It was just a thought. Perhaps you should make certain . . .'

'I have his money,' I repeated.

'. . . that no one else can get it.'

His brush flicked the page like a serpent's tongue, filling in the colour on the wild man's body. Seeing I would get no more sense out of him, I turned to go.

A glint of silver on the wall caught my eye, one of our Aachen mirrors: I had not seen it there before. I peered at my distorted reflection, and wished its holy rays could heal the gulf between us.

LXXVII

Oberwinter

A creak sounded from the stair. Nick and Emily froze. Outside, the wind blew snow off the rooftop and rattled the windows in their frames. They waited for the creak to come again, to grow into the tread of mounting footsteps.

Nothing came.

'Let's get out of here.' Nick put the toilet roll back and headed out. He locked the door behind him and didn't look back. He didn't want to think about what might have happened in there.

They tiptoed down the stairs as quickly as they dared. On the first-floor landing, Nick heard the murmur of a voice from below.

'We can't stay here,' he whispered. 'They didn't rip that room apart without the owner noticing.'

'Agreed. But where can we go?'

'Anywhere.'

The owner was in the lobby, leaning on the counter and muttering into the phone. He flapped his hand to wave them down, but between the cigarette in his mouth and the receiver in front of it he couldn't manage more than a grunt.

Nick dropped the key on the counter and breezed through the front door.

'We're just going out to get some dinner. We'll be back in about an hour.'

They found a *weinstube* in a house off the main square, overlooking the river and the railroad tracks. It was a cosy place, with bookshelves on the walls and old wine bottles on the windowsills. The waiter tried to sit them by the front window, but Nick insisted on a table at the back, tucked behind an antique wine press. He wasn't sure who he thought he was hiding from. It was probably the only place in Oberwinter that was open.

He hadn't planned to stay long, but the moment he saw the menu he realised he was starving. He hadn't eaten since breakfast. They ordered beef stew and *spätzle* noodles. When the waiter disappeared into the kitchen, Nick pulled the pieces of paper out of his pocket and smoothed them on the tablecloth.

'Is that Gillian's writing?'

Nick nodded. His tired mind tried to take in what was written on the creased sheets of notepaper. It was like a replay of his own recent past. Names that would have meant nothing a week ago leaped out at him, jarring memories that had barely had time to form. '*Vandevelde – B42 ink??? Other MPC images in G. Bible? 08.32 Paris arr. Strasbourg 14.29. Call Simon. Is bear key?*'

The notes covered three sides of the paper, scrawled at various times and in different-coloured inks, crossed out and circled, connected by arrows that branched out into new questions. A palimpsest of the last three weeks of Gillian's life.

On the fourth side they found something different. There was little writing; instead, a sketch that looked like the plan of a building. It was roughly pentagonal, with irregular sides and angular projections. A dotted line led to one of the corners, a red X inked heavily where it met the building. Gillian had written '*Kloster Mariannenbad*' in the margin beside it, and a brief list below:

> *rope*
> *shovel*
> *head lamp*
> *bolt cutters*
> *gun?*

'*Kloster* means monastery,' said Nick.

'That would fit with the picture Atheldene sent us.'

The waiter came out of the kitchen and laid two steaming plates of food on the table. Nick covered the paper with his sleeve.

'Can I get you anything else?'

Emily tried a smile. Her face was drawn, her mouth tight with exhaustion. 'We were just talking – we wondered if you knew – have you heard of a place called Kloster Marianenbad near here?'

'In Oberwinter?'

'A monastery.'

An apologetic shake of his head. 'I do not know this place.'

'What about castles?'

He laughed. 'This is the romantic Rhine. We have here castles every five hundred metres.'

'Any nearby? Any that aren't on the tourist trail?'

The waiter thought for a moment.

'We have the Castle Wolfsschlucht. But this is closed.'

'You mean for the winter?'

'For all of the time. Private. I think it is owned by an American.'

He put his hands on his hips and scanned the bookshelves over their heads. Nick and Emily waited. Eventually he reached down an old book with a frayed cloth cover and dog-eared pages. *Beautiful Oberwinter*, said the title.

'If you want to know more, maybe this has something.'

Nick thumbed through the book while Emily wolfed down her food.

'Here we are: "Castle Wolfsschlucht".'

In medieval times, the building was a monastery dedicated to the Virgin Mary. Tradition says it was built on the site of a local shrine, though this has never been proved. The monastery was obedient to the Archdiocese of Mainz, with one of the most famous libraries in Germany. Most such foundations were dissolved during the Protestant Reformation of the sixteenth century, but the monastery petitioned the Emperor Charles V and was declared *reichsfrei*, independent of all local authority and answerable directly to the emperor himself. Residents of Oberwinter are still proud of the tradition that the pope himself interceded with the emperor on behalf of their monks, promising Charles support in his war against France in return.

The monastery was finally dissolved by the Secularisation Law of 1802. The title passed to the Counts of Schoenberg, who converted the buildings into a castle. In fact, the monastery was perfectly suited to this role. It is built on top of a steep rock overlooking the Rhine, surrounded on three sides by the Wolfsschlucht or 'wolf's gorge'. When the armies of Napoleon marched through the Rhineland, they did not even attempt to capture it.

In 1947 the castle was sold to an anonymous benefactor. It is closed to the public, but one can still glimpse it from the river and wonder what history lies behind those ancient walls.

'The last sentence sounds rather plaintive,' Emily said. 'As if the author was almost as curious as we are.'

'It is a bad place.' The waiter had returned with another basket of bread. He lowered his voice, and looked around the empty restaurant for theatrical effect. 'My grandfather has once told me that in the wartime, the Nazis are going there often. Always in the middle of the night. He said that even maybe the *Reichsminister*, Joseph Goebbels, has been there.'

Nick was about to ask him how Goebbels had got in, but at that moment a woman's voice called the waiter into the kitchen. He excused himself. Nick looked back to the book.

'There's a picture.'

He spread the book flat on the table and turned it to face Emily. The image was dark and vivid: a lonely castle perched on an outcrop in a gorge between two mountains. Heavy lines scratched out a brooding sky, while a black river boiled in the foreground.

'Is that where we have to go?'

'If that's where Gillian went.' Nick laid the sketch map beside it. It was hard to see in the woodcut exactly how the castle was laid out, but there were two turrets that might correspond to the corners of Gillian's pentagon, and a squat tower rising from the back that could be the keep. He rotated the drawing until it looked right.

'Must be it.'

'It certainly sounds as though the Pope went to a lot of trouble to keep it safe. There must be something in there he didn't want the Protestant reformers finding.'

'Or the Nazis.'

Emily studied the plan. 'So how did she get in?'

'This tower here' – Nick indicated the X – 'around the back. Gillian must have found an entrance there.'

Emily read over Gillian's list in the margin. 'Or tunnelled her way in with her spade and her head torch.'

'Maybe we can improvise.' Nick signalled for the bill. When the waiter came, he said, 'Our car's stuck in the snow just outside town. I don't suppose you have a shovel and a piece of rope we could borrow to get ourselves out?'

The waiter looked surprised, but he was too polite to question Nick's priorities. He went outside, and came back a few minutes later with a garden spade, a torch and a length of blue nylon rope.

'Perfect.'

Nick paid the bill with the last of his euros. He felt bad that he couldn't leave a better tip. He put on his coat and picked up the spade.

The waiter held open the door as they left. Snowflakes blew across the floor on a gust of wind; the glasses on the table rattled. The waiter peered out into the dark street.

'Good luck.'

LXXVIII

Frankfurt, October 1454

When we revisit places from our childhood, most reveal themselves to be small and mean compared with the magnificent locations of memory. Frankfurt was different. It seemed that all the world had arrived that year for the Wetterau fair. In one square, the cloth makers' stalls became a tented city of every colour and weave imaginable: from heavy fustians and gabardines to the lightest Byzantine silks that shimmered like angel wings. From the covered market hall came the warm perfume of unnumbered spices: pepper, sugar, cinnamon, cloves and many more I had never tasted.

I tended our stall in a corner of the market between the paper makers and parchmenters. It was a lonely spot – for all the hundreds of merchants, we were the only booksellers at the fair – and I struggled to make myself heard above the clamour. After so many fearful years of secrecy, I could hardly bring myself to speak.

It should have been Fust. He was our salesman, and he had conceived this plan to show off the first fruits of our labour. But he had cried off the day before, complaining of a fever, so I had come in his place. It was good that I did. I had been too much in the Humbrechthof lately. Fust's deadline was approaching and the Bibles were still behind schedule. The constant awareness of it – calculating and recalculating schedules, supplies, man hours – had become a weight that hung heavy on my back. I dreaded the journey. I could not imagine myself away from the project, or it without me. But Fust insisted. 'Peter will come with you. It will do you good,' he told me.

After an hour on the road to Frankfurt, I knew he was right. The autumn air pinked my cheeks and cleared my head; the ripe smells of fallen apples and leaves unclogged my senses. Even the clamour of the fore-stallers, who risked the wrath of the authorities by offering goods outside the market, seemed more vibrant than irritant. That night I fell into easy conversation with the other merchants at my inn, staying up far later than I was used to, drinking too much and suffering a sore head next day.

On the first morning of the fair, a total of three men came to my stall. I almost counted a fourth, but he only wanted directions to the tanners. I had little to do but slap at the fleas who had warmed my bed the night before. My pleasure at leaving Mainz grew faint; in my mind I composed long cantankerous complaints to Fust of how this was a fool's errand. But that afternoon, the flow of visitors quickened. By next morning, I could barely keep pace with them. Many were priests and friars, but they must have reported what they saw favourably. Soon richer hands were picking up the pages, fat rings brushing the vellum. I saw abbots, archdeacons, knights. And, eventually, an unexpected bishop.

Every half-hour, something like this would happen: I would be standing behind the stall, commending the virtues of my books, when a young man with an ink-stained smock and wild hair would make a commotion, pushing through the crowd until he came to the front. He glanced at the Bible pages, then turned to the crowd and announced loudly, 'He is a fraud.'

He held the quire open so everyone could see.

'This man claims his text is perfect, but clearly he has not even read it. There is not a single correction.'

He fumbled under his smock and unrolled a scrip of parchment. He showed it to the crowd.

'My work, on the other hand, is perfect.'

The audience, realising what was happening, laughed. Compared with the milk-white pages and velvet-smooth text of the Bible, his parchment was a sorry sight. The edges were tattered, the hide yellowed (we had soaked it in beer the night before), and the words almost invisible under a scruff of amendments.

'Not one error remains,' he declared.

'Nor here,' I answered.

He bent almost double, pointing his buttocks to the audience, and put his nose to the Bible pages.

'I cannot find any fault,' he admitted grudgingly.

Murmurs from the audience.

'But any man can get lucky once.'

I picked up two more of the quires and displayed them. 'Thrice? And, indeed, if you come to my workshop in Mainz you will find one hundred more available for purchase, all identical in their perfection.'

Peter Schoeffer (for he was the indignant scribe) puffed out his chest. 'I could do you as many.' He flapped his fingers in wild arithmetic. 'They will be ready in the year 1500.'

'Mine will be ready in June.' I lifted my voice and addressed the whole crowd. 'Any man who wishes to buy one, or to see more of this miraculous new form of writing, can visit me until Tuesday at my lodgings at the sign of the wild deer; or thereafter at the Hof zum Gutenberg in Mainz.'

Many in the crowd pressed towards our stall, clamouring to know more. Schoeffer pulled off his smock, smoothed his hair and joined me behind the table.

'In two years, twenty men have made almost two hundred of these,' I heard him boast to a pair of Dutch merchants. Under the table I kicked him: I did not want him revealing too much of our art, or even getting men thinking how it might be achieved.

But before I could say anything, a new arrival demanded my attention. I saw him coming from a distance – rather, I saw the commotion he made in the crowd as it opened before him. All I could see of him was the crown of his mitre. Even that barely poked above the surrounding throng. I smoothed my surcoat and rearranged the quires on the table.

'The Bishop of Trieste,' a priest announced.

I bowed. 'Your Eminence.'

'Johann?'

The pointed hat tipped back. A clean-shaven, olive-skinned face grinned up at me. Even then I did not recognise him: his title blinded me to the man who stood before me.

'Aeneas?'

'Aeneas has become more pious. You swore you would never take holy orders.'

'Did I?' Aeneas looked genuinely surprised. 'I must have meant that I was not ready for it at the time.'

We walked in the cloisters of the cathedral. Across the square, a gaggle of priests and retainers watched from the door and wondered who I was.

513

'The last time I saw you, in Strassburg, you were working for the council to frustrate the Pope.' I gestured to his rich robes. 'Now you are his ambassador.'

'I deny nothing, but sinned in ignorance. I begged the Pope's forgiveness and he has granted it.'

He said it in earnest, but even Aeneas could not make it sound spontaneous. I had the feeling he had said those words many times.

'You were also trying to seduce a married woman. Did you conquer her?'

He had the grace to blush – though with embarrassment rather than remorse.

'Keep your voice down. You know there is more joy in heaven over one sinner who repents than ninety-nine who never stray.'

We turned a corner in the cloister.

'Truly, I am not the man I was the last time you saw me. The council of Basle . . .' He waved his hand as if wafting away a smell. 'They were so *tedious*, Johann. They could not see it was a lost cause. They denounced the Pope, they denounced each other. Some even denounced *me*. Eventually I was offered a post as secretary to the Emperor Frederick and I took it. I went to Vienna.'

He smiled at me, his anger forgotten.

'If there is a more boring city in Christendom I pray I never see it. The Jews in Babylon suffered less than I did in my exile. But God works in mysterious ways. It was there that I heard my calling. In that fractious, factioned, clique-ridden court I came to see that our friend Nicholas was right. Unity is everything.'

'In Strassburg, you cared more about perfection than unity,' I reminded him.

'But how can there be perfection *without* unity? Unity is the foundation of perfection. And with your books you have achieved both. They are miraculous.'

'If it was a miracle, it was worked by human sweat.' I thought of Andreas Dritzehn, of Kaspar's disfiguring wounds. 'And blood.'

He laid his hand on my arm. 'I take nothing away from you, Johann. You are a most astonishing man. *Multum ille et terris iactatus et alto* indeed. Let me see the pages again.'

I handed him the quire I had brought with me.

'Absolutely free from error,' he marvelled. 'And what you said in your speech – that you have a hundred others exactly the same – was it true?'

'Closer to two hundred.'

'How have you done it?' He saw my expression and retreated hastily. 'I know you have your secrets. But this is – I repeat myself, but there is no other word – miraculous. Can you make anything with this art?'

'Anything that can be written.'

This excited him greatly. Though still leaning on his stick, he seemed to dance down the cloister. When we reached the next corner he exclaimed, 'Imagine it, Johann. The same Bible, the same mass, the same prayers in every church in Christendom. The same words in Rome and Paris, London, Frankfurt, Wittenberg and Basle. Perfect unity. These columns on your page would be the pillars of a Church stronger, purer and more whole than anything ever seen. A delight to God.'

'It is only a book,' I demurred.

'But what are books? Ink and vellum? The accumulation of marks scratched by a reed on a page? You know better. They are the dew of the vapour of pure thought.' He paused for a second, enchanted by his own eloquence. 'Christ and the saints may speak directly to us, but more often they speak through books. If you can create them in such numbers, and with such immaculate text, all Christendom will speak with a voice so loud it stretches to heaven itself.'

His words warmed me all the way back to Mainz. I recounted them to Peter, and we passed a pleasant journey talking of all the books we might make and sell for the profit of the Church. I was glad, for it had never been easy between us. Often I found his enthusiasm for our work too aggressive, and rebuffed it; those times when I did try to encourage him, he took it as meddling. Looking back now, I think he nursed a deep passion for the work of the books and was jealous of it: he distrusted all motives but his own.

I was still dreaming of books to come as I rode over the bridge into Mainz and passed through the city gates. Peter took the sample quires back to the house; I returned our horses to the inn where we had hired them. It was almost dark, but I could not wait to share my success with Fust. I hurried to the Humbrechthof.

The gate was locked. When I tried my key it refused to turn. Irritated, I rang the bell hanging by the gatepost.

The window in the gate snapped open and a hooded eye appeared. It looked like Fust's face, though there was no reason why he should be playing the gatekeeper.

'Will you let me in?'

His face was hard.

'I am sorry, Johann. This is no longer your house.'

LXXIX

Oberwinter

The shadow under the gate was darker than anything Nick had imagined. He shivered as they passed through it. A few paces on, he looked back. The town was already fading behind them, wrapped in mist and the safety of its walls. Inside, soft light glowed behind curtains; a Christmas tree twinkled in a window; a recorded soprano sang a lonely song. Beyond the walls, nothing but darkness.

They walked up the highway. Habit kept them pinned to the verge, though there was no traffic to avoid. Soon enough, they drifted to the middle of the road and walked side by side. Their shoes crunched in the ankle-deep snow; the shovel slithered as Nick dragged it behind him. Once or twice they heard rumblings from the river to their right, and saw lights like distant stars as barges swept past.

Nick had no idea how long they walked. On a map it probably looked no distance at all, but in that cold, monochrome world, with only his footsteps to mark the time, it seemed an eternity. Lost in his thoughts, he might have missed the turning altogether if Emily hadn't tugged his sleeve.

'Is that a path?'

They'd come to a bend where the road swung sharply around one of the mountain's flanks. Just before the turn, a lay-by had been scooped out of the forest that ran up the gorge beyond. Where Emily was pointing, a dark cleft loomed in the ghostly snow-covered trees.

Nick turned on the flashlight. Before he could look for the path, something at the edge of the road caught his eye. It was a sign, barely poking out of the snow bank that the ploughs had heaped up. Nick went over and rubbed the crust of frost off it.

'Wolfschlucht Brucke,' he read. 'Wolf's Gorge Bridge.' He looked around for the bridge, then realised he was standing on it. He peered over the guard rail and saw the yawning mouth of a corrugated-iron pipe disappearing under the road.

'I guess this is the place. That path you saw must be a frozen stream.'

They climbed over the icy guard rail and slithered down the embankment. The frozen stream led away into the forest, a narrow ribbon of white.

Nick reached out for Emily's coat. 'You don't have to come.'

She shook him off without reply and headed up the hill.

Even with the stream to follow, the woods were all but impenetrable. The forest seemed alive. Low branches snagged his shoulders, snapped into his face, poked his legs and dribbled snow down the back of his neck. Underfoot was equally treacherous. The snow smoothed out all traces of the rocks and roots lurking beneath. He didn't dare use the flashlight in case someone was watching from the castle. Even where it was flat it wasn't safe, for that usually meant they were walking on a frozen pool. Once Nick's foot went through to the ice: he skidded, flailed, and was thrown onto his back. The shovel banged on a stone. He lay there and listened to the echo clatter through the forest.

Blinded by snow and branches, they almost missed the castle. The only hint was a glimmer of light in the otherwise unbroken darkness to his right. That was enough. Nick struck off towards it, blundering through the undergrowth like a wild boar. A blizzard whirled around him; tree limbs creaked and cracked. If he didn't find it soon, he thought he might be lost for ever.

The trees ended in a rock face. Nick leaned against it, breathing hard and shivering. Meltwater trickled down his back. The light had vanished, but if he craned back his head until his neck ached he could see stone walls at the top of the cliff, dark against the grey clouds. It looked a long way up.

There was a snap behind him as Emily emerged from the forest. She'd lost her hat; snow sprinkled her hair like diamonds.

'How do we get up there?'

Nick tried not to think about how high it was. 'Are you any good at climbing?'

'Not since I was ten.'

Gillian had been a climber, for a while at least. One of their less successful dates had been when she'd taken him to the climbing wall where she went every Wednesday. She crawled up to the ceiling like a spider, laughing, while Nick still hadn't figured out how to put on the safety harness. When he did finally make it onto the wall – about eight feet up – his wrists ached for a week.

'I guess I'd better try.'

He stared at the cliff, trying to figure out how Gillian could have got up. The black rock face offered no clues. He ran his fingers over the surface to feel for a crack or a ledge, anything to get him started. A small bulge, about knee high – that might do.

'Here goes nothing.'

He put his foot on the outcrop, pushed off and lunged up for a handhold. All he felt was glassy ice. He scrabbled for purchase and got none; lost his balance and fell to the ground. The snow probably broke his fall, though it didn't feel like it.

Emily leaned over him. 'Are you OK?'

He brushed himself off and got up. 'Gillian wasn't a mountaineer. Even she couldn't have climbed a sheer ice face.'

He went back to the cliff and examined it again, brushing his hands over it in broad sweeps. Emily hung back. She fumbled in her pocket and examined the sheet of paper Gillian had left, now creased and damp from the snow.

'Maybe she didn't go up.' She tapped Nick on the shoulder and pointed to the paper. '*Mariannenbad* means Mary's Pool. And the book in the restaurant said there was a shrine to her near the medieval monastery.'

'You think Gillian prayed her way in?'

'Marian shrines were often built over springs. They thought the water had healing powers.' Emily's words sounded quiet under the snow, as if the trees themselves were listening. 'We came up a stream bed. It must come from somewhere.'

They scrambled around the base of the cliff, wading through the deep snow. It looked so permanent. Any holes or caves must surely have been filled in weeks ago.

'What's this?'

There was hope in Emily's voice. Nick hurried over to where she was standing. Shading the beam with his hand, he shone the flashlight on the rock.

'Looks like some sort of landslide.'

At the foot of the cliff, a small heap of rocks spilled out across the ground. The snow that covered them was thin and broken, sinking into a shallow depression that snaked away from the cliff. When Nick put his foot on it, he felt ice.

'Here's our stream.'

Emily was already clambering up the rock fall. Lying flat, pressing her belly against the stones, she scrabbled the snow away.

'I think—'

There was a clatter, and a stifled gasp as the stones shifted under Emily's weight. She rolled back. Nick lunged forward to catch her.

'Are you OK?'

She brushed herself off. 'I think there's a hole up there. It's covered over, but the snow's not deep.'

Moving cautiously, Nick scrambled up the rocky slope. A couple of times the stones almost gave way under him and he stopped, his heart in his mouth. But Emily had been right. Between the top of the debris and the cliff face, there seemed to be a gap. Nick burrowed into the snow, scooping it away with the shovel. There was nothing behind it. When he stuck his arm in up to the elbow he felt only air.

Emily gazed up from the bottom of the slope. 'Can you get through?'

Nick felt around. 'Only one way to find out.'

Even with all the snow cleared out it was barely high enough for him to squeeze through. Rocks scraped his cheeks; snow dribbled down the back of his neck. He wriggled through on his belly. It was deeper than he'd expected; there was a moment when his whole body was under the cliff, and he had a sudden, paralysing vision of the stones giving way and crushing him.

And then suddenly the ground was dropping away. Nick pushed out an arm to steady himself but found nothing to hold. He tumbled down the slope in an avalanche of stones and bruises, until he landed with a splash and a thump on a hard floor.

He turned on the flashlight.

He was sitting in a stream that flowed through the bottom of a narrow cave, just wide enough for him to stretch his arms between the walls. Stalactites dripped from the ceiling like candle wax, leaving milky deposits in the water, which disappeared into a cracked pipe beneath the rubble.

'Nick?'

Emily's voice cut through the darkness, above and behind him. He swung the beam around to see her disembodied face peering out from the hole.

'Be careful coming down,' he warned.

She slithered down the slope head first. Nick caught her and helped her to her feet. If they stooped, the cave was just high enough for them to stand. On the back wall of the chamber he could see a carved image of the Virgin Mary cradling her infant son. The work was coarse, except for a smooth spot above the baby's head. It reflected the flashlight like a halo.

'That would have been from the pilgrims,' said Emily. 'There must have been some tradition in the Middle Ages that if you touched it you'd be healed, or have your prayers answered, or be lucky.'

Below the statue was a stone basin, a shallow pool. The stream spilled out over its edge, but something gleaming in the bottom caught Nick's eye. He knelt beside it and reached into the icy water. His hand came out clutching a flat silver quarter.

'It was one of Gillian's things – she always threw quarters in wishing wells.'

'Then where did she go?'

'Well, we know where the castle is.'

Nick shone the flashlight at the ceiling. Even though he knew what he was looking for, it took him a while to see among the forest of stalactites and the shadows they cast. But at the edge of the cave he found a dark spot that wasn't a shadow. A hole in the ceiling, a shaft rising towards the castle. On the wall he saw shallow ridges carved into the rock like a ladder.

Emily touched his arm. 'Are you sure?'

'Whatever they did to Gillian, they did it in the hotel. I saw it on the webcam, remember? If she got into the castle, she must have got out again.'

'What if they found out how she did it?'

'Then they'd have blocked up the hole.' *Don't let yourself think or you'll give up.* 'The snow must have covered it over before they could find it.'

He slung his backpack over his shoulder and started to climb.

The walls were slippery, coated in a powdery slime that rubbed off on his fingers, but the shaft was so narrow that he could brace himself against it. With the stone rungs to cling on to, he climbed quickly, flitting in and out of the beam of light Emily shone up. He tried not to look down.

By the time he reached the top the flashlight beam was a faint presence far below. He didn't even know he'd arrived until he reached up for the next rung and felt smooth stone blocking the way. He paused, resting his weight against the wall. *Yet another dead end.* But the adrenalin was flowing: he *knew* Gillian had come this way. He put his shoulder against the stone and heaved.

It lifted free with less effort than he'd expected. Braced

against the wall of the shaft, he almost lost his grip. He stiffened and steadied himself. Then he slid the stone aside, opening a narrow gap just wide enough to squeeze into. He hauled himself through and looked around.

He was in the castle. He'd come out into a small round chamber that must be the base of one of the turrets. A staircase spiralled up into the darkness. He craned his head back, looking for the telltale winking light of a security camera or an alarm. Nothing.

Emily clambered through the hole. She clutched his arm as she surveyed the high room, covering the flashlight with her fingers.

'Do you think anyone heard us?'

'Let's hope not.'

They tiptoed up the stairs. On the first landing, a door led through into a long low-vaulted corridor. Recessed lights, hidden behind the arches, cast yellow pools of light on the flagstones.

Emily shivered. 'It looks like some sort of dungeon.'

A row of oak doors pierced the wall, studded with wicked-looking lumps of iron and hung with heavy bolts. All the doors had grilles in them, presumably so that in ages past jailers could check on the miserable wretches in their charge. Nick went to the nearest one and peered in.

A body lay sprawled on the floor, arms outstretched in a pool of blood.

In that instant, all Nick's nightmares, all the fears he'd stifled, struck him in a single, shattering blow. He sank to his knees and puked. Everything was wasted.

But even in his despair, he knew something wasn't right. He pulled himself up and forced himself to take another look, peering through the bars into the murky cell.

Fear had played him false. It wasn't Gillian.

The body was wearing a long white gown, which explained part of his mistake – he'd thought it was a dress. Blood covered half the face, which had also misled him. But there was no way it was Gillian. It was a man, a monk in a cassock belted at the waist with a twist of rope. Nick could see the brow of a tonsure just above the single bullet hole that pierced his forehead.

Relief flooded through him so fast he almost puked again. He forced himself to think. The blood looked wet – the puddle was still spreading at the edges. Whoever had done it couldn't have gone far.

In the corner of his eye, he saw Emily coming up behind to take a look. He pushed her back.

'Don't.'

Emily shot him a searching glance, but stayed back.

He moved on to the other doors, steeling himself for more horrors. Thankfully, there were no more corpses. One room was stacked with oil drums, which struck Nick as dangerous in a castle housing a medieval library. He could smell the vapour leaking out through the grille. A second room was lined with steel bookshelves. The next room was empty, though dark stains splashed the wall. *How old were they?*

Nick approached the last door. His wet trousers clung to his legs, trying to hold him back; the adrenalin was draining out of him. A voice in his head screamed at him to retreat. He looked through the grille.

A young woman sat on the floor, her head pressed against her knees. Her hair hung over her face, and her bare arms were mottled black with bruises. She must have sensed the motion by the door. She looked up.

'Nick?'

LXXX

Mainz, 1455

'You cannot come in.'

Fust's eye stared at me through the window in the door, pressed so close that his knotted skin seemed cut from the same timber.

I didn't understand. 'Is this a joke?'

'You have broken the terms of our contract. I am calling in my loan.'

I still could not comprehend it. Like a chicken strutting around the farmyard spouting blood from its gizzard, I carried on as if it were a reasonable discussion.

'How much do you say I owe you?'

'Two thousand gulden.'

I laughed wildly; I did not know what else to do. 'You know I cannot pay. Every penny I have is tied up in the Bibles. Every scrap I own is mortgaged against them.'

The eye surveyed me dispassionately. 'If you cannot pay, then you forfeit everything. I will take over the works and finish the Bibles myself.'

'How can you?' A thousand questions distilled into one. Fust chose to answer its narrowest, pragmatic meaning.

'The men know who pays their wages. They will see the work through. I will meet you tomorrow to discuss it.'

He snapped the window shut.

Ten years of hope died in an instant. I slammed my fist against the gate so long I almost unhinged it. I denounced Fust to all the powers of sin and the devil, while passers-by gathered in knots and stared. No one took mercy; no one came out of the Humbrechthof, though every man inside must have heard me.

When I had spent every drop of my rage, I crept home.

We met in the vineyard on the hill near St Stephan's church. The last time I had been there it was a muddy building site. Now a stone wall enclosed it, and neat formations of vines grew waist high. Next spring, they would fruit for the first time; a year from now they would pour forth wine. I wanted to rip them out and burn them.

At Fust's suggestion, we each brought a witness. I almost chose Kaspar, but at the last moment thought better of it and invited Keffer the press master instead. Fust brought Peter Schoeffer. He and Keffer stood by the wall and watched, while Fust and I walked among the leafless vines.

'I am sorry it has come to this,' he said.

His gaze was unyielding: the carelessness of a man sure in his victory, already thinking of the next battle. On that hilltop there was nothing behind him except empty grey sky.

'Was this your plan all along? To lure me down this road and then set about me like a brigand when we finally sight our destination?'

He looked disappointed. 'I thought better of you,

527

Gutenberg. I thought we could have done something extraordinary together. I did not expect you to be stealing from me every night while I slept.'

I stared at him.

'While you were away in Frankfurt, I made an audit of the Humbrechthof. Everything relating to our common project. Do you know how much you stole? Two hundred sheets of vellum. A dozen jars of ink. Fifty gulden unaccounted for. Did you think no one would notice?'

'I never stole a thing.'

'Borrowed, then. No doubt you will say you intended to replace everything in due time.'

'I took nothing. Everything we used at the Gutenberghof was separate from what we used on the Bibles.'

'What about those indulgences?'

'That was a mistake I made two years ago. I never repeated it.'

' "Can the Ethiopian change his skin, or the leopard his spots?" ' He waved his stick at me. 'I have made enquiries about you. For such a long and unusual life you have left few marks on the world – but not all your footprints have vanished. The burgomaster of Strassburg had a few tales he was eager to tell.'

Now I was bewildered. 'The burgomaster of Strassburg? Who is he?'

'A man named Jörg Dritzehn. He told me how you snared his brother in a venture he did not understand, bled him dry and then stole his portion for yourself when he died.'

'Everything I did with his brother was faithful to our contract.'

'And everything I have done is faithful to ours. You swore that the money I loaned you would be put towards our

528

common profit. Not skimmed off to line your pocket while I carried all the risk of the Bibles.'

'I swear I did not.' A vision came into my head: my beautiful Bibles, my life's perfection, locked away from me inside the Humbrechthof. 'Even if I did, why insist on it now? In a few months there will be profit enough for both of us. Whatever you think I owe you, whatever will make it right between us, I will pay with interest when the Bibles are sold.'

A grim smirk was my reply. I saw he had taken it as a confession; more, that this was what he always intended. By bringing the suit now he had caught me without a chance to pay. The incomplete Bibles would be valued not for what they would be worth when finished, but what they had cost in materials. If the court awarded even half his claim, Fust could take them – together with the presses, the types and paper stocks – for a pittance. When he sold them, all the profits would be his.

I looked to the boundary wall where Peter Schoeffer waited.

'I suppose he will oversee the completion of the Bibles.'

Fust nodded. 'You have taught him well.'

Another coil of anger tightened around me. 'You will have to find new premises. I am the leaseholder of the Humbrechthof.'

'No longer.' Fust handed me a sealed sheet of paper. 'From your cousin Salman. He has cancelled your arrangement and transferred the property to me.'

'Why should he do that?'

'I promised to use my influence with the guild council to see that no harm came to his property. And I offered to pay double the rent.'

I wanted the earth to swallow me up, to knot me in vine roots until they crushed me. I leaned on a fence post.

'Please,' I begged him. 'There is no need—'

'The trial date has been set.' He cut me off and turned away. 'The sixth day of November, an hour before noon, in the convent of the barefoot friars. Whatever defence you have to offer, you can say it there.'

LXXXI

Oberwinter

Nick slid back the bolts. They might be old, but they were well oiled. The hinges squeaked, but only for a moment. Then the door was open.

'You came.'

Gillian flew across the room and flung herself against him. She kissed him on the lips and he let her. He'd wanted this moment for so long – way before he had ever heard of the eight of beasts, the Master of the Playing Cards or any of it. So many nights he'd lain awake, wishing for her, until dawn came up over New York. It had been worth it – as sweet as he'd ever imagined.

But he couldn't capture it. All too quickly, it began to fade, even as he held her. He found himself thinking about the danger, about how they would get out, about all the things he wished Gillian hadn't done, about Emily. Still hugging Gillian, he opened his eyes. He saw Emily watching, coolly sympathetic, and gave her an embarrassed smile.

He held on until he felt Gillian's grip loosen, then eased

away. There were a thousand questions to ask, a lot of answers he probably didn't want to hear. But that was for later.

'We need to get out.'

Gillian stepped back. Her face was drawn and haggard, her cheeks raw from the cold. The overhead light bulb made the shadows around her eyes even darker. She seemed to be wearing pyjamas.

'Are you OK?' Nick said.

'I've been better.' She straightened. 'No, I *am* better. Thank God you came.' For the first time, she noticed Emily. 'And you – I don't even know you.'

Emily gave a polite smile, as if they were meeting at a cocktail party. 'I work at the Cloisters. If I still have a job to go back to.'

'I don't remember you.'

'I started after you left.'

'Leaving would be good.' Nick looked at Gillian's bare feet. 'There's about two feet of snow outside and it's a long walk back to town. Do you have any shoes?'

'We can't go yet.' Gillian slipped a rubber band off her wrist and pulled her hair into a ponytail. Nick and Emily stared at her. 'The castle's empty. I haven't heard anyone since yesterday morning.'

'Bullshit,' said Nick. 'There's a dead man at the end of this corridor and he's still bleeding. The guy who shot him can't be far.'

'Come on, Nick. Don't you want to see what this was all about?'

'It was about you.'

Gillian flashed him her pixie grin. Once it would have made him glow with happiness; now it seemed contrived.

'I've spent almost two weeks in this cell – and a month

before that tracking these bastards down. They've done things . . .' She let her gaze slide towards Emily. 'If you two want to go ahead, go ahead. I'm not leaving without what I came for.'

'Of course not.' He was shocked to find he was actually tempted. He'd assumed it would be different, that gratitude would overwhelm everything. Instead, he found himself as confused as he'd ever been, the familiar feeling of always being two steps behind and looking the wrong way.

She's been kidnapped, locked up and God knows what else. Did you think she'd melt in your arms?

He glanced at Emily, who gave the slightest shrug in reply.

'It'll only take five minutes.'

Gillian seemed to know the way. She led them through a door at the end of the corridor, up a spiral stair and out onto a broad rampart. Nick flinched as the cold night hit him. To his right, he could see a small courtyard covered in snow, two pointed towers flanking a gatehouse and a square keep rising into the darkness. On the other side, far below, the snow-bound forest stretched down to the river. A foghorn sounded in the distance.

'Keep low,' Gillian whispered.

'I thought you said this place was empty.'

'No point taking risks.'

They crawled along the wall, keeping below the rim of battlements, until another flight of stairs brought them down to the courtyard. They skirted its edge, keeping in the shadows around the storehouses and sheds, under a trellis of withered vines and past a stone well. Tyre treads and footprints gouged the snow; Nick wondered how fresh the marks were.

He was so busy looking ahead for danger that he didn't

watch his footing. He kicked against something, tripped and fell forward. He pushed himself up on his hands.

A three-eyed monster, like some horror from the bestiary, stared at him out of the snow. Its skin was stippled blue and black, its lips locked in a silent scream. Nick opened his mouth, but no sound came out of his frozen lungs. He scrambled back, caught his knee on something else and rolled over. Face to face with another monster.

They were monks. Two more of them, each with a single bullet hole drilled in his forehead. There was less blood this time: the cold and snow must have frozen it almost instantly.

Nick got up. 'We really need to get out of here.'

Even Gillian looked frightened now. But she'd always thrived on proving she could do what others were afraid of. Before Nick could stop her she'd run along the foot of the wall to a doorway into the keep, turned an iron ring and opened the door. Nick cursed and followed.

'Don't they lock anything around here?'

'The only way into the castle – the only way they know about – is across a drawbridge over a hundred-foot gorge. It's worked for five hundred years.'

As she said it, she led them across a corridor and flung open a pair of double doors. Nick and Emily stared.

It was like a cathedral built of books. Gothic pillars eight feet thick rose to a dimly raftered ceiling high above. All the space between was filled with shelves, and every shelf was jammed tight with books. Every storey or so wooden galleries emerged, snaking around the pillars and in front of the shelves like the canopy of a forest. The floor mirrored the image back: interlocking swirls of many woods, inlay on a giant scale, twisted in scrolls like foliage.

'The *Bibliotheca Diabolorum*. The Devils' Library.'

As they advanced into the room, Nick saw that the books weren't free on their shelves, but locked behind a lattice of thin wire bars. Some looked impossibly ancient, with varicose cords running through their spines; others had the split cloth and frayed edges of old school books. The whole room was suffused with the musty smell of old paper – and something more acrid. Gasoline?

Emily peered through the bars and examined the names on the spines. She shuddered. 'No wonder they call this the Devils' Library. Pretty much every book ever written about the black arts is here. And some I've never heard of.'

'There's a reason for that,' said Gillian over her shoulder.

She walked quickly to the back of the room. The smell of gasoline was stronger here and some of the books looked damp. Before Nick could wonder why, Gillian was reaching for a small leather book, almost invisible between the massive volumes around it. To Nick's inexpert eye the books here looked older than in the rest of the room: he was surprised there was no grille protecting them. A second later he saw why. The book rattled as Gillian withdrew it. When it came free, Nick saw a heavy chain anchoring it to the wall. Most of the links were black with age, though one gleamed steely fresh.

'Bolt cutters,' said Nick, remembering her list.

'I don't suppose you brought any. They took mine away.'

Nick's brain ached from trying to keep up. He didn't know who he'd thought he'd come to rescue, but it wasn't this incarnation of Gillian, who strode around forbidden castles as if she owned them. He'd have taken more care in a video game.

'Who are *they* anyway?'

'The Church? The mob?' Gillian shrugged. 'The Italians have only managed to organise two things since the Roman empire: the Catholic Church and the Mafia. I guess it's not surprising they work together.'

'But why—'

Gillian rested the book on the shelf and slid it across.

'Take a look.'

LXXXII

Mainz, 6 November 1455

Fog came down in the night. When day dawned, the city had disappeared. From my bedroom window I could not even see the house opposite, except for the tip of its roof looming from the mist like a ship's prow. I pulled on my fur-trimmed coat and remembered the youth who had dressed in this same room thirty-five years earlier, waiting for a court to tell him he was insufficiently well born to inherit his father's estate.

The house was empty. I had told the others, those who stayed with me, not to come to work today. Even the servants were gone. I had not asked Kaspar to leave, but when I looked in his room he was not there. Part of me was disappointed, another part relieved. I drifted around the lonely house, too dispirited even to rouse a fire. I should have been working on some sort of defence for my trial, but each time I thought of it a great dread crushed my soul.

I went into the workshop and looked at the press. It stood in the middle of the room like a gallows, the platen raised, the ink tables dry, blank piles of paper stacked beside it. I ran my hand over the rugged frame. I pressed my fingers against the type in its bed and looked at the red indentations it left in my skin. I felt as I had that morning in Paris – void. I had stared into the flames and conjured the rainbow. Now all that remained was ash.

But I also remembered that day in Paris was when I first encountered Kaspar's art. I went to my bedroom and took down his bestiary from its shelf. I leafed through the well-thumbed pages, marvelling again at his skill. Many of the beasts looked almost human: the shy deer with its chin tucked against its breast; the lovelorn unicorn who stared at the virgin maid and did not see the hunter's net behind him; the bonasus who roasted his pursuers with fiery dung and mischievous glee.

I turned to the last page to look at the card, the four bears and four lions who had led me so far.

Written by the hand of Libellus, and illuminated by Master Francis.
He also made another book of beasts using a new art of writing.

I blinked. A second sentence had been added to the colophon, written in a hurried hand in watery brown ink. It was Kaspar's writing. He must have come straight from the press when he wrote it, for he had dripped press ink on the card below.

'I wondered when you would find my note.'

A tremor ran through me. Kaspar had appeared, silent as a devil, standing in the doorway and watching me with a crooked smile. I held up the book.

'What does this mean?'

'What it says.'

He stepped out of the shadows, revealing a slim leather-bound book in his hand. He gave it to me.

'A gift.'

My hands trembled as I opened it.

Nick's hand trembled as he opened the book. A second later, he felt unexpectedly deflated, an echo of how he'd felt in the hotel room in Paris, opening Gillian's envelope and laying eyes on the card at last. The first page was utterly familiar – a cleaner, clearer version of the page the computer had stitched together for them in Karlsruhe. The bonasus with the wicked grin, spraying its fiery excrement over the men behind it: a monk, a knight and a merchant.

'The lion is the strongest of all beasts and fears nothing.' Gillian reached across him to turn the page, brushing against him as she did. Nick flinched away. 'But how much braver is the worm, weakest of creatures, in constant fear he may be crushed yet humbly scavenging among the footfalls of giants and monsters. In time, he brings low even the noblest beast.'

'That's not how the text is supposed to go,' said Emily.

Nick looked at the next picture. It was a lion, but not like the regal animals on the cards. It lay on its side with its crown askew. Its mangy fur had been pulled apart and a colony of maggots ate out its entrails. Its dull eyes lolled in its skull, almost as if it was still alive. A cloaked figure lurked behind it, watching, its face hidden in the shadows of its hood except for a row of giant serrated teeth.

Nick never forgot what he saw that night. It read like a monument to grotesque obsessions: bestial sex, deformed bodies, malice, torment and decay. Thanks to Bret, Nick had seen some of the most graphic images the Internet had to offer. Compared to that lurid realism, the black-and-white engravings in the book were plain, almost naïve. But even after five hundred years they maintained a savage power, a heightened truth in the anguished faces and debased bodies that shocked more viscerally than any photograph.

Each page brought new invented beasts: the *monasticus*, a double-jointed eunuch who spent all his time feverishly licking the scars where his genitals should have been; the *equevore*, a man with a horse's head and a penis so large it required its own chain mail and helmet. A string of broken women lay behind him where he had raped them until they snapped in two. And in every picture, the cloaked figure, his savage teeth grinning in approval from under his hood.

On the penultimate page, a creature with a pig's body and a man's head, naked except for a hat, knelt on all fours. A dog in a crown squatted behind him and sodomised him, while another held him by his ears and thrust himself into the pig's mouth. From the look of wild ecstasy contorting his puffed face, the pig was enjoying it. It was hard to tell if he was man or woman: he had a man's genitals, but a woman's breasts dangling from his distended belly to suckle the pack of wild men who bayed at his feet. Behind them all rose the cloaked figure, now swollen to three times his height, leering over them like a plume of smoke.

'Who is that?' said Nick.

'The pig in the hat is the Pope,' Emily said. 'The dogs are the King of France and the Holy Roman Emperor of Germany. Knowing the date and the place, I'd guess it was intended as some sort of metaphor for the *Armagnacken* attacks of the 1440s and '50s.'

'What about the guy behind them?'

Gillian turned, her eyes shining with excitement. 'Can't you guess?'

The last animal in the bestiary was the rat. It seemed to have been added as an afterthought – the cloaked figure who haunted the book was absent from this page.

'The rat follows the goose to its nest and murders its young.'

Beside the text was a scene of domestic devastation. The rat, wearing a square cloth cap like Fust's, sat up on its haunches and tore the head off a downy gosling, still nestled in its egg. Its young eyes were wide with terror, staring at the mother goose, unable to understand why she did not come to help. The mother watched, helpless. Her wings had been ripped from her body and lay useless on the ground; blood poured from her breast where her heart had been gouged out. In her anguish she had not yet noticed. A rat pup with a face like Peter Schoeffer clung to her leg and gnawed it.

I confess, my first reaction was not outrage or a scandal; it was jealousy. While the quires of my Bible languished in the storeroom at the Humbrechthof, slowly mounting up, Kaspar had taken the first fruits of my creation. He had beaten me.

He watched me eagerly. 'What do you think?'

'It is . . .' I slumped on the bed as the full enormity of what he had done struck home. 'Obscene.'

'But beautiful. Everything we dreamed of, before Fust tore it down.' He knelt beside me and caressed the page. 'My pictures and your words.'

'Those are *not* my words.'

'Our two arts fused as one. This is our master-piece.' He pointed to the chapter heading. 'I even managed to press the rubrics in red.'

I turned through the book. In one sense he was right: the book was immaculate. The proportions were pleasing, the pages precisely aligned: every drop of ink seemed to shine from the page. The illuminated images shimmered in gold, but it was the gloss of pure poison.

'How many of these have you made?'

'Thirty.'

'Are they here?'

'Not far away.'

'Bring them to me,' I commanded. 'You must bring them back so they can be destroyed.'

The grin persisted, though strained. 'Why should I destroy them? They are perfect?'

'They are abominations,' I cried. 'You have taken everything about my art that was good or noble, that might have benefited the world's salvation, and debased it. You are the tempter, the serpent in the garden.'

'And you are a blind fool.' In an instant a terrifying rage transformed his face. 'A feeble-minded idiot who has stumbled on a power he does not understand. I have harnessed it to the one force in the world that deserves it.'

I sat on the bed, dumbfounded. In the silence between us, I heard the creak of footfalls on the stairs. We stared at the door, frozen in our battle like the beasts and hunters in the book.

Father Günther appeared on the landing. 'Johann? It is almost eleven o'clock. They are waiting for you at the court.'

All my bones had turned to wax. 'I cannot go.'

Günther stared between me and Kaspar, a witless spectator to our unfolding cataclysm.

'You must go. Otherwise, they will make a summary judgment against you and you will lose everything.'

I fell back on the bed. The court, the judgment, Fust – they were nothing. Kaspar had unscrewed the form of my being and scattered the pieces. Everything in me, all that had meaning, was lost.

'You and Keffer go. Report back what Fust says against me.'

He hesitated. 'If you cannot answer him—'

'*Go.*'

'Are you ill? Perhaps I can persuade the court to delay.' He glanced at Kaspar, imploring him for help. Kaspar played with the cover of his book and said nothing.

'Leave me alone,' I hissed. 'It is done.'

With a last, bewildered glance at Kaspar, Günther hurried from the room. I heard his footsteps recede down the stairs, the bang of the door as he left the house.

Through tear-stained eyes, I looked up at Kaspar. I felt the vellum of his hateful book, smooth as a lamb.

'All the things that Fust accuses me of: the missing parchment and ink, the types that reappeared in the wrong place. That was you.'

'Some – not all. The priest Günther has had a profitable sideline of supplying the scriveners of Mainz with paper for the last year. And often at night when I crept down to use the press, I found Peter Schoeffer practising his craft. Perhaps he knew this day would come.' He laughed at me. 'You were always a poor judge of character, Johann.'

I gazed at him, trying to hold together the shattered pieces of my heart. 'Why did you do this to me?'

'I did it *for* you. To show you the potential of what you have created. In the same way as it took the serpent to free Adam from the garden of perfection where God held him captive, I wanted to make you see what could be done.'

He pointed to the bestiary he had given me in Strassburg. 'Do you know how much that cost the man who commissioned it? Fifty gulden. And what is it but a mirror to flatter his vanities? I gave him what he paid for. But with your press, Johann, we can change the order of things.'

He touched the scars on his face. 'You know how I got these. Because a king, an emperor and a pope – Christians all – raped their lands in the name of God. But in my torments, the *Armagnaken* taught me there are other powers that hold sway over this earth. I learned things from them – secrets that even the Church fears.'

'Secrets?' I echoed.

'This book is just the beginning. With your press, we can write things and make so many copies that the rich and the Church can not stop it. We will sweep them away in a torrent of fire and paper. Do you know why churchmen are slavering over your Bible. Because they think that if they control the art they will control the world.'

I almost wept with frustration. 'That is what I wanted. Perfect unity.'

'How could a man like you, of all people, want such a thing?' He clenched his fist in fury. 'Obedience to a Church which bleeds the poor while its bishops wear gold and fur? A Church which would rather collect fees than baptise souls? Which will sell you a receipt to expunge the same sins its priests commit tenfold? They do not deserve this invention, Johann. With the powers we can summon up, we will use it to destroy them.'

He took the book away from me. 'I did not invent the beasts in this book. I drew them from life. I thought you of all men would see that.'

I buried my face in my hands. I heard a soft thud as he dropped the book on the bed beside me, then the creak of a floorboard. Perhaps I felt the soft touch of a kiss or a caress on my forehead; perhaps it was only a spasm. When I looked up, Kaspar was gone.

*

'I can see why the Church wanted to keep this secret.'

Nick closed the book. His skin itched, as if the maggots had crawled out of the book and started to devour him. It had been a long time since he had felt so dirty.

Emily looked bruised by the encounter. Her face had gone so pale it was almost translucent. 'It's brutal. So much hatred in it. It's hard to imagine it coming from the same man who printed the Gutenberg Bible.'

'The typeface proves it.'

'Do you think that's why they hid it?' said Nick. 'To protect Gutenberg's reputation?'

Gillian gave him a scornful look. 'Did you even look at the book? It isn't just satire. Look in the margins.'

Reluctantly, Nick opened the book again and peered at the decorated borders. The moment he saw the pictures, he knew he would never forget them. If anything, they were worse than the illustrations they framed, images he could barely describe.

'It's sick.'

'Sicker than you think. It's not just ornamentation. It's an instruction manual.'

'What do you mean?'

'The figure in the cloak? Why do you think he gets bigger in every picture? He's getting closer. There's a secret hidden in the pictures in this book, just like in the old alchemical texts. It's a book of power.'

Nick stared at her. As always with Gillian, he couldn't tell what she was really thinking.

'You don't really believe it works?' But he could see in her face that she wanted to.

'Somebody does,' was all she said.

Nick didn't know what to say. He looked at the picture and thought of the playful, witty beasts in the book they'd rescued from Brussels. 'It's so different from the other bestiary.'

Gillian stiffened. 'The bestiary from Rambouillet? You found it? Can I see?'

Nick pulled it out of his bag and laid it beside its partner. They looked almost identical. He opened the back cover and looked at the inscription over the card.

Written by the hand of Libellus, and illuminated by Master Francis.

He also made another book of beasts using a new art of writing.

'Which is hidden in the *Sayings of the Kings of Israel*.' Emily supplied the invisible words.

Gillian frowned. 'You know, I never figured out exactly what that meant. I suppose it must be something to do with this place – all the lost books.'

Nick looked up at the shelves towering over him. How many more secrets lurked among the old leather and rotting parchment? How many other terrible visions and diabolical rituals from men who had sought out the darkest powers of the earth?

A draught caught the back of his neck. The chill reminded him they couldn't afford to linger.

'How do we get it out of here?'

'You don't.'

Nick spun around. The double doors were open. For a moment, he almost believed that the incantations in the book had worked. A man with snow-white hair and eyes like coals stood watching them. His long coat flapped around his ankles in the breeze.

546

'I think you have something for me.'

I lay on my bed and wept. I was betrayed. Fust and Kaspar between them had taken everything.

I fell into a sort of sleep, a dazed nightmare of ravenous beasts, crazed men and debauched women who came alive from the pages of Drach's book. A diabolical mill swallowed men in its mouth and ground them to dust. A pope with cloven hooves sat on a throne and passed terrible judgement on me.

A vigorous pounding on the front door woke me. Was it over so soon? Had the court decided? I did not know how long I had been unconscious, and when I looked to the window all I saw was fog.

The front door crashed open. Footsteps pounded on the stairs, heavier than Günther's. Too late, like a remorseful suicide in mid-air, the scales fell from my eyes and I felt the full, breathtaking scope of what I had lost. I wished I had not been so careless of it.

Two men burst through the door. They were not bailiffs, but armed soldiers in the archbishop's livery. They shouted at me but I was too dazed to understand. They hauled me off my bed; one held me up while the other punched me in the face. I wondered if this was another nightmare, until I tasted blood in my mouth and decided it must be real.

They bound my hands and picked up my bestiary without looking at it. The other book, Drach's abomination, had slipped behind the mattress where they could not see it. Then they tied a sack over my head and took me away.

LXXXIII

The old man was alone. Nick made to charge him, but Gillian grabbed his arms and held him back.

'Don't.'

As she spoke, another man came through the door, the Italian with the broken nose, the man Nick had fought in Strasbourg. He aimed his gun at Nick and grimaced.

The old man advanced into the room. The closer he came, the more Nick noticed his eyes. Pitted deep in his waxy face, they glinted as hard and pure as diamonds.

'Father Nevado?' he guessed.

'*Cardinal*,' the old man corrected him. 'I have moved up in the world.

'I wasn't expecting the Spanish Inquisition.'

A chilling smile. 'We call it by another name now. But, broadly speaking, yes. You are very well informed.'

'I spend a lot of time in libraries.'

It must be nerves, Nick thought, adrenalin stringing out his battered mind before he collapsed. How else to explain how he could stand there trading wisecracks with the man who would kill him.

At least I found Gillian. It was a comforting thought.

'If this is the Devils' Library, who does that make you?'

'The angel who guards the pit where lost works are cast out.'

Emily looked around. 'Are all these books lost? I'm sure I've seen some of them before.'

Nick looked at her in surprise. Did she care? Even at the end, was the scholar in her curious? Or was it just a basic human instinct to keep talking, to delay the inevitable as long as possible?

Nevado seemed happy to humour her. 'Some of the books here do not exist outside this room, but many more are in the world. Some have even had influence. Contrary to ignorant supposition, this library is not merely a prison for condemned books. It was established by Pope Pius II as a school against error, where those who fought in the vanguard against sin and the devil could study their foes more closely.'

'That's funny,' said Nick. 'I looked in one of those books and all I saw was the Pope.'

'The first book in this library was the *Liber Bonasi* in front of you. Not the oldest, but the first. It had personal significance to Pope Pius. He knew Johann Gutenberg; he championed him because he believed that the printing press would beget a more perfect faith. The Church had many wounds at that time. He thought the press would cleanse them. Instead, it proved more suited to spreading lies and error.'

'Malware,' said Nick. 'The book's a virus. The press spreads it quickly – much faster than before. People read it and get infected. Eventually you end up with a whole network of infected people who you can use to launch attacks.'

'The Reformation,' said Emily.

549

'I doubt that Pope Pius would have thought of it so – but yes. Truly, there is nothing in the world the Church has not seen before. Pius knew that if Gutenberg's monstrosity became known, the printing press would have been condemned as an agency of the devil. He suppressed all trace of the *Liber Bonasi* and left a decree that every copy should be wiped from the earth. Thirty copies were made. One remains here as an exemplar. Twenty-eight more have been hunted down over the centuries, dug out of the libraries and collections where they lay buried, and destroyed. Only one remains outstanding. And now you have brought it to me.'

Nick was feeling faint. He looked up to try to clear his head, but the towers of books looming into the darkness only made it worse.

'Why do you even bother?' said Emily. 'Gutenberg, the Master of the Playing Cards, whoever made that book: they won. Any worthwhile technology can be used the wrong way. However many copies of the bestiary came off that press, you've still printed more Bibles. Isn't that a better trade-off?'

For the first time, Nevado looked angry. His ageless face suddenly became old. 'This is an ancient war between good and evil. You cannot compromise with Satan. Pope Pius was wrong. The Church was never stronger than when books were rare and costly, written individually in a language only a learned fraternity could understand. To keep these books here was nursing a serpent in our breast. They should have been destroyed.'

'I never knew the Church was so squeamish about burning books.'

The anger ebbed. The blood-red lips twisted into a cruel smirk. 'Everything in its time. Why do you think I suffered you to come here?'

The adrenalin was running out. Nick could feel the crash coming. 'We broke in.'

'Why do you think you found the hidden map, the ladder leading you into the tower? Did you think we are so trapped in the Middle Ages that we do not even know how to lock a door?'

'Wouldn't surprise me,' Nick muttered.

'This moment, with Pope Pius's charge at last complete, is a fitting time to end his folly. The library will burn, and you will burn with it. They will find your bones in the ashes and you will be held responsible.'

'Why not just do it yourself?'

Nevado held up his hands. His skin was parchment thin, veins like rivers just below the surface, but they were steady as ice. 'You think I am old and feeble? I have achieved much, but I have not finished my journey. I still have ambitions.'

'Will letting a priceless collection of books burn help you become pope?'

'Few cardinals in the conclave will ever know of it. Those who do, most of them will be glad it has happened. They will hear that a gang of international art thieves broke into the library to steal the manuscripts, overpowered the monks and the guards and could not be stopped. In their greed they grew careless. They dropped a cigarette; papers caught light; the library was lost. They were caught in the fire and burned almost beyond recognition.'

'And we're supposed to be a gang of international art thieves?'

'Why not? A man wanted for murder in New York: a computer expert who could disable our security systems. A medieval scholar with a known animus against the Church. And a disgraced auctioneer who stole from the properties she

551

was supposed to be valuing. You came here of your own will, following your own trail of evidence.'

'For someone who wanted us to come here you spent a lot of time trying to kill us.'

'I was over-hasty. You would have been killed in New York if my associates had managed it, or Paris or Brussels or Strasbourg. Always, you escaped. I wondered how you could prevail against forces so much greater than your own; I prayed God to deliver you into my power. Finally I understood. He has brought you here to bring me the book and fulfil my purpose. His purpose. Truly, He moves in mysterious ways.'

He took a cigarette out of his coat and lit it. A nostalgic smile spread across his face as he took a drag. 'I quit fifteen years ago. As my doctor said: they will kill you.'

'There's only one problem,' said Emily. 'You've got the wrong book.'

'Where are the rest of these books?'

Always the same voice. Always the same questions. I longed to answer but I could not. A crushing weight bore down on me. It milled my wretched body, choking my lungs, bending my bones until they snapped.

'I don't know.'

I did not know anything. Where I was. How long I had been there. Who held me captive, and how they had come by the book. All I knew inside my sackcloth hood was the rattle of chains, the smell of wet stone and burning pitch, the ceaseless questions I could not answer.

I was naked – I knew that – tied to a frame like parchment being stretched to dry. A flat board rested on my stomach, held down by a great and increasing number of stones. It was an exquisitely apt punishment – that I who had devoted myself to

552

pressing ink, lead and paper should now go under the press myself. I wondered if Fust had told them.

'Men speak of the new art you have discovered. Was this what you intended? A tool for heretics?'

'I wanted to perfect the world.' It had seemed so vital to me, a burning purpose. Now it sounded feeble.

'Did you seek to destroy the Church?'

'To strengthen it.'

'To summon the powers of darkness?'

'To spread truth.'

The inquisitor leaned over me. I knew, because I could smell the onions on his breath. Air fanned my neck as he waved something – the book? – in front of me.

'Is this what you call truth? The most diabolical lies and filthy slanders that the devil ever planted? Even to look on this book would be mortal sin.'

My chest burned. 'I did not make the book,' I gurgled.

He ignored me; he always did. The pain of torture might break a man's body, but it was the futility that destroyed his soul. The questions never changed; the answers were never believed.

'How many did you write?'

'Thirty.' I spoke eagerly, almost grateful for the chance to answer his question. 'He said there were thirty.'

'One was sent with an obscene note to the archbishop. Another was found on the step of St Quintin's church – a perfect copy. Is that the devil's work?'

'My art,' I gasped.

'So you confess?'

Panic gripped me. Had I confessed? I tried to explain; I heaved against the board to get air in my lungs, but all I managed was a strangled groan. Then I realised how ridiculous it was and lay back. I could not condemn myself any more than they already had. I would die there.

I heard a grim laugh. 'You will not die here.'

I must have spoken aloud.

'When we have learned what we need, we will burn you in Mainz as a heretic.'

A small sigh escaped my body, perhaps the last breath in me. It was the end I had always known would come, the lesson my father had tried to beat into me that day in Frankfurt. I would die a heretic, a forger who had debased his currency.

Despite everything, I found myself laughing: the mad cackle of my rotten soul fleeing. I had lived half my life haunted by fear of burning for the mortal sins I had committed against body and nature. Now I would burn for a book I had not made. I suppose it was a sort of justice.

My laughter enraged the inquisitor. He shouted to his assistants. I heard the grate of stone, and two ribs cracking as the weight bore down.

'Where are the rest of these books?'

The pain consumed me, pressing me into oblivion.

For a second, Nevado was absolutely still. Then he pushed past them and strode to the shelves at the back of the room. The gunman by the door edged closer.

Nevado picked up the bestiary. 'This was the book you brought?'

Nick didn't answer. He had a terrible feeling nothing he could say now would save them. The overpowering smells of gasoline and tobacco made him sick.

Nevado opened the cover. One glance was enough.

'This is the wrong book. A simple bestiary.' He swept the book aside and turned to Gillian, his waxy face flushed with rage. 'You told me they would bring the *Liber Bonasi.*'

'There's a colophon,' Gillian stammered. 'It mentions the other bestiary. That's how we knew. It led us here.'

'This is *worthless.*' Nevado leaned on the shelf, seemingly oblivious to the cigarette dangling inches from the packed books. Nick barely noticed. Something the cardinal had said echoed in his mind like a gunshot. *You told me.* He turned to Gillian.

'You told him we were coming?'

'Of course not.' She reached to her shoulder and began twisting a lock of hair around her finger. 'I told him the book I found in Paris was the one he wanted. I had to. He must've thought you'd bring it if he lured you here.'

She looked him straight in the eye, begging him to believe her. Nick wanted to; he almost had when Emily said quietly, 'How about the note? Your set of instructions on how to break in.'

'I don't know. He found them when he captured me. Planted them where you'd find them.' She saw Nick's expression. 'What?'

'Do you know where he hid them?'

Gillian stared at him. He recognised the look: he'd seen it before. In trouble with someone, searching for the answer they wanted to hear. She began to speak, then checked herself.

'He hid them in the toilet roll,' said Nick. 'Did you tell him about that?'

She crumbled. He'd seen that before too. 'I had to, Nick. He'd have killed me if I didn't go along with it.'

'And what did you think he'd do to us when he caught us and found it wasn't the right book? Tell us it was all a misunderstanding and let us go?' His head pounded; his eyes hurt just to look at her. He felt as if he'd turned to stone.

'Enough.' Nevado turned, his face hazed in the smoke of the half-smoked cigarette. He shouted something in Italian to the guard at the door. 'I have decided—'

Without warning, Gillian flew at him. Before the guard could react she had snatched the cigarette from Nevado's mouth, pivoted away and hurled it into the bookshelf. The oil-soaked papers took the flame eagerly, as if they had waited five hundred years for the consummation.

'*No!*'

Too late, Nevado seemed to change his mind. He ran to the shelf and pulled the burning papers to the floor, frantically stamping on them. A gust of wind from the door picked up the loose leaves and blew them against the shelves, starting new fires higher up, out of reach. The hem of Nevado's coat caught fire.

Then the whole wall exploded in flame.

LXXXIV

Through the gathering smoke, Nick saw Nevado run for the door. He tried to follow, but a rattle of bullets answered him almost immediately. He dived for cover, pulling Emily down with him and covering her with his body. When he looked up, he was just in time to see the door slam shut.

Where was Gillian? He looked around through the black smoke pouring off the books and couldn't see her. Had Nevado taken her with him? Was that part of the deal?

Then he saw her. She was lying on the floor near the shelves, propped up on her arms trying to crawl away. Hot ash and embers rained down on her, curling like petals on her back, but she didn't move any faster. She couldn't: when she tugged her leg forward a dark river of blood smeared behind her. Nevado's parting gift.

Nick ran over, hooked his arms under hers and dragged her to the middle of the room. Emily tore a sleeve off her sweater and tied it around Gillian's thigh to staunch the bleeding. Her face was white with shock.

'I'm sorry,' she mumbled. 'I'm so sorry, Nick.'

There wasn't time. The flames were already beginning to spread from the back around to the sides of the hall. Smoke was filling the chamber. Nick pulled his gloves out of his pocket and handed one to Emily.

'Hold this in front of your face.'

Breathing through the soggy wool Nick raced to the door. The surface was smooth and featureless, with neither lock nor handle visible.

Did you think we are so trapped in the Middle Ages that we do not even know how to lock a door?

He gave it a kick, but it didn't so much as creak. He only hurt his foot. He pressed it with his hands and felt the grainless strength of metal. They would burn long before it did.

He ran back to Emily and Gillian. 'Bad news.'

Without taking the glove from her face, Emily pointed up. Thick clouds of smoke swirled among the rafters. She snatched the glove away just long enough to say, 'The smoke. Going out.' She took another breath. 'Must be an opening. In the roof.'

Was there? Nick had his doubts. But there wasn't any other way out. He stared up at the shelves, like a giant stair scaling the high wall. Ladders and galleries connected them, though some were already dangerously close to the encroaching flames. Even if they made it to the top, they'd probably just find themselves trapped.

Got to keep trying, he told himself. He put his arm around Gillian's shoulders, lifted her up and headed for the nearest ladder.

The cold air in the courtyard was a mercy. Nevado dropped to his knees in the snow to extinguish the last embers smouldering in the hem of his coat, and to cool the burns that scalded his legs. Ugo watched him uncertainly.

'Should we put out the fire?' he asked.

Nevado looked back. From the outside, the inferno inside the keep was all but invisible. The windows in the tower had long since been blocked up. Only the smell of smoke, almost comforting on this snowy night, gave any clue. The plume pouring from the roof was lost in the darkness.

'Are you OK, *Monsignóre*?'

Nevado realised he was trembling. He had not meant it to end like this – rushed and sloppy, out of his control, Pope Pius's commission still incomplete. And the sight of all those books burning – evil though they were – had shaken him more than he had expected.

But the Lord moved in mysterious ways. Perhaps it was a gentle correction, he thought, a warning to his pride that only God was perfect. His plan would still work.

He turned to Ugo. 'Give me your weapon.'

Ugo looked surprised, but handed him the pistol without complaint. Nevado felt the weight of it. It was so much smaller than the guns he'd used in his youth, protecting himself against the republican gangs who lurked in the forests around his father's church in Andalusia. But the mechanism was the same. He checked the clip and the safety.

'Bless you.'

He fired two shots into Ugo's chest. The Italian collapsed without a sound, his blood seeping into the snow like ink.

They overpowered the guards and could not be stopped. It was regrettable but necessary. No one could blame him for inadequate precautions.

Nevado gave him one more bullet, just to be sure, then threw the gun into the snow by the keep. Whoever came to investigate could draw their own conclusions. Then he hurried to the stables where his car was parked.

The back wall of the tower was awash with flame, like a stained-glass window leaded black where the shelves had not yet collapsed. It sucked in air and turned the whole chamber into a vast oven. At the far end of the room, Nick had stripped to his T-shirt and was still soaked through with sweat. His shirt was tied around Gillian's leg, strapping on a makeshift splint made from two lengths of bookshelf. She clung to the shelves as she hobbled along the gallery.

The walkway was metal, a cast-iron lattice so that when you looked down, you could see how far you had to drop. It wouldn't burn, but it might fry them. Nick could already feel it getting hot through the soles of his shoes. So far, the stone pillars had stopped the flames from spreading to their part of the library, but it couldn't be long. A blizzard of burning paper scraps swirled in the hall on currents of smoke and scalding air.

Whoever had designed the library hadn't made it easy: the ladders were placed at alternating ends of each gallery, so that you had to zigzag your way across each level to reach the next. It reminded Nick of a primitive video game, working your way to the top while a gorilla threw bananas and fireballs at you. Only now, the fireballs were all too real.

The ladders were the hardest part. Emily went first, then lay on her stomach and reached back down while Nick supported Gillian, holding her hips to steady her. She tried to help by pulling herself up the rungs, but smoke and pain and loss of blood made her giddy.

Once she slipped, lost her grip and almost plunged backwards over the edge. Nick held on grimly and hauled her back.

'Leave me.' She reached out a hand and stroked his cheek. 'Save yourself.'

If there'd been any prospect of actually saving himself, perhaps he would have been tempted. Instead, he hoisted her onto his shoulders and climbed the ladder. She didn't resist.

Emily yelled something to Nick, but the roar of the fire drowned her voice. Instead of trying again, she simply pointed down. The fire had leaped around the pillars: eager flames raced up the shelves below them.

Now they were in a deadly race. They took Gillian between them and dragged her, stumbling, to the next ladder. Smoke rose all around them, sieving through the holes in the iron-work like poison gas. Nick's lungs ached; his skin sizzled with raw heat.

At last they came out on the top balcony. When Nick looked down he had the impression he was standing atop a column of flame. Smoke made it a dull, bloody red: it was so thick up here that he could hardly see.

But Emily had been right: the smoke was moving upwards. Squinting through his tears, Nick saw a dark opening in the ceiling. It was too high to reach, and too far from the wall for the shelves to be any use.

'Wait here.'

Nick dropped to the floor and crawled along the gantry on hands and knees. The hot metal scalded his hands; he grabbed two books and used them like oven mitts to protect himself. At the end of the row of shelves, tucked in behind a column, an old wooden school desk sat gathering dust – perhaps so that anyone who came up this far didn't have to carry his book all the way down. Nick grabbed the desk and dragged it back along the gantry, closing his eyes against the smoke. Books fell unheeded from the shelves; once the desk skewed around and jammed against the handrail. A desperate heave brought it free.

He didn't even realise he'd reached Emily until he felt her hand on his back. She understood at once. She scrambled onto the desk, raised her arms and reached for the skylight. Still she couldn't quite reach. Nick wrapped his arms around her legs, squeezed and lifted.

She swayed; for an awful moment he thought she'd topple and take both of them over the edge. Then she steadied as her hands gripped the side of the open skylight. Her weight rose away. When she was up, Nick manhandled Gillian through, then followed himself. His head popped out through the hatch and felt cool air. He drew a deep breath, and immediately choked on a lungful of the smoke pouring out around him. He looked around.

They'd arrived in a thaw. The fire was melting the snow from the roof and sending it pouring onto the stone walkway where they stood. He scooped some up to wash his eyes and realised it was warm. The puddles began to steam.

Nick left Gillian with Emily and ran around the tower, wading through slush, peering over the wall for any sign of a ladder or a fire escape, even protruding bricks they could cling on to. There was no way down.

The water on the roof was bubbling now. In horror, he realised it wasn't just water. The lead itself was beginning to melt, blistering off the roof and running down into the overloaded gutters. It wouldn't be long before the whole thing went. He rolled Gillian over to the balustrade, trying to keep her from the river of molten metal. He hugged Emily to him but didn't speak. There was nothing left to say.

He heard a throbbing in his ears, a pounding that swelled until the roar of the burning library was entirely drowned out.

562

A blinding white light appeared in the sky above, sweeping over him like the eye of judgement.

I was close to death. The weight on me was so immense I thought it would split open my skin and burst my heart. My head felt as though all the blood in my body had been squeezed into it, inflated like a bladder. I hung in a balance, as finely calibrated as any goldsmith's scales. In one pan, the stones; in the other, my life. Even the addition of a single coin would be enough to crush me into oblivion.

'What is the meaning of the other bestiary we found in your house?'

The questions never stopped. The weight on my chest had long since left me speechless. Yet I had to groan, to gasp and babble wordless nonsense, to convince them I was trying. If I stayed silent they would only add more stones.

'Who else helped you?'

I said nothing. In all my torment I had never answered that question.

My silence displeased the inquisitor. I heard the familiar, dread command. '*Alium* – another.' The obedient slap of foot-steps. The rasp of stone.

And then a bang; muffled shouts that grew suddenly louder; a rush of air. The clatter of a stone being dropped. Had the board that flattened me broken and spilled its load. It did not feel that way. Had I died?

I tried to hear what was being said. After the inquisitor, any new voice was like a cold stream in the desert.

'You must stop this at once,' someone was saying. 'Remove those stones.'

'This is the archbishop's castle.' You have no authority here, Bishop.'

'Cardinal,' the new-but-familiar voice corrected him. 'I am moving up in the world. And you will be dropping like one of your stones down a very deep well if you do not free my friend this instant.'

'This man is a heretic.'

'He is a truer servant of God than you will ever be.'

There followed a pause, filled with a hope more excruciating than any torment I had endured. Then – praise God! – the sound of a stone being taken off me. I tried to breathe and found my chest lifted a hair's breadth further than before.

'Faster,' the cardinal insisted. 'If he dies now, you will take his place.'

The trickle of rocks became a cascade, crashing onto the floor like a tower being torn down to its foundations. Stone splinters ricocheted against my cheek but I barely felt them.

The board lifted off me like a door opening. Fingers fretted at the cords around my neck, prising loose the knots.

A dazzling light blinded me, like morning sun on the Rhine. It made a halo around the face that peered into mine. Even in that cruel room he managed an impression of his usual smile, though it was heavy with care.

'Truly, you are a most extraordinary man.'

The car fishtailed as Nevado swerved into another corner. He knew he was driving too fast. The road switched and twisted through the forest, steep hairpin bends dropping suddenly into icy straights tucked among the trees. In the headlights, the world became a corrugated tunnel of trees and snow. He kept his eyes fixed ahead.

The road straightened and he began to relax. The highway to Mainz was shut, but his boat was moored in Oberwinter. He could be in Frankfurt by dawn, then a fast train to Basle and a friend who would swear he hadn't left Switzerland in two days. The police would call, and he would reluctantly telephone the Vatican with the terrible news.

He realised his attention was wandering and snapped it back to the road. He was approaching a bend where a landslide had carried away the trees to offer an open view back across the gorge. He pressed the brake – gently – and felt the car shudder to a standstill. He stared across the valley. A vast plume of smoke choked out the stars; flames glowed red through the skylights he had left open to fan the fire. He smiled, trying to steady his breathing. Everything had worked.

A brilliant white light passed over him like an angel. The whole car shook with the vibrations of the aircraft passing overhead. Whose could it be? Had they seen him? Suddenly his whole plan was in doubt.

Gripped by panic, he hit the accelerator. Too hard – the wheels spun, whining in protest as they sprayed snow behind him. He pushed harder, stamping the pedal and rattling the gearstick. The wheels howled, then bit the frozen earth. The car lurched forward. Still dazed from the searchlight, he didn't see the bend ahead until it was too late. He tried to turn; he slammed on what he thought was the brake, not realising it was the accelerator still locked to the floor.

There were no crash barriers, no trees to catch him. The car flew over the cliff and plunged head first into the gorge. The last thing Nevado saw was his headlights reflected in the snow, twin points of light rushing towards him, the eyes of a vengeful God. He screamed.

A small puff of fire erupted in the trees on the southern slope of the gorge. It burned like a ball of paper for a little while, then died, leaving a black blot on the virgin snow.

Nick shielded his face against the spotlight and peered into the sky. Through the whipped-up snow he could see helicopter blades spinning like giant scissors, the glint of a glass canopy and a square of light where a door had opened. Someone was standing in the opening, looking at them. He waved frantically, screaming for help. The rotors drowned his cries and flung them into the darkness.

But someone must have seen him. A cable snaked down. A moment later he saw a man attached to it, descending like a spider. He touched down on the roof and waddled over to Nick. He wore a green jumpsuit that looked vaguely military, though his face was hidden under an enormous helmet.

Nick pointed to Gillian, lying behind the balustrade. Blood had soaked through the makeshift bandage and clouded in the puddles around her. The man in the jumpsuit gave a thumbs-up. Together, he and Nick lifted Gillian upright and wriggled her into a harness.

Emily cupped her hands over his ear. 'Who are they?'

Nick shrugged. With the spotlight shining in his eyes he couldn't make out any markings on the helicopter. It crossed his mind that perhaps these were Nevado's men; that they might take Gillian away and leave him to burn on the rooftop. But a minute later – it felt like an eternity – he saw the spider-man coming down his thread again. This time he'd brought two harnesses, and ear protectors. Nick and Emily clipped in and were hoisted up, while below them gouts of flame erupted from the collapsing roof. It was like flying over a volcano.

The noise of the rotor hammered with a new intensity as they reached the helicopter. The air itself seemed to be against him, a great weight battering his shoulders, trying to hold him down. The cable swayed – but strong hands were waiting. They hauled him in.

At the back of the cabin, Gillian lay strapped to a stretcher. A medic inserted a drip into her arm and slipped on an oxygen mask. Her face was blue with shock, but when the mask went over her mouth he saw it fog up. She was breathing.

He felt a hand tap his shoulder and turned. Sitting on a bench opposite, one looking anxious and slightly ill, the other with a grim smile on his face, were two of the last men he'd expected to see.

LXXXV

I lay on a bed at an inn – I do not know where. The hard bed offered little straw to ease my limbs, but after the agonies I had suffered it was like a sack of feathers. Aeneas held a cup of water to my lips. I could barely drink; half of it splashed down the front of my tunic.

'Are you really a cardinal?'

He put a finger to his lips, though there was no chance of being overheard. 'I will be soon. Until then, these fools have no way of knowing.'

'Thank you.'

'You saved my life once. Now the debt is repaid.'

He picked up the book he had taken from the inquisitor and read in silence for a moment. The gleam in his eyes turned grey.

'How did they find it?' I asked. I knew from my interrogation that they had not discovered the copy that had slipped behind my bed. If they had, I would probably be dead.

'It was left on the cathedral steps for the archbishop. He had seen pages from your Bible – he recognised your art. He guessed at once you must have made it.' Aeneas gave me a look that seemed to penetrate my soul. 'Did you?'

'It was made in my house, with my tools.'

'But not by you?'

I shook my head. 'Do not ask me to say who.'

It was an unreasonable request, and Aeneas bridled at it. But a second later the anger passed, replaced with weary resignation.

'If you held your tongue under that ordeal, I will not use friendship as a lever to prise it out of you. We will find out.'

I thought of Drach, of his ever-changing character and quicksilver affections. If ever there was a man who could make himself disappear, it was he.

'You will never find him.'

'We had better. Many in the Church will think he is the most dangerous heretic since Hus. Worse, perhaps. At least Hus could only write his sedition one copy at a time.'

He laid the book aside. 'Remember what I told you in Frankfurt? Your art is a way to speak into the hearts of men. This book is a contagion. By the power of your art, it could carry the plague of heresy further and deeper than ever before. It could tear Christendom apart.'

'Or bind it together.' I pushed myself up and gripped his arm. 'What I have discovered cannot be unlearned. You will not stamp out heresy by being rid of my art. It is a tool. Perhaps I would have been more careful if I had imagined how powerful it might be, but it is still only a tool. Words are pressed onto the page but men compose them. Better to fight their ideas than the tools they use.'

My feeble voice faded as I saw he was nodding with me.

'That is why we must protect it.' He slipped the book into a leather bag and knotted it shut. 'We will root out this evil and destroy it utterly. We will find the man who did it and erase his name from the pages of history. I will do my best to protect you – as you see, I have some influence – and you will never speak of it to anyone.'

It was the only time I ever heard him sound so serious – a glimpse of the inner strength that had carried him so high.

'As for you, I think you deserve better than you have had from your friends. I will see what I can do.' He reached onto a side table and pressed a book in my hands. For a second I thought it was Kaspar's; I shuddered to touch it. Then I realised it was my bestiary, still with the card pasted into the back. The two books were easily confused.

'The inquisitor had it. I return it to you. Presently, I will try to restore more of your fortunes.'

He gave a thin smile. 'Though you will find the Church is not your only enemy.'

Nick looked into the faces opposite him: two of the last men he'd ever expected to be rescued by. Atheldene, incongruous in a wool coat; beside him, in a blue parka and an NYPD baseball cap, a face Nick thought he'd left behind for good in New York.

'Detective Royce?'

He might as well have been miming: the noise in the cabin meant he could barely hear himself. One of the crew passed him a headset.

'Have you come to arrest me?'

Royce shook his head and pointed to the back of the cabin. 'Your girlfriend.'

'Gillian? She—'

'She's a thief.'

Nick couldn't believe it. 'You're going to prosecute her for

570

taking the card from Paris? After all this?'

'It's not the card. Simon here's been tracking her for months.'

Nick glanced at Atheldene. He didn't look the part. 'You're a cop?'

'I'm an auctioneer. But I've got friends in the Art Squad at Scotland Yard. Sometimes I do them the odd favour. A few months ago they asked me to keep an eye on Gillian. Things had been going missing from the Cloisters in New York and turning up for sale in London, but the museum could never prove anything. In the end they wrote her a first-class reference and packed her off to Stevens Mathison. Soon afterwards it started happening to us.'

Nick jerked his thumb at Royce. 'Was he involved?'

'Only when you showed up in Paris.' Royce flashed him a grin: it looked less unpleasant than it had in the interrogation room. 'Simon called London, who of course had the heads-up on you from Interpol. They called me. I got that special feeling I get sometimes. Instead of booking you for murder and obstruction of justice, I figured we might get something interesting by following you.'

'And Atheldene? Almost getting killed in Brussels? Was that part of the plan?'

Atheldene played with the button on his coat. 'That was genuine. I was terrified. I usually get called in to tell the Art Squad when someone's selling something they're not supposed to own, or to see if the object in an insurance claim is genuine. I'm not used to this sort of thing.'

The helicopter banked around the mountain. The clouds had parted and a cold moon appeared.

'What's that?' Atheldene pointed to the hillside below. A fire burned among the trees, a golden bead in the silver forest.

The pilot's voice, German accented, came over the headsets. 'Maybe a car crash? I call Oberwinter to send the police.'

'Can they send a fire engine too?' Atheldene craned around so that he could see the castle. The roof must have collapsed: the flames now rose unhindered out of the shell of the tower.

'On that road, it is not possible. Maybe in the morning.'

'The Devils' Library,' Atheldene murmured. 'Imagine even half an hour in that place.'

'I'd have swapped with you,' Nick muttered. 'You wouldn't have liked the librarian.'

'Point taken. But it is a shame about all those books.'

Emily reached inside her shirt and pulled out a battered brown-leather-bound book.

'Not all of them.'

Atheldene almost lunged for it across the cabin, then remembered his manners. 'Is that the one . . . ?'

'No. It was chained to the wall – I couldn't. But I managed to grab this. Anyway, I prefer it.' She passed it to Nick. 'It's for you.'

Nick shook his head. In the back, he could see Gillian breathing fitfully as she slept under a blanket.

'I got what I came for.'

COLOPHON

What I say to you in the dark, tell in the light; and what
you hear whispered, proclaim from the housetops.

It was strange to be back in the Humbrechthof. The clatter
of the presses; types clicking together in their sticks; the
shouts and banter of the apprentices calling across the
yard for more paper, more ink, more beer. But it was no
longer mine. The purpose that animated the house had
changed: practical, routine, no longer charged with the
excitement of discovery. Kaspar and I, Götz and Keffer and
the others, we had charted a new country. Now a second
generation had arrived to lay down roads and barns, drain
marshes, plant crops, tame the wilderness. Many of the faces
I saw were new: they glanced at me as I passed, but only idly.
A few recognised me, and looked away or shook my hand as
their consciences allowed. Peter Schoeffer was not among
them.

'He went to Frankfurt,' said Fust, when he received me in
his room. 'He has some business there with a bookseller. He

should have returned by now. He will be sorry to have missed you. No doubt some woman delayed him.'

I let the lie stand, and wondered if Fust knew that Schoeffer was sleeping with his daughter. Fust misread my expression.

'He thought the world of you. As an artist, as an inventor. Nothing pained him more than having to choose between us. He is my heir, but yours also.'

He picked up a small block of engraved metal from his desk and gave it to me. It came apart in my hands: I began to apologise, then realised it was meant to. One part, the smaller, was a bulbous letter B, intricately carved so that within the strokes of the letter itself flowers grew, branches blossomed and a hound chased a duck over a meadow. It fitted into a slot in the second piece of metal, engraved with a lush border of foliage, to make a seamless whole.

'Peter's invention. You ink the inner part red and the outer blue, then drop it in among the black-inked forms and print the initials. We are using it on a psalter for the cathedral.' He showed it to me imprinted on a piece of paper, sharper than any illuminator or rubricator could produce.

'Beautiful,' I admitted. Perhaps I had been wrong. Perhaps there were still discoveries to be made in this house.

'It is still too slow. Peter is like you that way, obsessed with quality and no thought to cost.'

An awkward silence hung between us. Fust escaped it by shuffling papers on his desk until he found the one he sought.

'I suppose we should finish our business.' He gave me the document to sign and seal. 'I am sorry this is necessary. The psalter is late; the Church is slow to pay, so I must borrow more money. The Jew had heard about our disagreement and demanded an assurance that you accepted all the terms of the court's judgment. It is only a formality.' He lit a candle and reached for the sealing wax.

'You will forgive me if I am cautious about anything you give me to sign.'

'Of course.' A sharp-toothed smile. I could not wound him so easily.

I read it through. Fust took the contents of the Humbrechthof, the presses and types, the ink and paper, the furniture, down to the last composing stick. He also kept the finished Bibles to sell at his own profit. The Gutenberghof, its press and everything in it remained mine. There was a time when I had burned with the injustice of it; now my anger had cooled. It was past.

I signed my name at the bottom and pressed my seal into the soft wax. Punch and form. Fust did the same.

'You have a new seal,' I noticed. A black bird with a yoke around its neck, supporting two black shields blazoned with letters and stars.

'The Fust and Schoeffer Book Works. Peter designed it. We will stamp it in all our works, a hallmark of our quality. Customers will demand nothing less.'

I did not like it. In its way, it seemed a greater blasphemy than anything Kaspar ever did. To put your mark on a piece of art, to claim it for your own, was to appropriate it from God.

Again, Fust misinterpreted my frown. 'I am sorry,' he repeated. He wanted me to believe it. 'The street between our houses is not so very long. No doubt we will see each other. I hope we can be friends.'

I was old enough that it barely hurt to lie. 'I hope so. But not now. I am leaving Mainz for a time.'

There was no missing his relief. 'Where will you go?'

'I have an errand in Strassburg.'

*

April sunshine bathed the city. The half-timbered houses and Gothic turrets shone with a warm light; bright colours festooned the square where racks of tea towels, postcards and guidebooks had sprung up like spring flowers. Crowds of tourists milled about, enjoying the Easter holiday, while kings and angels, lions, knights and serpents watched from the stone above.

No one paid any attention to the young couple who walked hand in hand across the square. They entered the cathedral by the west door, under the monumental facade, into the deep twilight that kept perpetual hold on the interior. To their left, on the north wall, a row of stained-glass kings glowed vivid with the light behind them. Nick's pulse quickened; he squeezed Emily's hand.

Atheldene was waiting for them about halfway along the nave, just before a side chapel interrupted the procession of kings. A fluorescent vest was draped awkwardly over his suit, and a hard hat perched on his head. At the base of the pillar behind him, a stone mason in overalls stood in a hydraulic scissor lift.

'I hope you're right about this. You can't imagine the paperwork involved in pulling apart one of the masterpieces of Gothic architecture. Especially when the people who want to do it are all *personae non gratae* with the Church hierarchy. I've had to call in a career's worth of favours and tell the most outrageous fibs.'

Nick took the bestiary out of his bag. The corner of the battered card poked from behind the last page. He tucked it back in. Soon he'd have to surrender both – the card to rejoin the deck at the Bibliothèque Nationale in Paris, the book to the British Library in London. It had all been discreetly arranged

576

courtesy of Stevens Mathison. Nick, who had never owned any book older than a *Superman* #61 Issue, would be sad to let them go.

But the bestiary had one last secret to give up. He opened it to the restored front page, cut out by Gillian but now expertly sewn back in. In the bottom corner was the sketch of the square building standing in the arms of a cross which they'd noticed on the boat to Oberwinter.

It was Emily who had finally deciphered it.

'It's not a building with a cross,' she'd said, one evening back in New York. 'It's a building at a crossroads.'

Nick hadn't been impressed. 'That narrows it down.'

'It does if you know anything about Gutenberg's life.' An exasperated sigh. 'Strasbourg – the city of roads. The crossroads of Europe.'

'And that building . . .'

'The cathedral.'

It was a doodle – it could have been any building with an arched door. It didn't even have much of a tower.

'It all fits. The crossroads. The kings on the walls and the *Sayings of the Kings of Israel*. Gutenberg.'

And so they had come back, to the church at the crossroads where two dozen kings of uncertain realms stood entombed in glass.

'Manasses was the sixteenth King of Israel.' Emily counted off the kings in the windows, four at a time, until she came to the window opposite where they were standing. 'Louis the Pious.'

'Seems appropriate.'

'Gillian's going to be kicking herself if we're right,' said Atheldene.

Nick went quiet. He'd crossed Europe to find Gillian and,

unbelievably, he'd rescued her. He still wasn't sure what he'd found. He no longer lay awake at night wondering what might have been. He no longer wanted her to hold him and whisper she was sorry for everything, begging him for a second chance. But some questions couldn't be answered. She would always be the wild woman, untamed and unknowable, dancing in the margins.

Nick and Emily put on yellow vests and hard hats. The lift carried them up the side of the column, high over the heads of the tourists below. One or two looked up, but the sight of reflective clothing seemed to reassure them that nothing interesting was happening. High-visibility camouflage.

'How could Gutenberg ever have gotten up here?' Nick wondered.

'They were still building and rebuilding the cathedral when he was here. There was probably some scaffolding around the pillars.'

The lift eased to a stop. They were almost at head height with the kings now, face to face with the carvings on the pillar. A man's head pushing through thick foliage. An eagle with a snake in its beak. And . . .

'The digging bear.' Nick had known it would be there: Atheldene had spotted it from the ground and sent a photograph. Even so, he felt a shiver of unexpected awe. This close, he could see how similar it was to the animal on the card. A little squashed, maybe, to fit the space on the pillar: a flatter back, a sharper bend in its knee that made it more purposeful. In the bottom corner, a small hole had been bored in the stone beside its burrowing snout.

Bear is the key.

The mason took out a thin metal hook like a dentist's pick. 'If I find any cement, we stop,' he warned.

But there was no mortar holding it in place – only generations of accumulated grime and soot packed into a treacly black muck. The mason worked it free with his tool. It left a thin crack outlining the stone.

'Squeaky-bum time,' said Atheldene. He took the bear by its snout and inched it towards him. It came smoothly, almost eagerly. He and the mason lifted it down onto the floor of the lift. A rectangular hole yawned in the pillar.

'There's something in there.'

Emily reached in. Her hands came out holding a rusted metal box, about the size of a biscuit tin. Big enough to hold a book. Hands trembling, Atheldene inserted a blade into the lid and prised it open. All three of them craned to look in.

'It's . . . disintegrated.'

The box contained nothing but a deep layer of scraps, like soap flakes or autumn leaves gathered up for the bonfire. Most bore traces of writing; some flashed gold or red where fragments of illuminations caught light from the stained-glass windows. None was more than an inch across.

'Water vapour must have got in. If the parchment had been exposed to sunlight at any point previously, moisture would have broken it apart.'

Emily pulled on a latex glove and picked up one of the fragments. Even now, the ink was black and glossy.

'This is the right typeface for the *Liber Bonasi*.'

'Some of it's different.' Atheldene pointed to another fragment where the words were in brown ink. Even Nick could see it was handwritten, not printed.

'. . . many names . . . goose meat . . .' Atheldene let it fall back in the box. 'I don't know what this is.'

Emily sifted quickly through a few more of the pieces. 'It

looks as if there were two books in here. The *Liber Bonasi* and a much longer manuscript. They're all mixed up.'

Nick stared into the box. He couldn't begin to count how many fragments there must be. Thousands? Millions? Some had probably disintegrated completely; others might be illegible. But he had time.

He smiled at Emily. 'We can piece it together.'

I stepped into the Gutenberghof for the last time, glancing as always at the pilgrim on the lintel. I resembled him more after my ordeal with the inquisitor. My back stooped, my neck drooped. On cold days even breathing was painful. But the load I had carried hidden under my cloak so long was almost done.

The others were waiting for me upstairs. Saspach and Götz, Günther, Keffer and Ruppel – and half a dozen others, men whose names have not figured in my chronicle, though I saw them almost daily as we worked the press. Mentelin the scribe, who had begun work on a new set of types since Fust took mine; Numeister, Sweynheym, Sensenschmidt and Ulrich Han. Only Kaspar was absent. In the middle, towering above them all, stood the press. Like all of us, it had aged: stained with ink, dented from all the times we had needed to hammer out jams, its screw no longer quite straight – but still capable of sixteen pages an hour in the hands of good men.

'I am going away,' I said without preamble. There were murmurs of disappointment, but no great shock. Since the trial, and all that followed it, they had watched me slowly unravelling myself from the business of the house. After the great work of the Bible, I had no enthusiasm for calendars and grammar books.

'Keffer will run the workshop in my absence. For the time

being, he will focus on texts we already have set – indulgences and so forth – while we build up capital and train new apprentices.'

'For the rest of you, you are welcome to stay in my house as long as you wish. But do not waste your time. Teach yourselves the arts you do not know. If you are a compositor, learn type-founding; if you have only ever boiled ink, learn how to spread it so that it makes an even impression every time. Share your knowledge freely. Then go back to your home towns, or cities you have always dreamed of, and establish workshops of your own. Train apprentices, and let them train apprentices of their own. Join no guild, but challenge each man to make his master-piece. Spread this art the length and breadth of Christendom so that all men may read, learn, understand and grow. You will make mistakes; only God is perfect. Some men, perhaps even some of you, will use this art we have devised for wrong ends. That is inevitable. This tool is too powerful to be kept in the hands of any one or two men. As long as we imprint more good on the world than would otherwise have been, this art will be a blessing.'

I left them there and went out into the warm April sunshine. I had given up my dream: I would not make any perfect thing. I was merely a man. At a younger age it would have devastated me; now I felt only the relief of a great burden lifted. I was at peace with an imperfect world.

I had not gone five miles from Mainz when I thought of a way I could make the press better.

HISTORICAL NOTE

For a man whose invention transformed the world, Johann Gutenberg left remarkably little of his own life imprinted on history: a few receipts, a couple of mentions in civic documents, and partial records of the four court cases referenced in this novel. Most of them raise more questions than they answer. The reality they reveal – industrial espionage, non-disclosure agreements, intellectual property rights, demanding venture-capitalist investors, precarious financing, lawsuits – would be familiar to any Silicon Valley entrepreneur today. They remind us that printing was a uniquely complex and expensive undertaking, requiring vast sums of capital to be invested over many years, as well as management skills and a production-line organisation almost unknown in the Middle Ages. Gutenberg's genius must have been for financial engineering and logistics, just as much as his technical mastery of inks, metals, mechanisms and paper. In this book, I have allowed my imagination free reign over Gutenberg's early years. The later chapters, in Strassburg and Mainz, are more anchored to the few facts that are generally agreed.

But Gutenberg's life is an open book compared to that of the Master of the Playing Cards. Nothing survives except for his work, a vague idea of the time and place where he lived, and the consensus that he was the first man to print images from copper engravings. Like other artistic breakthroughs, not least Gutenberg's Bible, the cards are not just technologically innovative but genuine masterpieces.

The idea that these two giants of early printing could have met and collaborated is compelling, though unprovable. Both were active in the first half of the fifteenth century in the Rhineland; both used presses in some of the earliest examples of mechanised mass-production. As described in the novel, several of the Master's images appear in an illuminated Gutenberg Bible now at Princeton University, while others appear in a giant handwritten Bible which must have been produced in Mainz at the same time as Gutenberg's Bible was coming off the press.

If the ideal of the medieval artist was to leave no trace of himself on work that ultimately derived from God, then both Gutenberg and the Master of the Playing Cards succeeded almost too well. The Master's name is lost to history; Gutenberg was equally forgotten for almost two hundred years, buried by Fust and Schoeffer's propaganda. But for their passion to mass-produce text and images, the modern world is their monument.

ACKNOWLEDGEMENTS

I'd like to thank everybody who helped and encouraged me in writing this book. Dr Natalia Nowakowska of Somerville College, Oxford for sharing her research on early printing; Maxime Préaud at the Bibliothèque Nationale in Paris, who generously allowed me to examine the original playing cards; Dr Allen and the Mystery Writers' Forum; Oliver Johnson, collaborator and editor; the Banse family and Isabella Paul for their hospitality in Germany and much else; my family, especially my father for his German expertise; Jon, Sarah and Agnes Hawkins, for whom *The Rhineland Testament* remains one of the great fictive might-have-beens; my agent Jane Conway-Gordon, despite her threats to withhold chocolate cake; the Inter-Continental Literary Agency; John Kelly; Charlotte Haycock and everyone at Random House; the staffs at the British Library in London and Boston Spa, the York Minster Library, and the JB Morrell library at the University of York.

After eight books, it would be easy to take my wife Emma's patience and support for granted: instead, it only seems more extraordinary. She made what could have been a particularly challenging writing period one of the calmest I can remember.

My son Owen arrived a month after I began this book. He came along on my research trip, charmed his way across Europe, and was exposed to more Gothic architecture than is safe for any five-month-old. He also contributed random punctuation in the moments when he got through my defences to the keyboard. Born into a world where the communications revolution begun by Gutenberg is reaching unfathomable new dimensions, this book is for him.